LANDFALL

The Stranger Trilogy: Book Three

SONIA ORIN LYRIS

Knotted Road Press

Landfall
The Stranger Trilogy: Book Three
Sonia Orin Lyris
Copyright © 2020 Sonia Orin Lyris
All rights reserved
Published by Knotted Road Press
www.KnottedRoadPress.com

ISBN: 978-1-64470-163-8

Cover art:
Mark Ferrari - http://www.markferrari.com/
Interior design copyright © 2020 Knotted Road Press

Want all the maps?
https://lyris.org/seer-saga-maps/unmoored

Want the entire trilogy? Get your copies here:
Unmoored
Maelstrom
Landfall

It's True. Reviews Help.

If you liked this book, please consider giving a rating and a review. Even a short "Can't wait for the next one!" will do nicely, and help the author to make more books for you.

A note from Sonia:

Thank you for being part of my creative process. I have regular chats for subscribers, on my Patreon account, here:

https://www.patreon.com/lyris

Never miss a release!

I announce new projects on my Facebook feed:

https://www.facebook.com/authorlyris

You can also sign up for my newsletter:

https://lyris.org/subscribe/

Also by Sonia Orin Lyris

The Stranger Trilogy

The Seer

Touchstone

Mirror Test

It Might be Sunlight

The Angel's Share

Blades

Chapter One

GRAY, this early hour of this spring day. Cold and damp, as Tokerae sat with his sister Ella on the roof of Etallan's main house.

"Hirelings across the city," Ella said.

Tokerae gazed at Etallan's sprawling grounds, structures small and large. The smithy belched smoke, wafting through the branches of a huge tree in the courtyard that had grown for generations. Beyond all of it was the high, pointed wrought-iron fence that marked the boundary of Etallan's land. And beyond that, down and down through the city, was the Yarpin harbor, thick with ships.

"Hirelings across the city," Tokerae echoed.

"Key in-palace contacts made alert and ready," Ella said.

Sitting here, considering strategy and forging plans, made Tokerae nostalgic. So much like his years in the Cohort, with his sibs and their predilection for rendezvousing—and dueling—in odd, hazardous places. They were proud to see how dangerously they could tread.

A simpler time, though he didn't realize it then. For the

boys and girls of the Cohort, everything seemed possible. The way was open, limited only by nerve and wit. Any of them could achieve the greatest prize of becoming Cern's consort and fathering royal heirs.

So they studied, fought, and fucked. They vied for leverage and influence, intending to need it in the years to come. Whatever the future held, one thing seemed certain: they would be spending the rest of their lives working together, Cohort brothers and sisters, scions of the Houses.

Of course, it had not turned out that way. Some sibs had died being stupid, others through bad luck. But most held steady and survived, even thrived.

Like the mutt brothers. They seemed inextinguishable, tenacious survivors, with a streak of luck that stretched past the horizon. Then, one day, out of the blue, Innel took his brother Pohut out of the game entirely, saving them all the trouble. Leaving only Innel.

Who was now gone, hard as it was to believe. Disgraced, fallen, and executed. Tokerae and Ella had managed to accomplish what had seemed impossible: get rid of the mutt for good.

"Are you listening to me?"

"Key in-palace contacts made alert and ready," Tokerae said.

"Money to Garaya," Ella said, "to seal the agreement."

He nodded. "Garaya."

When enough coin was involved, the Garayan council was impressively flexible about their loyalties. Toss in the possibility of forgiveness and good standing, and they were eager to cooperate with Etallan.

"We must begin moving the rest of our forces from the provinces," Ella said.

This was where it all got tricky and expensive. Tokerae

considered the money played out across decades to assemble, train, house, feed, and hide these private and illegal soldiers, then to pay Helata to transport them. It really was an impressive amount.

"Are you certain?" Tokerae asked softly.

"Months," Ella said with feeling. "We are mere months from being ready, if we put all into motion."

"Our eparch-mother disagrees about the wisdom of this timing."

"Then we act without her."

Tokerae shook his head. "We don't have enough money, and no one gives that kind of credit, even to the presumptive eparch-heir of Etallan."

Her gaze swept the grounds before them. "How long can she hold the eparchy, do you think?"

Tokerae shrugged. "Kincel's eparch is nearing ninety. Mother has a ways to go yet."

Ella gave a frustrated exhale. "Everything is ready. It must be this year. It cannot be later."

Tokerae held his hands wide, indicating helplessness. "We can't do it without the funds of the House."

"Everything must end, sooner or later," Ella said, turning an intent look on him. "Let's make it sooner."

He turned to face her. "What are you saying?"

"The mage. Hired for wisdom, he said. Go ask him for some." Her look turned fierce. "What have we got to lose?"

He snorted at the thought of his mother's reaction should the mage relate that particular conversation. "We have everything to lose."

"Well, brother, so does she."

"She'd name another heir," he said quietly, speaking his fear.

"Who? A cousin? Their spawn? You know she wouldn't.

It's me or you." Ella shrugged. "Let her give it to me, if she's in a snit. I'll take it, then abdicate to you. I've given you my word on that. My word, Tok."

Tokerae turned to stare out at the distant harbor, hoping to hide the welling emotion he felt at this reassurance. He gave a single, short nod.

His sister put a hand on his arm. "Brother, listen: we must act. Our House's reputation weakens daily, while mother sits idle, arms tight around herself, like a frightened child."

"Is it that simple, do you think? Is she not possessed of some... prudent, elder wisdom?"

Ella smirked, shook her head. "It's the fear that her decline brings, the frailty of shortening years, and nothing more. She should be sitting by a warm stove, with sweet, hot wine, to enjoy her remaining years instead of standing in our way."

Tokerae said nothing.

"We know what is possible, you and I," Ella continued. "We have the fire and metal inside to forge Etallan's future. All mother has is fading embers."

"She seems full of vigor, for all that," he said bitterly.

"Ask the mage," Ella repeated. "Unless you're afraid of him?" The taunt was simple and obvious. She gave him an amused, affectionate smile to soften it.

"We've had nothing useful from the arrogant, condescending creature. Not even a clever Rochi card trick."

"Ask him."

Undul Etris Tay had explained all of the ways that he could not help them. Then he ate their best food, consumed expensive twunta, and wandered Etallan at all hours, like a curious, undisciplined child. The elder cousin trailed along, but kept losing him. Ella and Tokerae were forced to send another family member as well, while at the same time trying to pretend that this stranger who could somehow walk into any room was unimportant. Certainly was not a mage.

One day, the Forge Master had come to Tokerae.

"Ser. Your guest? Using rare and expensive metals. Gonna burn himself," the Master said. "Or someone else."

"Let him," Tokerae had told the Forge Master. What choice did they have? "I don't care if he burns himself. Keep everyone else well back. Just in case."

Tokerae could easily imagine the mage destroying the forge entirely, then walking out, unscathed, to ask about dinner. It was unnerving to have the mage wandering House Etallan; they wondered what he might stumble across or find that they would prefer hidden, but at least they knew where he was.

Then, suddenly, they didn't. The mage was gone from sight, leaving those tasked with following him in a panic.

But he showed up for the evening meal.

Undul Etris Tay was either the best swindler to ever stumble over Etallan's threshold, or he was the most dangerous threat the House had ever faced.

Either way, could he help them with the problem of their mother?

"Ask him," Ella said for a third time.

Tokerae nodded. "If I can find him."

∾

Undul Etris Tay raised his fingers from rinsing them in the ever-present bowl of warm water. He flicked away the excess, spraying lavender and orange scent into the air, then dried his hands with meticulous care on a small towel. A crumb fell from his beard onto his lap.

How, Tokerae wondered again, could the mage be so fastidious about some things and so uninterested in others?

The mage looked at Tokerae with distaste. "And what?"

To the point, then.

"Have you been to the palace, High One?" Tokerae asked.

"Your mother asked me the same thing. Wretchedly poor listeners, you Iliban. The monarch and unborn child are healthy. Likely to stay so."

Tokerae took a moment to digest this disappointing news.

"And what?" the mage snapped.

"You have said, High One, that you make no Iliban monarchs. I hear you. I hear you well."

"Some of much," the mage replied, looking bored.

"But..." There would be no turning back, not after this. Tokerae's voice dropped. "Would you consider making an eparch?"

The mage's look was suddenly sharp. For a moment Tokerae felt a warmth pass through him.

"I thought that you were kin."

"We are. Of course we are. My mother, after all. But elderly. In need of a rest. It's just a matter of timing."

A snort. The mage wiped his mouth with the towel. "Perhaps I tell her of this conversation."

Tokerae fought a desire to swallow nervously. "Perhaps you do. But how would that serve you, High One? I will be eparch after her, and when I am, I can continue to offer you the finest meals in Yarpin at any time."

"With this chef? You will keep her?"

"Her position is permanent." It wasn't, but it could be made so.

"You live so short," the mage said, frowning.

Was that a complaint? Or a threat? Tokerae decided to take it as a positive step in negotiations.

"I expect to live a very long time," Tokerae said with feeling.

The mage shrugged. "Yes, why not."

Tokerae blinked. That sounded very much like an agreement. Was this what passed for a formal contract with mages? *They think of you as cattle.*

"Just a little nudge," Tokerae said quickly, barely believing his luck. "Nothing that harms her."

The mage laughed, gave him a long look, then laughed again. "You are certain that you are next in line?"

"Without question."

"A little nudge. Hm. Some of much. When I get to it."

When I get to it?

Tokerae opened his mouth to object, then thought better of it. "You will inform me?"

"I think you'll notice."

That was not reassuring. Or was it? "What are you going to do?"

"Not to mind," he said with a wave of his fingers. "Don't forget your promise. I wouldn't like that."

"Never ever, High One."

The mage rubbed his nose with the back of his hand and looked at Tokerae, then flicked his fingers at him, though they were now dry. "And what? Go away."

"High One," Tokerae said. He began to bow, aborted it, then did it again, just like his mother had. He clamped his jaw shut, turned, and left the room. Behind him, the mage chuckled.

An unsettling conversation, but it seemed to have been a successful one. First he would find Ella and tell her the good news. Then he'd get to the kitchen to tell the chef that she had a new home.

Finally, he'd leave the House, very quietly, and unseen, for his evening with Lilsla.

~

Tokerae gripped a handful of Lilsla's thick honey-brown hair and brought her face to his. He kissed her deeply, then did it again.

He rolled off to lie by her side. He had not felt this good since... when? Since the last time he had seen her.

Sweat trickled down his ribs to the sheets. He turned to look at her. In the firelight, her stomach glowed with a sheen of sweat. He stroked it, marveling at her soft skin.

"Lilsla, something is..." He trailed off, not sure what he had been about to say.

She turned her head to look at him, attentive.

"Going to happen," he finished. "Things may change."

"The eparchy, at last? Oh Tok, that's—"

"Yes, that. But maybe more than that."

She looked confused. "More than the eparchy?"

No, he shouldn't have said that. He stopped stroking her. "Lilsla, you must not repeat that."

"Of course not. Never."

What was wrong with him, that he had said anything like that?

Well, it was Lilsla. She was not just anyone. She would never betray his trust, though Ella would, of course, be furious if she found out that he was here, let alone what he had just said. He must be more careful.

"More than the eparchy," Lilsla said thoughtfully, turning her body to face him, one hand tucked under her ear, the other on his thigh, stroking.

Tokerae had thought himself spent, but found that to be

untrue. Feeling the tightness and hunger spark in his groin, he inhaled sharply and began to reach for her.

Cohort training kicked in, and he reviewed the timing. She had stroked his thigh just after he had said something that he shouldn't have. Was she trying to seduce him into saying more? He searched her eyes.

She smiled at him. "After things change, maybe you could help those of us in the trades, the way that other man said he would."

"What other man?"

"The one who used to speak to crowds in the market square. At night? The one who pretended to be the Royal Consort?"

Tokerae's heart pounded. He sat up. "Pretended? What do you mean?"

Seeming puzzled, she drew herself up alongside him. "I thought you knew, because you grew up with the real Consort, that he wasn't...he wasn't..." At his expression, she trailed off.

"Why would you think this?" he whispered.

Her mouth quirked a little, amused. "I saw him up close, one time."

"What does that mean, you saw him up close? What did you see?"

"His shoes, Tok. His clothes were fine. So beautiful. But I know shoes, and his were... well-made, certainly. Good shoes." She shook her head. "But not the sort the royal Consort would wear."

"What do you know of such things? You who have never even been to the palace? Maybe he put on poor ones, to talk to poor people."

"Well, yes. But why would he dress so fine, head to ankle, and wear lesser shoes? It makes no sense."

Because the idiots whom Tokerae and Ella had chosen to dress him that night hadn't thought it through.

Tokerae took her shoulders in his hands and brought her face close to his. "You've said nothing of this absurd idea of yours to anyone, have you?"

She replied, but it was an instant too slow. "No, of course not." His grip on her shoulders tightened. She swallowed, eyes widening. "I haven't. Tok, I haven't. I swear. Not a word."

Ella had been right. What a fool he'd been to come to this woman, even in secret. And then, to speak so openly, to hint at their plans... With what he had just said to her, and what she had guessed about the mutt's twin—anyone who had both of those facts could put the rest together.

He pushed her away, and she rolled to her knees on the bed, hunching over.

"Tok, really and truly, I've said nothing, not to anyone. You're right, I see that now—he wore those to walk in the commons and the mud. Why, if I had such fine shoes as he must own, I would never wear them out into such a—"

He slapped her across the face. Then again. "You will say nothing of this, not ever again."

In a whisper, she echoed him. "I will say nothing of this. Never again."

He stared at her.

No, it wasn't good enough. Because she *had* said it, just now, to him. And when he'd asked her if she'd told anyone else, she had hesitated. So she had told someone, and was lying about it. She thought he couldn't tell. She was wrong.

Or maybe she thought he could tell, and was being obvious on purpose.

Tokerae had been raised on just these sorts of games. This was simple blackmail, she was telling him that her good behavior relied on something. Something he had yet to give her.

He would give her nothing.

He got up from the bed and began to dress.

"Tok?" she asked softly. "Tokerae? Please. I'm sorry. I didn't mean... I don't know anything about anything. I'm a silly woman. I...Tok?"

He stood at the door, hand on the latch to open it, his head low. Her voice was a silk rope tugging him back.

"Tok, please forgive me. I'll do whatever you want. Anything."

And what would she want, in return for that anything?

He snorted, then left, shutting the door hard behind him. His most trusted armsman stood outside, guarding the door.

"Send her away," he said to the first. "Far away."

"Yes, my lord." The first armsman frowned. "Ser, do you mean send her away, or do you really mean..."

The armsman trailed off, watching him, waiting.

Tokerae took a breath. What else did Lilsla know? What had Tokerae foolishly admitted, unthinking, after hours of her intoxicating body next to his?

All his plans depended on the right people knowing what he wanted them to, when he wanted them to. And the wrong ones knowing nothing.

Tokerae's money and power was nothing compared to what it could be. Lilsla would need to be a halfwit not to see the advantages of keeping him in her debt.

Not the sort the royal Consort would wear.

What a fool he'd been. It was blackmail. If she said anything to anyone...

"See to it," he said soberly, "that she speaks to no one, ever again. If you can manage that and still let her breathe, do so. If not...if not..."

Tokerae looked around, swallowing, unable to complete the sentence.

"I understand, my lord," said his armsman softly. "I will take care of it."

"Don't hurt her."

A slow, confused blink. Then another one. "Yes, my lord."

Chapter Two

UNDUL ETRIS TAY had slid comfortably into a palace routine.

First, he would change from the fluffy robes he'd convinced some mid-city Iliban to give him into his green-and-cream servant's garb, which he kept stashed in a high cupboard in what was now his storage room. Much easier to wander dressed this way, and not have to keep up the shadow and light that shielded him from Iliban eyes.

Not that Iliban noticed very much, even when they looked. Still, a few did, especially children, and there was no advantage to alarming them.

Next, he would stroll the palace halls, touching walls and tapestries to hear what wood, stone, plaster, and fabric had to say. Mostly it was Iliban confusion and fear, desire and avarice. Muddles of messy emotions, splattered everywhere like a toddler displeased with his food.

He would then go to the massive palace kitchen, there to visit with the queen's second chef, a woman that Undul Etris Tay had persuaded to adore him beyond reason, despite his seeming to be a mere servant. The chef was entirely infatuated with him now, judging by the markers in her blood, changes in temperature, and the glowing at her groin. She eagerly offered him generous bits of whatever she happened to be making, which made the decision as to whether to stay for the royal meal, or to return to Etallan, much simpler.

After that, Undul Etris Tay would visit the library. There he would lose himself, quite happily, for a bell or two, combing through books and scrolls, cubes, and even the very rare knotted poems that the Iliban kept in locked boxes.

Finally, he would wend his way back to his storage room, which through no accident was just under the queen's apartments. Unguarded, unlike all the rooms above and besides her apartments, because, apparently, Iliban—like some sort of vole—knew how to dig, but not how to climb.

Iliban. Not at all clever. But then, with such short lives, one could hardly expect them to learn much before they died.

This line of reasoning reminded him of the rumors of fascinating conversations taking place, possibly right this moment. He could, no doubt, join those dangerous discussions, if he wanted to. Deep underground, below the ocean, questions were being raised about the Dictates of the Council of Mages.

In the safety of his own mind, he could admit that he felt the draw to such a meeting. Few among the magi would argue that Iliban were their equal, and those were the ones who had entirely lost their minds. But there agreement ended. Should Iliban be allowed to do as they pleased in this world that mages must share with them?

Or should the pretense and exhaustively circuitous engagement with Iliban at long last be dismantled, and Iliban treated as the lesser creatures that they were? Indeed, would it not be in everyone's best interest to give the Iliban proper laws, reliable control, and stop them from killing each other?

They might even be put to good use. Mages needed to eat, and someone must grow the food, after all. They did this already, Iliban did, but how much more effective could they be with mages in command?

He sighed. It always came back to this: overseeing a world of Iliban sounded like drudgery of the worst kind. He had his doubts that such a plan would play out quite as neatly as the Reversionists and Archists claimed.

Who would oversee the Iliban, after all? Not himself, if he could possibly avoid it.

Undul Etris Tay kept his opinions to himself. While he might be tempted to join the Reversionists and Archists for conversation, he was not tempted enough to actually show up. Not while the Council was still at thirteen.

Thirteen of the world's most powerful mages working in concert was plenty to fear. Even if you discounted their many magi supporters, tucked away across the world.

It was a miserable wager, if a mage wished to live. Which he did. Most certainly.

No, Undul Etris Tay would follow his aetur in this matter, who urged his alignment with the Council, and a strict adherence to the Dictates.

The Tay magi lineage tended toward the practical, and he and his aetur, Urtar Tay Ert, as a matter of simple sense, stayed as far from the attention of the Council of Mages as all effort would allow.

So much for that plan.

For a moment, Undul Etris Tay entertained thoughts of reporting Etallan's illegal hiring of a mage to the monarch's Minister of Justice. That would certainly be amusing, but would accomplish nothing; Iliban didn't care about anything as banal as their own laws. Not when there was coin to be made by ignoring them, and Etallan had money. Enough to afford a mage.

Coin was not why Undul Etris Tay had come to Yarpin. Coin could be had anywhere.

It was the food and the smokables, as splendid and singular as reputed. He had been pleased, not only with the cuisine but with the twunta. Despite the annoying Iliban, he had been having rather a good time, right up until the moment when the wretched spawn of House Etallan had asked him to unseat—or better yet, kill—their queen for them.

Just like that, he was squarely in the middle of an overthrow scheme devised by Iliban who, to his surprise, might actually be able to pull it off, putting Undul Etris Tay directly in the causal line of monarch-making, in high breach of the Dictates.

Should the Council investigate—and they would, sooner or later, if Etallan achieved its goals—the fact that he had been there when it happened would become clear to them, and then the Council would closely examine the involvement and conduct of one Undul Etris Tay dua Mage.

That was not an experience he wanted to have.

He'd thought about leaving and going far away, but it was too late: he was too close to the matter to pretend he had not been here. It would be very clear that he was present when the deed happened, and that would be known once the Council decided to investigate.

But he could protect himself. If not from the regard of the Council, at least from their castigation.

Like all mages, he knew the Dictates through and through, and it was only an offense to take down a monarch, or raise one up. There was no offense in maintaining one.

And so it was that Undul Etris Tay, after his desire for excellent food and rare books had been momentarily sated, snuggled into his cozy storage room nest with the fine amardide blankets and silk pillows that he'd taken from across the palace, wriggling to obtain a most comfortable position in his makeshift bed, and closed his eyes.

From there he would examine the queen through two walls and twenty feet of elevation. When something wasn't quite right in the bubble of her pregnancy, he would adjust it. When the growing creature within pressed too tightly in one direction or another, he would gently nudge.

Indeed, when anything troubled her royal majesty's physical body, Undul Etris Tay would make it right.

Every few days he would come back. To enjoy the food. To peruse the library.

And to make certain that Undul Etris Tay could not be accused of making or unmaking the queen of the Arunkel empire.

"A marvel, Sacha," Cern said, glancing out the sitting room window at the points of color that were spring flowers in the lush gardens below. She rubbed circles over her huge belly. "No pain at all. Barely any discomfort. So unlike last time, when..."

When she had nearly died. No need to finish that sentence.

"A blessing," Sachare replied, distracted by Estarna who was wriggling under a couch to get a ball she had misplaced. A moment later, Sachare brought out a pink ball from the other side.

A fire burned in the hearth. The dogs, Chula and Tashu, sprawled in front of it, their black-and-tan brindled faces full of sleepy contentment, black-tipped ears twitching as Estarna squealed, tugging on Sachare's other hand, voicing her nickname. Rather relentlessly, Cern noted.

"Saka, saka, saka, saka!"

"A moment, Esta," Sachare said. "Perhaps you're getting the hang of it, now, Your Grace."

"Ball, ball, ball, ball." Estarna jumped for what Sachare held in her hand.

The child was learning words at a stunning rate. Also running and falling. Then getting up again, which was, to Cern, watching closely, the skill one most needed to rule.

And screaming. Cern had not realized how loud such a small creature could be. Ah, the education of motherhood.

At least the child and dogs were getting along well. Chula and Tashu seemed to understand instantly that Estarna was theirs to protect, and took to the work readily, getting between her and any stranger, growling when anyone new entered the room.

"Perhaps I am," Cern answered. Indeed, if the rest of the babies that she had planned were this easy, it made the Grandmother's many offspring seem far more plausible.

"Hungry?" asked Sachare.

"Always. But I only want to keep them waiting so long."

Cern needed Anandynar family backing almost as much as she needed the Houses. Her kin, both distant and near, needed reason to support her. *Bound in word and blood.* It was time for the blood part.

"They will wait a bit longer for you to have food," Sachare said. "Not you," she said to the dogs, who had lifted their heads hopefully at the mention of food. Chula gave a huff, reclining again.

Sachare was holding the ball just out of reach until the child quieted, then she dropped it into Estarna's open hands.

Food came promptly. Cern ate more than she would have thought possible. Estarna put more food onto her face than into her mouth, and squealed in delight at Sachare's playfully reproachful expression. Sachare then joined her in the minor mess.

When Cern judged the child fed, she spoke. "Bring them in now."

Sachare wiped her own face and Estarna's clean of food. More toys were brought, and the two of them settled on blankets by the dogs.

"Are you certain that you want us here for this, Your Grace?" Sachare asked.

"Yes. They need to know who they're protecting."

At Cern's order the two doors into the room were opened simultaneously. From one entered Nalas. Through the other came Cern's aunt Lismar and her uncle Lason.

Sachare put a hand on the softly growling Chula, who quieted.

All three of Cern's visitors bowed low, then stood, their gazes flickering to each other. Lason's return to the palace had been kept a secret, so Nalas was surprised, his look bordering on alarm. Lason had not known what this meeting was about, and was scowling at Nalas.

Cern studied them closely. This moment of raw reaction gave her a window into their minds, but also meant that she must take control quickly.

"Listen to me," Cern said sharply. "I need you. All of you. None of you are expendable."

It had come to Cern that as precarious as things were now, she could not afford the struggles of the old system, the one that the Cohort was built on. She must fashion a new one.

Nalas was well-liked, and growing fast in capability. But he was not an Anandynar.

"Nalas," she said, "you have served well as Lord Commander, but you lack the seasoning I require." And the name, but she would not say that, though he was clever enough to understand. "You are now responsible for in-palace security. This is no demotion; my safety and that of the heir—the very monarchy—depends upon you and the queenguards that you command."

"General Lismar," Cern continued, "your leadership on the field of battle has been proven again and again. I assign you to oversee all of the crown's external forces."

Lismar, whom Cern had spoken to before, was unsurprised.

"Uncle Lason," Cern said. "Welcome back to the palace. I name you Lord Commander of the Host of Arunkel. Lismar and Nalas will report to you."

Lason, narrow-eyed and by all appearances ready to be angry at Nalas for having taken his former position, looked stunned, his fury forgotten.

"They will also report to me," Cern added. "Your work, uncle, is to assure the integrity of the whole of the Host. Mine is to oversee the entirety of this new triad of command."

Cern gave the three of them a moment. In their faces she read everything she'd expected: confusion at this odd division; suspicion, uncertainty, mistrust, and—there it was, now, just rising—piqued interest.

They stopped looking at each other, and began to stare into the distance. Considering the implications. Planning.

Good.

Lason was now nearly smiling. He had been replaced by Innel at Cern's command, and had been loudly unhappy about it. This reinstatement was all the redress he could have asked for. But the smug look he gave Cern now told her that she would need to keep him in line.

It had been Lismar's idea. Cern had been surprised, knowing what Lismar thought of her brother.

"Lord Commander? Why?" Cern had asked.

Lismar had grinned. "It's a target position, Your Grace. Why do you think we gave it to him in the first place?"

A target position. Cern understood.

Now the royals who had been furious at Cern appointing the commoner mutt Innel as Lord Commander would be appeased as well.

"If you have any questions," she said to the three of them, "you will come to me."

Slow nods all around. Unlike the old system, where a single Lord Commander oversaw all of their new duties, each of them now would come directly to Cern. That would mean more work for her, with everything she must attend to including this creature growing inside her, but it also meant that she would know far more about what was going on than she used to.

It was about time.

"My breath as law," she said, formalizing it, seeing their expressions settle into acceptance. "You have work to do. I release you to it."

~

"Adra, I have some news."

They lay in bed together, staring at the sparkling, colorful ceiling overhead.

The Domina had a particular way of speaking when she was following some long, complicated trail of thought, the sort of trail that Innel might have easily followed once upon a time. He found that he rather enjoyed her tone. It came from the back of her throat, as she drew the vowels of each word long and low.

He had also, across these months, found some pleasure in his work here in her eight-sided room. Mostly, the work was silent. He knew what she wanted, and it was no hardship to show her the many things the Cohort anknapa had taught them so well and so long ago, when they had come of age. In return, she showed him how each of the devices on the walls was used.

In truth, the most difficult part had been discovering that Zeted was keenly and loudly pleased with some of the very same things that Cern had liked. In those moments, the memories came back, pounding on the door of his mind and drowning out all else.

"What is it?" Zeted had once asked. He struggled to answer, his tongue caught. Finally he managed, "more kanna, Domina."

She snorted in amusement. But after that, back in his room, Ralafi supplied Innel with a range of intoxicants. Like a buffet. Duca, kanna, twunta. Sometimes even phapha. It settled him, mind and spirit.

Yet the voices came, sometimes when he least expected them. His brother's. Cern's.

I condemn you as a traitor.

Sometimes, in the moment before sleep, his daughter's face swam into his mind, and his eyes leaked.

Now he stared at the sparkling ceiling. The Domina had been very generous, asking in return only that he attend to her, which he was happy to do. His Cohort education, finally good for something.

He startled at her touch on his naked shoulder.

"Adra."

She's talking to you, brother.

Innel turned his head toward her, his mouth working, trying to apologize for having mistaken her voice for the ones in his head. But the words he might once have used stacked atop each other, wiggling around, fighting for dominance. He worked his mouth in silence, then gave up.

"What a fabulous mess it is," Zeted said at last in her musical voice, "the capital of Arunkel. Adra."

Arunkel.

That word now sat at the top of the heap. In his mind's eye, Innel saw the bright Yarpin harbor thick with docks and colorful with ships' flags. He saw palace hallways, wide and well-lit from windows that looked out onto palace gardens, then up and up into blue skies.

He saw his daughter, whom he had failed. A wordless moan escaped his throat.

"Here, Adra. Have some of this." Zeted offered him a delicate porcelain plate on which was a fortune of thinly sliced, milky white qualan, like a tiny loaf of bread. Innel took a slice and put it on his tongue, letting his head fall back to the pillow.

"A fabulous mess," Zeted repeated. "Even the Perripin Congredia with all its dramatics cannot compare. If someone were to describe to me the histrionics taking place in the empire to the north—the queen's new heir, the execution of that child's father—I would suggest that they change the names and take it to the Kelerre Grand Stage, where I would gladly back the production."

The new heir.

A throbbing, dull pain warred with a sudden rush from the qualan. The pain gave way, washed over by a puff of sea air through the windows, and the delicate paintings of hummingbirds and fornicating figures worked into the sparkling, illuminated ceiling.

Innel swallowed, the taste of qualan an ecstatic bitterness at the back of his throat.

He turned slowly to look at Zeted. Her skin was marvelous and dark, like oiled wood, and soft, like plush silk velvets. He traced fingers across her cheek, down her neck, to her collarbone.

She wrapped his wandering fingers in her hand. "The queen's child, Adra. Was it really his, do you think?"

Innel blinked away his daughter's green eyes.

"Yes."

"Ah, how interesting. Then, do you think it is true, what they say, about the crimes he committed?"

"Reckless. Clumsy. Not a traitor."

"Ah," Zeted replied.

She sat up against a wealth of pillows, taking from a side table a glass riddled with lines of gold, and swirled thick, brown-green liquid. From the pungent scent Innel knew it for a rare, imported liqueur, made from pine needles that grew on the Spine of the World.

He knew this, because Cern had tried it once and had not liked it.

Cern.

Zeted, however, did like it. She made an appreciative sound and held the glass to him. He sat up, took a sip, then handed it back. The sweet liquid combined pleasantly with the qualan in his stomach. For a moment, he could almost forget that something sick also lived there.

"The news," Zeted continued, "is that the Arunkel queen is again pregnant."

Innel sank down into the bed and stared at his fingers, where his nails were still cracked and thin.

"Adra. There is more." She reached down and took his chin, gently turning his face to hers. "He was executed."

So beautiful, the Domina was. A stunning woman, from her wild thick black hair to her great breasts. Even her toes were marvelous, and he ought to know.

"Who?" he asked, having again lost the trail of the conversation.

"The traitor mutt. The royal Consort. Innel sev Cern esse Arunkel. He was executed."

Innel was suddenly aware that Zeted was watching him very closely. He stared back, reviewing the words she'd said, making sure that he had heard them right.

Careful, brother.

"Executed?" he managed.

"Yes. Hanged, his hands and feet chopped off, his body burned."

Innel tried to imagine it, could not. Was it possible that it had happened, and he had forgotten?

No, that was absurd. He'd be dead.

"Hooded," Zeted added.

Clever, came the clear thought, unbidden. Cern had needed the traitor executed, to go forward and maintain control. But he wasn't there. Hooded.

Well done, Cern.

Then the realization landed on him: he was dead to all. He would never be able to go back. He would never see his daughter again.

Innel trembled, hunched tight, eyes shut against tears, shut against knowing what he already knew.

"There, there, Adra," said Zeted, stroking his head. "It's only the Grand Stage of Arunkel. It doesn't affect us here in Bayfahar, not in the least. Have another sip of this marvelous brew, my pretty one. Sit up. There you go. Drink it. Drink it all. Then we'll return to some of what you do so well."

Chapter Three

A RUSHING SOUND. A throbbing. The ocean. Her heartbeat.

It seemed to Amarta that her feet walked without her will.

They passed low buildings in dim twilight, smoke rising from squat chimney stacks atop structures shaped like low hillocks, covered in dirt.

Tayre spoke to someone. Money. Credit. He pressed a pack into Amarta's arms and it moved.

Tadesh.

Amarta held it tight to her chest. Not too tight.

It trembled.

Could she be trusted with Tadesh, given what she had done?

That thought brought her alert. She looked around, feeling lost.

Tayre gave her a touch to reassure, then handed something to the woman with whom he had been speaking. He pressed Amarta down into a low doorway, where steps led underground.

A narrow passage. A small, low-ceilinged room. On the floor, a cot. Amarta sank down, setting the pack gently on the floor.

"Drink this," Tayre said.

She didn't ask. She didn't foresee. She drank.

She slept.

~

"Keep going," Tayre said, pressing her forward. The way was up, and steep. Tight switchbacks climbed a high cliff, out of the harbor town where they had spent the night. Tayre carried everything.

The rising sun laid every shadow bare.

"I killed him," she said. Her first words since they left the ship.

Morning, but it was already hot. With each step, Amarta's feet raised puffs of dirt.

"He killed himself, using power he didn't understand," replied Tayre.

"He sacrificed himself for nothing."

"To save us. That's not nothing."

One step after another. A slow, grinding ascent.

"I killed him."

"Keep going."

~

In the moment before waking, Amarta knew, but also did not.

The blade of memory. The cut about to come.

She clung to wisps of sleep's solace, but it was as if she stood on a spike and must fall.

Olessio.

She blinked awake.

The room was hot, a line of sun on her face from a gap in a wooden shutter overhead.

She shut her eyes again, but memory found her.

Huge ocean waves. Great capsized ships. Shouts, cries. Islands rising and falling, seawater sluicing across mountain sides, through forests. Beaches stripped of sand. A sheen of something pale, where fields and meadows now cracked open.

Olessio.

A whimper escaped her. A series of shuddering, gasping sobs took over.

Tayre pressed a warm, quivering Tadesh into her arms.

"I'm sorry," she whispered to the trembling animal. Tadesh curled, her thick tail covering her face. Amarta wet her pelt with tears.

~

O lessio.

Amarta pushed off the covers, stumbled to her feet. The lack of him was a gaping, seeping wound that refused to finish its business and let her die.

Half-naked, she stumbled out the cabin's door, onto the road, dimly aware that Tayre followed.

In the east, a crescent moon shone through shreds of clouds, putting the land in deep shadow. She ran toward it until the road ended at the edge of a bluff. A silvery, moonlit ocean stretched into the night.

She howled. Once she started, she could not seem to stop.

When at last she had no more voice, Tayre took her by the hand, and led her back, as the twilight began.

Villagers stood outside thatched houses, and watched the two of them pass.

The lands of Seute Enta were spare. Dusty, rutted roads were dotted with tufts of grass that held stubbornly to life. Scraggly trees marked dry streambeds where boulders gathered, waiting for rain.

In the distance, brown and blue mountains wavered in the day's heat.

Amarta walked, aware only that the land beneath her was as unlike the Island Road as any land could be.

A remembered flash: her feet sank into vibrant green moss.

That was before. Before she had urged Olessio to open a hole in a sack of spider silk and release the island's eggs.

Olessio! Yes! More!

Before Amarta had tried to liberate people who didn't need it, didn't want it, and ended up destroying them instead.

More!

His skin sagged like a melting candle. He looked toward her, blinking blood. His last act, to throw Tadesh clear, must have taken everything he had.

On the ship, Tayre had gathered Tadesh and gently dabbed at her fur, cleaning her pelt of Olessio's bloody handprints.

Amarta blinked into the present. She looked around, frantic.

"Here," Tayre said. He held out the pack. Amarta took it, cradling Tadesh within. The animal shuddered through the fabric.

"Why didn't I see it coming?" she asked, her voice hoarse.

"There was a good deal to see, Amarta."

"Why?"

"Many things were in motion, all at once. No one sees everything."

As if they belonged to someone else, her feet kept walking.

She wept. Tayre took the pack from her arms.

"I didn't see it."

"Amarta."

Before he went under, Olessio balanced on the remaining two boards, blinded by his own blood.

"Why didn't I see it?" she yelled at the bleak Seute Enta lands, at the washed-bright sky, and into the heavy air.

She didn't remember going to the ground, but Amarta was on her hands and knees, pounding the dry dirt, her teardrops raising puffs of dust, sobs gripping her body.

He waited until she was done, then took her arm, drew her to her feet, and pressed her forward.

"Keep going."

$\sim$

"Why am I here breathing, when he is not?"

A dark, lamplit, low-ceilinged room. Amarta sat on a cot, staring at stone walls.

A few feet away, Tayre was mixing something in a bowl.

"Life," he said, "is not a prize bestowed upon the deserving. It simply is."

He held the bowl to her. Thick, white, lumpy.

Like Island Pearls.

"I'm not hungry."

"Olessio," Tayre said slowly, each syllable cutting into her like a knife, "would have wanted you to eat."

Just a bite, hmm?

She took the bowl, stared into it, then felt sickened, and set it down.

"Tadesh must eat, too." Tayre gently drew the small animal from the pack, put her next to Amarta, and set down bits of cheese.

Tadesh made a sound between a whine and a wheeze, turning her head away when Amarta tried to feed her, then slunk back into the pack.

That night, Amarta woke to the whistling howl of the wind.

No, it was not wind. It was Tadesh, searching the corners of the room and making small sounds as she failed to find what she was looking for.

Amarta called to her, then crawled to her, but Tadesh kept searching.

"Where is she?" Amarta cried out, waking suddenly, and scrabbling to her feet to search. They had camped on the banks of a nearly dry stream.

Tayre was at her side.

"Amarta."

"Where is she?" Amarta demanded.

"You don't remember?"

A dream. A nightmare.

"No, no." She looked around and around. "Where did she go? Where?"

Tayre pointed. "That way. Toward the mountains."

"We go after her."

"Do we?" His voice was soft.

"He gave her to us, to take care of. It was the last thing he did."

"That is true. But you can't care for someone who doesn't want it." His hand snapped out and grabbed her arm before she could run. "Listen. We could follow her, yes. It would be a hard trek into those mountains. We'd need guides, pack animals, supplies. We'd risk coming across the deadly beetles they call the Eufalmo. Yes, we could do this, Amarta, if you are absolutely certain. First tell me: will we find her?"

Amarta stared at the mountains. Time passed as she sought vision for the first time since she had lost Olessio, searching every future. Searching, searching.

Tadesh was not there.

He released his grip on her arm as she sank to the ground.

〜

They walked. In the heat of the day, because Amarta could not sit still. Like fools, like lunatics.

At each step, their worn and grimy boots kicked up dust. Agony propelled Amarta forward, the pain in her legs and feet a balm to the wounds that bled her spirit.

There is always a path to failure, is there not? she had said.

Who would say such a thing? A child, no more thinking than a foolish beast, thrashing its way through delicate lives, breaking everything it saw.

Always a path to failure. Had she taken every one of them?

How could she have been so stupid?

Her lungs burned in the hot air. She stumbled, caught herself, did it again.

At last Tayre drew her, unresisting, to shade. He made her drink and rest until she was recovered enough to insist that they return to the road.

〜

Another town. This time, low, square houses sunk into hard, carved stone. They were cool inside, with ceilings so low that Tayre could not stand.

On a cot, they lay together, the room lit only by pinpoints of light around the edges of the door.

"I failed him."

"I think he would say that he failed you." Tayre replied softly.

"He succeeded. Too well. Because I pushed him. I should have been the one to die."

"He would not have wanted that."

"I want to die."

"It will pass."

She turned to him. "You could do it."

"No."

"But it would be so easy for you."

He let out a long breath. "It will pass."

She sat up, angry. "What do you know? You feel nothing."

He drew himself up to sit beside her.

"Amarta. It will pass."

"You mean I'll stop wanting to die?"

"I mean you'll stop ripping yourself apart for what you did, or did not do, as if such self-wounds could change the past. Then, perhaps, you'll begin to understand what really happened."

"Is that what you did, when tragedy shredded your young life and tore away everything you knew?" A guess built of something Olessio had said.

His face changed in the dim light. Only now did she realize that he was rarely truly expressionless. His eyes and mouth always contained at least a hint of intention, emotion, pretended or otherwise.

Only now, because she had never before seen his face so utterly blank. Had she gone too far? Said too much?

Well, when hadn't she?

Then a small, shocking smile came to his face.

"He was a worthy companion," Tayre said gently, and Amarta knew from his face that he understood the genesis of her guess. "And wise."

Again she wept.

～

"We could go back to Arunkel," Tayre said as they walked. "You could see your sister and nephew."

"No."

"A return to Maris's homestead, then. She could help you heal."

"No."

"Western Perripur. Somewhere new, but a place where the language and people are familiar."

Familiarity was the last thing Amarta wanted. She shook her head.

"Where, then?"

"Keep going."

～

The road curved, turned, rose and fell. How long had it been since they had walked straight?

They passed an empty town. Sun-bleached stone rubble surrounded abandoned mound-houses. Brown-green tangles of plants clawed life from dry land, wrapping themselves around the stones. Heaps of horned skeletons that might once have been oxen marked the edges of what might once have been fields.

They passed a shallow watering hole, where black and white horned goats drank, watching them warily.

The road took them up another hill, down another valley. Again and again.

Tayre left her in the shade of a great boulder as he followed a hawk circling overhead. She couldn't stop the colorless memory, when Tadesh followed Tayre into the woods, and Olessio wove strands of ginger and yam into bits of edible beauty.

It is not enough to simply eat.

Tayre returned with a lifeless raccoon, tucking his sling back into his shirt. At a cookfire, the meat bubbled, set to cool on rocks. Tayre tore off bits, put them in front of her.

"Eat."

A thought came to her. She stared at him, mouth agape.

"You knew."

"I knew what?"

"You knew what would happen. You told me. I didn't listen."

"I did not know."

"You must have. Why else would you have warned me, again and again?" Then, when he did not answer immediately: "Why didn't you stop me?"

Somehow, she was inches from his face, breath coming hard, without any memory of how she'd gotten there.

"Advising caution is not the same thing as knowing," he replied mildly.

She saw in his eyes the reflected land around them, the barren landscape, the rocks and scrub. Had she ever been this close to him before?

All fear of him was gone.

"I was a fool. A child. Why in all the Hells didn't you stop me?"

"Because you were neither."

"I made a horrible mistake."

"And you learn."

She sat back, blinking hard. "Nothing I could learn from this is worth what it cost." She looked around, unseeing. "If you knew, and you didn't stop me, then you killed him, and I damn you for it."

He shrugged slightly. She wanted to hurt him. Close enough to hit. If she went at him, full out, with enough intent, might he kill her?

If he saw the craving in her eyes, he didn't show it. Instead he tore off a small leg from the roasted meat. With it, he gestured to the bits that he had set out for her.

"Eat," he said.

~

Amarta woke to her own whimpering. An underground room, dark on black. Tayre stirred beside her.

"It hurts," she said to the darkness.

"It will pass."

"When?"

She heard him inhale.

"It will pass."

~

Tayre did what needed doing. Negotiations, packing, carrying. Amarta became increasingly disgusted at her own uselessness.

At a hilltop way-house that they had just entered, she set about to unpack a bag. Tugging on a leather thong, she managed to tangle it further. She yanked again. It stuck tight.

"Shall I do that for you?" Tayre asked.

Subtle but unmistakable, the hint of condescension in his tone.

Amarta tried to force open the knot with her teeth, but the leather turned wet and swollen.

Tayre watched her struggle, then brought out the knife with the jade handle, offering it to her hilt first.

"Go on, cut it. A faster solution."

She stared at him, confused. Something inside her tightened.

"What are you saying?"

He snorted in amusement. "Slice it open. The cords will be useless after that, but the problem will be solved, yes?"

A nameless pain kindled inside her. A wordless moan escaped.

"You mean the islands," she breathed. "The children."

She had cut through a tangle of futures to save them, cut through their very lives to find a solution, and that same cut had killed Olessio.

Tayre shrugged, as if he did not care.

"Why would you say that?" she cried.

"I'm tired of your whining."

Fury unfurled like a beast inside her, a hot wash of blinding anger, and she struggled to hold herself back from launching at him.

Then it was doused by the realization that he had kindled her outrage deliberately, making himself her target, to give her someone to be angry at besides herself.

No. There was only one suitable target: herself.

"Is it sharp enough?" she asked. The knots were made of leather. Leather was skin.

"Yes."

She took the offered knife, wondering when he would stop her. Vision attempted an answer. She pushed it away.

Where to cut? Stomach? Throat?

What did she know about knives?

In her mind's eye swam the faces of the island children she had tried to save, only to lose them everything. Olessio, who had given his all to help her.

What did she know about anything?

Nothing.

She blinked her eyes clear and levered the tip of the knife under the knot.

Churning, empty ocean. With his last breath, he called her name, then hurled Tadesh to safety.

Amarta had failed him.

And to what grand purpose had all this sacrifice been put?

Amarta had wanted to even the scales, to fix the accounting. Perhaps to find justice for those who needed it. And yet the cost was paid by those whose greatest mistake was to trust her.

No more tears, she decided angrily. She had cried enough.

Nor would she give herself the release of death. For a long moment she stood there, the knife tip under the knot, poised to cut.

Then, very carefully, she drew it back and returned it to Tayre, leaving the knot to stay tangled.

~

The days were unstrung, like beads scattered across a floor, but the winding road forward was the only string that mattered to Amarta.

When they came across the people of Seute Enta, in their sun-cloaks and reddish skin, their faces long and thin, Amarta let Tayre do the talking.

Tayre continued to manage the details of their lives;

shelter for the cold nights and the days when the sandstorms bit. He nagged her until she ate. Pressed a water bag to her mouth until she drank.

Walk. Drink. Eat. Sleep. Walk again.

Slowly, she began to take interest in the lands around them, the thin trees, the rugged grasses. Sharp-edged mountains against pale sky.

"Do you want to go home?" he asked.

It had been a long time since either of them had spoken, and his question itself seemed a knot that she couldn't untie, didn't know how to sever.

Home. Where was home?

Memories of Dirina and Pas came to her, but sluggishly, like a wagon with a rusted axle pressed to move. Her affection for them was a distant memory, as if it belonged to someone else. Pale and colorless.

Arunkel, the land of her birth, seemed a distant place, where cruel, senseless things were done by those who could, to those who could not stop them.

Olessio.

One name to blot out all the other memories.

"There is no home," she replied, her mind returning to the gray place.

"Where are we going?" he asked.

She didn't answer, and again they both fell silent. But the question burrowed into her mind, tearing tiny holes in the walls she had built around the pain. It grabbed threads of thought, drawing them through the holes.

Hours, days, or weeks later, she answered.

"To Seuan. To examine the Heart."

The day-scent of hot pine surrounded them as they lay on the ground in the shade of the heat.

"I've killed more people than you have," she said.

"By accident. All at once. Not quite the same thing."

"I killed him."

"He killed himself."

"It hurts."

"I know."

~

Another underground room. Walls and ceiling of daub on stone, bits of which had fallen to the tile floor, where the dust of years accumulated in the corners. The cracks on the ceiling were like lines on a map that went nowhere.

"Amarta," he said softly, and put a hand on her stomach.

She blinked.

The hand began to move, gently, the fingers traveling up her front, to her face. Tips stroked across her cheek, down her neck.

It was slow. It was shocking.

She blinked again.

"Now?" she asked, looking for outrage—any emotion at all—and not finding it. "Now you say yes?"

His hand paused.

"Now I say yes."

"Why now?"

"You are sick with grief. Touch can heal."

"All the times before, I did not need such healing?" She attempted to spark anger, but it fizzled and went out like wet kindling, leaving only mild bitterness. "Why only now do you offer me this precious elixir?"

"Because your fear of me is overshadowed by your grief. Now it makes sense."

Her choked reply turned into a sob. She caught it before it escaped, stuffed it deep inside.

"I killed him, just as I killed..."

Nidem.

She stared distantly, remembering foresight's vision of her friend Nidem with an arrow through her. The memory of that painful vision, she drew out, drew close, making it vivid in her mind's eye.

Amarta's own cloak, trimmed in blue, across the girl's body, an arrow in her chest. The cloth was dark where blood seeped.

An odd sort of memory, this memory of a vision of what would happen, that she had never seen. And yet, entirely real; Nidem had died.

A small grief now, by comparison to every waking moment. Tayre was right: her wretchedness was a darkness in which no shadow could be seen.

She rolled onto her side to meet his hunter's brown eyes.

"Did you kill her?" she asked.

"No."

She sat up, cross-legged, and turned to face him. "The girl who wore my cloak," she said, punctuating each word. "Her name was Nidem. *Did you kill her?*"

"No."

"Another lie?"

He inhaled, rolled from his side onto his back, and stared at the ceiling. "I did not kill the girl you name Nidem, the one who wore your blue-trimmed cloak, outside Kusan. But I did see her die. I thought she might be you, so when I saw two men attacking the Kusani wagon, I rode down to intercept, to stop them. By the time I arrived, she had an arrow through her and was dead."

His tone held no emotion at all, no persuasion. Perhaps it was true.

"What happened to those men, who you say killed her?"

He sat up on the bed, crossed his legs, facing her. "I ended their lives."

"Did they suffer?"

"Yes."

It was not justice. Justice would need to account for Amarta having put Nidem in the path of that arrow to begin with. After that, justice would need to account for the many whom Amarta had let come to harm and death at the Tree of Revelation.

Then justice must address the thousands of islanders whose homes and lives she had destroyed when the islands dove for their eggs.

Finally, justice would need to account for Olessio. And Tadesh.

Amarta understood now that justice could not do all that. It was too small. It was a tiny, weak thing that broke at the lightest of challenges. Justice was hardly anything at all.

Olessio.

With some effort, she brought her attention to the living man sitting in front of her, and what Olessio had said about his shape in her eyes. Had it changed?

She had craved this man for years. Now, it seemed, she could have him. Did she still want him?

She chuckled at the irony, at the bitter, bleak truth that nothing she had ever gained through vision or effort, had been, by the time she held it, the same thing that she had struggled so hard to get.

The sound of her laughter shocked her even more than Tayre's saying yes.

"Healing, you say." Her voice sounded odd to herself.

With no modesty at all, she pulled off her shirt and shrugged out of her pants. Olessio was dead. What else could matter?

She lay back on the bed and stared at the crumbling ceiling.

"Show me."

Tayre was quite as skillful at sex-touch as Amarta recalled. In truth, his ministrations took the pain away for whole moments at a time, moments in which she could sink into a world of gliding caresses. What Maris had called Amarta's body hunger was finally and daily satisfied.

At those times of the month when her body wanted to make children and she was most hungry, Tayre showed her other ways to be sated.

It came to her that there was something darkly seductive in the flashes vision gave that led to her holding a small child to her breast. Something powerful within her wanted to be known.

But no; it would be an act of deplorable cruelty to bring an innocent into this world, especially now that she had demonstrated how poorly she protected those closest to her.

She recalled her sister's unasked-for pregnancy that had become her nephew Pas. If she felt anything at all toward Dirina and Pas now, it was a dull gratitude that they were far, far away from her, and spared the cost of Amarta's affection.

Tayre was right: day after day, their slick bodies sliding together, this simple yet compelling animal need to which he drew her, was indeed a sort of healing.

Her body had its own will and now seemed to have a reason to sleep, to wake, to eat.

"The pain," she said, one dark night as they lay together in another underground room.

"Yes?"

"You said it would pass." She felt him nod beside her. "In what way does this transformation occur?"

For a time he said nothing. Then: "Imagine that you have a piece of broken glass in your pocket. For whatever reason, you can't take it out. Each day, you reach inside, and the glass cuts you. You might forget for moments that it's there, but put your hand in your pocket again, and you know the pain."

Olessio.

"A year passes," he continued. "A decade. More. You forget entirely. One day you put your hand in your pocket, and you'll find it there. But the shard has dulled. It will always be there, but it dulls. It is easier and easier to touch."

This did not seem possible.

But then, Tayre was no longer who he had once been to her, and that also seemed impossible. Yet it was so.

What's between you two?

The shard was still sharp. The gaping tear that was Olessio, gone, ached beyond bearing.

"Anything," she whispered. "I would give anything to have him back."

"If some entity were offering that bargain, at any cost, the line of people to take it would be very long."

She sniffled. "I won't forget him. Not ever."

"I don't doubt that. Nor will I."

She curled on the bed, her mind full of images of churning seawater and broken glass.

～

They passed villages. Silent faces turned to watch them go by.

At a long-abandoned town, every door had been broken from its frame, human bones embedded in the baked dirt.

"The Eufalmo?" she asked, when it was far behind them.

"That would be my guess."

The land became hilly. Thickening patches of green wove together. Far distant was a hint of forest.

"What is between us?" she asked.

For a time he did not speak, but his silences no longer troubled her.

The road led east, then north again. It occurred to her that perhaps his silences had nothing to do with unnerving her, and had not for some time. Maybe he was sorting things out inside, his thoughts as tangled, in their way, as her own.

"You own the contract that binds us," he said at last. "A contract I am sworn to serve. There is that between us."

"There is that," she agreed.

"Now there is sex as well."

"Yes."

They walked.

"What is between us," he said, "is whatever we decide it is."

We.

Far to the north, snow-tipped mountains seemed no closer than they had days ago. But wasn't that the way of the world? You walked paths that seemed endless. Then, one day, they ended.

"He once told me," she said, "that you must have a gift, one that was also a curse, that drove you to your exceptional skill."

"Did he."

He had also told her that she was his family. The shard was still sharp enough to cut.

It seemed to Amarta that her life before the Island Road was a different life. Then, if someone had asked Amarta to name the hardest moment she'd endured, high on the list would have been the hours—or was it days?—that she had spent in a dark, candlelit room, subject to terror and agony crafted by the man walking at her side.

No longer. One horror to wash away the memory of another?

She should have let them die, Beloveds and islanders all. Let the monks of the Revelation walk their path of righteous falsehood, dragging along their querants in comfortable ignorance. Who were those people to her, anyway?

Strangers. Nothing more. Let every one of them die. An easy trade for one small Farliosan man.

An erroneous accounting, that. As Tayre had said, no such trade was being offered.

Looking back, she saw all her mistakes, among them the taking of halfway measures, the cutting of the problem with the sharp knife of her foresight, while disregarding all the other parts of the knot.

Whatever Tayre said, she had killed Olessio.

"You were right," she said. "Your touch heals. How you smell and taste. Your body against mine. I like these things."

It seemed a long, long time ago that she wondered, incessantly, if he desired her, if he liked her, or if his actions were merely contrived, his words only tools.

Wisdom had come to her, it seemed. Or at least enough experience to realize that words themselves never carried truth. All words were tools.

"Tayre," she said.

"Yes?"

"All the times you said no to me..." she trailed off,

considering how to conclude that sentence.

"Yes?"

"You won't refuse me again."

Without turning to look at him, without altering her pace, she reached out a hand to him. It was the very hand she had refused to let Maris heal, the very fingers he had broken so long ago.

For a time they walked in silence. She kept her hand extended, not because she knew what he would do—she would not leave this moment for long enough to foresee—but because she was certain, somewhere deep inside, that he would do what she wanted him to.

At long last, she felt his fingers. They entwined with hers. She smiled.

～

On the horizon, angular shapes rose slowly. They were the color of the beige-gray land around them, and resolved into distant towns.

Step by step, a dark rectangle grew, becoming high and wide, then clarifying into a wall. In time, a gate became visible. Only as tiny figures, so small that they might have been ants, entered and exited at the base, did Amarta begin to comprehend how high the walls were.

Tayre began to ask questions. What did foresight tell her? What would they find in Seuan?

What did she intend there?

She considered the many answers she could give him and dismissed them all. Vision itself was a mystery, a tangle, a cauldron of snakes. To give voice to what she saw would be to reduce it to the venal, and solve only the parts of the knot that she could yet see, as she had before: cutting in ignorance.

Never again.

No one sees everything, Tayre had once said. True enough, and besides, there would never be time to find all answers, because events did not wait to be understood.

Thus, where she looked mattered. She must craft herself, down to her very eyes, to look in the right places to see the right things.

Always paths to failure, she had told him. Childishly foolish words, the way she had used them to justify her actions, but there was also something to them that stank of wisdom.

Seek doorways, not dead-end alleys.

Some dead-end paths were inevitable, but Olessio's death had not been one of them.

That burden, she would bear for as long as she lived. It could never be made right, any more than she could stop the arrow through Nidem's chest, or preserve the islanders' lost lands and lives, or the monks and those who attended the Revelation.

There was no evening the tally, no making right the accounting of lives. But Amarta could face her culpability without blinking. She could see what it was that she had missed before.

She could begin to understand.

~

The city-state of Seuan sat atop a vast rise, half hilltop mesa, half wide-open ground, sloping down to the west.

They passed wagons, most covered, but one open, drawn by an ox and filled with strange produce, long and neatly laid in rows. Something that came from the islands, perhaps for the last time.

For miles around, the land was nearly bare, littered with tree stumps, crab grass, and bushes, showing the dips and rises of the earth, the smoke of far villages beyond.

To the west of the walled city was a large, sunken arena, cut into the earth. Black outlines moved, heat-flickered animals in a shape Amarta had never seen before. Small eyes, and snouts that came to a curved point.

She looked a question at Tayre.

"Sorogs," he said "I've only heard of them. Rumored to be fast, deadly, and well-protected by thick hides."

They walked another hour, then another. The walls grew higher, a huge metal gate growing in size. Inset, a smaller, wagon-sized door at its base allowed carts to come and go.

Amarta felt tired and thirsty, but would not pause, not even for a sip of water.

When at last they arrived at the walled city of Seuan, the wagon-sized door, some twenty feet high, was closed. As they approached, it slid smoothly to the side with a sound of heavy stone and metal rolling. It came to an open position with a heavy clang.

Walking through the opening toward them was a small woman wearing loose clothes of pale blue, brocade cuffs of black, and a hood-cowl laid back from her head onto her shoulders. Her face was thin, her features delicate, and eyes bright against her red-hued Seute Entan skin.

She stopped some ten paces from them and bowed, touching her forehead, throat, and sternum.

"Welcome to Seuan, travelers," she said in perfect Arunkin, then turned to Amarta and bowed again. "You must be the Seer of Arunkel. We make you welcome. We have been expecting you."

Gesturing for them to follow, she turned and led them into the city of Seuan.

Chapter Four

DIRINA WOKE to the sound of her bedroom door opening. A soft creak and floorboards shifting as someone stepped into the dark room.

Dirina slipped out of the bed on the far side, picking up from the floor the heavy stick she kept there for this purpose. She rose and began to creep toward the door, eyes struggling to make out a shape in the dim room.

"Mama?"

"Pas!" She exhaled relief and frustration and dropped the stick. "Pas, what are you—"

"Mama, I had a bad dream."

"Come to bed and get warm."

They climbed under the blankets. Dirina wrapped herself around him and put her head to his, inhaling the scent of him.

"Mama?"

"Yes, my sweet?"

"All those times that we had to run to get away. How did you know when it was right to leave?"

"I didn't. Amarta knew."

"But how did she know?"

"She had visions."

"I know that, mama, but how did she *know*?"

Dirina considered, made a thoughtful sound. "She didn't, not always. She doubted what she foresaw, and what it meant. But then, when the moment came, she..."

Dirina trailed off. There was something strange about the way Pas was asking. It was not typical for him to have bad dreams, and he didn't usually wake her in the night for comfort any more.

Dirina felt a trickle of dread.

"Pas."

"Mama."

A long silence.

Dirina would never forget the night when a young Amarta—younger than Pas was now, though not by much—crawled into her bed, in the hours before dawn. *I had a dream, Diri. Ma and Da, they...*

Only a dream, my sweet. Only a dream.

If only Dirina had not been so quick to disregard Amarta's visions.

Was this moment like that one?

Dirina opened her mouth to ask Pas about this dream, then she shut it again.

He was a smart child. He had seen what Amarta could do. Was it wise to encourage her bright, eager child to take what was only a dream and imagine it as something portentous?

It was no way for a child to grow up. Dirina had seen what it had done to Amarta.

"Mama, I was thinking."

"Yes, my sweet?" she asked lightly, softly, forcing a smile into her voice.

"We could take a trip, couldn't we? We've mules, a

wagon, lots of food. Blankets. We could ride out for a while. To see the land. Now that it's warming up again."

"I suppose we could," Dirina said slowly at this odd suggestion. She thought fast.

Nalas had sent them to live in this house, providing six guards who were always here. Would they let the two of them go off on their own? Would they stop her from leaving?

Nalas had instructed them to obey Dirina, but what else might they have been told, by someone else? Life at the palace had made her distrust all things and people connected to it.

"Mama?"

If Pas were fashioning himself after Amarta, emulating her the way any child might copy a beloved elder... but what if he weren't?

"That sounds lovely," she said, choosing her words with care. "I wonder if we should take some of the guards, too, so they can share in the pleasure of our trip." She rather doubted the guards would see it that way, but one problem at a time.

"Yes," Pas said, "I think that would be good, to have them with us."

Either Pas was foreseeing—and the guards were trustworthy—or he wasn't, and it wouldn't matter. A few days out on the road and back again. What was the harm in that?

If Nalas came to visit, and found them gone, he would be wretchedly worried. She would leave a note, explaining that they were out to see the countryside, to enjoy the spring, and would return soon.

Dirina felt an all-too-familiar ache. They had never, not once, returned to a place they called home after they had needed to flee. What made her think this would be different?

And so to leave meant she might never see Nalas again.

Her husband, since the small, hurried wedding. Was she really going to leave him, and the finest house she'd ever lived in—with enough food in the larders that every meal was enough—on a child's say-so?

She had done just that, time after time. After their parents had died, Dirina had sworn to herself never to disbelieve Amarta again.

Pas—clever boy—wasn't even claiming foresight. He was talking around it. That decided her.

"We'll go tomorrow," she said. "Do you suppose that tomorrow is soon enough?"

"Yes, mama, I suppose so."

"Then we'd best get some sleep now, while we can."

"Yes, mama."

In moments, his breathing had changed such that she knew that he had fallen into slumber.

She lay awake, considering the practical matters of what to bring, what to leave, and how to make it seem that they were only gone temporarily. In case they were not, in case someone came asking questions, trying to decide whether to pursue them or to wait.

Such familiar thoughts. If there were one thing Dirina was practiced at, it was leaving the place they called home, quickly and forever.

All of this reminded her keenly of Amarta, who had not come to the wedding that hadn't happened. Which, in retrospect, was probably a good thing, because Amarta might not have been any safer at the palace, with all this turmoil, than Dirina and Pas had been.

Amarta hadn't even sent a letter.

The familiar ache and fear at the pit of Dirina's stomach uncurled and rose, filling her; it was the fear that said Amarta hadn't written because she couldn't, that her visions had failed her at last.

But there was no way to be sure, and nothing to do about it now other than worry. Dirina resolved to set it all aside and rest in this comfortable bed with her beloved child before they went on the run again.

Silently she blinked back tears and prayed.

My dearest Amarta: may you be warm, fed, and surrounded by those who care for you as much as I do.

~

"I've found her." His mother's look was triumphant.

"Who have you found, mother?" Tokerae asked warily.

His mother, the Eparch of House Etallan, dismissed the servants from the sitting room, leaving the two of them alone. "The traitor's whore, my boy. The seer. Look at this."

She held out to him a letter. He took it, read it, took a breath.

"Anyone could write this, and Seuan is sufficiently far away to make confirming it exorbitantly expensive. Mother," he said, hoping for a patient tone. "Do you really believe that she's a seer?"

Her eyes narrowed and she took his arm in a tight grip. "The Houses are after this woman and willing to drop large purses of coin in the hunt. I don't care if it's true or not. Get her, claim anything, and the other Houses will be unnerved. It is not yet time for the grand plans of which you dream, boy, but anything that rocks the other Houses makes us more secure, and brings that time closer. You understand me?"

"Yes, of course." Sort of, anyway. "Shall I address the details of this matter for you, my eparch?"

She gave him an assessing look that turned sour. "This is not a practice drill. I will take care of it myself."

What was there to say to yet another insult?

"Tokerae, my son." She took his hand in hers, patted it affectionately. A chill went through him. "I am told you are sending messages to Garaya and some of the other provinces."

His skin crawled under her touch, but he dared not pull away. "Minor matters," he said flatly. "Nothing more."

That she had heard about these communications was troubling. It meant that somewhere in the chain of people between Tokerae and Ella and the city of Garaya was a rotten link.

His mother gripped his hand more and more tightly, digging her nails into his skin. He nerved himself not to react.

"Do you have any idea how much has been spent? How many people across decades have given lives to prepare the way for us? If you act against the Anandynars now, you waste all that—every drop of blood, every ounce of precious metal, and you put our House at risk. Tell me that these rumors are not true."

"These rumors are not true."

She scowled, examining his face as if she might read the lie there. "I forbid you to make any moves against the crown without me. Is that clear enough, even for your muddled thinking?"

"Yes, mother."

"Our time will come, Tok. Be patient and obey my orders."

"Yes, mother."

Ella was right: the time would never come. Whether the cause was his mother's devotion to her father's opinions, her obsession with Innel's whore, or simply an aging woman's fear of risk, she would never act.

Her glare was piercing. It took every bit of Cohort training he had to meet and hold it across moments.

He looked away first, angry at her, angry at himself. She released his hand.

"I am going to have the mutt's whore dragged back to Arunkel," she told him. "Then we'll find out what she is, seer or pretender. Not that I much care; we'll get something useful out of her, either way. And that's a prediction you can rely on."

Tokerae recognized the expression on her face. It meant that someone was going to pay a high price. For a moment, he almost felt sorry for Innel's whore.

His mother turned away, muttering to herself about men, ships, and weapons. It was, oddly, an echo of the conversation that Tokerae had lately had with Ella.

If he and Ella moved quickly enough, by the time their distracted eparch-mother became aware of what they'd done, it would be too late for her to object. They would have succeeded, and Tokerae's mother would be forced to admit that Tokerae had been right all along.

That would be a moment to savor.

U ndul Etris Tay had mixed feelings about the capital city of Arunkel, through which he regularly made his way from House Etallan to the palace and back again.

On the one hand, Yarpin had, without question, the very best twunta on the entire continent. That included Perripur, north and south.

They didn't know what they had, these Yarpin denizens. They thought that Perripur grew better stuff, because rumor held it to be so. It wasn't true.

And the food—exceptional chefs across the city, Etallan's among them. Every city Undul Etris Tay had visited had a distinct style of food, based on culture and source ingredients that could be gotten in hand. He had very much enjoyed the meals he'd been fed, but they were beginning to repeat.

Undul Etris Tay was ready to leave.

Soon, he told himself, as he stared at the ceiling.

A level up, and twenty paces to the north, a woman was breathing very hard and occasionally yelling in pain. He brought his focus fully into her room and into the woman, assuring himself that all was well.

From the room next to her came another sort of complaint: two dogs who whimpered and yipped every time Cern cried out. Their vocalizations annoyed him, and might be distracting to the midwives, so he dipped into the dogs, calming them into a light doze in which their voices softened and did not carry.

Better.

Where to go next, was the question. What great city might be eager to show a mage like himself a truly splendid time?

Obvious choices included Kelerre and Senta, both Perripin cities, where mages were treated better than they were anywhere in Arunkel. But despite a thousand miles and a border they were too close.

Undul Etris Tay wanted to be far from whatever carnage was about to blossom here in Yarpin, and that meant either crossing the Rift to the eastern lands, or venturing into Southern Perripur. A much longer journey, but—

Another shout from the queen. She sounded angry, which, as he recalled, was just about right for this point in the process.

He touched in with each of the three midwives. Often this was the better way to see how things were going. From the etheric scent of them, they were pleased with the birthing.

A longer journey. Also Southern Perripur was hot, and he

didn't like hot. Then he thought of Vilaros. Might a seafront city be more temperate? He'd only seen it once, passing by in haste to pursue a rare invitation to a gathering on the island of Ilesea, but he'd glimpsed the tall towers of the university from his ship.

Suddenly everyone in the room overhead was very excited. The baby's head was crowning. The mother was in a state of intense agitation, but also euphoric. The mage calmed the first part and intensified the second.

Another thought occurred to him, that the Perripin chefs living at the edge of the warm waters of the Temani Gulf would have special dishes to offer, probably ones that Undul Etris Tay had never before tasted.

Vilaros it was.

The newborn baby emitted a long piercing cry that turned into a determined howl. Then the boy was out of his mother, slick, healthy, and continuing to be quite, quite loud.

Most of all, Undul Etris Tay would miss the twunta. He could take some with him, but the amount that could be carried would not last long, not at his current rate of smoke. On the other hand, now that he had a destination, perhaps a shipment could be arranged.

A horse-sized box. Or two. Why not three? Four, and he could afford to be generous to those who pleased him. He smiled at the thought.

Everyone in the queen's room was very busy. The woman who was her closest companion still had scars that caused her pain. From some injury, likely someone trying to kill her with a sharp object. Bored, Undul Etris Tay worked her, loosening the tissues so that they would heal faster, brightening the area so that her blood knew better what to do.

He checked the newborn boy, from blood to heart to

bone to brain. All seemed where it was supposed to be, and ready for what came next, which—as soon as the child stopped howling—would surely be sleep.

Undul Etris Tay roused himself from his comfortable nest of pillows and blankets, took a long stretch, and scratched his beard. He'd have to shave it for the heat, he thought dourly. But at least in Perripur, he wouldn't need to hide his magic as he was doing now.

When the blood and the baby were all out of the healthy Arunkel monarch, the little thing snug in his mother's arms, both of them beginning to doze, Undul Etris Tay left the palace, making his way into the city to The Sanctuary where he would arrange for a large shipment of twunta. Four of them.

After that, he'd return to House Etallan, and let them feed him again.

He must stay a few days longer in this wretched city, just long enough to be sure that the queen and child were well—exceptionally well—so that when the Council of Mages came to find out what had happened here, there would be no question that one Undul Etris Tay had had nothing at all to do with taking down the monarch of the Arunkel empire.

◠

L ason looked around the large room. It was entirely right that he was back in his old office again. Very right. He smiled.

He had needed to insist on it. No, he had told the queen's seneschal firmly, he did not want a new room. It must be the very same one. It had been his before—should have been his all along—and it would be his again.

He wanted it cleaned, he had said, every inch of it, to

remove the stench of the traitor. He wanted it done yesterday.

In the end, it had taken five days. Should have been faster, no doubt, but Lason had decided to be gracious. After all, despite being more than twice the traitor mutt's age, he had outlived the bastard. He had won.

Lason sat at his desk which had been brought out from storage, cleaned, and polished. His maps were again on the walls, alongside his favorite weapons. Things were as they should be.

He smiled and ran his hands over smooth wood, letting the silken texture comfort him. This was a good start on wiping away the humiliation of having the traitor take his position. Cern had come to her senses, finally. The mutt was gone now, good and truly.

A knock at the door. Lason nodded to his guard, who opened it. In came Nalas.

Lason stood. "You? What do you want?"

Nalas bowed. Not very deeply. Not deeply enough.

Nalas was another problem: he should never have been made Lord Commander, not even temporarily. Not with his youth, inexperience, and lack of aristo standing. Another misstep from the young queen. But she had corrected it.

Nalas looked around the large office that had, until days ago, been his.

"Not yours anymore, boy," Lason said. "Stop gawking. Show respect."

"Lord Commander, where is your guard?" Nalas asked.

"What?"

"Here. In the hallway. Standing ready to protect you. These are not the men I assigned to you."

"Of course not. I changed them out."

Nalas opened his mouth, shut it again. "Why?"

The queen had put Nalas under him, so Lason was,

properly, his superior, but she had also given Nalas unprecedented authority over palace security, which was more than a little unconventional. Lason knew what he'd say right now to a proper underling. But Nalas wasn't that. Not quite.

It made him hesitate.

"I don't need to explain myself to you," he grumbled.

The other man exhaled audibly. "No, Lord Commander, you don't. But those men were chosen specifically—"

"By you. I have my own people. Loyal people."

Lason had summoned back the guards who had served him before. Seeing their faces light with gratitude and loyalty had been a distinct pleasure. Loyalty was key. If you didn't have that, you had nothing.

"Anyone who reported to the traitor must be replaced," Lason said sternly, quite aware that Nalas himself had been the mutt traitor's second in command.

"You propose to replace the entire army?" Nalas asked.

Lason bit down on the retort that came to his tongue. "We'll see."

"I only meant to protect you, ser."

"I have that under control. You may go."

Dismissed, but Nalas stared at Lason for a moment instead of leaving.

Wondering how far you can push me, boy, since you can talk directly to the queen? Go ahead, find out.

Nalas turned and went to the door. Coming in as Nalas left was Lason's steward, Malio, who bowed very nicely indeed.

Lason sat at his desk. Malio poured wine. Good wine. Palace wine. He'd missed all this.

Then Malio hovered.

"What is it?"

"A House Kincel envoy, Lord Commander, asking to see the queen. Redirected to you instead, ser."

"Rightly so. Her majesty just gave birth, and must be spared unnecessary strain." He nodded permission for the envoy to enter.

Her livery was the color of stone and flesh—basalt and ecru—her surcoat hemmed with a messenger's cloud-white. She bowed smartly.

"Lord Commander, I stand here representing my eparch, the Eparch of House Kincel, and to convey a message for Her Most Excellent Majesty."

She held out her hand, fingers curled in a light fist, then with a flourish opened them, revealing a heavy stone ring.

A bit showy, but Lason didn't mind. He took the offered object, a black, glinting feldspar that would fit a large man's thumb. It bore the stone archway sigil of House Kincel. Proof that she spoke for the eparch.

Beautiful work, the ring. One expected no less from the House of Stone. He handed it back and gestured for her to continue.

She bowed again. "For Her Majesty's ears only, Lord Commander."

Lason waved his guards outside, leaving only Malio. "We are alone. Tell me, and I'll pass it on to Her Majesty at an appropriate time."

"Lord Commander, forgive me, but the message is only for—"

"The queen has just given birth," Lason snapped, "and must be undisturbed. Say it or leave."

The messenger made another bow—not so deep this time—then drew herself tall, taking a breath, and speaking in the cadence that typified formal House communications.

"All honor and submission to Her Great and Excellent Majesty, from the Eparch of House Kincel."

Lason motioned for her to continue.

"My Eparch ardently desires Her Excellent Majesty to be well-informed, and thus conveys to her this information, that has come to him through various means. It is this: men travel to Yarpin from points across the empire in large numbers. Some are Arunkin, some Borderellos, some Perripin."

"So?" Lason asked. "It is the nature of our great capital to attract strangers for all sorts of reasons. In what way is this remarkable?"

"I am given to understand that my esteemed eparch felt it worthy of note, especially if these were fighting men, which they might be."

"Might be? What, are they armed?"

"No, Lord Commander, though illegal weapons are not hard to come by, under inappropriate circumstances."

Inappropriate circumstances. Only House Etallan was allowed to make bladed weapons, and only for the crown. The envoy meant to imply—or rather, her eparch did—that Etallan was providing illegal weapons to unnamed someones.

Lason sat back, glowering at the envoy. It was a vague accusation, a political missile, intended to sow distrust between the queen and the Great House of Metal. Surely there was already enough of that, with the obscene execution of one of Etallan's own by the traitor mutt, which had forced Cern to authorize it or disown him.

Damn it, she should have disowned him.

Another matter that the Anandynars would need to address and soon, this insult to Etallan. Cern must make amends—they needed Etallan—but without allowing the royal family to seem weak.

Cern marrying Tokerae would do it. When she was recovered, Lason would urge her in that direction.

"How do you know all this?" he demanded. "Did these

maybe-fighting-men camp in one of Kincel's quarries, demanding stone swords?"

At the jab, her expression went messenger-blank. "No, ser. We have our information from our cooks and courtesans at House Passare's waystations."

Passare, House of roads, bridges, and waystations. Kincel and Passare were close by the standards of Great Houses. Too close, Lason had always thought. Another thing he must mention to the queen.

"I am not going to trouble the queen over gossip from servants and whores."

"Kincel cooks and courtesans," the envoy said in a strained voice.

"Watch your tone, messenger."

"Yes, ser." Another bow, hardly a dip.

Lason snorted. "Relay to His Illustriousness Eparch Kincel the queen's gratitude for this most detailed information." From her expression, the envoy didn't miss his caustic tone. Good. "Tell him, if you think he can stomach it, that if he wants to pick a fight with Etallan, do it without the crown. The queen desires to unite the Houses, not divide them." He waved a hand in the air. "Make my words sensible and elegant. Also relay our best congratulations for his eighteenth grandchild born last week. Or is it nineteenth?"

"Nineteenth, Lord Commander," she said tightly.

Lason nodded. "You are dismissed."

"Yes, Lord Commander." She bowed, stepped back, once, in precise formality, turned, and left.

Chapter Five

THE HOUND and Rabbit tavern was packed, no stools or benches to be had, barely a wall to which a back might be put. The tenders were hopping—nearly climbing over feet and knees to get to those demanding food and drink.

Shae waved at Rose across the room again, but the harried-looking tender was busy. All these men—Shae didn't know them, had never seen them before, and they had too much money to spend.

"Foreigners," Shae whispered disgustedly, peering into the mug of the man next to her to see if there was anything there worth stealing.

She took the mug from his slack fingers and downed the last bit, sludge and all.

"Hoi," he objected weakly.

"You want me steady tonight," she assured him, "In case you need me to take you home. Remember?"

"Oh. Did I say that?" he asked, words slurring.

Shae had been drinking for hours, but the scene before her left her feeling too sober.

"Where they all coming from?" her companion asked. "Big fellows, some of 'em."

Shae nodded glumly. They were nothing like the usual tradesmen and tourists that Yarpin summers drew. They were big. They moved as if they knew how to scrap.

Shae had spent most her life watching people and turning observations into food, drink, and shelter. To her eyes it was obvious: they were also waiting.

Waiting since they got to Yarpin, the earliest a good tenday ago, and more arriving all the time. Some exchanged glances, nods. They might be strangers to the capital city, but not all of them were strangers to each other.

The Hound and Rabbit was Shae's second home, but she got around, and she knew that they were everywhere. Tens of them. Hundreds. Maybe more.

It was wrong. She could feel it in her bones.

"Strange," said her companion quietly, following her look. "Should we tell someone? Someone who might care?"

"No one to tell," Shae said.

He made a disgusted sound in his throat. "Ain't that the way of it."

He had no idea what she meant by her words. He was just being agreeable.

Be careful, ser, she'd told the former Lord Commander.

The crowd in Execution Square had been thick and loud, jeering and calling as he was paraded up the steps. A great show, after all. Always cause for celebration, to see the high dragged low.

Some in the crowd remembered him another way, Shae among them, and there were ugly looks at the highest balcony where the queen sat.

Next came the ponderous reading of the crimes. Then the noose and the kick that removed the elegant stool on which the hooded man had stood.

His legs worked frantically as Shae held her breath, then slowed and slowed some more, until they, too, simply hung.

The cheering went on for an hour.

Her own people. Commoners who had been willing to applaud him when he spoke of how he would help them cheered when his death was offered as cheap amusement.

She was sickened. The people of Yarpin, she decided, deserved what they got.

Fates, she needed another drink to quiet these ugly thoughts rattling around in her head. Where was Rose?

There, looking across the room at Shae. Finally. Shae raised her mug and Rose gave a nod.

Shae was still spending the money that Innel had given her, but that would soon run out. Without his generous patronage, there would be no keeping her parents in their nearby cabin. She would need to take them into deep country, to see how far what she had stashed over the years could stretch.

It was time to be somewhere else, anyway. Leave these louts to their own business. Whoever they were. Whatever they were up to.

Shae looked to her side at her drinking buddy and felt sad.

"I'll miss you."

"What's that?" he asked foggily.

She thought of the man who had been Innel sev Cern esse Arunkel, of the last time she had seen him, walking away in the heavy rain. Raised in the palace, but born common. He had been one of them.

Be careful, ser.

He had waved at her over his shoulder. *Always,* he had said.

Clearly he had missed a moment or two of diligence.

And now, what was left for her, here in Yarpin?

"Nothing," she replied to her own question, looking into the empty cup in front of her as Rose struggled toward her through the crowd with another one. "Nothing at all."

~

Tokerae was woken from a deep sleep. It was dark, and well before dawn. The knocking was urgent. His mother's chamberlain entered.

He followed her to his mother's room. There the Eparch of House Etallan lay in her bed, motionless.

"Tell Ella," he hissed at the chamberlain. He himself took off at a run to the mage's suite, banging on the door. When there was no response, he worked the handle.

To his surprise, it opened.

Undul Etris Tay lay upon his bed, yawning. Tokerae slammed the door behind himself and strode to the bed.

"A gentle nudge, I said, damn you," Tokerae hissed.

"Talk to me that way again, Iliban," the mage said pleasantly, "and I'll be chatting with *your* heir."

Tokerae's mouth opened and closed, and opened and closed. Suddenly he felt terrifyingly adrift.

"My mother," he said hoarsely.

The mage adjusted the pillow under his head, his gaze on Tokerae.

"Yes, your mother. I went by her room late last night." He shook his head, then tapped his chest. "Not flowing right here. All gummed up. I thought about fixing it so that I could give her that gentle nudge you kept me begging for. Then I thought, why take a step back only to take another forward?"

"What?"

"This is what you wanted, no? Good timing. Lucky you.

So, instead of fixing, I took a walk around the grounds. Late night. No one out. Only the forge going. What a forge. Best I've seen."

"But... my mother."

The mage sat up, swung his legs over the side of the bed. "Yes, you said. And what?"

The door opened. Ella stepped inside, shut the door. Her face was pale, her eyes flickering between her brother and the mage.

"Did he...?" She began, coming to Tokerae's side. Then, without waiting, turned on Undul Etris Tay a look of blinding fury.

Tokerae could see this situation going wrong, badly wrong, and fast. "Not him," he said quickly. "It was a natural death, sister."

Ella glared at the mage, and Tokerae earnestly wished that the mage were not staring back with such curiosity.

His mother.

His mother.

The enormity of it flitted around him, like a swarm of gnats refusing to leave, refusing to land. He felt disconnected, as if this were all a continuation of the dream from which he was awakened. Could it be?

Did he want it to be?

"You did nothing?" Ella demanded of the mage. "Nothing at all?" She was breathing hard, her tone menacing. Tokerae gripped her arm tight in a sharp warning.

Tokerae and his sister stared at the balding man with his thick middle and uncombed beard. He grinned back, as if he were actually hoping that they would lose their control. Maybe he was.

"He did nothing, sister." Tokerae whispered, entirely willing to believe it now, true or not.

The mage's words came fully into Tokerae's understanding. The mage had looked into his mother's body, into her very heart. He could have healed her.

He could have killed her.

And this was why Arunkel had outlawed these creatures for so many years.

Undul Etris Tay looked even more amused now than he had before. "And what?" He asked Tokerae. "Are you Eparch now?"

Tokerae could not answer.

"Yes," Ella whispered. "Yes, he is. Eparch of House Etallan."

She turned to him. Her eyes were red. She had been crying.

She wasn't now. Instead her face held a fierce expression, and something more, in her eyes, that fortified him.

Eparch. He was Eparch.

~

In the hallway, Tokerae dele Etallan was swarmed.

His mother's chamberlain was fighting with the bursar over three different matters at once. Urgent conversation crashed across the hallway as people began to accumulate in knots. He heard his name, again and again. Questions. Demands.

Yes, some matters were clearly both necessary and urgent, like his mother's funeral. More urgent yet: the ceremony that would confirm him as Eparch. But surely everything else need not be handled as immediately as the din around him would imply.

He met Ella's eyes over the crowd. Seeing him, she pushed her way through, close, and began to direct people, telling them where to go and what to do. As they peeled off, she drew Tokerae forward and into action for what was truly necessary.

Minutes became hours, and Tokerae had only a moment to see his mother's body again, and barely that to console his father, who sat at her side, holding her hand, nodding vaguely at Tokerae's condolences.

The eparchy ceremony was hastily arranged and executed. This was not the first time an Eparch of Etallan had died suddenly, so there was precedent. Tokerae sneezed out the accumulated dust of decades on the ancestral eparch robe now laid across his shoulders—a heavy charcoal velvet, embroidered with copper in the House sigil of crossed sword and pickaxe. The very symbol worked into the center of the Anandynar crest, and that no accident.

A whirl of fast ceremonies began and ended. More discussions, decisions. All essential. Hours passed in which Tokerae had no moment alone.

Then Undul Etris Tay, in his food-stained accountant's garb, appeared at the door to the eparch's office, at the edge of the gathered crowd. Tokerae felt alarm. He caught Ella's gaze, intending to convey to her that the mage be addressed, that to have him here, with all of Etallan's most influential, was inviting disaster.

It shortly became clear that it didn't matter what Tokerae and Ella did.

The mage walked directly through the surrounding throng toward Tokerae. People parted as he came close, as if they preferred another place to stand, or wanted to be extremely close to someone nearby. No one seemed the least bit surprised that this was occurring, and none looked at the mage.

Tokerae was stung by an unwelcome sense of being a

child in a dress-up game. He hastily pulled off the ceremonial cloak and let it drop to the floor.

From his side, the mage spoke. "I require a conversation. Here or privately. Your choice, Eparch."

"Not here," Tokerae breathed. He and Ella made quick excuses, following the mage, who still seemed invisible to everyone else, back to his room.

Once inside, the mage spoke. "I am sated. With your House, your city, your politics. I leave."

"What?" Tokerae said.

"Ah, no. Please, High One," Ella began. "We—"

"Yes, no," the mage said, holding up a hand. "You'll offer more money. Another chef. I want it not."

"But—"

"Thank me for inconveniencing myself to find you in the middle of your annoying day, rather than leave unannounced."

Tokerae parsed these words. He felt the blood drain from his face.

"Thank you, High One," he whispered.

"Thank me for my help these last months."

"So grateful, High One," Ella managed.

Undul Etris Tay smirked at her, then at Tokerae. "Don't forget your promise, Eparch. A binding, mage-witnessed contract."

Witnessed by the very holder of the contract, and without even a token to seal it, but Tokerae wasn't inclined to quibble. "Most assuredly," he answered.

"Contract?" Ella asked, an edge to her voice. Tokerae gestured her to silence.

"Some of what," Undul Etris Tay muttered, looking around the suite: "I feel moved to offer you something more."

Tokerae could nearly read Ella's furious thoughts: *More than what?*

A small shake of his head. Don't antagonize him, sister.

The mage picked at his teeth with a fingernail. "Wisdom, Iliban: your kind will believe anything, even the implausible, if it is said loudly and often; repetition plants the seeds of doubt, advances may be achieved with a mere expenditure of words."

At Tokerae's confused look, the mage sighed. "For your simpler ears, do not slight the power of a simple lie." He took them both in with a smirk. "I never lose when I wager on the disorder of Iliban thought."

Tokerae could not tell if he'd been insulted, which would not surprise him, or wisely advised, which would.

He decided that wisdom, if there was any to be gained here, would start with a simple and respectful bow. After a moment, Ella followed suit.

The mage's expression went distant, as if Tokerae and Ella were now the invisible ones. Without further comment, Undul Etris Tay dua Mage left House Etallan.

~

"It is time, Helata," Tokerae said. At his side was Fadrel, Cohort brother and the presumptive Eparch-heir of House Helata.

"Is it now, Etallan?" Fadrel replied, stroking his beard, and staring out from the dockhouse balcony where they sat, drinks and smokes at their sides.

The sky had darkened to azure as the dying sun cast glowing orange through pale clouds that stretched over the ocean.

At his words, worry shot through Tokerae. Was Fadrel having second thoughts?

"The list of names," Tokerae reminded him softly.

This was the most important part. To know who, in-palace, could be relied on via Helata's influence would nearly double Etallan's numbers there.

As the silence stretched, Tokerae wondered if Fadrel had heard him. He opened his mouth to repeat himself. But no —an eparch did not do such things. He held his tongue.

Fadrel continued to stroke his beard. "Yes, the list. Arms to your people waiting outside Garaya, to make your bribe to that erstwhile loyal city more persuasive. Transportation for your many, many friends to our glorious capital."

Tokerae hid relief. "Yes."

"In return, trade tariffs lifted. And..." Fadrel turned in his chair to look at Tokerae. "Phaltos."

Phaltos. Helata wanted Phaltos most of all, which would require prying the Lesser House from Kincel. It could be managed, if all went as planned.

To this demand, there was only one answer, and Tokerae had better sound entirely certain of it.

"Yes," he replied firmly.

Fadrel gave a nod, began to groom his mustache with his long nails.

"Don't forget the birthmark," Tokerae said.

"That I am unlikely to forget." A short laugh that turned quickly sober. "You realize that this is all grossly illegal, Cohort brother."

Tokerae gave a snort. "Affronts to our empire's security cannot be swallowed like overcooked pieces of meat, as has been recent practice." Blaming, by implication, either Cern or Innel or both. Let Fadrel decide. "In uncivilized times, such as these, we cannot be constrained by the rules that govern civilized nations. The remedy must be immediate and convincing. Thanks to the traitor mutt, we have lost the immediate part, but we can yet make the cure entirely convincing."

"Rehearsed those pretty words, did you, Etallan?" An amused smile. "Studying the Grandmother Queen's speeches, hmm?"

Tokerae gave his Cohort brother as austere a look as he could manage, hoping to imply that he had not done exactly that.

"All right, then," Tokerae replied primly, "let me put it more bluntly, in a manner that, I am certain, Niala esse Arunkel would have found most agreeable: victory writes laws. Garaya's betrayal of the crown cannot be allowed to stand. It will not be allowed to stand."

Because money would end what arms alone could not: Garaya's infuriating negotiations with Perripur.

"You are a patriot, ser," said Fadrel with a straight face. Ironically? Mockingly?

Damn the man's beard and mustache; Tokerae could no longer read his face as he had in times past.

"I most certainly am."

Fadrel looked out to sea, where the deep blood red of sunset was fading into gray as clouds gathered. He was quiet for long enough that Tokerae found himself again becoming uncertain, then unnerved. He reached for his drink, took a swallow.

The last bit of sun winked out. In the dimming light, Fadrel gave a slow nod.

"Let us proceed at good speed, Etallan, into tomorrow's glorious dawn."

～

Tokerae sat with Ella on the roof of Etallan's main house, his arms crossed over his knees.

Was this what an eparch did, make plans on a roof?

Who were they hiding from now?

It felt right to sit here and look down at the grounds of Etallan. Since he was Eparch, what felt right was surely right. Wasn't that what his mother had done all his life, all her eparchy? She never seemed to waver, to doubt.

Why did Ella's words sit so heavily in the air between them?

He craned his neck to the lip of the roof and looked over. How many fears had he faced down, across a lifetime in the Cohort, from heights to blades, from exams to royal interviews? Why was this one so much harder?

Because planning was not the same thing as stepping past the point of no return.

"You're sure," he said.

"I am, Tok," Ella replied. She was watching him. "While we can hold everything in place for perhaps another month, after that, it will begin to cost us dearly."

It was already costing them dearly.

"Timing is key," she added, still watching him.

"I know that." He tried to keep irritability from this voice, but probably failed. Ella knew him too well. Timing was not merely key; timing was all. "And what of those in-palace?"

"They stand alert and available."

"And the elixir?"

Five hundred small corked bottles, full of a thick bitter liquid. Each bottle had been made with a ceramic metal wash to glint pale green, to make it seem exotic. The elixir was Seuan truly in origin—that part was true—but its effect was nothing like the immunity promised by rumor. Rather, it would sedate.

"The bottles are secreted in hundreds of places across the palace."

"Mice," Tokerae said.

"Ready. Hungry."

He turned to meet her look at last.

"It has come," she said softly, with something like awe. "This day has come at last."

Tokerae drew a deep breath, turned to look behind himself, up slope, to the top of the roof.

Every Great House had line-of-sight to the palace. The hillside on which the palace and Houses had been built had been planned that way from the founding of the empire. On the roof, each House displayed something that spoke of its produce and its pride.

Up the slope that rose behind them, at the very highest part, was a flat on which was a great metal fountain. From a centerpiece came wrought brass and iron, the orange and charcoal metals wire-fine and arcing, twisting in the air to seem like liquid that fell and poured into a large pool of red and black glass.

Etallan might have shown blades or pickaxes. A mock-up of a mine. A forge. But no, it was a fountain. Every child of Etallan knew what was on the rooftop of the main house and why.

The fountain said that House Etallan, embodying as it did the might of forged and worked metal, fed the black-and-red pool that represented the Anandynar monarchy. For hundreds of years the rooftop had provided an enduring visual message to the crown: *You need us.*

It would be the work of a few minutes to change the message. A bit of paint, and the smooth glass surface would go from red and black to gilt-gold. At that moment, every in-palace contact upon whom the plan relied needed only to look out the window to see the signal. To know that it was time.

For Tokerae and Ella, the message went deeper: Etallan created the monarchy, and always had. No longer would it be red and black.

When the pool turned gold, the planning of decades—of generations—would become action.

Tokerae turned back to look over the grounds of his home. A rare moment of quiet came over the grounds. Even the ever-present pounding of the forge had paused. It felt peaceful, as if nothing truly needed to change.

Was it really time?

His mother had thought not.

"How do we know... " he began, then shook his head, searching for the right words. "When, exactly? There must be someone we can ask."

Their eparch-mother was dead. Their father would never counsel risk, no matter what might be gained. The mage was gone, and wouldn't have cared in any case. Who?

They met each other's looks.

"You are Eparch." Ella's tone held no doubt. "You are the one to ask. You are the one to answer. No one else. I say we are ready, Tok." A deep breath. Her voice dropped. "All you need say is 'go.'"

Tokerae found that he was breathing shallowly, as if he were under water. He stood, agitated, walking to one side of the sloped roof to look at the grounds, then to the other, as if the answer might be somewhere down there in the dirt, or trees, or metal fences of House Etallan.

Below him two levels was a large room. On the mantel his mother had kept her bells, his entire life. The mantel was now empty, waiting for whatever Tokerae, as Eparch of House Etallan, might decide to put there.

Eparch of House Etallan.

In the sky, a flock of birds winged north, then abruptly changed direction, winging west instead. How did they know when it was time to turn?

They knew because one bird led them through the sky, led them into their future, and the rest followed, fanning out behind.

"Go," he said.

Chapter Six

"COME WITH ME, PLEASE," the Seuan woman said.

Amarta and Tayre following the beckoning Seuan woman through the huge gate, anchored in towering walls, into the city-state of Seuan.

As Amarta's feet fell on stones so well-fitted that they might as well have been one rock, she sensed the future shifting. Inside, some thirty paces of stone paving separated the walls from the rest of the city.

They walked a wide, clear boulevard. On either side were tight clusters of houses, seeming to be villages complete with lanes, rooflines, and high bridges.

They crossed another wide boulevard. At the center of the streets, a spiral of stones was neatly arranged on a bed of sand. Two new clusters arose, on either side. The smooth road banked to the sides for drainage, and was meticulously clean, bare of weeds, and lacking any hint of horse or oxen leavings.

Amarta puzzled over all this, but what struck her most was the lack of sound beyond their footfalls. No market conversation. No laughter or children playing. No curtains pulled aside to reveal faces of curiosity at these strangers.

Amarta caught glimpses of trees and sloped gardens on tile roofs. The clusters were not empty. People lived here.

The Seuan woman walking before them led them to a stone building. Inside, they climbed a flight of stairs, and entered a large, well-lit apartment. Windows faced the street. Another set faced a small inner courtyard garden at ground level.

"I am called Zung-Urfan," the Seuan woman said, turning to face them, "which means five-tongue. It is not a name, but rather a title that may change with circumstance. There is no need for you to remember this title. During your stay, I or one of my brethren will be your guide. We all speak your language. Simply say what you wish, and we will answer."

The apartment was pleasantly cool, yet bright with sun. Tile floors, a bed, a table, chairs. The courtyard below was verdant and lush, with white and orange flowers arranged in circles. In this dry land, the garden spoke of lavish and meticulous care.

Under Zung-Urfan's silent direction, five Seuan men and women, dressed much as she was, came into the room. With smooth, practiced movements, they set bowls and trays of food on the table, then left.

"Do not wander the city without escort," Zung-Urfan said. "Seuan produces powerful compounds. Even one inhalation at the wrong moment during our necessary processing would make you grievously ill or worse."

A warning? A threat?

Zung-Urfan touched her forehead, throat, chest, and bowed. She turned and left.

Amarta stared, bemused, at the food. A bowl of something long and thin, pale and glistening. Buttered dough, a vegetable pod, some kind of baked worm—she had no idea.

She shook her head slowly and snorted, amused.

"What?" Tayre asked.

"A year ago, this whole exchange with Zung-Urfan, and this food, would have seemed impossibly strange to me. Now it only seems a little strange."

She quickly checked the future for the outcome of eating from these dishes. Nothing here would harm them. And yet she hesitated.

"What would he have said now?" she asked softly.

Tayre picked from another bowl something soft and white and round. A piece of fruit, perhaps. Or some creature's eyeball. He held it up.

"I will tell you what I think," Tayre said, in a shockingly good imitation of Olessio's voice and manner. "Since we are here, let us discover just how very strange—and perhaps wonderful—this food really is." He waggled his eyebrows at her. "I say we eat."

It hit her in the gut, this stunningly accurate, uncanny mirror of Olessio. The pain was sharp, sharper than she would have expected. It rippled through her, and up to her eyes, which filled with tears, then down again through her chest and stomach, all the way to her feet, in a healing wash that left her feeling warm and tender.

"I say we eat," she echoed, wiping her eyes.

❧

After months of walking across Seute Enta, to simply wait was unsettling. Amarta paced the room, looking out the window at the empty wide stone boulevard, beyond which was a cluster of small houses.

All at once, from the houses in the cluster across the way, some fifty or more Seuan in light brown clothes emerged, marching up the boulevard, and passed out of view.

She turned to Tayre. "I haven't traveled nearly as much as you have. But this seems a very odd place. Is it?"

"It is." He tapped the plaster base of the window. "Nothing here is made of wood or thatch."

"What does that mean?"

"It means nothing to burn," he answered. "not even windowsills. They have storms and floods, earthquakes and Eufalmo. But this is protection from fire, and it is expensive. Why?"

Amarta had no answer. Or rather, she had flashes of answers, none of which told her very much.

By sunset, Zung-Urfan had returned with more food. This time the plates were brought and laid out by five pale-skinned and pale-haired Emendi, each dressed in asymmetrical beige tunics, one arm sleeveless, revealing the slave brands on their arms.

Amarta felt herself go cold, then hot, her face flushing as she watched.

The Emendi arranged the plates. Amarta's mind spun back to Kusan. Almost without thinking, at her side, she made a subtle Emendi hand sign.

I see you. I know you.

None of them responded, their gazes staying forward.

Zung-Urfan lit three lamps. "Is there anything else you require?"

"The Heart. When do we meet him?" Amarta asked.

Zung-Urfan tilted her head toward her in a slight bow. "Seuan welcomes you as honored guests."

Not an answer.

Tayre snorted softly, infusing his words with an edge of offense. "Does your leader know that the Seer of Arunkel is here?"

A small bow to him that might have meant yes. "We are busy preparing for Kailo, our sacred annual rite in which we select the Heart who leads us forward."

"Your leader changes every year?" she asked, confused.

Zung-Urfan made a fist with her right hand, tapped her chest lightly. "We are always led by the Heart, Seer, and that never changes. But in the way that you mean, our Heart has resided in one great man for ninety-seven years."

"Ninety-seven years?" Amarta asked, surprised.

Zung-Urfan made her three-touch bow and left.

Through the window, Amarta watched Zung-Urfan climb into a wheeled seat-cart, long handles lifted by the Emendi with whom she had come. They trotted forward and out of sight.

Amarta recalled the stinking slave ship at Senta, then the branded Arunkin men who pulled the Domina's carriage, and last, the Emendi children in the room behind the auction block.

"Are there slaves everywhere, across the world?" she asked tightly.

"Where there is money, yes. Sometimes they are called by another name. Criminals, set to unpaid labor. Debtors, required to work off an obligation. But it amounts to the same thing."

She looked at him searchingly. "Why do people do this?"

He returned her look. "Because they can. It's not much different than owning an ox to pull your plow so that you don't have to."

Her mouth dropped. "You equate an enslaved human to an ox?"

Tayre shrugged. "There are hundreds of thousands of people across the world who you don't know, Amarta, who are told where to live and what work to do. Consider Souver, who you cared enough about to pay a large sum of money to board, possibly for the rest of her life. Does Souver have a choice about where she lives? What work she does, or for whom she does it?" He paused, watching her. "What did you rename Horse?"

How did he know?

"Promise," she whispered.

Tayre nodded. "In all the years that Promise carried me, he did what I wanted him to do, and he did it well. In return, I fed and cared for him. But if he had not fulfilled my needs, I would have sold him."

She looked away from Tayre, then out into the street now darkening into the night, a lump in her throat.

"It is not the same."

For a long moment he said nothing. "Perhaps not."

At the next meal, as the Emendi laid out dishes of food, Amarta made the hand sign again.

No response.

"Stay and eat with us," Amarta urged Zung-Urfan as she turned to leave. "Teach us the language of Seuan."

"I speak yours fluently, Seer. There is no need."

A flash of memory: She hung on a ladder on the side of a ship. Her life, Tayre's, and Tadesh's all waiting for Amarta to get them on board. The feel of the strange Seuan syllables coming from her mouth.

"We are not accustomed to sitting so idle," Tayre put in, his smile brightening into a completely charming expression. "Surely you can take a bit of time to tell us about the Body of

Seuan and your marvelous city. This sacred Kailo, about which we are so curious."

Zung-Urfan looked undecided, but Tayre's full-on charisma was hard to resist. She gestured for the Emendi to leave. "Only a moment, though. I have so much to do."

Amarta watched as Tayre asked her questions, every one of them subtly flattering. He began with the city's exports— the elixirs, antidotes, healing salves, and intoxicants for which Seuan was world-famous. She noticed that he didn't mention the poisons for which Seuan was also known.

Zung-Urfan's use of language was so adept and smooth that she might have been raised in Arunkel. But her answers were vague, as if scripted. Was she being particularly cautious with these strangers? Did they treat all foreigners this way? Or had reports of the disasters Amarta had left behind preceded her to Seuan?

"What of the Kailo?" Tayre asked.

Zung-Urfan's eyes flickered to each of them. "It is a gathering of the Body of Seuan wherein the sacred orders of Eye and Ear examine the previous year's predictions to confirm the Heart in his leadership. Then the castes perform devotions and renew their oaths."

"Predictions?" Amarta asked softly.

Zung-Urfan nodded. "Every life in the Body depends upon the extraordinary foresight of our Heart. We would be no more than the dust of bones if he could not truly say what was to come."

"How are these predictions assessed?" Tayre asked.

"The Heart writes. Each is sealed and dated in advance of the Kailo." Zung-Urfan's expression was proud. "It is easy to say what will happen, but to be held accountable for it..." Her eyes swiveled to Amarta. "That is another thing. Is it not?"

Amarta heard the challenge in Zung-Urfan's soft words.

Amarta would always need to prove herself, she realized. Every time. *How many tests do you need, Farliosan?*

As Amarta looked back at the Seuan woman, she realized, strangely, that she felt no compulsion to prove anything. There was, she now saw, an advantage to letting others wonder if she were a pretender: it gave her time to understand them.

It was now clear that to understand the knots of Seuan, Amarta would need to learn their language. She tugged at the memory of clinging to the ship's ladder as the islands were beginning to submerge. Gently, because of how tangled it was with the shard of glass that was Olessio, that was still so sharp.

She had it, almost. And then again. She opened her mouth. She made sounds.

Zung-Urfan's eyes widened. She gave a respectful nod. "You speak some Seuan already, it seems."

Amarta had no idea what she had just said, but best not to let on. "Yes, but we want to learn more. Will you help us?"

The Seuan woman made a polite fist-touch to her chest. "Nothing would please me more, honored Seer, but now I go." She touched her forehead, throat, chest, gave a small bow, and turned and left.

"I think I surprised her a little."

Tayre nodded. "I'd wager that she's going to ask someone if these particular foreigners should be allowed to learn the language of the Body of Seuan."

The two of them, restricted to their apartment, settled into a routine.

It was a luxury to sleep with him by her side in a bed, and stay there for as many hours as they liked. No hard ground below, no dark burrow in some dusty Seute Enta village. A good bed.

In the hours together, nothing was rushed. Amarta learned a new sort of patience in this land of desire.

No, it wasn't quite patience. More, it was a slow, slow dance. His attentions were as capable and smooth as everything else he did. Nothing was withheld, and there was no teasing in his touch. Rather, each moment was filled with a potent and unhurried exploration that filled her body and spirit with visceral joy.

Speaking seemed entirely unnecessary. It was as if this touch was a quiet conversation whose meaning she understood but could not put into words, and didn't care to try.

His spoken words had never felt so genuine as what he said in these quiet hours.

Nor, perhaps, upon reflection, had hers.

To lie beside him after the two of them had played out their passion was another kind of satiation, an additional meal. His body was endlessly fascinating. The lithe muscles, the curled hairs on his chest, the soft down of his taut stomach. The scars.

Many, many scars. A record of his life, written in yet another language she did not understand.

Something aged him young. Olessio had said. No one, on a whim, becomes what he is.

"How did you get this?" Amarta asked softly, tracing her fingers down his chest, where an old, raised scar stretched from ribs to just under his left nipple.

For a moment she thought he wouldn't answer, as he so often had not, when she asked questions about his past.

Then he did.

"My teacher, who was also my uncle. I was young. His blade was much longer."

"That doesn't seem fair."

He looked amused. "That was the point. My uncle showed me why backing away was a poor response to that attack."

"It was an accident?"

"No. It was not his habit to cut anyone by accident."

"He did this intentionally?" She frowned, following the scar that must have been a deep slice into him. "You hold no grudge against him?"

"It was a lesson I would never forget, one that saved my life again and again. A scar is a small price to pay for such a gift."

She tried to imagine the hard way in which Tayre must have been raised. What had driven him to become what he was? His gift-curse? But that, she knew, he would not tell her, not today.

Her thoughts turned to herself and her own training. There had been no training.

"I must become better at what I do," she told him. "Much better. Advise me."

He nodded slightly. "You must practice in new ways. As long as you repeat what you already know, that's all you'll ever know."

Amarta stared into his eyes, trying to read who he was, and failing.

"You never make mistakes. How is that possible?"

"I make mistakes all the time. I change how I think of them, so that they turn into something else."

"What? What do you mean?"

"I ask, what if they are not mistakes, but paths I have yet to walk? Puzzles to solve?"

"Knots to untie?" she suggested.

"The right knot at the right time is no puzzle, but a tool.

If you're dangling from a rope, the right knot saves your life. Not all knots need untying."

His look at her told her that he meant the Island Road, the knot that Amarta had cut. If she had understood that knot instead—perhaps even left it alone—Olessio would be still alive.

Remember us, the Islanders had said. Looking back, those words took on a different meaning.

But she could look back, she realized with some surprise. The memories still ached deeply, but not beyond bearing. The shard did not slice quite as deeply when she touched it. Tayre had been right.

"How do you make sense of a knot's nature?" she asked. "And whether it is a puzzle or a tool?"

His lips quirked in a slight smile. "I look at the well-worn paths of my thoughts and find a new route. Then I look at the knot again, from another angle." For a moment, his gaze on her intensified. "Don't look at what you can see, Amarta. Look at what you can't."

She sat up, bemused. "How do I see what I can't see?"

"That's the question."

She exhaled frustration. "You say things that are at odds with other things that you've said."

He chuckled, and put his hands behind his head, staring at the ceiling. "My uncle used to say that adages were useless, unless you had more than one and they contradicted each other. Then you might have the beginning of wisdom."

"Where is he now, your uncle?" she asked softly.

He replied without looking at her. "Do you remember my answer to Olessio?"

Where are your people, Guard-dog?

Dead.

She changed her question. "How did he die?"

90

He stared beyond the ceiling and shook his head. He would not answer.

Well, so be it; she did not need to know. At least not yet.

She lay her head on his chest, a hand on his belly, and listened to the beating of his heart. As she lay there, she brought to mind the names and faces of those who had paid for her missteps with their lives.

~

At the table after the meal, Tayre's words circled in Amarta's mind. What was it that she couldn't see? What was she not looking at?

There were countless futures, that she knew. Even for this tabletop's tile, under her fingertips. Go far enough forward, and it would be dust.

But then, that was true for everything, wasn't it?

She puzzled over what little she knew of Seuan. It seemed to her that to understand a people, it wasn't enough to see the tangled knot, as she had with the Island Road. She must also know what the cords were made of. Leather? Silk? Hemp? How were they tied, and why?

By the time Zung-Urfan returned with her Emendi slaves and the evening meal, all Amarta could be certain of was that she didn't know enough.

The food was set out. Zung-Urfan turned to leave.

Find a new route. Her body, Amarta decided, was a harp, its only task to play a tune that would keep Zung-Urfan from leaving. She made a sound. Vision would not provide meaning, but it gave her clues as to what the outcome might be.

A moment forward. A moment back. Amarta let new sounds form.

Zung-Urfan twisted back, her polite facade cracking into

shock.

"What did I just say?" Amarta demanded, standing, stepping toward her. "What?"

Zung-Urfan gaped. "It is what we say, in-caste only."

"What does it mean?"

"It means, 'I need you, as no one but your own can need.'" The Seuan woman tapped her fist to her chest, then again, in a gesture that seemed more for Zung-Urfan's reassurance than the foreigners she faced.

"I want to attend the Kailo," Amarta said.

"It is sacred. For the Body only."

"I am the Seer of Arunkel. I go where I wish."

A moment. A blink. The thrice-touch bow, too fast. Zung-Urfan nearly fled the room.

Amarta exhaled. Was her approach a misstep, to be so adamant and seem so arrogant? Or was it the right tone to take to make sure that the message got back to the Heart?

Tayre gave her an inquiring look. "Can you take on the whole city, Seer?"

She shook her head. Not yet, she couldn't.

In vision, a slow drumbeat. A distant, shrill scream.

∼

Amarta and Tayre stood just inside the doorway of their building, which opened onto an empty, wide stone boulevard. Before them was nothing but sun-baked streets.

"There is no cover here," Tayre said softly. "And thus no stealth. What do you intend?"

"I am done waiting," Amarta answered, then strode forward.

Tayre followed close behind, perhaps remembering the last time she had strode off and he had hesitated, on Punaami.

They walked the broad, smooth stone road, passing clusters of houses, and seeing no one. The wide boulevard crossed another, and they passed another village-like enclave.

Suddenly a child's face from a window, her mouth a wide circle of surprise. Amarta stared. The face vanished. A common occurance anywhere but Seuan.

Another part of the knot that she must understand before she touched it.

Then, ahead, some fifty figures spread across the road in a line, advancing. Each wore rough-hewn, tan clothes, and held a long stick with a sharp, curved end. All wore expressionless leather masks.

Amarta's heart sped. These were the men from her vision, that day when she had been blindfolded under wet Perripin skies, when she had learned to evade thrown rubber balls.

She knew these warriors. She knew what they could do.

Zung-Urfan stood at the center of the line, which stopped as Amarta and Tayre did, some ten paces away.

"With respect, Seer of Arunkel," Zung-Urfan said, her voice raised, "this is not your city. These are not your ways. Go back to the dwelling we have set aside for your living pleasure."

"I hear you," Amarta said, matching Zung-Urfan's volume. "We comply. But tell your Heart that I will not wait much longer to meet him."

"I will relay your words, Seer."

"Lend us slaves to teach us your language."

Amarta dipped into foresight. We cannot, Seer. We are all very busy, preparing for the—

"Preparing for the Kailo," Amarta said sharply, as Zung-Urfan opened her mouth to reply. "You have said. But you can spare two slaves from among your hundreds. It would keep us entertained. Perhaps we will be discouraged from wandering."

A pause as Zung-Urfan digested this, then the three-touch bow, as the warriors of Seuan watched from behind their masks.

Just before Zung-Urfan was about to turn, to leave, Amarta did so, putting her back to them and returning with Tayre to the apartment.

∼

Another meal, this one set by new Emendi. Zung-Urfan gave a three-touch bow and left. The two pale-haired slaves, a man and a woman, remained. They sat at the table and began to speak.

The lessons were simple. Body parts, pronounced differently from the similar caste names, such as the caste of the Ear and Eye, the Tongue and Hand. The Thumbs. There was, Amarta gathered, something special about the Ear and Eye. Sacred orders, their teachers told them, but did not explain what that meant.

The Emendi refused to answer questions about themselves. No names, not where they came from. They did not respond to Amarta's Kusani hand signs.

Finally, Amarta asked them outright about Kusan. They assured her that they did not know it. Kusan—a famous, hidden city and sanctuary for Emendi world-wide, and they had never heard of it?

They refused answers about the upcoming Kailo, the Heart, and the habits and ways of their owners.

And yet Amarta and Tayre learned.

When they were alone again, Tayre said: "Much can be inferred. Notice which words are never used. 'Coin.' 'Market.' 'Child' is used in conjunction with caste, implying that children are born into their castes."

Amarta learned from the Emendi, and even more from

what Tayre saw. She pushed herself to practice in new ways, connecting the feel in her throat of the new words to vision.

One day, Amarta spoke a sentence of words that the Emendi teachers had never voiced, and perhaps never intended to. On their faces was undisguised shock.

Let them report that to their Heart.

"Next time," she asked, "please bring something to write with."

When they came again, they had stylus and wax, and Amarta began to learn the written language of the land.

"Our esteem to you, Seer," Zung-Urfan said to Amarta. "We will show you the surrounding towns so you may see the produce they provide. The sandstone cliffs, where huge faces are carved by ancient artists. Our great *sorogs* and how they are trained."

"When do I meet your Heart?" Amarta asked.

Zung-Urfan's fist went to her chest. "That is not for me to say."

"When is the Kailo?"

"You must remain here during the Kailo, honored guests."

Zung-Urfan made her three-touch bow and left the room.

Amarta exhaled frustration. "Does it seem to you that this Heart does not want to meet me?"

"Delaying, at least," Tayre said. "Perhaps for the Kailo. Perhaps to put you off-balance."

"It won't."

Amarta stood at the window, looking across the boulevard to the nearest enclave. Who were these people, in this city of castes named for human body parts? Who was this Heart, who claimed to predict the future, but would not see her?

"What is your intention here?" Tayre asked.

"To understand the knots."

"And then what?"

Every decision Amarta made changed the future, and thus changed what was visible. Every decision meant the ending of countless other possibilities, never to be glimpsed again.

Don't look at what you can see.

Amarta was coming to understand that the scope of any single question was huge.

"I haven't decided yet."

～

A marta asked herself questions.

If focus itself was a choice, and every choice created new futures, then what she looked at mattered more than almost anything.

How to decide where to direct her attention?

Did that very question spawn new futures?

She sat at the apartment table and thought about thinking until her mind swam. Then she put that aside and considered this place. She recalled the cities she had visited—Munasee, Kelerre, and Senta—and how quiet Seuan was by comparison.

Except Kusan. The underground city of the Emendi had also been silent. In the dark stone hallways of Kusan, Amarta had learned to listen for the softest of sounds, for footsteps in dust, or the scrabbling of the ferrets.

She listened here as well, to the tiny creaks of the building, the rush of wind, a bird from the courtyard garden below. A fly buzzing across the room.

It occurred to her that it was not enough to meet the Heart, to examine him. She had examined the monks of the Revelation and the Mothers of the Islands. Then she had done them grievous harm.

No, she must also understand the Heart deeply before she acted, which meant that she needed to know his city and his people, in all the ways that she had failed to understand before.

It seemed a huge undertaking. If the scope of the knot was larger than she could take on, perhaps she was still looking too hard at what she could already see?

She stared at Tayre, who silently watched her in return.

Don't look for the ball. Look for where it isn't. Look for the open spaces.

Amarta decided to see nothing, as if she were blindfolded. She stood and slowly began to walk the edges of the room. Her gaze fell on various items. A plate. A cup. A chair.

She touched a spoon, moved it slightly on the tile. Each small change meant the birth of new futures. No matter how small, every decision altered what could be decided next, or be seen. Or be understood.

Each person, aware of their choice or not, in each moment, decided what to look at, and thus altered what they saw.

No one sees everything.

No one?

She moved the spoon back to where it had been. Where was it, in the moments to come?

From the street below came soft, numerous footfalls. A caste unit returning to their homes, perhaps, or a changing of the guards who now surrounded their building at all hours to make sure that Amarta and Tayre stayed inside.

Tayre glanced out the window. In this moment, she knew where his attention was. Where would it be next?

Her hand on the chair's back, she moved it so that the legs scraped softly on the tile of the floor.

Tayre glanced back. His gaze slowly raked across the room, looking for her.

Looking and not finding.

Amarta counted to three before his eyes came to her. He stared, expression blank, then nodded very slightly, acknowledging what she had accomplished. He turned back to the window.

Elation filled her.

~

Amarta studied minute details of the world, looking for what she could not see. The shadow the sun cast on the wall. The breeze from the open window. Empty plates from the last meal. Tayre's motions.

He practiced daily. In the apartment or out in the small courtyard below, where they were always alone.

When he practiced, Amarta did as well. He would jump, spin, and roll while she walked from shadow to light, corner to bench, tree to bush. She stood, or sat, or lay prone on the thick green groundcover.

What was she not seeing?

What was *he* not seeing?

She learned. So did he, only he learned faster. The next time she tried to escape his attention, a count of two was as high as she could go before his gaze found her. Then it was a count of one.

She honed her attention, slowing herself, then slowing more. What was the nature of the moment between being seen, and being something else?

The count rose. Two. Three. It went down. Up again. It wavered between one and two.

To fool Tayre, who knew what she was attempting to do, for even for a single count, was beyond what she would have thought possible.

But what about those who were not looking for her at all?

One morning, at dawn, they were awakened by a distant, steady, deep drumbeat. Outside, caste units walked the boulevard, all dressed alike, pouring from clusters of houses, walking in snug knots toward the sound.

Amarta dressed.

"Where are you going?"

From his tone she knew that he already knew, but she answered anyway.

"The Kailo."

He began to dress, too.

"You can't come," she said, though surely he knew this as well. "I can barely keep myself unseen. With you by my side it would be impossible."

"Amarta."

"No stealth without cover, you said. You're right. There is no way that you can go out there without being noticed."

"Your ability isn't infallible, Amarta. If I'm not with you, I can't protect you."

"I won't need it. I go to watch, not to act."

"Decide to go, use your foresight, and see what you would have seen. Stay," Tayre said. "This is dangerous."

She had considered this approach, which she had used before. But to use foresight was like trying to hold a thousand squirming, living maps. She had walked the world enough to know how flawed maps really were.

What she said was simpler: "No knot can be untied in imagination, or even in foresight. There is only one place to untie a knot: where it lives. I only go to watch," she repeated. She stepped close to him, her nose to his neck, inhaling his scent, remembering this morning's sex. His hands went to her back in a light embrace and soft circles.

He was attempting to seduce her, and it was working. Desire rose in her, a gentle, thrumming pull, so unlike the insistent craving that had been the buffeting wind of her awareness for so long. At least, whatever happened today, she would have him to come back to.

A thin slice of bleakness cut across that thought.

It had to be the glass shard that was her memory of Olessio, but Tayre had been right: day by day, the shard was a grain of sand's weight easier to carry.

From the future a chill whiff of something wretched.

It wasn't Olessio.

"What is it?" Tayre asked as she tensed in his embrace.

It was gone. She shook her head, then pulled away.

"I'll be back," she promised.

"What am I to do while you're gone? Wait?"

She blinked, thinking it through. There wasn't much else he could do. They might allow him to leave the city, if he attempted it, but she knew that they would not allow him to follow her to the Kailo.

"I need you here," she breathed. She needed to know that he was safe.

She turned to the door, wondering if he would try to stop her. He did not, and she descended the stairs and stepped out into the dawning day, following the caste units, who did not see her, toward the steady drumbeat that came from the center of the city.

Relief went through her that Tayre had not tried to keep her from leaving, followed by a brief pang of sadness that she couldn't place.

Chapter Seven

"THE EAST GARDEN TODAY," Sachare said, quietly relaying Cern's order to a waiting cadre of nursemaids and queensguards, who all began to make necessary arrangements.

Nothing was simple, Cern reflected. Not even choosing which palace garden to take the children to.

Cern's own calculations had grown more complicated, too: time of day, thus the sunlight available, sunlight that she craved more than ever, now that she was breastfeeding again.

Also, from another part of her mind, drilled across years to think this way: defense. However unlikely a palace garden attack might be, she considered the probabilities. Thus, predictability: when was the last time they had taken an outing to that particular garden?

And what about history? What had happened in that location, across Anandynar generations, that someone with bad intent might think about and wonder if they could make it happen again? Such stories were passed by word of mouth, even when not recorded.

In no written history would anyone find the knife attack

on the Grandmother Queen in the South Garden. But it had happened, and Niala bore a scar on her thigh her whole life to show for it.

Also, never recorded, was what had happened to the attacker. But that story, too, had been passed down through the Anandynar line, in vivid detail.

Cern sighed, wondering if her concern was excessive, the dark nature of her thoughts a consequence of the physical changes that being a mother brought. She looked at her two children, now being readied for this outing. So fragile, these young ones, and needing extraordinary attention and care.

Not much different from the council, now that she thought about it. Or the aristocracy. The empire itself. Cern's mind ranged across great cities of Munasee and Erakat, and what they needed most. The wayward Garaya that must be brought back into the fold. The towns, the roads that connected them. Her subjects, laboring in fields and trades. The Teva, who must be kept secure as allies.

In years to come, what would Queen Cern be known for? What sort of ruler did she want to be? These were not new questions to her, but having children changed the answers.

Estarna screamed and dashed around the room, shattering Cern's thoughts. The child loudly resisted the efforts of the nursemaids to put the naked two-year-old in clothes.

Cern took her baby boy from Sachare to give Sacha free hands to help with Estarna. Cern looked down at the baby in her arms.

She could see his father's features in his face, though she had the advantage of having studied them up-close and recently. It would be some time—years, if Cern could manage it—before anyone else would see the resemblance.

Her newborn boy had finally been named. After much debate—mostly with herself and some with Sachare—Cern had named him Nipatas Three, after a distant ancestor king who had the distinction of being the first Arunkel monarch to make a peace treaty with the Teva. As an added benefit, the Teva would not miss this gesture and the respect it implied.

She had to admit that one of the things Innel had done right had been to reconstruct the Teva treaty, and add on the fostering exchange provision. A royal child to be raised in exchange for a Teva child.

That royal child might even be Nipatas himself, when he was of age. She wondered if it would amuse the Teva to have an Anandynar youth to raise who bore the name of the first Arunkel monarch with whom they had had beneficial dealings.

Estarna screamed again, the sound briefly muffled as a tunic passed over her face. The squeal turned to delight as Sachare started juggling brightly colored balls to distract the child while the rest of the clothes went on her. Meanwhile two nursemaids took Nipatas from Cern and set him in an amardide and ebony carriage.

"Ball-ball-ball."

"Please?" Sachare prompted Estarna.

"Please-please-please!"

Estarna was learning words at a stupefying rate. The range of plants, flowers, fish, and birds in the east garden would be a suitable study for a young royal mind, and sunlight would be good for all of them.

Having at last assembled themselves, trailing the dichu dogs, Cern's retinue strolled and rolled out of the antechamber and into the hallway. Nursemaids, attendants, and guards deployed around her and the children in concentric circles up and down the hallway. At Cern's side, Estarna walked, her head held high, a confidence in her gait that made Cern proud. She pointed and named everything they passed, from tapestries to shoes to people moving aside to let Cern and her retinue pass.

The dogs wound their way through people's legs to walk at Cern and Estarna's side. Suddenly Tashu took off, bounding up the hallway.

"Tashu-Tashu-Tashu!" called Estarna.

Along the walls, palace denizens watched them all go by. They bowed. Many smiled, gasped with delight, whispered and pointed as they caught their first glimpse of the newborn in the carriage.

"What's he doing?" Sachare asked, as they passed a hallway alcove. There Tashu was snapping and pawing at the floor. As Cern slowed, the entire retinue slowed as well. A subtle parting of her people gave her a narrow corridor of visibility while yet still keeping her enveloped.

Something small dashed out from the wall and through the opening her people had made, directly toward Cern.

"Mouse-mouse-mouse!" Estarna cried delightedly.

A guard stomped on the ground to block it. With a small squeak, the mouse deviated, running in another direction. Tashu barreled through legs, cornering. There were soft but ardent curses as people were forcibly parted by the determined dichu dog, then mouse and dog were far up the corridor in a chase.

A moment passed, and they were gone, the minor drama concluded. All eyes went to Cern. It was part of her work, she knew, to respond to events, to set an example. Her mood, whatever it happened to be, would be taken as direction. Echoed.

She gave an amused smile. A small chuckle.

Around her, soft laughter arose, ripping out to those lining the walls.

Again, they began forward. Tashu returned, looking disappointed, but in a few minutes, his ears perked up again, and he bounded off in pursuit of another small shape dashing across the hallway.

There were always mice in the palace—there was simply no keeping them out—but Cern could not remember ever having seen two, in such quick succession, in daylight hours. She looked again at the walls. Were there fewer people here than usual for this time of day?

Another cough. A snuffle. A sneeze.

Watch for the odd thing, daughter. What is out of place? Big events are built from small ones.

She gave a look to her seneschal. "Examine the matter." He gave a set of fast hand-signs to an assistant, who rushed off.

As they all made their slow way to the main staircase, Cern's circles subtly changed shape, preparing for the stairs, where it all must shift as they descended. Always the dance.

Far down the hallway, a figure abruptly emerged from a doorway and began to run forward.

Cern stopped. Guards deployed sharply. She was keenly aware of her one hand on the carriage, the other on Sachare, Estarna snug between them.

Three guards drew blades and ran forward to meet the figure, who she now saw was the guard Radelan. He whispered urgently to his fellows.

"I don't care how important," one snapped at him, the words carrying. "You idiot, you don't run at the queen. We kill people for doing that."

The man was gulping air, nodding, but looking past them to Cern.

"Your Majesty, I must speak with you."

"Now what?" she muttered. Was he here to tell her of some new betrayal?

She gave a cautious nod of permission. Radelan was searched, his pockets emptied, and he was let to step a bit closer, though still surrounded. At five paces, the guards stopped him.

Radelan met her eyes with a haggard expression. "One in twenty, Your Majesty. Maybe one in fifteen."

"What?"

"Disloyal. Ready to move against you. Within the palace walls. Now. Today."

Twitches rippled across her guards. She raised a hand to hold them.

"How can you know such a thing?" she demanded.

His face sagged. "Exactly as you suspect, Your Excellent Majesty."

Because he was one of the traitors.

The guards ringing him came to the same conclusion, tightening, watching her for a signal.

Cern thought fast. *One in fifteen.* If it were true...

"Fetch the triad." She meant Lismar, Lason, and Nalas. "Not the garden, after all," she said with open regret. "To my office. Bring him."

Radelan was grabbed, a little roughly, a little uncertainly. Cern could see her people wondering. Was he a trusted informant? A turncoat? They didn't know.

She didn't, either.

~

Cern's office was packed. The children. Sachare and attendants. Lason and Nalas and all their people.

Cern's own queensguards. A good twenty-five or more. Her eyes flickered across faces.

"Explain yourself," she said, her attention moving to Radelan, who was now ringed by six of her best.

The man gave a ragged exhale. "I am to deliver a message

to you. I—" He swallowed. "—I've been paid by Helata and Etallan."

Helata *and* Etallan?

A guard at Radelan's side, shocked enough to speak, blurted, "You took coin from the Houses?"

"Quiet," Nalas snapped at him.

"A betrayal of your oath," Cern said to Radelan. She felt weary.

"Yes, Your Majesty," said Radelan. He was a big man, now slumped, expression fallen, seeming to be suffering.

Seeming.

Twice paid—thrice, if she included the crown—meant that he was being paid to lie to someone. Could anything he said be trusted?

He licked his lips, spoke again. "Sent me to deliver it. Because I had gotten in to see you before, so I could do it again. Seemed a sign from the Fates, Your Majesty. I knew I had to..." He trailed off, eyes darting around the room.

Whatever he was about to say, he was losing his nerve.

"You've done well," Cern replied encouragingly. "Tell us the message."

Radelan shook his head. "I have friends. Family." His voice broke. "Has to seem I delivered the message, but not so early. Next bell, soonest. And then—I can't be allowed to—to—" He was breathing hard. He was terrified.

Cern exchanged a quick look with Nalas, whose confused expression told her that he understood no better than she did.

"Of course," Cern told Radelan, hoping to reassure him, though of what, she had only morbid speculation. "We will do what is necessary to take care of your friends and family. You have my word." Suitably vague, but spoken with royal authority. "Say what you came here to say. Say it now."

Radelan looked to one of the guards who had taken his possessions. "The rock."

The guard brought from his pocket an object, presented it to Cern with an open palm. Cern looked it over, but did not touch. Seuan contact poison was expensive, but the Houses were wealthy.

It was a rock. Or rather, it was in the shape of a rock, but from how it caught the light, the thing was clearly fashioned of metal.

She recalled the conversation. "A rock," Cern lied with a royal smile. "Simple basalt. Not even polished. Why, Tokerae, do you have something better to offer me?"

As she understood the meaning of the object, she felt as if a new weight had landed on her shoulders.

Here's your rock, Cern, the object seemed to say. Made of Etallan.

"The message," Cern said flatly.

Radelan took a breath. "'Your Excellent Majesty: relinquish your throne immediately. If you do, your life is assured, as well as the lives of the many now in jeopardy. You will be allowed to marry the new king of Arunkel, and you will publicly assert his authority. All for the good of the state, by my honor. Here my symbol: know me as Tokerae dele Etallan."

The room went deathly quiet.

Cern was keenly reminded of the vicious, brutal games that the Cohort used to play, the moves her siblings made to see how far they could go and what might be gained from some audacious risk. During the Cohort years, Cern had been an observer of this swirling intrigue, of ambushes, alliances, and betrayals.

It was never aimed at her, because she was the prize to be won. But she always knew that someday it could be.

That day had come.

"Outrageous!" Lason shouted, face red, mouth opening to say more. Cern gave him a tight head shake. To his credit, he clamped his jaw shut.

Lismar entered. Lason took her by the arm, whispering urgently, recounting events.

Cern turned to Radelan. "Now that you've broken your oath to multiple masters," she said bluntly, feeling the press of time, "why should I believe you at all?"

Radelan blinked, as if only now considering this. "I suppose I wouldn't, Your Majesty. But..." He looked around the room, then back to her. "Can you see Etallan's roof from here?"

The monarch's offices looked down upon the Great Houses. Atop each one was a renowned, extravagant display that showcased the House's unique produce, as well as demonstrating its loyalty to the crown. It was understood that the monarch's gaze honored the Houses, as the Houses' displays honored the crown.

Nalas was already at the window, yanking back the drape. His expression changed. Stunned? Alarmed? Both.

Cern walked to join him at a normal pace, more slowly than her internal state urged. It was essential to seem in control. Around her, guards shifted to shield her from Radelan, retaining their configuration as best they could to keep Cern at the center.

She watched peripherally. Did any guard hesitate? She listened to the soft sounds of their boots shifting on the floor, saw the motion of armed men reorienting to protect her. Or to target her.?

At the carriage, Sachare stood with Estarna at her side. Cern knew the guards closest to her children very well.

One in fifteen.

Or did she?

At the window, Cern looked, having braced herself to see.

On Etallan's roof, the familiar brass and iron fountain still arced down, like water, but in the pool below, the red-and-black Anandynar colors were no more. In the sunlight, the surface glinted gold.

This meaning, too, was entirely clear: Etallan meant to obliterate the Anandynar monarchy and create their own.

From his uneasy look, Nalas understood at least some of what was clear to Cern. "I'll be back with force, Your Grace." He dashed from the room.

Cern let the drape fall, turned her back on the window.

"What does this mean?" Cern asked Radelan, though she understood Etallan's message perfectly.

"The signal to begin, Your Majesty," Radelan answered.

"To begin what?" Of course she knew, but it had to be said.

"For those in-palace, the double-paid," Radelan answered, his look full of shame. "To stand ready."

"Tell me everything, Radelan."

He nodded. "Don't drink the elixir. Ignore the mice." He gulped. "Surround the queen."

Her guards tensed. Their eyes flickered around at each other.

Was she already surrounded?

She must seem confident in them, now more than ever. "The mice?" she asked calmly.

"Rumors that they carry plague, Your Majesty. Not true. The elixir, said to prevent you getting sick. That's not true, either."

"I've men down today," Lason interjected. "Coughing. Complaining of fever."

"Pretense, Lord Commander. They've been bribed to act

as if they're ill," Radelan said. "Most of them don't even know who bribed them."

"What does the elixir do?" Cern asked.

"Makes you stumble. Talk to yourself. Hallucinate. That part's true."

One of her guards spoke softly. "I've seen a lot of the regulars sucking it down, Your Majesty."

Clever. Those not in the know would willingly consume the elixir, taking themselves out of the fight. Evening the odds.

So very Cohort, this plan.

She turned to her uncle, who answered the question she was about to ask.

"We still have the numbers," Lason said. "Easily."

"You might not, Your Majesty," Radelan said heavily. "A western window?"

Lismar dashed from the room, through a side door that led to the large, adjacent audience chamber. As Cern followed, so did Sachare and the children.

Cern was keenly aware of her guards reconfiguring around her. Innel had chosen and trained the queenguards, and after him, Nalas had reassessed and reconfirmed every one of them. Cern had put her life and her children's lives in the hands of a traitor and his second.

Was it possible that they were all above reproach?

Or perhaps now, having seen Radelan and knowing who had bribed him, they would resolve to be?

The audience chamber had high, decorated ceilings, trimmed with rich red amardide wood, and polished black stone floors. The room was rich with history, even in Cern's own lifetime.

On that section of stone, Innel had laid Pohut's wrapped body before her father the king, as he sat on a heavy ebony and bronze chair on the dais with Cern at his side.

And there Innel had beheaded Eregin de Etallan, splattering blood, sending the head rolling.

Cern looked through the large western window, seeing exactly what she had been hoping not to see.

Beyond the defensive walls of the palace, hundreds and hundreds of pikes and helmets glinted in the sun. They wore no uniforms. But high on a pole flew a banner, with a crossed sword and pickaxe, orange on black.

Etallan.

Cern took in the scene.

At the now-barred palace wall gates and atop the walkway, guards gaped at the army gathering under the Etallan banner. The guards drew weapons, raised bows.

Cern had studied countless battles in minute detail. Her tutors had included generals and captains, cavalry and soldiers.

It had all been theory.

She glared at Lismar and Lason, stifling an urge to yell at them. *How is it possible that you let us be surprised?*

But there was no need. Both looked ashamed and furious. Lismar turned, gave hasty commands to her second, who took off at a dead run, while Lason hit the wall next to the window with a balled fist once as he cursed, then turned to Cern.

Cern counted her blinks, to keep herself from a stunned immobility. *One. Two.*

She was sure Innel would have seen this coming. Fates damn him to many Hells, but he would have known.

Then again, would she even be here if he had not so offended Etallan?

Three.

She thrust away that line of thought.

Inside the walls, her soldiers gathered, streaming into

view from the direction of the garrisons, in various forms of undress, weapons in hands.

"Your Majesty, we must act," Lismar said.

Four.

Cern's gaze flickered to the dais, where her father had so often held court. *Always have a second plan, daughter.*

Then to her children. At the wall stood Estarna, tugging Tashu's ear. Chula sat to the side of the carriage, panting and drooling, Sachare's hand on his head.

Five.

Her mind seemed to snap out of its terrified stupor. One part of her began to play out force and defense. The other went to the hand that held the sword: What did Tokerae want?

If he meant to marry her and take over the monarchy from within, then he would want as little bloodshed as necessary to win. He was Cohort; he would be thinking about what to do after, when he would imagine himself in command of the men he now stood against.

His first plan would be for Cern to capitulate willingly. *What you've got in you—keep it if you wish—but all the next ones are mine.* He would not trust an easy surrender, but surrender was his goal.

"Defense only, until I say otherwise," Cern told Lismar.

A bow. "Your Grace." Lismar left the room.

Below, hundreds of Anandynar soldiers and armed guards assembled, readying themselves for a battle that no one had expected.

If Cern could decisively win this encounter, then action was the clear course. Overwhelm the resistance, dominate the treason. Be ruthless.

Again, her father's words: Once the killing starts, it will spread like wildfire. Even survivors are never again whole. But sometimes it must be done. Be certain.

She was not certain.

"Do we have the numbers, Lord Commander?" she asked.

Lason spoke to the window. "Arunkel soldiers are the best fighters in the world, Your Grace. Even equal numbers do not trouble me."

"They trouble me," Cern snapped. She turned, edge on, so that she could see Radelan, her back half to the window. The skin between her shoulder blades crawled. "One in fifteen, you said. My queensguards in this room number twice that. Which two are compromised?"

Around her, guards shifted uncomfortably, eyeing each other.

Radelan's eyes went wide. "I don't know names, Your Majesty. They might all be loyal." Apparently he felt the inadequacy of his words, and added, "We have a sign to know each other." He raised his hand, making a circle of thumb and small finger, middle fingers gathered.

Cern stifled an exasperated rebuke at what could have been useful information, had he thought to give it to her in private.

Not Cohort.

"Now that you've betrayed every side, Radelan, how do you expect to survive?"

He shook his head. "I don't. I deliver the message. You slay me."

Her guess confirmed, she affected to be affronted, and sharply reprimanded him: "We do not harm messengers."

His expression went stark. "You must. If they find out that I warned you before the bell, my family and friends are dead." He reached behind his ear, took out a small pastille, gray-and-brown. "From Seuan. Fast and painless, they say." To the nearest guard: "Will you run me through after, brother? One last favor? I beg you."

The guard nearest him snorted angrily.

"I am your queen," Cern snapped imperiously. "You die when I give you permission to die."

Radelan dropped his head in startled submission. Good; her authority was still potent.

Around him, her guards readied to take the pellet from him. She held them with a gesture; she needed him willing.

Sounds from outside drew her attention. Beyond the walls, a platform. There, a man stood high on a makeshift stage, in Etallan's colors and a speaker's livery. He threw his arms wide and began to shout.

Nalas crossed the large chamber to Cern's side. "I have one-hundred-fifty of my best outside, Your Majesty. Sober. Ready."

"Loyal?"

"Absolutely."

No sense in asking twice; he was right or he wasn't.

Lason's ear was against the window.

"What is he saying?" Cern asked.

"Bizarre lies, Your Grace."

"Don't make me ask again, uncle."

Lason glowered through the glass. "The halfwit speaks of an impostor queen. A birthmark on your thigh, known to those who have bedded you. Tokerae says that anyone loyal to the empire must demand an examination to be sure you are Cern. Pay it no mind."

"The double-action," Cern said.

"What?" Lason asked.

Not Cohort, either.

"With one hand he pressures me to surrender my position. With the other, he questions my right to the position at all."

"An obvious lie. No one will believe."

It did seem weak—the council knew her by sight, as did thousands of other palace denizens and aristos.

On the other hand, none of them had seen her naked. Tokerae could claim to know about a supposed birthmark from his many years in the Cohort. From his times in her bed. A bit of doubt might be all he needed.

How many of the other Houses were aligned against her? How many were not? She remembered her dinner with Fadrel dele Helata, a year ago, and wondered if he had been planning this even then.

Down below, her soldiers assembled into lines, facing the gate, weapons ready.

It came to Cern that Tokerae had slightly handicapped himself by choosing to attack at this gate. The side gate would have been a more effective entrance. He knew the palace and he was no fool; he wanted Cern to see all this as it played out.

Thousands of armed men, all converging at once. Mice. Intoxicants. Cern's excellent view. This was the work of years. Tens of years. Maybe longer.

There are more plots yet, Your Majesty. Innel had said. *Had he known?*

No time for that now.

"We can stand against this rabble," her uncle said, waving a hand dismissively.

Cern looked again at Estarna, Sachare, and the carriage holding Nipatas, and suddenly knew that Tokerae would never let her children live.

If she did not surrender, what was Tokerae's second plan?

Force and blood: a monarchical coup. It had never been achieved, not in nearly a thousand years of Anandynar rule, because the palace was strong and Lason was almost certainly right that their defenders were better armed and better trained than the attackers.

"Your Majesty," Lason said urgently, "give the order."

But the worst outcome would be for Cern to fight today and lose. Tokerae would force her to wed. It would be the end of the Anandynar line, the death of her children. Even when the other Houses came with support—if they came—it would be too late.

"I have decades of experience, Cern," Lason said. "You must listen to me and—"

"There," Cern said, pointing.

At the rear of the troops facing the gates, a line of soldiers stepped backward and out of place. One made the conspirator's hand-sign. Then another.

"Get Lismar," Cern said heavily.

The thousands of battles that Cern had studied—down to details of weapons quality and quantity, cargo manifests, and supply lines—had taught her to quickly and precisely consider every angle, no matter how hungry, tired, or afraid she might be.

So this moment was eerily familiar, from her years of Cohort drills and tests. The fact that it was not practice meant only that her heart was pounding, her mouth dry, not that the calculus was unclear.

In terms of force, what she was looking at below was not complicated. She had the numbers. With reliable troops, her side had an excellent chance.

They were not reliable.

Lismar was at her side. Nalas stood ready. Lason's arms were crossed as he glared out the window.

Another cluster of armed soldiers wearing red-and-black uniforms stepped backward, flashing the conspirator's hand-signs between them.

Cern's gaze found Sachare, who held baby Nipatas in one arm, and Estarna's hand in the other. Estarna stared back at Cern, a thumb in her mouth, her eyes wide.

Guards, attendants, assistants, nursemaids looked back, waiting for her to make an order. Judging by their faces, Cern was still giving every indication that she knew what to do next.

If only it were true.

～

The bell of the hour rang. Radelan twitched visibly at the sound.

Cern judged him to be genuinely ragged with fear and despair, to be a man who had told the truth at last. But she must be sure.

"Your bell has rung," she told him. "Deliver your message to me, as you were instructed."

"But I did already, Your Majesty."

"Do it now."

Haltingly, Radelan repeated the words he had memorized. They were the same.

Cern nodded. "You will return to those who hired you and relay my response. Return to me with his reply."

Radelan shook his head. "But I must die. It's the only way to protect my—"

"I hear you, Radelan. Now hear me." She pitched her voice and cadence, loud and regal. "I am Cern esse Arunkel and my word is law. I will give your family and friends the chance to survive, but not if you waste your life by dying in dishonor. Serve me. Redeem yourself."

He was breathing hard. His fist gripped the gray-and-brown poison pastille tight.

"He won't believe me."

"He will, because you will speak the truth. Just not all of it."

She stepped to within a few paces of Radelan, making the guards surrounding him visibly nervous.

"Radelan, don't lay down your life before your duty is complete. I need you. Say that you will serve."

He bowed, trembling. "I will, Your Majesty."

"Then take a message to Tokerae dele Etallan. Tell him that I want to negotiate."

Chapter Eight

TOKERAE DELE Etallan studied the trembling Radelan. The large man was dressed in the queen's colors but had also been given a jacket with a white hem, signifying that Cern accepted him as a legitimate messenger.

Radelan's face was ashen, his shoulders hunched. He was terrified.

For a moment, Tokerae didn't understand. Then he did: Radelan was not House-born, and he was not Cohort-raised. He lacked both blood and forging and could hardly be expected to know how to hold steady in times of change and challenge, as these were.

Tokerae looked at the armed force that stood between him and the palace. This was history, and Tokerae was making it so.

This very moment. He felt exhilarated.

"The queen's words?" Tokerae asked. "These were her exact words?"

"Yes, your Illustriousness. Yes."

"Say them again."

The message began with a bid for negotiation, then went

on to speak of civilized discussion, of sparing the many from grievous harm, and of avoiding divided loyalties throughout the Houses. She invited Tokerae to the palace, promising him safety and honor.

Divided loyalties, eh? She was Cohort and knew the cost of battle. She would have looked out the window and seen that the odds were nearing even.

Maybe she didn't have the stomach to bring it to blood, after all, despite the Cohort years.

He turned to Ella at his side and spoke low, only for her hearing. "She's ready to talk terms, sister. What do you think?"

Ella gave him an acerbic smile. "The moment you step foot into the palace, Tok, she'll imprison you if she can, slaughter you if she can't, regardless of her promises. Wouldn't you?" She gestured to the huge space where they had gathered their substantial force. "Out here, our advantages number in the thousands. Why give up position and strength, brother? What is there to negotiate?"

"Her children," Tokerae replied. "I know her. They'll be the key. I could promise to keep the two she's got whole, but she might not believe a messenger for something that important."

"You're not going to keep them whole after your own are born," Ella said. It was not a question.

Tokerae snorted softly in reply. "No. But as you told me, all this would be easier from within the palace, with her surrender and cooperation. She'll insist on seeing me, before she agrees to anything like that."

Ella made a thoughtful sound. "Let's see how sincere she really is."

∾

C ern found Tokerae's answer unsurprising and insulting.

Negotiation was possible, he said via the guard Radelan, but only after Cern set to rest the distasteful and troubling rumor that she was not who she claimed to be.

The solution was simple, the message went on, and Cern need not even leave the palace grounds. Simply strip naked before the steps of the palace, where all could witness and confirm the existence of the royal birthmark on her thigh. If she refused this easy proof, Tokerae dele Etallan must assume that the birthmark was not there, and then he would have no choice but to defend the honor and dignity of the empire and address her as the pretender she was.

Radelan spoke these words, but reluctantly, his head hanging.

Lason shouted into the room. "That brazen, contemptible, wretched—"

"What birthmark?" Lismar asked.

"No birthmark," Cern replied. "He invented it." She gestured her command triad closer.

To Lason: "Lord Commander, what do you advise?"

"Attack now. Our numbers are still even, and I'll wager his poorly trained mercenaries turn tail the moment they face the finest military of the world."

Would you wager everything, uncle?

"Nalas?" she asked.

"I'm certain we can push them back from the gate. If other Houses are sending force, Your Majesty, that would make the difference. Are they?"

At this, Lismar shook her head. "We can't count on that. They'll have been bribed and threatened to stay away, and Etallan and Helata will have blood hostages to make sure of it."

A motion caught Cern's eye: down below, a man flashed the conspirator's hand sign again.

"Our forces are riddled with traitors," Cern said.

"I blame the mutt," Lason spat. "Hard to be loyal to a—"

Then, from Nalas: "He had more loyalty than you ever—"

Cern clapped her hands. "No time for bickering." She barely held her own clutching panic at bay, yet somehow her voice remained steady. *You trained me to act the adult, father. Who knew I'd learn so well?*

To Lismar: "General, what do you advise?"

Lismar growled at no one in particular. "I've sent for outlying troops, but they're days away. I say accept no part of Etallan's terms. We have not held the throne this long by giving in to every House tantrum. We lock down for a siege. We can hold steady for at least—"

Nalas gasped. They all turned to look.

A line of royal soldiers had threaded themselves backward through their fellows, becoming the rearmost line. The motion itself caused some confusion. Some objected. Some resisted.

The back line was suddenly a melee. Soldiers turned, saw that something wasn't right, and became confused about who and where the enemy was. Some were utterly unnerved to find their own turning on them.

They went down. Throats cut, bodies pierced.

"Sacha," Cern said sharply, without taking her eyes from this new horror. "House Nital has stayed out of this treason. Return to your House of birth if you wish; I release you to it. Do it now."

"It would tear my soul in half, to break my oath to you," Sachare replied. "I will not leave your side."

Cern hoped the emotion she felt didn't show. She didn't have time to feel it.

Lason gave a wordless, pained sound, and began to swear.

Atop the palace wall walkway, Arunkel guards were turning and turning, their bows pointed within, on their own. At the gate, a quin of soldiers unbarred the gate and yanked it open.

Outside the walls, the invaders cheered, and thrust through. The battle began.

Cern's breath came hard and fast. "Give me options."

From outside came shouts, roars, and the clanging of metal. No one needed to look to know what was happening.

"The tunnels," Lason said quietly.

Cern's father had forced her to memorize an astonishing number of hidden passages through the tangled palace, including ones that led nowhere. It had been a dank, dark, unpleasant study. She still remembered her father's taunting voice guiding her through the most confusing of trails, those given only to the heir.

"You advise me to flee?" Cern asked. "Abandon our forces? A coward's run?"

"We have to save our lineage, niece," Lason answered.

"Your Majesty," Nalas said. "We are outnumbered. Command us to stay and fight and we will. To the last breath. But it is no coward's run to take your children somewhere safe. Wherever you go, you are still queen."

Lismar gave a bitter nod.

Cern's command triad was united in their advice at last.

She looked out the window, and saw the truth of it: her forces would not be able to resist long. Then the palace would fall.

The Cohort-trained part of her marveled at how quickly things could come unraveled, at how fast everything she knew could shatter.

Deep inside, a grief so large that it held the voices of generations of ancestors threatened to overcome her.

She pushed it away. She would feel it later. If there were a later.

Cern gave orders to her seneschal and the elite guards holding Radelan.

～

Below the seat of the heavy ebony and bronze chair was a disguised blood-lock, much like the one on the lockbox under Cern's bed.

Cern touched it and the lock clicked open. At her command, guards tilted back the huge chair on its disguised hinges, revealing an inset door below. Opened, it revealed a ladder descending into darkness.

Men began streaming down into the hole, following Lismar, whom Cern had instructed as to how far to go and where to wait so that Cern could direct them through the branching passageways and lethal traps.

Cern met the gaze of her turncoat guard, Radelan, and gestured him close, holding his guards back.

Radelan hesitantly came forward. Seeing Cern's trust, he sank to his knees.

"If you come with us," Cern said to him, "they will kill your family and friends."

His eyes were wide as he nodded.

A booming sound, as something pounded on the locked palace doors below. Cern could feel it through the floor.

She put her hands on Radelan's shoulders, feeling the skin and muscle beneath the fabric.

"You served me bravely today."

"Thank you, Your Majesty," he whispered.

Cern searched his face and judged that in his

hopelessness, he was eager for redemption. *Know what nightmares control those you rely on most.*

"I must ask of you one more thing," Cern said, injecting vulnerability into her tone and a shadow of her true need into her expression. "Will you serve me a final time? You are my very last hope, ser."

A glimmer of surprise lit his eyes at this unexpected term of respect.

"Anything. Anything at all."

"After we are gone, lower the chair until it locks shut. Then find Tokerae dele Etallan. Tell him that we have escaped through the east riverside kitchen tunnel. He will know what you mean." It was a tunnel well-known among the Cohort, who had laboriously mapped its treacherous holes and traps. "He'll want to know how you know. Tell him that I sent you to—" To what? She thought fast. "To retrieve the lockbox in my bedroom, then to meet us at the fifth fork."

Cern ached at the thought of Tokerae knowing where her lockbox was, but this would not work unless Tokerae was convinced that the item Radelan was sent for was something Cern found precious.

In any case, he would find the lockbox, sooner or later. It was now as far out of Cern's reach as it would be at the bottom of the Nelar ocean.

Cern twisted off a ring that her father had given to her, that his grandmother had given him. Cern had worn it for many years, and Tokerae knew it well. "Tell him that I gave you this to show to the guards, so that they would let you into my bedroom. Say that, out of loyalty, you went to him instead to report that I was fleeing."

"He'll kill me," Radelan said.

"No. He'll take you with him into the riverside kitchen

tunnel, because he's never been past the third fork. At the fourth fork, tell him the rest of the pattern."

Tokerae would find it irresistible, especially if he believed that Cern fled that way.

Radelan could buy them hours. Days, if they were lucky.

Toting hastily obtained supplies, more of her people climbed down the ladder. Then Estarna and Sachare, baby Nipatas strapped to her chest.

"He'll interrogate me," Radelan said.

"No. He won't have time, not if he wants to catch us. He'll force you to lead, to test that what you say is true. Listen closely: right-left-right. Right-left-left. Do you have that?"

Radelan nodded, repeated it back.

"Your Majesty," Nalas said urgently, "You must go."

Cern ignored him as she took Radelan's hands in her own, and captured his upturned gaze in her own.

"In that tunnel," she said with a gentle intensity, "are wide holes that drop into deep waterways." She gripped his hands more tightly. "Fast and painless, you said. Take your tablet and then stumble into one of those openings. Do it before the fifth fork so that Tokerae and his people go on without you."

"And my family and friends?"

"Make him believe you, Radelan, and he will not touch them." She said it as convincingly as she knew how. In the confusion that would follow, it was even possible that she would turn out to be right. Possible, but not likely, if she knew Tokerae. But Radelan must be persuaded. "Serve me in this one last thing, Radelan, and your transgressions against crown and country are absolved, your honor fully restored."

"Is that possible?" His voice was small, like a child's. "Truly?"

"It is. My breath is law. I proclaim it so. Do you give me

your sacred oath to complete this task I have set you, Radelan?"

His hands trembled in hers. "I do, Your Majesty. I do." He was crying softly.

She gave him her best smile. "Stand, now." He did. "The moment you complete your task, Radelan, you will have not only the gratitude of the crown of Arunkel, but be fully reinstated as a queensguard. Make me proud, queensguard."

Radelan was now entirely entranced, filled with hope for redemption. With luck, his elation would last long enough for him to do what Cern needed him to do: lead Tokerae astray, then fall into a hole.

Finally—and to Nalas's obvious relief—Cern climbed down the ladder. As she descended into darkness, she thought of the many very useful things she was leaving behind. Her mind spun on the challenge of hiding and feeding nearly two hundred people as they fled the palace and city underground. Rings, coins, maps—so many things that she wished she could have brought.

Yet it was her father's letters that she most regretted having to leave.

Chapter Nine

"A VALUABLE SLAVE, YOU SAID, DOMINA."

Zeted stared out her vast window at the ocean. The sunset was lovely. Pink-hued clouds reached for each other across an orange canvas, like the fingers of lovers.

"Yes, Ralafi," she said.

She took a sip of the Arapur-Bruent lilac mead, which had been custom brewed for her from lilacs shipped to the island from her own orchards. The mead was solidly acceptable. Better than last year's, though not as good as the batch three years ago. Something about the weather or the soil. She must ask her orchard master what she thought.

"Why not brand him, then?"

There was a not-too-subtle whine in her majordomo's voice. Jealous of the strange Adra?

"And why would I do that?"

"To protect your investment! You've branded other unmarked slaves. But this one—you put a gold chain around his neck. Domina, a gold chain! He could escape. Sell it. You would have no recourse at all!"

"I am not worried about his escaping, Ralafi."

Adra had shown little interest in anything, let alone his own freedom.

"Domina, he's an addict. You don't know what he might do." Now Ralafi's tone held undisguised complaint. "I don't understand."

Adra was no fool. Where would he go? He was safe here, well-cared for, and he knew it.

Zeted had always felt that the best captivity was when someone preferred their life in her employ over another one.

In that light, perhaps it was unsporting to brand and chain even slaves. She could save herself the trouble.

She smiled a little, thinking of how it would rattle her majordomo.

She reached over and patted his hand. "Ralafi, my darling boy, you don't need to understand. Just make sure he's fed, watered, and clean when I want him. Oh, and keep his consumption of intoxicants to a sensible level. That's all you need to be concerned about."

"Yes, Domina."

"Don't sulk, Ralafi."

"Yes, Domina."

～

Innel sat on his cot. He stared into space. The door to his tiny room opened. Ralafi entered.

"God's nipples and damn you, you're stoned again!"

This statement did not seem to require an answer, so Innel did not offer one.

The majordomo took Innel's head by his again-bearded chin, and dabbed at his cheek with a warm, wet cloth.

"You took it all at once, didn't you. I told you not to. Remember? She wants you. Can't you stay sober at least some of the time?"

"Makes you think she wants me sober?"

"Ah! Words! From his very mouth! *I* want you sober, you Arunkin trash. Tired of cleaning up your baby drool and steadying you while you lurch down the hallways to the bath, then trying to keep you from drowning in the water. I ought to let you sink. Get up, she wants you."

Innel stood unsteadily. The room spun. He sat down again.

An exasperated sigh from Ralafi, who bent over, his face close to Innel's. Too close.

"What is it about you, boy? What makes you so special?"

"Nothing."

"On that we can agree. But the Domina..." He stood, snorted frustration. "Give her time, she'll get over you. Now, up. Take my arm. Let's get you clean and sweet-smelling, the way she likes you."

Innel wanted only to sit where he was, and stare at the lavender wall. Or perhaps sleep and dream of nothing.

Time to earn your keep, brother. Pohut's voice whispered from somewhere.

Innel wondered, if he behaved particularly well, if Ralafi might give him more duca and kana. He was about to ask, but at Ralafi's scowling expression, he thought better of it.

At last, his sense won out. All good things flowed from Zeted, including Ralafi's largess that kept Innel in intoxicants that defended him from too much thought.

Innel struggled to his feet again, leaned on the swearing Ralafi, and let the other man take him to the bath.

~

Ralafi opened the door to the Domina's great octagonal purple room and glared Innel inside.

Innel shuffled in, bowing as steadily as he could manage

to Zeted. He caught his balance against her desk, an extravagant, ornate mix of mahogany, amardide, and amethyst.

"Domina," he muttered, making his way unsteadily toward the large, central bed.

"No, Adra. Not just yet. Sit over here, next to me."

He frowned, looking for her. There she sat, at the very desk, in a huge chair, a lesser one by her side.

"Yes, Domina," he muttered, gratefully sinking into the smaller chair.

She dismissed the sour-faced Ralafi with thick, ringed fingers, then sipped from a long-stemmed glass of something in a liquid shade of plum. For what seemed to Innel a long moment, she said nothing.

"Adra, can you read?"

Innel's mind worked the question, though sluggishly. Of course he could read, and in a couple of different languages, Perripin among them. But should he answer? He turned her words over in his mind. Was there any reason to refrain? He failed to find one, and so he nodded.

"Good," she replied. "I have a contract offer in hand, unlike the usual that I receive. Not only do they want to rent one of my ships, but ask that I hire a team of mercenaries to ride it, some of whom must speak Seuan. Quite the ask." She paused. He felt her staring at him. "Do you understand what I've said thus far?"

A crew. A force of fighting men. A ship to take them across the ocean to Seute Enta. The Seuan-speaker part was unlikely, but possible. It was not that complicated.

Even in your current state, brother.

Innel nodded, agreeing with Pohut.

"They are offering me many times what I would usually charge for such a thing, and my rates are hardly low to begin with. This seems very odd to me. Adra, what are they doing?"

Unbidden, the cost of such a venture began to unroll in Innel's head. Mercenaries. Weapons and tools, depending on the work required. Food for the voyage, and sufficient for the return, in case provisioning at the destination proved problematic. A captain, crew, cooks.

What sort of operation would be worth that much money, at such a distance?

"High-value illegal goods," he suggested. "Some rare mage-work item. Something that coin alone will not buy."

"The target is a person."

"A rescue, then. Or an abduction."

"I think you have it exactly." Zeted made a thoughtful sound. Even in his dulled state, he could tell that she was studying him closely. "Here's a picture of the one they seek. Take a look, Adra."

Zeted held out a piece of paper.

The image hit him like a blow. Recognition must have shown in his face, because Zeted smiled wide with her ample lips.

He should have been able to hide his reaction. Gone, it seemed, were the days when he easily wore a mask of indifference.

Gone, gone. All gone. He felt himself tremble, tried to suppress it, failed, gave up, sighed, and stared again at the picture of Amarta al Arunkel.

"You know her," Zeted said. "Who is she?"

Someone you released, brother. Someone you intended to be free.

Innel shook his head.

"Tell me, Adra." Zeted's hand was on his, warm, her hold firm.

"A figment," Innel replied. "A story. Some say that she can tell the future. Some say she's the old king's bastard daughter."

"A swarm of wasps, Arunkel politics," Zeted said, an amused look on her face. "Becoming more so by the day, from the news. Is she royalty?"

Innel shook his head.

"Someone in Arunkel thinks she's quite valuable."

"The Houses," he muttered.

"My thought as well, given the amount of coin involved." Zeted thoughtfully tapped ringed fingers against the mahogany flat of the desk. She took another sip of her wine.

"It pays exceedingly well," she continued. "With what I clear after expenditures, I could buy myself three new ships, and I like ships very much. But I have a reputation to protect, Adra. Is this going to create problems for me with the Houses, if I take this contract?"

Innel slowly shook his head. Any House funding such a venture would want to keep it quiet, no matter how it played out.

"They specify Perripin mercenaries," Zeted added.

"Of course they do," Innel said. "Anything goes wrong, blame it on Perripur."

An invasion of Seuan would not sit well with the Houses. A dangerous play, to make Seuan unhappy, at least for those who enjoyed the best healing, fertility, and feel-good elixirs that the world knew. Whoever was behind it would want to stay in the shadows.

Helata, who traded with Seuan regularly and lucratively, would be especially unhappy. It wasn't Helata, in any case; Helata was too proud to use any ships but their own.

Innel tried to dismiss these annoying thoughts, but they kept returning, like hungry squirrels determined to find every dropped nut.

"Should I send a mage along?" Zeted asked, "to help apprehend this woman?"

"Won't help," he said.

"A friend of yours?"

Amarta dua Seer, a friend? He thought of Pava, the Emendi who had named him Adra.

No, the Seer was nothing like a friend. He shook his head.

"Then you won't be upset, if she's... apprehended? Harmed in the attempt?"

It was not his concern. He had done what he could for her, back when he'd been... what had he been, again? Who had he been?

Someone.

"Adra. Answer me." Zeted's voice was sharper now. Demanding. "Will you be distressed if this woman is taken, or harmed? Does it matter to you?"

The seer would get away. She always did.

"How many mercenaries?" he asked.

"Fifty. But there's one more part I haven't yet told you."

She was silent for long enough that Innel found his gaze drawn inexorably to her. As he met her gaze, she stroked his bearded face gently, affectionately, then tapped a pile of papers.

"They provide a map of her location in Seuan, and I'm assured of local cooperation, including an unlocked side-gate at a signal from my ship. This means someone there wants her gone. This makes obtaining her seem far more likely, does it not?"

Fifty armed and capable men. That's what Innel himself should have done, back when he was looking for her, instead of hiring individual hunters, however grand their reputations might be. She could see a single mercenary coming. But fifty, all at once?

"Not my concern," he said.

"She might die, Adra."

"Not my concern," he repeated.

Zeted looked back at the picture again. "Then it's settled: I'll take the contract." She downed the rest of the thick, plum liquid and looked back at Innel. "Now we can go to the bed, Adra."

"Yes, Domina," Innel replied automatically, his mind still on the ship and the problem of capturing the uncapturable.

He did not think that Amarta dua Seer had ever been pursued by this many mercenaries in a coordinated effort, all of whom knew exactly where to find her. It might actually work.

Not his concern, he told himself again.

❧

"They'll never lay hands on her," Innel said to the pale lavender wall.

Fifty well-armed men with a map and an open gate? I wouldn't wager on her, brother.

"Not my concern."

What do you think they'll do to her, once they have her?

He knew exactly what they would do to her. He himself had ordered it done.

Capture. Chains. Questions.

A finger on the scale in her favor is all it would take, brother.

Innel made a thoughtful sound. "Possibly so."

You could give her that.

Innel lay back on the bed, which was, he had to admit, extremely comfortable. He had no reason to leave it, ever, except in service of satisfying Zeted, which was itself not so unpleasant.

He had come to appreciate the regular baths, despite

Ralafi's grumbling. And the food, which was tasty, satisfying, and plentiful.

Then there was the generous supply of those substances that made it possible for Innel to forgo thought. To find sleep.

Escaping the villa would be the easy part. His room was never kept locked, probably because he had never attempted to leave it on his own.

It would be simple: he would walk the hall, head held low and subservient, yet with posture and pace that conveyed that he was on an errand for someone in authority. Perhaps it was common knowledge that Zeted favored him—a matter of gossip and speculation. If he held himself just right, he could be assumed to be doing her bidding.

Then he would take some of the extra over-clothes that hung by the kitchen door, clothes that would make him look less like a slave and more like one of the citizens of Bayfahar. Next, down the stairs to where the trash was staged. A smelly area, typically deserted. Once outside, he guessed that finding his way down off the road into town would be fairly easy.

A little harder would be to convince the ship's captain and the mercenary commander to let Innel on board for the journey to Seuan. But even that could be done, he was nearly certain.

It was a plan. Almost.

"I could do it," he muttered, a little surprised.

The man you used to be could, perhaps. But now?

"I could. If I wanted to."

Talk is for spectacle, brother.

"Not my concern."

Wasn't it you who brought her to the attention of the Houses in the first place, by openly taking her to the palace?

"I released her."

Rather publicly.

"I was generous," Innel said, annoyed, jabbing at the ceiling with a finger to make his point. "I released her from the contract with me—a priceless contract, too. Generous. I offered her anything to stay."

She said no.

"She said no. I gave her a horse, anyway. A gift. One of the queen's finest. You know how much that creature was worth?"

And an escort.

"To protect her."

A royal escort. The queen's Rusties. In full daylight. You might as well have sent a speaker along to announce her to all she passed. If that wasn't your intention, it was sloppy work, brother.

It had been a chaotic time, and Innel's attention had been stretched thin. Among other matters, he had been juggling the delicate Teva treaty negotiations that would gain Ccrn a powerful ally in the mining towns. That morning, when Amarta had come to him to ask him to free her, Innel suddenly realized that he could not hold her against her will for long.

An excellent decision to free her, as it turned out, because it had gained him the goodwill of Marisel dua Mage, and that had led to Cern being healed, and surviving her pregnancy. In truth, Innel's daughter's very life sprang from his decision to release the Seer.

His daughter's life.

The ache washed over him like a suffocating wave that nonetheless refused to drown him.

"Sloppy," he agreed at last.

Now, the Houses seek what you once held dear. She saved your life at the battle of Otevan, then saved the battle itself.

"But I don't owe her," Innel said. "We're even."

All right. Let her die, then. It's all the same to me.

Innel snorted, waved a hand at the wall. "Of course it is. You're not even here."

From the corner of his eye, a shadow moved.

Innel snapped his head around to look straight on. Shock prickled through his entire body.

A murky shape—his brother, or some convincing semblance—crouched on the floor, near the bed, one long arm draped across one knee, head cocked at Innel. The blurred expression seemed amused.

That the best you can do, brother? Dismiss my words by discounting my existence? Surely, after killing me, the least you could do is to consider whether my points have sense to them.

Innel breathed raggedly. Had his mind finally snapped?

His brother's words were as compelling as they had ever been. Ghost or mere lunacy, it would be just like Pohut to put the argument first and himself second, to insist that Innel think more deeply and consider all sides of the matter.

Pohut had not only been his brother. He had been Innel's friend. His first friend. His best friend.

Innel looked away from the shape, shame filling his eyes, tears wetting his face.

He curled in on himself, turning to the bed, arms over his head.

Some time later, he started awake. Sounds came through his small window. Pots banged, loud cursing from the kitchens. He sat up, looked around. He was alone.

His head ached. His mouth was dry and tasted terrible.

A dream?

Did it matter?

"I could do it," he repeated.

The challenges rolled around in his head. How to get aboard? How to convince the mercenaries to believe him?

"No, damn you. I want nothing to do with this."

Where was Ralafi? Innel would beg for extra, so that he could sleep without dreams. Sleep forever.

But as he looked around the room for any sign of his brother, his mind, the damned thing, chewed and chewed and chewed, like a dog with a bone.

After a while, Innel realized that he really could do it.

Then, as the night wore on and sleep did not come, that he would.

Chapter Ten

TAYRE WATCHED AS AMARTA STARED, unseeing, at the untouched food on the table.

"They killed an Emendi slave," she said at last.

The words were beyond inadequate.

The Kailo ceremony had been—what? Sickening, yes. Bloody, too. Also, tedious and hot. Amarta hid on a rooftop, lying flat to watch, some hundred paces distant from the outer circle of Seuans.

That morning, as she had made her way to the rooftop, the drums had begun. Slow and steady, they had continued for hours, a strong beat and a weaker one, like a heartbeat. So well-timed were the drummers that the sound seemed to be one drum, coming from many places.

Within the circle sat thousands, perhaps the entire Body of Seuan. Each caste fanned out in a wedge-shape of tight, neat rows from the center stage. At the back were the children and the Emendi slaves.

Three people stood on the circular center stage. Four, if she counted the blonde figure lying on a stone table to the side.

At the very center stood a man. He wore a simple gray robe, his bald head reflecting the sun. To one side, a woman in rags of brown, black, and dun wore a veil across her face. To the other, a man in a mottled plum tunic, with bare hands and feet stained the same color.

They were doubtless the First of the orders of the Ear and Eye, the ones that Zung-Urfan said would confirm the Heart, the bald man at the center.

From this distance it was hard to tell if the bound, supine Emendi figure was male or female, alive or dead, but Amarta guessed male and alive.

"Did they cut the heart from the Emendi's body?" Tayre asked.

"How did you know that?"

"A guess. It fits what I've heard and seen here."

On the stone table, the Emendi screamed and bucked and writhed as the Heart cut up through his belly with a knife. While the man howled, the Heart set the knife aside and took up another. The howling turned inhuman. Blood flowed. The Heart cut up and up.

At last the Emendi fell silent. The Heart dug his hands deep into the still-shuddering body. He pulled out each organ, setting it into sunlit silver bowls.

Amarta had been biting her knuckles to keep herself silent.

"It was..." There were no good words. "Horrible. He held the man's heart over his head and turned in place, the blood trailing down his arms." She took a gasping breath. "Why do they do this?"

"To make sure that those who are watching them know that they can."

"No one in the crowd seemed disturbed. They were riveted. They almost looked pleased. I don't understand."

"They see it yearly," Tayre said softly. "To them, this is the way things are properly done."

"You accept this?"

"I neither accept nor reject it. You want to understand the knots of Seuan? Understand this. What happened next?"

"The Kailo was... circles in circles. The front five of each caste stood and walked around the stage, in the direction opposite to how the Heart was turning. His hands were still high, still holding the..." She shook her head, unable to finish the sentence. "The castes began to sing."

First one, then the next, and the next. A wordless song, each caste's song different, yet folded into the previous, a melody alongside the drumming. The sound rippled around the circle, opposite the direction to those first five.

Circles within circles within circles.

When all the gathered thousands were singing, Amarta realized that the totality of the sounds wove into an overlapping, rippling drone, as if an undulating motion. It tugged at something deep inside her, and though she lay flat on the rooftop tile watching, she felt as if she were in motion.

"The only things that didn't move," Amarta said, "were the Eye and Ear, who stood on either side of him. All at once, the Heart stopped. Everyone stopped. The drums stopped."

She was silent for a long moment.

"And then?" he prompted.

She shook her head.

Tayre nodded. "The Heart, Eye, and Ear ate the Emendi's heart."

Amarta gaped at him. "How do you know that? Were you there?"

"No," he said. "But they are not the first to do such things."

"I had to turn away, so I didn't..." she swallowed bile, even now, remembering how nauseated she had felt. "When I looked back, they were still passing it from hand to hand, mouth to mouth, Heart to Eye to Ear, and back again. When it was gone..." She took a breath. "The first five from each caste dropped to their knees. The Heart went to stand before them. There were words. An oath, I suppose. Then they cut their palms and dripped blood on his feet."

"And the prediction?"

"The Eye brought out a scroll and read it. He passed it to the Ear, who did the same. They raised their hands, palms facing the Heart."

"Affirming him," Tayre suggested, and Amarta nodded.

"Then the drums began again, and the singing and chanting, but it was all reversed, the circles unwinding. Then each caste went silent. And then they started leaving, in lines. They were very quiet."

Completely quiet. No discussion of the Heart, and how fine he looked, or how poorly some other caste had performed in comparison. No hopes for the next year's predictions. No jokes. Only footfalls below her, as she waited on the rooftop.

"Do you suppose they do say such things, in private, to each other?" Amarta asked.

"Probably," Tayre answered.

"I wonder what they talk about."

He regarded her silently, but she heard what he did not say: *Not all knots need untying.*

~

In the mornings, Amarta left Tayre in their apartment-prison while she explored the city. In the afternoons, they practiced on the lush green of the garden courtyard. Practice turned into a game.

He would move. He dropped, rolled, kicked, or sprinted

across the yard. Amarta pointed to where she foresaw him being next, waiting until the last moment.

He was very good at the game: he would change directions, sometimes so fast that it seemed barely possible.

Amarta improved until she could see ahead, not just one move, but two. Then three. She learned to avoid making small motions with her eyes or body that warned him too soon about what she had foreseen.

Their morning conversations with Zung-Urfan repeated.

"Will the Heart see me today?" Amarta asked, as outside, the wind gusted.

Zung-Urfan touched her chest. "A storm comes. The cisterns must be addressed. Water-doors and sluices selected, arranged."

"Will the Heart see me today?"

Zung-Urfan put a fist to her breast. "He attends the sacred rite of passage for those children coming into adulthood, some of whom may go to the holy orders."

"Will he see me today?"

Zung-Urfan thumped her chest. "A sorog is ill. The Heart must say if he is to be healed or ended."

The sorogs were the great black beasts they had seen from a distance when they'd first come to the city.

Amarta asked again, every day, and every day one excuse after another.

And then, simply: "No."

This morning, after Zung-Urfan left, Amarta went to the door. She paused, meeting Tayre's eyes, remembering when he had been the one leaving to do reconnaissance, and she was left at some inn or barn to await his return.

Years of warnings and cautions, but now he said nothing. In all possible moments leading from this one, he also said nothing.

Tayre was unique in Amarta's experience; he could keep

his silence in the now, and in the future, holding his intention pure. A disciplined mind.

She left, creeping down the stairs to the outer door, and stepping outside to weave a path through the unseeing guards.

Today, though, something had changed. Someone had decided something. Futures shifted, unlikely ones thickening, strengthening. To make decisions was difficult, but every time Amarta wavered, the fogs of possibilities grew new tendrils that she must track.

An undisciplined mind, hers, with messy thoughts. So many of the ills surrounding Amarta had been caused by her own half-measures, and that must change; she must learn to keep her mind and purpose pure.

She walked into the city to study the knot of Seuan.

Tayre watched Amarta as she began to sketch a map of the city in crumbs and grease on a smooth ceramic plate.

"An attack," she told him, "From the east gate. From the harbor."

"Who?" Tayre asked.

"Perripin, well-armed, capable."

"How many?"

She blinked, looked into the future. "Too many."

"Numbers."

"At least fifty."

He blinked. "Why are they not stopped at the gates, by the Seuans who stand guard there?"

"I don't know. But they enter the gate without challenge."

He made a thoughtful sound. "Is their intention to capture you, or to kill?"

"Capture," she said softly. Vision warned of a dark, rocking cabin, stinking of mold. A drearily familiar future.

"We are forewarned, so we have time to act," he said. "We can leave the city before they arrive, yes?"

Amarta took a breath. "I have a plan. I need your help." He would not miss that she had not answered his question.

He spread his hands. An invitation to continue.

She pointed to a spot on her plate. "This is the temple of the Heart—that tallest tower, the one you can see from everywhere. These, to either side, are the temples of Eye and Ear. Nearly every caste produces something, sealed in ceramic, or metal, or wood. Powder, salve, liquid, jelly, and so on."

"For export."

She nodded. "But some of these substances never leave the city. Two, in particular, go to the temples of the Eye and Ear. Regularly, because they spoil so fast. The plan requires them. I can get us inside those temples and out again, easily, but I can't carry both urns without your help."

"What's in the urns?"

She had hoped he wouldn't ask. But of course he would. She could not answer because foresight made it clear that if he knew, this soon, he would actively resist her, and that she could not allow.

When she did not answer, he seemed unsurprised.

"Again," he said, "I ask you: why we can't avoid this attack entirely by leaving Seuan?"

That had been among the possibilities that Amarta had considered. To keep seeing the various and conflicting futures, she had refrained from selecting. Now, in order to move forward, she must step into one, and let the others fall away.

"I will proceed with my plan," Amarta said slowly, resolving this as she spoke. "If you want to leave the city without me, I understand. Go, and I will defend myself as best I can with what you have taught me."

She'd chosen the words carefully, knowing where his mind went when he thought her in danger.

As she steadied her decision inside, the future shifted again, some possibilities becoming dominant, others weakened, and others vanishing entirely.

The plan was risky, but not reckless. Not like what she had done at the Island Road and the Tree of Revelation.

No—those hadn't been plans. They were nothing like deliberate. Rather, she had let herself be swept away by outrage, bringing devastation to the very people she had been trying to save.

Never again would she let outrage guide her hand. No matter how grievous the knot. No matter how sharp her knife.

As Amarta swam in a miasma of future visions, looking for the one in which Tayre did as she wanted him to, a distant-yet-sharp sorrow pricked at her, carrying the familiar stench of grief.

She would not look at it. *Always a path to failure.* She must avoid the mistake she'd made with Rhaata, of attending overmuch to an unlikely future, and thus helping to create it. Yet she must not disregard it entirely, lest it wriggle to life while she was distracted.

A delicate balance. A knife edge of focus.

"This is barely a map, Amarta. Not a plan. Tell me the rest."

But she could not; too many details and he would call the plan insane. She studied his face, saw the doubt. Given the destruction that she'd left in her wake, his skepticism was understandable. Entirely reasonable.

She must seem confident, without seeming foolhardy. Words would not sway him. She would need to show him that she knew what she was doing.

How to keep his mind open long enough to offer him that proof?

Ah, there was the answer: the thin thread of his curiosity. Fine, but strong.

She took a breath. "The Eufalmo are coming."

Chapter Eleven

CERN and her company descended the ladder from the grand audience chamber where Radelan remained, hopefully to do as he had agreed and cover their tracks.

Cern and her hundreds crept along narrow corridors. Another ladder down. Another corridor.

Had she brought too many? Or not enough? A good two hundred and more, by her estimate, once she counted the queensguards, various staff, and seneschal.

And the children, who brought the count even higher. Many of the guards had come back from obtaining supplies, their own families in tow. Cern had no choice but to welcome them all; she could hardly force them to leave their own behind yet expect the loyalty she required.

Now Cern breathed orders to be sent back down the line, that their route would be soon interrupted. They would need to exit a cold storage vault in one room, cross a rarely used palace hallway into another room, and there find a hidden panel that would allow them to continue.

To cross a hallway in the very palace that they were fleeing—all two hundred of them—would be a moment of profound vulnerability. Even so, this was the most direct pathway out of the palace and city that Cern could have selected.

Once they were in the open, she told her people, they must move fast and quietly. The children especially, whose high voices could carry, must be silent. If even one person wandered off, or were caught and forced to talk, they could all die.

One by one, they climbed out of the cold storage vault, left the first room and streamed across the hallway. Sounds of fighting reached them through the floors above. Distant and muffled by stone and plaster, but there was no mistaking it: the palace had been breached, and many still fought on to defend their queen.

Cern clamped down on her rising emotions at these thoughts. She stepped into a hidden panel, where there was a small chamber. She gestured to those around her—Sachare, the children, guards—to go forward and follow Lismar into the passageway.

Nalas and Lason stepped to her side. Cern watched as her people went by, laden with weapons and packs of food and water—whatever they could gather in the few minutes they'd had—children's hands gripped tightly. They were frightened. But silent.

She met all of their gazes, giving encouraging smiles before they went forward into darkness, demonstrating a confidence she didn't feel. A lifetime of practice meant that she knew how, not that it was easy.

All it would take would be one crying child, heard through the walls.

"You must go, Your Grace," Lason whispered. "You're not safe here."

"They need to see me, to know why they risk so much."

Lason scowled. He hissed at the line of people: "Faster!"

Cern put a quelling hand on his arm.

Shame washed over Cern as the muffled sounds of yelling and fighting—of the resistance to the treason—surged. Shame at her own flight.

Never run, daughter. But if you must, you must.

I must, father, to save my children. The traitor's dirty feet soil my palace floors, and his stinking ass will sit on my throne, but I will reclaim it all. I swear this, on my lineage, my country, and my children. I swear to avenge those who fight and die for me this day.

Lason turned to go the other way, out the hidden panel, back into the store room. Cern caught his arm. "Uncle, what are you doing?"

"Someone must be last," he said, watching the tail end of the line of people go by. His gaze followed two children, hand in hand, as they passed. "Someone must erase the signs of us having been here. See that the doors are properly closed, that the dust on the hallway floor does not point to our passing."

"I have people who will do that," Nalas whispered.

"I have people, too, damn you," Lason snapped. He gave his steward Malio a glance, then shook his head. "None of them have my eyes. It must be me. I am to blame, in any case. If I had listened..." He fell silent.

"Uncle? What?" Cern asked.

"I will tell you later." He pressed her firmly forward into the dark corridor. "Go on, Cern. I'll be along soon."

Cern hesitated, then strode forward to catch the others, Nalas close behind. She pressed past each of her people, until she was again at the front of the line, where she could lead them safely forward.

The tunnel sloped downward, and they descended, staying silent as they passed under the palace. It was hard to say how much time had passed, with no bells to mark the hours, and little light to see by, but it seemed quite some time later that Lason's steward Malio managed to reach Cern at the front of the line.

Malio's face was tight as he told her what had happened. Lason had left the storage room, into the hallway, to check one last time, ordering Malio to stay inside with the panel in place until he returned.

Shouts in the hallway. Malio heard Lason roar with anger, escalating into the unmistakable sounds of a fight.

It went quiet. Malio waited for his master to return. Finally, Malio secured the panel from within and ran to catch up with the end of the line.

Lismar gave a long exhale. "He is lost, Your Grace," she said to Cern. Malio sobbed softly.

~

W *hat now?*
Cern stifled annoyance as she was forced to a plodding stop by a tight knot of queensguards and servants in front of her.

Days of traveling in dusty, grimy, lamplit tunnels, with forks and traps that only Cern knew about, had made for slow, tense progress. But there should be nothing unexpected in this particular stretch of narrow tunnel. Why were they stopped?

Behind Cern, more people pressed forward, discovering that no one was moving in front of them, packing in too tight.

Cern did not doubt her memory. She had walked this tunnel numerous times, and more than once in full dark, her father behind her the whole way, barking at her to recall the maps she needed to memorize, reminding her of the cost of failure. *You'll die, daughter,* he'd say.

He had impressed upon her that these tunnels must never be used. *Then why learn them?* she had wanted to shout back, but no one shouted at Restarn esse Arunkel, not even his daughter.

A dark gratitude had been taking root inside her these last days, as she considered the alternative to this flight, a too-clear future with Tokerae dele Etallan.

She resolved not to even think his name again, not until the day that she had him at her mercy.

Estarna was quietly complaining, showing off a rather impressive vocabulary. Sachare hushed her, hugging her as they leaned against the tunnel wall, along with many others. A few managed to sit on the ground, but there was not room for all.

Nursemaids had shared responsibility for baby Nipatas, struggling to keep him comfortable despite his snuffling reaction to the dank tunnels. Cern had fought to ignore his wheezing sounds, to keep her focus on the journey, lest any of her party take a wrong turn, or fall prey to any of the traps along the way.

The tunnel was tight, the air dank and thin and stinking of too many people. Claustrophobia threatened. Cern thrust it away. No time for that.

The usurper would be stunned to know how little progress they had made; they were still in-city. With luck, he would never find out.

Nalas squeezed through bodies to stand in front of Cern. Even in the dim lamplight, his face was haggard and dirty. Very likely she looked no better.

"A tunnel collapse ahead, your grace," he said softly. "We think we can dig through."

Cern reviewed maps in her head. By her reckoning, they were past the edge of the palace, deep into the high-city, and most likely under House Nital. Where exactly, she could not say. Deserted cold kitchen storage? Busy servant's quarters?

Cern exchanged a look with Lismar.

"Do we have a choice?" Lismar asked in response to Cern's unspoken question.

Lismar knew as well as Cern did just how the story of their numbers and provisions would end: either they would make it through to find the food and water they needed, or they would die here in the tunnels.

Or they would surrender.

There would be no surrender.

Nital might have stayed out of the treason, but that didn't mean the House wouldn't turn her in, if they noticed her digging. Who knew what leverage the Usurper had over Nital? Cern doubted that Sachare's presence would matter much.

"Permission to dig through, Your Majesty?" asked Nalas.

"Be quick. Be quiet."

Nalas bowed his head and left the way he'd come.

At Cern's feet sat Tashu, panting. Chula whined. The dogs were hungry and thirsty, and they were not alone. Rationing had begun immediately. There just wasn't enough of anything, and the food caches along the way were past desiccated, or gone to rodents and bugs.

They must get out of the city. Yet here they all stood, waiting. Tired, hungry, thirsty, and unmoving.

If Nalas and his men couldn't clear the tunnel, they'd be forced to backtrack. That story did not end well.

Cern felt eyes on her in the dim light. She summoned her most assured expression.

A s she waited, Cern's mind played out everything that might go wrong. A few feet away, baby Nipatas wheezed.

Cern turned to Lismar. "Did Lason know this route?"

Lismar shook her head, shadow on shadow in the dim light. "Our brother the king wouldn't have trusted Lason with something that important."

Some comfort, at least; Lason could not have been forced into revealing a route he didn't know to begin with, though he could reveal that Cern was fleeing the palace. They would tear the room apart to find the tunnel and they would. Cern reviewed the forks that defended them from pursuit and wished that there had been more of them.

"Do you think that he talked, aunt?"

Lismar exhaled. "No, Your Grace. From what Malio heard, he was discovered in the hallway. I know exactly what that idiot would have done: charge them with everything he had, forcing them to kill him. He's dead."

"A hero, then."

Lismar sniffed once. "A doddering old fool. But loyal."

In front of Cern, Nalas squeezed through.

"Your Majesty. The way is clear."

Relief flooded through Cern. "Nalas, well done," she said with feeling.

Packs were hefted, and the line began to move forward again.

Lason, for his many flaws, was no traitor. He had done what family sometimes must: sacrifice everything to give the lineage he cared so much about the chance to survive.

In return, Cern must do better than survive. She must find a way to compensate Etallan and Helata for their treasons.

Many, many steps stood between where they were now—

plodding forward, hungry and tired, their lives in peril—and the future in which Cern might slake her thirst with the blood of her enemies.

No matter; Cern was Anandynar and Cohort. She knew how to plan and wait until the time was right.

She thrust away the seductive imaginings of vengeance and focused on keeping herself and her people alive.

~

C ern emerged into the sunlight. Following from the cave mouth at the foot of a rocky hillside of tangled brush and loose rocks, came the rest of Cern's two hundred queensguards, attendants, officials, servants, and families.

The line became a cluster, then a wheel, then a spiral, as people gathered under the thicket of trees or simply stared up at the sun.

Cern blinked in the bright light, eyes watering, as she greedily inhaled clean air. She blinked her eyes clear and examined the treeline of the hill from which they'd emerged. It looked as she expected it to. She knew where they were, more or less. Hopefully more.

She snapped her fingers at the dogs, who looked around, clearly tempted to run off, and they stayed close.

Reluctantly. They wanted food and water. They were not alone.

In the faces of her people she saw profound relief. Some were sobbing quietly. Many stared at the sky, joyous to be free, to breathe air clear of the dank, ancient tunnels and each other. They hugged. Some sat on the ground.

It did not take long for looks to turn expectantly to Cern.

She huddled with Lismar and Nalas. "We must find water, food, and a safe place to rest. Soon."

"Outlying villas with families, loyal and true," said Lismar. "We'll go to them."

Cern shook her head. "We must be miserly with our trust, aunt, lest we find more traitors than we can count. No room for missteps. Nalas—" Cern bit off what she had been about to say. Her keen edge had dulled across days of fear that must be masked as they crept beneath House after House and a second tunnel collapse through which they had to dig.

Not acceptable. She could not afford any slips.

"Lismar," Cern corrected firmly. "Assemble a small scout team to visit some of these perhaps-loyal families. See about getting us supplies to hold us while we go forward. Tell them as little as possible."

Lismar's gaze flickered fast between Cern and Nalas. She bowed quickly and left.

"If you don't trust me, Your Majesty—"

"I'll be blunt, Nalas: your wife and son's location is now surely known to the treasonists." Was her voice harsh? Probably. Cern felt ragged, her self-control stretched thin.

Nalas's expression tightened. "I assume they are dead, Your Majesty."

Of course he did; he was not Cohort.

"No," she said, "they are almost certainly alive. Hostages, to inspire your cooperation."

His betrayal, she meant.

She watched his face go through the changes she expected: hope, then hope torn asunder, as he understood that he would need to choose between his family and Cern. That was quickly followed by the stark look of a man who has unearthed his beloveds only to find them dying.

She waited until his expression settled into a bleak understanding. It didn't take long. Good: he was as smart as she'd hoped.

"What would you do in my place, Nalas? Your monarchy and empire assaulted, the Houses on your trail, and treasonists eager to slaughter your children. Your people hungry, tired, and afraid. What would you do?"

Nalas blinked, visibly blinking away his misery. No doubt reburying his wife and child in his mind.

"I would move," he said, voice hoarse. "And fast. Divide the company into three parts, perhaps four. Head them in different directions to confuse pursuit. Whatever your intention, or final destination, Your Grace—a place to hide, reach out to those still loyal, assemble a new army—tell no one, not until the last possible moment."

It was good advice, and much along the lines of what Cern had been thinking. Nalas might not have been Cohort, but he was clever. No surprise that Innel had chosen him to be his second.

Innel, who had been both Cohort and clever. What would Innel—traitor and father to her child— have advised her now?

He would have said that the second to a traitor is a questionable asset.

She studied Nalas carefully. "What shall I do about you?"

He swallowed, then again. "It seems to me that you must either send me far away, or keep me very close, to spare yourself the doubt that I might choose my wife over my queen."

"And would you?"

He lifted his chin. "Never. My oath and honor bind me to you, Your Majesty, first and always. Dirina knows this, and would expect no less of me."

"Even at the cost of her life? And her son's?"

"I cannot speak for her," Nalas said. "Only myself. I hold firm to my oath."

Very moving. *Innel, you trained him well.* But was it true?

True or not, Cern needed him, so it was time to give him a touch of hope.

"They may still be whole, Nalas," she said gently. "It is not beyond possibility that they escaped the grasp of the traitors entirely, and now walk free, as we do." Possible, but not likely. From his expression, he suspected as much. "Until we know for certain, your loyalty to me is your best chance of seeing them alive again."

A grim business, this, knowing what nightmares controlled those closest to you. But she had no choice.

From his expression, Nalas didn't, either.

He bowed very low. "Command me."

Chapter Twelve

"THE EUFALMO ARE COMING," Amarta said.

She gestured to the map of crumbs and grease, at the harbor some distance east of the city, where the attacking Perripin force would land. Then to the north, where the Eufalmo would come from.

He listened. Without objection. Without agreement.

When she stopped speaking, he shook his head. Had she said too much?

It didn't matter; words and maps would not convince him.

She stood. "I can do this. Let me show you."

Amarta descended the stairs and paused at the threshold of the building that led into the street. Whether he was curious or restless from not having left this building in some time, he followed. She felt the light touch of his fingers on her shoulder as she stepped forward into the dim shadows of the night.

Overcast skies gave a vague outline to the dark city. Amarta paused until something distracted the guards. A sound, a motion—she did not know what, and did not need to. She led Tayre across the boulevard, in what would have been full view of the guards, if they had been looking.

Tayre followed unhesitatingly as they made their way through the city, his fingers reading her motion through her shoulders. He was attentive; he slowed when she did, stopped immediately, and matched her pace.

A side street. A curved walkway. They passed under a stone bridge.

At a small door in the deep dark of an alleyway, she signed into his fingers: *here*. She led him around the temple of the Heart to another building, with a similar door, and signed it again.

Now that she stood here, knowing that what she sought and would need in only a couple of days was inside, she realized that she could fetch it right now, tonight, with his help, storing it until the time came. Having it now would save time and trouble later.

She looked at Tayre in the dark, a dim outline, and decided against it. She needed to demonstrate to him that she could lead him through the city and back again safely. Proof that she was steady and reliable.

And every step that he followed her made it more likely that he would follow her again.

For now, that was enough.

Amarta sat at the table and stared into the distance, her mind moving from the plan as it stood, to the future, then back again.

She paused in the middle, straddling both. Which futures changed, moment to moment? Which ones did not?

All at once she felt ready to face another direction entirely. With a dispassionate and ruthless regard, she looked backward. As memories played out across her mind, she understood that her own wavering focus had been her worst enemy, as if she were a passenger in a small boat who would not sit still, foolishly straining from one side to the other to peer at some sight, causing the vessel tip and lurch.

What she needed now was to be steady in intention, yet keep a light grasp of the distant and outlying possibilities.

One part of her mind assembled facts, the way Tayre might: what she learned from the Kailo, conversations overheard across the city, the words and silences of their Emendi teachers.

Another part of her watched the future and the many trails that spread forward.

A third part of her wove through the lessons she took from her past.

It was a lot to hold, and Tayre must surely feel her tension. If not in her silences, then in her touch.

There was touch. A feast of sensation in his arms helped keep her mind moving.

They lay together, skin on skin, limbs tangled. Her body sang with satiation as her mind spun hot with plans. As daylight brightened the room, her mouth and fingers found their way across his body, enveloping him, and drawing him closer.

Every now and then, her mind went to images of choppy, swirling water, vortexes of ocean sucking down ships and lives along with some part of herself that could never be restored.

She clutched Tayre tightly. He must notice the urgency of her grip, but he said nothing, only holding her gently in return.

Amarta must not lose this man to her own clumsiness, or to the tumult that surrounded her, as she had lost Olessio. She must not.

~

S he waited until the last moment to give him the rest of the details.

"We'll need more time to get into the rooms where the urns are kept," he said.

"We won't. There isn't theft in Seuan, so few doors are locked, or guarded."

He studied the map of crumbs and grease. "Your plan requires many pieces to come together at the right times. If a single one fails, we are dead."

There was no denying this, so she didn't try.

He looked back at her. "Why not leave Seuan, Amarta? We still have time."

"When the Eufalmo come," she replied, "there is no better place to be, anywhere on this continent, than inside this walled city. Seuan knows how to protect itself."

He gave her a sad smile, indicating that he found her argument unpersuasive. "Scouts and forayers only, you said. Months before a full swarm."

"Yes, probably, but—"

"Also, *probably*, the Seer of Arunkel could arrange for us to avoid Eufalmo scouts and forayers entirely, while we find a way off the continent, for which we have more than sufficient funds."

She met his gaze. She would not leave Seuan. He knew this. They were dancing around the argument.

"Safety is not enough," she said, standing. "If it were, we would still be in Perripur, where Maris dua Mage could tell me how to live."

He stood to join her. "There are other answers, and you know it. Are you looking for a fight, Amarta, to redeem your losses? It does not work that way."

He was right. Or he would be, if she were doing that.

It struck her, what a beautiful man he was. His face, his eyes, his body. It gladdened her spirit, just to put her gaze on him.

Quite extraordinary, isn't he? Olessio had once asked.

"Yes, he is," she answered under her breath, fending off the remorse that threatened to follow any thought of Olessio.

No distraction, not now. At this point, the most dangerous thing she could do was to waver. To tip the boat.

"I understand, Amarta," Tayre said, his tone earnest and compelling. "After what's happened, you want to win something. But this plan." He shook his head. "One misstep, and the game is over."

Amarta looked around the apartment, wondering if she'd see it again. Or him. She refused to let vision attempt an answer.

"I go now," she said, going to the door. "Come with me or not, as you wish."

She descended the stairs. At the threshold of the entryway, out of the guards' sightline, she waited. One moment. Another.

She exhaled softly. Could she make the plan work without him?

Time to find out.

As she stepped forward into the night, his fingers touched lightly on her shoulders, ready to follow.

It surprised her, how deep the touch seemed to sink.

$\sim$

They must get both urns, one each from the temples of Eye and Ear.

An external door left unlatched allowed easy entrance to the temple of the Ear. In a hallway lit with blue lamps, the two of them backed into an alcove as a unit of Ears walked by. Once the Ears had passed, Amarta led them down into an unlit basement.

This reminded her of the hidden city of Kusan's unlit world of stone. With that and vision, she led them silently to the urn. Tayre hefted it and followed her up and out of the temple, to the relative safety of the street. They left the urn in shadow and entered the second temple.

Where the Ear's temple was lit with blue lamps, the Eye's hallways had no light at all. It did not slow them in the least.

With both urns in Tayre's arms, under the light of a moon half-shrouded with clouds, Amarta led them near the east gates of the city. Where she inspected the two sealed, undecorated metal urns. In the silver-gray of night, one might have been brass, the other steel.

"This one," he asked quietly, "the repellent? That, the attractant?"

"Yes."

He gave her a long, assessing look. "You are absolutely certain of which is which?"

"I am."

Nothing about his face or posture changed, only the intensity of his stare. "Half-knowing," he said, slowly but forcefully, his gaze on her hot, "you have, again and again, gambled your life and the lives of others to achieve your goals. This time, Seer, your certainty—your knowing—it is whole. Is it not?"

"It is whole," she said. She meant to sound confident, but it came out as a whisper.

"Your life and mine," he said, pointedly.

She looked at him. Through him. Through this moment, to the hours before dawn, and those following. To the patterns of day, of night. The forces coming toward them. The lives that continued. The ones that ended.

Possibilities spread before her like a fog. A mist. An ocean.

She gave a sober nod. "Your life and mine."

∽

Outside the high walls of Seuan, in the colorless, intermittent moonlight, Amarta felt exposed.

At the east gate, she had spoken to the guards in their own language. They were from the caste of the Right Thumb, Amarta knew from her explorations, but a subset called the Small Thumbs, who were set to work the walls and gates, and who did not wear the flesh-colored masks.

Tayre and Amarta were let through without hesitation.

"What did you say to them?" Tayre asked her quietly.

He must understand some of the words, having studied the language alongside her, but as he had said, it was one thing to know the words and another to understand the speaker.

Amarta found herself breathing shallowly, looking around at the bare lands that surrounded them, for any sign of movement.

"That we are with the incoming Perripin force, sent to help smooth their way into the city."

"They are either very trusting," Tayre said, "or are delivering us directly into the attackers' hands. The latter is a much simpler explanation."

Amarta shook her head. "They believe their caste leaders, who know that we never left our apartment, so we must still be there. Thus you and I are some other foreigners, aligned— as we told them—with the invading force, which their leaders have told them to support."

His gaze swept the empty land. "No suspicion? No speculation?"

"No. They trust their leaders utterly and do what they are told."

He snorted softly, skeptically. She understood; the Seuan people were beyond unusual.

"This trust," she added. "It makes them fast. Fast enough to survive the Eufalmo."

She pried open the lid of the first urn, revealing a dark powder. Tayre held it for her as they walked south along the wall, allowing her to play out lines of powder onto the ground.

From atop the wall, a lone Thumb watched them go.

"Seeing us do this," Tayre said of the Thumb, "would he not doubt your story? Report this action to his commander?"

"He won't."

"Why not?"

Amarta continued to tip the powder of the urn that Tayre held into lines on the ground. "Because we are not the threats they have been instructed to watch for."

They doubled back. Amarta drew another line of powder, away from the wall, outlining both sides of a deep-cut gully that descended east from the city's rise and toward the harbor.

At last, the urn was empty. Tayre set it on the ground where Amarta pointed.

Now the more dangerous part. The second urn held the attractant unguent, and it was thick as honey. Amarta dipped a stick inside, then touched the stick to one stone and another, then the wall itself, as they walked north.

Tayre let out a soft hiss as the pattern of Amarta's work became clear to him. "You expect this incoming force to approach the city, in a single file, scrabbling up that gully, rather than to take the road?"

More touches. Here. There.

"Yes."

"That makes no sense, Amarta. If they come in any other manner, this plan of yours fails. Why would they do this?"

She looked at the sky, judging time from moon and stars, assessing wind, and laying these facts alongside foresight to be certain that what had changed and what had not were still known to her. Well-known.

Your life and mine.

So completely was her focus on these things that it took her a moment to make sense of Tayre's words.

He was right, she saw. Entirely right. She had not quite realized her own plan, as deep as she was into its execution. Any configuration of the incoming Perripin mercenaries other than the one that foresight predicted, and the plan failed.

"I don't know," she said. "But it is so, in all likely futures."

"In all *likely...*?"

A mistake to phrase it quite that way, perhaps, but she did not have time or focus to do better.

Quiet, she signed, as she continued to drop gobs of viscous unguent onto the ground, following vision's map. Just so, and so.

They walked along the wall far enough north that the wind would find the scent of the sticky stuff, and take it where it needed to go.

"Pour the rest here, and leave the urn."

Tayre did as she directed, his expression as masked as any Right Thumb.

Now to get back to the gate and inside. Fast.

They walked quickly.

The guards would open the gate. She knew this to be so. In all likely futures.

~

A marta pounded on the gate's solid metal door. Despite her plan, despite her vision, she was shaking with fear.

It opened and they were let inside. She was more relieved than she would have thought possible.

The Thumbs seemed confused by her return this soon, but accepting. Amarta made the right sounds, the right words, which she herself only half-understood. The guards, visibly reassured, gave her a respectful three-touch bow, and pointed to where, apparently, she had told them she wanted to go.

She led Tayre to a doorway into a wall-tower. They began to climb the inner circular stairwell to the top.

Only now that everything was set in motion did Amarta realize just how tired she was. If only she had thought to steal a vial of stimulant while she was doing the rest of her thieving. Next time, she thought with dark humor.

But there would be no next time, not after a plan like this.

The climb up the stairs was harder than it should have been. She pushed herself; she must not slow, nor give Tayre reason to help her, not now. At each narrow tower window, she looked outside to see the skyline of the city, to see the dark of the night.

At the top of the wall, a sharp, ocean breeze met them, along with two guards. She spoke to them out of a weary foresight, finding herself using odd sets of phrases, sensing the deeper meanings beyond the words. Seuan euphemisms, about pride of caste, about circles, about duty.

The guards seemed pleased, their bows and smiles effusive. They offered chairs for Amarta and Tayre on the walkway, bringing blankets to keep them warm from the cold ocean air.

How odd it was, that these guards, these Thumbs, who

could turn lethal in an instant, at an unquestioned command, were otherwise inclined toward easy generosity. What a strange people, these who called themselves the Body of Seuan.

She looked at the city, shadow on shadow, the Heart's high tower rising darkly above the rest, then turned back to the distant harbor, to the ocean, from which her future came.

Outside the wall, the ground was bare, the countryside clear. The road from the east gate descended into tight scrub and trees, curving down and out of sight, eastward, where the sky had yet to lighten. There the horizon grayed with clouds, hovered over the dark of the Nelar ocean.

Beyond that, well beyond, were the lands of Arunkel and Perripur, where the invading force had come from.

Where Amarta herself had come from. She had traveled a very long way to shake the hunters from her trail. Not far enough, of course, but then nowhere would be far enough for that.

Amarta did not realize that she had fallen asleep until the moment in which Tayre gripped her arm, briefly, firmly, and woke her.

"Amarta. They come."

Chapter Thirteen

TOKERAE NOTED the solid sound of his footsteps on the marble floors of the palace hallway.

The Etallan Monarchy, he mouthed, just to see how it sounded.

It sounded splendid.

For nearly a thousand years, Etallan had been forced to stand aside for the Anandynars, to stand well below the crown, for no reason beyond an accident of timing and history, one that could have gone the other way.

And should have. A mistake about to be set right. The histories would name Tokerae the agent of correction.

Tokerae had been raised in these halls, and never had he seen them so empty. Usually they were filled with motion and voices—children chasing each other, messengers dashing between floors. Now no one.

A shame. He would have liked to have had witnesses for this walk.

"Search the kitchens again," Ella said, walking alongside. "There are hundreds of storage rooms down there, and this place is riddled with hidden rooms. A meticulous search. Who knows what we might find?"

Every room had already been searched, emptied, the unused ones nailed shut so that no one could hide within and be tempted to foment further resistance. They had had enough of that.

"If you think so," he replied.

His mother, that was who Tokerae really wanted watching him make this walk. He would have given a great deal of anything he could lay hands on to have had her live long enough to see him now, striding past the very audience chamber where Eregin lost his life, toward the Ministerial Council, where he would be made king.

It was the moment he had lived for, when all the insults that Etallan had borne for generations would be rectified.

"They put up a good fight, the palace guards," said Ella.

He glanced at her, frowning. "So?"

Fighting for a queen who had vanished without a trace. How many would have kept on, if they had known she'd fled? He almost felt sorry for them.

"If only we'd taken him alive," she groused, and he knew who she meant.

The old Lord Commander. A stroke of luck, finding him in that hallway. Tokerae's soldiers knew Tokerae wanted him alive, but they had not been able to disarm or reason with the old man. He'd fought like a demon, mortally wounding one of Tokerae's men, then cutting down two others. They had killed him.

An infuriating loss. Lason almost certainly had known something about where Cern had gone.

All of this would be much simpler, if they had Cern in hand.

"You knew her," Ella said. "Were familiar with her thinking. Where is she?"

"Tunnels," Tokerae said shortly. "My teams are out searching. We'll find her."

That was, if the tunnel escape hadn't been an elaborate diversion. But he wasn't going to share that speculation with Ella.

It had been high-value Cohort information, to know the various passageways under and through the huge, sprawling palace, tunnels that could branch and circle and be full of deadly traps.

Tokerae himself had gone along the riverside kitchen tunnel with his men, Radelan leading the way. After they lost the clumsy guard down a hole into into a fast-moving waterway, they had been forced to turn back. The guard's body was later recovered from the Sennant River.

She hadn't gone that way. Cern had people with her, and more than a few. That many feet could not walk a dirty, dusty underground tunnel without leaving a trail of some sort, a trail they had not seen.

But she was somewhere. Could Cern and her children have fallen prey to her own escape? Encountered bad luck, and all be dead and rotting somewhere under the palace?

He didn't think so.

"When, brother?"

"I don't know," he said tightly.

"You were her Cohort."

"Oddly, sister, this didn't come up in any lecture or discussion, what hole an Anandynar snake might slither into when she decided to abandon her throne."

"The palace guards," Ella said, "tell them they have amnesty, if they swear a new oath. An impostor queen—they couldn't have known. Not their fault."

Could she be quiet, even for a minute? A walk through what was now his palace, to the Council that would soon crown him, was not something that happened every day.

"A demoralizing and debilitating shock," she continued, "to be attacked by their own. They need to know you understand this. Tell them—"

"Is your advice endless, Ella?"

She gave him an annoyed look. "There is much to discuss, Tok."

"It can wait," he snapped.

She quieted. Sullenly, but it would do.

Tokerae had taken the palace, this so-called Jewel of the Empire. The Ministers would soon proclaim him king. What else could they do, with his men through the palace, and Helata and Sartor at his back?

Once the council ratified the power that Tokerae already held, he would make changes. Rewards and punishments. The Houses who had supported Etallan's path to the throne would know Etallan's gratitude, and that was no small thing.

And the rest, well. They were Cohort. They knew what to expect.

The hallway at last silent, Tokerae slowed his gait, so that the sound of his heels on the floor was more pronounced. Ella kept pace.

It was a very good sound, his footfalls. A solid sound.

~

"Simply declare it so," Tokerae said, for the third time. The Ministerial Council returned weak smiles.

"There is no precedent for this circumstance, your Illustriousness," said the First Minister.

Outside this room, Tokerae had eighty armed men. At a shout, they would be inside. It would be the work of minutes to have every one of these ministers retired. Permanently.

"Make the precedent," Ella said from his side, far more

pleasantly than Tokerae would have. "Proclaim him king, hand him that huge, gaudy scepter, and it's done."

"Ah...." The First Minister said. "Even if the queen is truly dead, as you say, there is a legal succession list that we are by law required to follow. Your Illustriousnesses."

He looked at his sister and wondered if she was ready to reconsider having the Council tortured to see what they knew. He'd suggested it to her already, but she'd talked him out of it. "We'll need them, brother," she had said. "They will confer legitimacy upon you."

"The real queen is long dead," Tokerae said to the First Minister. "The woman you have been erroneously calling Her Majesty is—or more likely was—an impostor."

"Ah, yes. We understand this, Eparch," the First Minister replied to him. "A terrible thing, such a deception. Even we were fooled."

"Understandable," Ella assured him. "Quite a lookalike, we hear. No one holds you responsible."

Around the table Tokerae saw a few relieved looks.

"Thank you, Eparch-heir," said the First Minister to Ella. "But should the queen be legally declared dead— which action this council may be able to conclude— there still remains a succession list to which we must adhere."

That middle phrase did not escape anyone's notice.

"He'll be marrying Citriona Anandynar," Ella said. "Is she not next on the succession list?"

The Minister of Justice spoke up. "No, she is not. She is placed twenty-three."

"Ah, I see," Tokerae said, as if this were news to him. "Well, then. A solution suggests itself: deliver to me the names above Citriona, and I'll have a little chat with each of them. Give them the opportunity to remove themselves and clarify the matter."

"That is not how—" the Minister of Justice began, then fell abruptly silent.

Good—the man was starting to think clearly. I'm Cohort, you fool. I know the legalities of Arunkel royal succession at least as well as you do.

Or at least, how it was yesterday.

"Ah, but." The First Minister spoke. "The official list is in the lockbox of the queen, and thus quite inaccessible."

Tokerae already had that lockbox in his possession, and not one of his men had yet been able to open it. Was this an insult? He examined the man's face closely.

"You have copies of the list," Ella interjected, her tone cool enough that Tokerae knew she, too, was annoyed with this runaround. "For that matter, I'm confident that every one of you has the list memorized."

No one spoke.

"I'll need that list immediately," Tokerae said. He turned in his chair to give each minster a look, ending on the First Minister, who in turn cast his gaze desperately around the table. One by one, the other minister's gazes found various locations in the room of enormous interest.

At last, his expression wooden and tone resolved, the First Minister gestured to the secretary in the corner, who stood ready with paper and quill.

"Estarna Anandynar," he began.

～

Citriona Anandynar's eyes were wide as Tokerae strode into her sitting room. At the young woman's side sat Ella, holding Citriona's arm affectionately and snugly.

Ella smiled conspiratorially and whispered into Citriona's ear. Was Citriona blushing? Yes, she was.

His sister gave him a small nod. Tokerae stepped forward

with a warm smile, opening his hand to reveal a stunning, sparkling wristlet.

Citriona gasped.

"An engagement gift, my dear Citriona," he said. "Will you give me the honor of allowing me to place it on you, so that we may see if it fits you properly, or must be resized to joyously embrace your elegant wrist?"

Citriona nodded eagerly.

The key, unsurprisingly, had been Tokerae and Ella's chat with her parents. Her mother was a second cousin to the old king, Restarn. Tokerae and Ella had explained that their lovely and clever daughter Citriona had the chance to marry right into the monarchy, skipping all the fuss of succession.

Did they want this future for their most excellent daughter? Or should Tokerae make other inquiries among the royals?

They had been enthusiastic. Their consent was effusive.

Now, by clasping the perfectly fitting bracelet around Citriona's wrist, Tokerae drew her one step closer to her own consent and his throne.

"Act the part, brother," Ella had told him earlier, "and everyone will bend over backward to see how all the details seem to fit."

"Behave like a king, you mean," he replied.

"Exactly."

"I am already Eparch."

"Yes, you are," Ella had said, smiling proudly.

Tokerae took Citriona's hand, turning her arm gently, this way and that, to admire the trinket.

"Exquisite," he said, then stared into her eyes and let what he knew was a charming grin spread across his face, as if he could not restrain himself. "The wristlet as well. Shall we walk in the gardens and talk about your future?"

Chapter Fourteen

"DOMINA! DOMINA!"

Zeted had been enjoying what was turning into a truly magnificent sunset. Fine strands of clouds were drawn across the horizon, turning the sky stunning shades of magenta and orange, building toward Zeted's favorite moment when the Dragon Sun doused herself in the ocean, washing away the day's struggles, and reinvigorating herself for the morrow.

"Domina?" Now a loud knocking followed the voice on the other side of the door.

She had a fine view, not only of the sunset, but also of the harbor. Zeted found deep satisfaction in this vista. Nothing compared to owning ships. They were beautiful, devoted creatures, each with will, passion, and character, ready to glide into the unfettered ocean and change the world.

Zeted could almost feel in her own body, as she reclined here, each one of her ships, sensing them as if they were her fingers and toes, dipped into the cool, fresh ocean, ready to journey across the world and gather the many things that brought her money and delight.

She was most pleased with one ship in particular: *A Splendid Catch*. He was a striking vessel, powerful, fast, and ocean-ready, his sails just now catching the deep yellow of the setting sun as the crew readied to leave before dark enveloped the land.

The urgent knocking came again.

"Yes, Ralafi," she called. "Come in."

The door flew open and he nearly dove to her side.

"Domina!"

She gestured to the window. "Do you see this, Ralafi?"

"I can't find Adra. Not anywhere. A scullery saw him passing by the kitchens, carrying a bundle of clothes. Domina..."

"You're not even looking. Ralafi, the sunset does not wait."

"I think he may have run off!"

Zeted sipped her adept-wine. She made a long, appreciative sound, allowing the liquid to evaporate deliciously on her tongue into the rest of her throat.

"Domina? I think he may have gone to the *Splendid Catch*.

"I suspect you're right, Ralafi. Ah! The Dragon Sun touches the water! Do you see? Look at the colors!"

"Shall I send a runner, Domina? I think we can still catch them before they cast off."

Zeted had been mulling this same question for some time now, since she noted how many of her things were missing, including the picture of the woman that *Splendid* was off to fetch.

On the one hand, Zeted had enjoyed Adra in her bed. He was skillful in all the right ways. Furthermore, it had been useful to have his insights into the wasps' nest that was Arunkel politics; however laconic his words might be, his face and body were eloquent and informative.

Such a drug-addled creature, so damaged by whatever had happened to him, that Zeted had been surprised at this turn of events. She had not thought him capable of summoning the focus needed to leave the villa, let alone to make his way to the docks.

And then, to talk his way on board, with a clever captain and experienced mercenary commander to block his way?

It seemed beyond possible.

"Domina? Shall I send a runner?"

But then, given who Adra once had been, perhaps not.

Zeted found herself intensely curious as to what plan he might even now be enacting.

"That shade of lilac, Ralafi," she said, "Right there. Around the evening star? You see it? I can't get my silks in that color, no matter how many chats I have with the Arunkel House of Dye. Isn't it exquisite?"

"Domina... the ship? I think we could still..."

Perhaps it was that, despite the many favors she had bestowed upon him, The Den of Innocence was his true destination. Close to Seuan, he would find qualan as plentiful as wine. Easily affordable with what he'd stolen from her.

Splendid's captain would not be easily bribed—Zeted made a regular practice of attempting it herself, to be certain —and the mercenary troop on board were Perripin veteran fighters, hardly inclined to give a ride to an Arunkin stranger.

Yes, Adra would need a great deal of charm and cleverness to get on that ship, and stay on it until it reached its destination. If he were merely looking for more intoxication, it seemed probable that he would fail, and be back at her side in short order.

No, Adra, she felt certain, had some other fantastical plan in mind. Perhaps he had not given up on life, after all.

Zeted smiled wide as the sun sank into the ocean,

painting the sky in splendid hues. She might not find out what Adra meant to do with his freedom, but if she drew him back now, she would never have a chance of knowing.

"Domina. The ship."

"Yes, yes, Ralafi, the ship. I see it as well as you do."

At his despairing, distraught expression, she patted his arm. "Refill my glass, Ralafi, and let us watch as the sun dives deep into the Nelar Ocean."

"They're casting off now, Domina."

"Don't whine, Ralafi. You must learn to take pleasure in life."

Ralafi heaved a sigh.

"Here, drink the rest of this, and tell if that is not the finest adept-wine you've ever tasted."

"Yes, Domina." He took the offered glass.

"When you're done with that, send in one of the new boys. I think I'm ready for a change."

~

Innel kept his head down as he made his way through the docks, using the posture and stride that spoke of greatly annoyed haste that encouraged people to stay away.

He was at the ship's ramp before anyone thought to stop him.

"Hoi. You. What do you want here?"

"I'm late. I know, I know," Innel said irritably, which needed no pretense; everything was irritating since he'd started hoarding the intoxicants Ralafi had brought him instead of ingesting them. It had taken all his will not to dig his hand into his pocket for a pinch of the gritty mix of phapha and duca on the way. "But I'm here now."

The Perripin sailor scowled. "Everyone on my list is accounted for."

"Last-minute addition," Innel said, matching the other's tone, "I'm no happier about it than you are." Innel thrust a piece of paper at the man. On it was a name and the Domina's seal. "There: your list has one more."

Innel had taken a number of things from the Domina's desk after writing this letter and using her seal. In his pockets were a palm-sized golden cat and some other small items. If he were caught, he'd be in serious trouble.

Never mind the theft of a slave, brother.

Never mind that.

The sailor examining the seal shook his head. "Captain won't like this. Minutes from cast-off. Wait here."

He was right, the captain did not. Nor did the commander of the mercenary troop, who clearly considered himself nearly equal in authority to the captain.

Innel repeated his story, acting for all the world like someone who didn't want to be here. "Domina's orders," he said. "You want to tell her no? I already tried, but by all means feel free."

The mercenary commander—a graying Perripin man with even more scars on his hands than Innel—looked him up and down in such a pointedly unimpressed manner that Innel began to consider his alternate plan to head to the borderlands and go into hiding. With what he had stolen he could buy refuge, at least for a while.

Returning to Zeted's villa was out of the question; she would not treat gently someone who had stolen from her.

He was surprised by the pang he felt; he had become fond of her without even realizing it. Sobriety, he reflected, made for more agony than his improving memories were really worth.

"Got fifty-seven men on board," the commander said. "Fighting men. What in Hells are you?"

Innel nodded, and uncurled a second paper, the one with Amarta's face on it, showing it.

"I'm here because of this. I know her. I'll be the only one on your ship who does. The Domina sent me to make sure that when you get her in hand, she doesn't slip from your grasp."

"She won't."

"Fates, man. Do you really not know who this is?"

Uncertainty in the man's frown told Innel that he didn't.

"It's the Seer of Arunkel," Innel said with unforced awe. "You are not the first to try to take her, I assure you. I'm here to make certain that you're the last."

Still doubting but sufficiently won over, the commander abruptly gestured him on board. The captain, not particularly happy with this change, found a tiny cabin for Innel, barely large enough for a small bed.

Then the ship was under way.

As Innel began to meet the rest—sailors, crew, mercenaries—he was unsurprised to find that he was the only Arunkin among them. One by one, they gave him the same puzzled, slightly repulsed look that their commander had.

It had been a while since Innel had faced a mirror, but he had a good idea of what they would see: a pale, thin, hunched, limping man with the scars Taba had given him across a roughly bearded face.

That evening, as he stood on deck and watched the night's ocean churn around the prow of the boat, he wondered how he would steer fifty-seven fighting men. And in what direction.

"Tell us again how you know this woman we're to fetch from Seuan, Pewyan."

Pewyan. Innel had told them that he had been named after the famous Arunkel commoner general. He could hardly call himself Adra, a slave name, but he found that he was more than a little unsettled to use his father's name. His father the hero.

He was no hero.

Make me proud, brother.

Innel looked over the men, packed into a cramped mess hall. Outside, the wind picked up, howling, battering the ship with anything that was not tightly tied.

Those who could sat on stools. Most stood, huddling snugly along the walls.

Innel met the looks of these many Perripin men, then slowly rolled a shoulder, wincing visibly at the pain. A small drama, though in fact it hurt plenty, the knee and foot as well, not to mention the catch in his side that never went away.

But none of them were the result of battle, as he was implying. Taba's work, mostly, though the shoulder was from his sister Cahlen's arrow at Otevan, never quite healed.

You've got a way with women, brother.

At that, Innel wondered if his mother and sister had survived his execution.

Cahlen, possibly. Mother... well.

Well, indeed. He'd lay odds their mother was rotting somewhere. She'd have been lucky to have a burial.

Cahlen, though, you never knew. She had a way of slipping through the cracks in expectations.

"I was at the battle of Otevan," Innel began, as his momentary silence drew the attention of the gathered crew. "A regular, under the Lord Commander Innel, who—"

Careful, brother. "Who served with General Lismar. The Seer of Arunkel was there."

He gazed around at their faces, letting a look of realization come over him.

"What, you didn't know that she was the reason that the battle of Otevan ended as it did?" he asked, as if surprised.

Heads shook.

He laughed a little, gave an amused look. "This is why I was sent along. You see? You can't just march in there and take her. I don't care how many maps and open gates you have. She won't be there when you arrive."

"Where will she be, then?" heckled someone.

Innel scoffed. "You've heard, at least, of the rain of gold?"

Many nods. The story of the rain of gold had spread like fire. No one could hear it without dreaming. He had their full attention.

"Never seen anything like it," Innel told them, "Not in my whole life. Glittering flakes, raining down like snow. Everyone scrabbling on the ground, stuffing handfuls into their pockets, into shoes and scabbards. Even dropping their swords to the ground to make room." He stared distantly. "What a battle. The Teva on their astonishing shaota warhorses. Wickedly good aim with those bows, did you know that?"

"That we knew," one mercenary said. "It's only you Arunkin who don't know about the Teva who live inside your own borders."

General laughter. Innel joined in good-naturedly.

"Commander," piped up a tall man in the corner, looking at the old veteran who led them. "Once we've got her, can we take a day or three at the Den of Innocence? Get a taste of Seuan qualan?"

"Given that we're there, anyway?" added another, hopefully.

Enthusiastic mutterings took the room, all eyes on the commander, who smiled a little. "I think we might."

A cheer went up across the room.

Innel had slowly eked out what little he had hoarded from Ralafi across these many days. All that was left was crumbs. The very thought of an unlimited supply of the bitter qualan put an ache in his chest and set his mouth to watering.

"Tell us about the gold," someone said.

"No, tell us about the woman we're to fetch. She's *our* gold."

Looks came back to Innel. He knew, because he'd seen Zeted's contract, that each of these men stood to gain an impressive bonus if they brought Amarta back.

If. A finger on the scale in her favor is all it would take, brother.

Innel nodded slowly, as if remembering, a smile creeping across his ruined face. "That's a long story, fellows."

"A long crossing, Pewyan. We have time. Plenty of it."

Someone filled Innel's cup, and he downed it. It was not duca or kana, but ale would do, at least for the telling of stories.

His first task, Innel knew, was to get them to like him, then to trust him. After that, to get them to doubt themselves.

A delicate dance, to impress on them the difficulty of this operation and his deep knowledge about the seer without saying too much too soon.

But Innel was Cohort, and the telling of tales was a skill they studied at length, in and out of the palace library, from histories and journals and poetry. Some of those stories were very long indeed.

He considered the length of the voyage in days, and how

he wanted to leave these men wanting more each time he finished the meal's entertainment.

Innel took another sip of his ale, gave them a wide grin, and began to speak.

~

A cross weeks and meals, Innel played out tales about Otevan and Arunkel, folk tales from his youth, and anything else he could think of to both entertain and inspire.

Pohut had always been the better storyteller of the mutt brothers, but judging by the eager looks of his daily audience, Innel was doing well enough.

Next, Innel began to ask questions about the men, and their pasts. The mission. The city of Seuan. Bit by bit, he led the mercenaries to consider the possibility that the challenges they faced were more complicated than they thought—which was true—and began to imply that he had the answers they needed—which wasn't.

He prodded them subtly, at first. Then more obviously, examining their maps of Seuan, noting what could go wrong. At last, even the commander began to display misgivings about the simplicity of the operation.

"Fifty-some men to take a single woman?" Innel asked them in the cramped, crowded mess. "Didn't you think there might be a catch?" He chuckled and the mercenaries echoed him, a sign that he'd won them over.

And what exactly did he hope to accomplish?

As Innel understood her, Amarta might well have trouble escaping some fifty armed and capable men who intended to abduct her, especially in a city that had already turned against her. Most particularly if they surrounded her, came from all quarters, as would be sensible.

But if he could arrange to collapse them into a single

force, one that she would not only see coming, but could easily elude, that outcome could shift.

The continent of Seute Enta began to show dimly on the distant horizon.

"Hoi, there," Innel said to the many gathered in this meal. "It's now time for me to earn *my* bonus. Let me tell you about the Seer of Arunkel, and how to apprehend her." He gave a respectful nod to the commander, who gave him one in return.

"Tell us."

Innel looked across all the rest, exchanging smiles and nods with each one.

You've done it, brother: they trust you. Now ram it home.

"First," Innel said, "you must understand how this strange foresight of hers works. She sees things as if looking at a cave wall in firelight. That is, she sees shadows of what is to come. It is easy for her to step around a single attack, so easy that she doesn't worry about them. I have seen it many times."

"What do you mean?"

"Is one person a threat to her?" Innel asked. "It might be to me, but not to her. So, all of you, spread out, as you had originally planned? You announce the level of threat. She sees you on the walls of her vision, and is long gone when you arrive. Then where is your prize? Fled. Uncatchable."

There was unhappy muttering.

"What do we do?"

Innel held up a finger, let a grin spread across his face. "Make her think you are only one, so to give her no reason to flee until it is too late. You know exactly where she is, so approach the city seeming to be slow, to be small, and thus to cast a single shadow. A tight, low line, perhaps. Then she will think you are one, maybe two, and no threat at all. Easily danced around. Stay low and tight, until you are right in front of her."

"And then what?" asked the commander.

"She is not invincible, my friends," Innel said with a widening, confident smile. "There is no magic to her. When you can see her as you see me now, she is easily had. Fifty and more of the finest mercenaries in the land? She can only run so fast. That's your moment. Take her."

If they all approached together, slowly, as he was advising, then the Seer of Arunkel would have time enough to foresee and run in the other direction.

And when they returned empty-handed? Then Innel would need to have a truly compelling explanation as to why his plan hadn't worked, one that left him alive and healthy. That might be a challenge that even Pohut couldn't have managed.

Perhaps better to be away by then, hiding somewhere on shore.

Perhaps so.

"Take her," shouted one of the men, echoing Innel. The rest took it up. "Take her, take her!"

Well done, brother.

"Then the Den of Innocence! Our deserved reward!"

Howls of enthusiasm and table-pounding took the room, shaking the floor. Innel joined them.

The Den, perhaps the end of his own journey as well, was certainly worth howling about.

Chapter Fifteen

TAYRE WOKE HER. "AMARTA. THEY COME."

The two of them stood to look over the eastern parapet. There, the first spark of the dawning broke free of the Nelar Ocean.

On the ground below, outside the city wall, in the predawn shadows, a dark line of men crept slowly up the gully, crouching and single-file, despite that not far away was a far more convenient road leading to the gate.

Tayre gave a soft exhale of surprise.

Next, from the north, came a sound so soft that it took Amarta a moment to realize that it was not the wind. A muttering, perhaps. A distant hiss. As it increased, it might have been the noise a bumblebee would make. A mosquito. A hummingbird. Multiplied by thousands.

The sound grew and grew. She watched them hove into view: a thin line of Eufalmo scouts, chittering and hissing and clicking as they streamed forward along the ground from the north.

They were the size of fists, these scouts, their black eyes glinting in the dawning light.

It struck Amarta that this humming undertone was like the droning of the Kailo. Very like. Seuan and the Eufalmo had known each other for a long time.

The line of scouts followed the path Amarta had laid down of attractant and repellent. She knew that a full swarm would break the lines, ignoring the hints and nudges of her work, but these scouts were happy to follow the trail.

The line passed by the wall, under where she and Tayre stood. From the north, beyond the city, the sound swelled.

Horns blared from the walls as Seuan sounded its patterned alarms, relaying information across the city about what was being seen from atop the wall. Amarta smelled torches, oil.

Visible now was the source of the rising sound: the forayer line of Eufalmo.

Had she thought the fist-sized scouts large? These, many abreast, were the size of melons. Of dogs. They glittered in the morning light, in vivid colors, backs in patterns of stripes, dots, and solids, wings and legs blurred with motion, some with pincers, some without, all with heads that might have come from a nightmare.

Amarta felt the drone and buzz in her body, in her bones, as it became so loud it nearly drowned out Seuan's blasting horns.

To see and feel and smell such a thing in vision was nothing compared to the reality.

This moment, right now, was an inflection point. Likely, the forayers would follow the scouts where they led, but it was also possible that the rush of Eufalmo had become too thick, the line too wide, and they would instead overrun both the attractant and repellent.

The outcome would be the same, at least for the Perripin mercenaries, who now stood from their crouches to look around at what was coming, their confusion turning into terror.

They shouted. They drew weapons. They scrambled out of the gully for higher ground and scattered. They ran.

Too late.

The Eufalmo forayers followed the scouts exactly, in a thick, colorful line of iridescence, like some fantastical rainbow river in the rising sun, flowing in the path that Amarta had outlined for them when she and Tayre had walked where they ran, mere hours ago.

The entire line made a turn from the wall and splashed down into the gully.

Any elation Amarta might have felt as her plan began to unroll exactly as she had designed, turned rancid and sick in her gut as the Eufalmo poured over and through the armed men.

The mercenaries beat at the huge bugs with weapons and hands. They thrashed, they bucked, they fell, they flopped.

They shrieked and screamed and howled.

Amarta shook violently, swallowing bile, her stomach heaving, again and again.

But no, she would not look away from what she had wrought. Not this time, not ever again. She would see her actions through to the end.

One by one, the screams ended.

∿

The Eufalmo swept across the lives of fifty and some Perripin mercenaries, leaving only glistening bones and the steel of weapons. All else was consumed: skin, organs, fabric, leather. Even amardide armor.

After they consumed, the Eufalmo milled for a time as if to be certain that they hadn't missed anything. Then they withdrew, retreating exactly the way they had come, as if a tendril of tide pulled back into the ocean from shore.

The horns of Seuan fell silent.

Amarta and Tayre descended the stairwell from the wall. No one barred their way.

The city was active as they had ever seen it: Seuans moving in caste units, weapons and tools in hand. They moved fast, intently. Some ran.

Amarta and Tayre got quick looks but nothing more; they were not the danger Seuans were looking for.

Weak comfort, that they did not connect the Eufalmo scouts and forayers with Amarta. But after this morning's bloody dawn, their leaders most certainly would.

A curious land, this, where rumors did not fly, where people knew their place and did not look beyond it.

Again in the apartment, Amarta sat heavily at the table. Her head ached. Her eyes and limbs were weighted with exhaustion.

"I have killed," she said. "No accident. No half-knowing. My knowing is..." her voice cracked. "complete."

Tayre's expression held no pity. "How does this knowing sit with you?"

"Not comfortably."

An understatement. Amarta felt that she'd been wrenched into an entirely new self. The world around her felt gritty and rough-edged.

Amarta's life had been full of horrors, whether witnessed or foreseen, yet this one—she had no idea where to place it. It was a new thing entirely, and as it sat inside her, it did not seem to fit.

They were not empty creatures, the men she killed. They had families. Children. Friends. Hopes.

Futures.

"To take one life is no small thing," Tayre said. "To take fifty at once...that will change you."

Amarta shook her head. "I don't know if I like what I am becoming."

"Give yourself time to find out before you decide."

That sounded like wisdom. As she thought about irrevocable changes, she came across the memory of the Teva and their *limisatae*, the inked scars that circled their forearms to mark major life events. *A life taken to keep our people whole,* Jolon al Otevan once had told her, *that is* limisatae *as well.*

She stared at her forearm.

"Amarta," Tayre asked. "What next?"

She heaved a ragged breath. "We wait. We rest."

"What are we waiting for?"

"The Heart of Seuan." Amarta drew herself upright, despite how hard it was. "He will want to see me, now that I have shown him what I can do."

They went to bed. Somehow her hunger was even greater than her exhausted mind and body's need to rest. She reached for him.

She was too tired to keep vision away, and as her hands touched his body, vision served up a multitude of scenes in merciless clarity. It took all her fortitude and resolve not to recoil from him.

In the years that they had traveled together, Amarta came to understand that it was Tayre's nature and work to live close to peril, that disaster would always flicker at the edges of his actions. Time after time, she had foreseen him mangled and dead, but had always managed to draw the threads of his life, along with her own, past the threat.

Something had changed with the night's events, with the Eufalmo attack that Amarta had brought to pass, and with its gruesome conclusion. Something had changed, and the threads of Tayre's life were fast fraying. A wall approached.

Tayre leveraged himself up on one arm. "What is it?"

She could not tell him. He had lived with the threat of death so long that he would see it as irrelevant and discount it entirely.

"Amarta?"

She looked back at him, realizing that her face was, for him, no longer a window. He could tell that she was upset, but did not know why.

"A long day," she relied, "with a longer night." She rolled away from him.

~

In the morning, Zung-Urfan came.

"The Heart calls you to his presence."

They followed the Seuan woman into the street below. There an open carriage waited with six Emendi slaves gripping the handles, ready to pull.

Amarta's mouth fell open as she stared at the brands on their arms marking them as slaves.

"We will walk," she said.

"Seer." Zung-Urfan touched a fist to her chest. "The temple is no small distance away. This is much faster."

"I know where it is. We will walk."

"But... the Heart will be kept waiting."

"Then he will wait."

~

Zung-Urfan led them into the Temple of the Heart. A tencount of Right Thumbs flanked them, their expressionless masks tilted to keep Amarta in view.

Amarta trailed her fingers across plastered walls, stone arches, and metal-banded doors.

Was it, she wondered, too late to pretend that Tayre was nothing more than a servant, as he had acted at the House of Sun and Moon? Might that change his narrowing future?

"What is in here?" Amarta asked of a closed door behind which she could almost hear singing.

Zung-Urfan, agitated at the delay, touched her fist to her chest nervously, twice. "I cannot say."

But in some farflung, far less likely future, she could, and did. *Young adults, trained for the Eye and the Ear, Seer.*

Amarta would come back to this one.

"What is behind this one?"

Zung-Urfan gave a three-touch bow. "I cannot say. Seer, please: the Heart waits."

You may not pass into that room. It is forbidden.

Amarta would come back to this one as well.

The hallways of the temple curved and snaked, perhaps as tribute to the ways blood traveled to and from a heart.

Or perhaps to confuse the unwary. Amarta was not confused.

At a window that looked out onto a sandy courtyard, stones laid in spiral caught Amarta's attention. She stopped to look, as Zung-Urfan rocked from foot to foot. Amarta turned to stare at her. Zung-Urfan began to babble softly in Seuan, begging Amarta to hurry, and looking entirely miserable.

Amarta waited to see what would happen.

From the end of the curving hallway strode another

woman, dressed as Zung-Urfan was. She gave Amarta a three-touch bow, and spoke in Arunkin.

"I am Zung-Resch. We ask you, Seer of Arunkel, to please come with us now. The Heart is eager to meet you, and surely this delay benefits no one."

Zung-Resch. Amarta now knew enough Seuan to know that this woman ranked third in the caste of the Ear, two steps above Zung-Urfan, who might not be there for long, given how unnerved she had become at Amarta's slow pace.

They were sending their very best to deal with this strange foreigner woman.

Amarta answered Zung-Resch, in Seuan. "I accept your request for speed."

Zung-Resch blinked, not quite able to hide her surprise at Amarta's precise cross-caste use of Seuan.

The whole while, Amarta made a point not to look at Tayre. A servant, she tried to say with every motion, each step. Nothing more.

They climbed a spiral stairwell, flanked and led by the Ears and masked Thumbs, to enter a large, circular stone room of windows and doors.

Everyone in the room except Amarta and Tayre dropped back into a surrounding circle, oriented toward the man at the center. As one, fists went to chests, one foot dropping back, lowering themselves slightly in a precise ripple around the room.

In rank order, from highest to lowest, Amarta noted.

The Heart was robed in gray, as he had been at the Kailo. Unadorned, bald, his eyebrows lacked hair. His skin was barely lined. He did not look old enough to be sixty, let alone ninety-seven. Was he a mage?

The Heart spoke in Seuan, his voice deep and resonant, the words welcoming, formal, and polite. Zung-Resch translated into Arunkin.

Amarta ignored it all, and walked toward him. Directly.

Within castes, Seuans were comfortable in tight proximity. Between castes, less so. With foreigners, more distance yet was required.

Amarta expected to be stopped. But in what manner?

Thumbs lurched to intercept her. The Heart fell silent. Zung-Resch spoke urgently, telling Amarta to stop, to back away, that this act was beyond the bounds of propriety.

Amarta stopped, standing still some five short paces from the Heart, her question answered: in no future did the Heart use magic against her. He was not a mage.

She retreated to the distance that would be appropriate between equal castes.

If he noticed, or thought her distance more than an accident, he didn't show it.

Amarta tried to imagine how he saw her, this young, pale foreigner woman who claimed extraordinary powers, and might have just proven them.

She addressed him directly, in formal Seuan: "Again and again, Great Heart, you make me wait. You must now understand that yesterday's Eufalmo attack was no coincidence. It was my foresight and will, made manifest. Do you not want my favor and good intention?"

A moment of stunned silence took the room at her use of a Seuan dialect no one had taught her, and at words no one would ever say to the Heart.

He blinked, seeming to gather his thoughts. "We wish your favor and good intention," he said slowly. He held out a hand to stop Zung-Resch from translating, then gestured through the windows to the city. "Welcome to Seuan, Seer of Arunkel. Your presence lends us grace."

A door in the wall of the circular room opened. In came the First of the Ear, dressed in shreds of rags with a gauzy veil across her face. She stood at the Heart's left side. From another door entered the First of the Eye. He wore a blotched plum tunic, his hands and feet stained in the same color, and stood at the Heart's right.

Amarta examined the trio.

Which of you betrayed me to the Perripin easterners, and for what payment?

She would not say those words. But she could.

And if she had?

A test, Seer. Easy for one such as you claim to be, yes?

They doubted her, even now, after the Eufalmo came.

Well, she was used to having to prove herself, though not usually so lethally. Gone were the days of coin tosses, she supposed.

The Heart's head twitched slightly at the Ear. A signal.

The Ear spoke, her voice melodious. "We offer to you the role of Advisor to the Body, Seer of Arunkel. It is a rare honor, bestowed upon unique foreigners who offer council to Seuan."

"I will consider this," Amarta said, "But I will want something in return."

"In return?" the Heart said, clearly taken aback. "For this rare honor, you make a demand?"

Over the Ear's veil, Amarta met dark eyes. The man who was the Eye tilted his head at her quizzically.

Every motion here was strange, from head tilts to the tracking of a gaze. Only now did Amarta realize that Zung-Urfan had done more than speak perfect Arunkin; her very movements were Arunkin, smiles and nods so familiar that Amarta had not even been aware of them.

Amarta did not understand how they stood, why they turned their looks or heads as they did, or any of the other small movements that were the subtle forms of communication. No matter; she would learn.

"What do you want for this rare honor?" asked the Ear, her voice like a flute.

"I will tell you that when I have decided," Amarta answered.

Suddenly the Eye broke from his position at the Heart's side, walking toward Amarta in a manner strikingly similar to the one in which she had approached the Heart moments ago.

Amarta did not move. The Eye stopped only two paces away and circled her and Tayre both, his gaze strikingly intent. He returned to the Heart's side.

"Tomorrow we show you our great city," the Heart said. "Our cisterns, the *magi-khrastos* bequeathed to us by Raydafir Ire dua Mage, that keep the Body watered. Then, outside the walls, we will show you the villages and their produce upon which we depend. The pits where the great *sorogs* are bred and trained. Next you will see the—"

"When I am ready to see all this, I will tell you," Amarta cut in.

From the Heart's expression, Amarta now knew what Seuan affront looked like. A future trail thickened, one that led to her being surrounded by masked Thumbs and sharp, curved blades.

It was a moment that she had seen before, when she had been dodging balls and learning to fight, when Tayre and Olessio tutored her, under warm, wet Perripin skies. She had been so much younger then.

Various futures played out before her. She could, she was nearly certain, untie the knots that were Seuan.

The cost was not yet quite so clear.

Even in her dreams, she and Tayre coupled hungrily. In the dream, she knew that every kiss brought the wall of his death closer.

She shook herself awake in horror. Through the window, the sky was tinged with the first blush of dawn.

A new-spun web. A spider, unknowing its fate.

Tayre woke. "Amarta? What is it?"

Every time she touched him, she foresaw the many ways that he could die. She turned away, the ache of the dream heavy in her chest.

He settled behind her, close, a hand on her shoulder. "Amarta?"

No: she must stop looking at the many ways that could die, and find the ones in which he lived.

"Only a dream," she said.

$\sim$

Was the Heart a seer, or wasn't he? Amarta considered the evidence.

He had known who Amarta was, from the moment that she and Tayre had arrived at the gates of Seuan.

But that had been no secret. Amarta had been identified at Turia in the Overlook room, and it was no stretch to imagine that after she had wrecked the Islands, overland and sea travelers would spread the word about her. *Famous, Olessio had said, nudging her.*

She pushed the memory away.

The Heart had correctly predicted a storm. The wind had been gusting that day, the sky thick with clouds. It was not a hard guess.

Yet the Heart of Seuan had not known that Amarta would arrange for the Eufalmo line to obliterate the Perripin force he had expected. If he were a true seer, he would have warned the Thumbs at the gate not to let the foreigner woman and her companion outside. Or he would have told the Perripin force to spread out, and come from other directions.

He would have made Amarta's plan impossible, if he were a true seer.

A dull, unsurprised disappointment settled on Amarta.

But Seuan itself held something for her. It was a mysterious tangle, this place of castes and hierarchies; of Emendi slaves, imported from Arunkel and Perripur; of children selected for the orders of Eye and Ear, and those rejected used for something else entirely.

Blood. So much blood.

You want to understand the knots of Seuan? Understand this.

Long ago, or so it seemed, in a room at an inn, Olessio and Tayre had told Amarta about the Heart of Seuan and his predictions.

Seuan survives rains, floods, earthquakes, and the Eufalmo swarms. They're doing something right.

Speculation was not enough. Amarta needed to know if he was a seer or not. She must be sure.

~

It was night. Amarta wandered the Temple of the Heart. Masked Thumbs walked the curving halls, in twos and threes. Had they moved in sets of ten or twenty, Amarta would have had a harder time arranging to be where they were not looking. But as it was, she barely needed to slow as they passed her, unseeing.

She opened doors. Wisps of the possible thickened from threads to ropes. Some doors came open easily. Others required angle and pressure to unlatch. A few needed keys. She found them and used them.

Behind the door where she had heard distant singing, a hallway opened to rooms that held cots on which boys and girls slept. One girl awoke, met Amarta's gaze, then lay down and returned to sleep. Here in Seuan, even a child knew that what was out of place was simply not so.

At the end of the hallway, in a large room, sat a device for which Amarta had no name. It seemed a metal cistern of some sort, with pipes that issued outward with nipples on the end of each. She touched it. She foresaw blood.

In a corner, an open box seemed to be a repair kit, containing tools and piping. Amarta selected some bits and put them into her pocket.

She left this section, returning to the curving hallway.

Inside the forbidden door, long shelves were thick with vials. From the written labels, which she only partly understood, and the hints of each one's future, she knew them to be exceedingly rare substances, a treasure trove of Seuan's most precious elixirs, salves, powders, and pastes. Cures, antidotes, stimulants. Poisons. None of them, she foresaw, would ever leave the city.

She walked deeper and higher, through the winding passages of the temple, opening door after door.

Still she sought something. An inner room. The innermost. Where was it?

Here.

The door was well-formed and well-locked, resisting her attempts to enter. She followed one future thread after another, swelling each to see if it might carry her inside, discarding it when it did not.

Not long ago, she would have been impatient with the multitudes of lines, and would have taken the first one that might work. Now she knew what a trap that could be, and how it led to a cascade of problems. She would be as patient as she must.

As she searched the many possibilities to get inside this room, she realized that tumult always surrounded her. Wherever she went, futures changed their shape. The closer Amarta dua Seer came to any single future, the more that cracks of possibility turned into doorways, that small pebbles became avalanches.

It hadn't been Rhaata, she suddenly saw. It was Amarta herself who made the events too large.

The ripples from Amarta's own ability were why Olessio had died.

It would never happen again.

She came across a thread that suited her, and grew it bigger and bigger. When it was clear, she took from her pocket a bit of thin, woven material that came from the repair kit. It was hard enough to be amardide, thin enough to be fabric. She had no idea what it was, and didn't care.

She inserted the flat fabric into the space between door and frame, and moved it just so, following into the future in which she would be inside.

And then she was.

Chapter Sixteen

INNEL STOOD at the railing of *A Splendid Catch*. At his side, the Perripin captain anxiously scanned the shore.

"Four days," the captain said, scowling deeply. "They should be back."

Innel did not argue. The mercenary force should have returned days ago to report that Amarta wasn't where they expected her to be. Escaped at the last minute, Innel expected them to say. He had been fine-tuning his reply, preparing for the mercenaries to return and demand to know why his advice had failed them.

"I'd wager," Innel said, with more certainty than he felt, "that they disregarded my guidance. She must have slipped through their fingers. But they're strong and clever, and likely giving chase and running her down as we speak."

The captain's scoff was louder than the waves crashing on the shore. "Or maybe you gave them bad advice, Pewyan. Paid a pretty purse to come with us, were you?"

Innel turned to face the captain. "I wish." He shook his head. "If we don't bring her back, I get nothing more." That was certainly true. "Captain: I know this creature, and there's nothing easy about obtaining her. I can't account for everything that could have gone wrong. I wasn't there."

The captain's expression turned sour. "Maybe you should have been."

Innel turned back to face the harbor. "They wouldn't take me." He made sure his tone was both bitter and resigned, but the truth was that despite arranging for the mercenaries to think of Innel as physically worthless—the lame, unsteady advisor—a part of him ached to be where the action was.

"You would have slowed them down," the captain said, not unsympathetically.

"That's certain," Innel admitted. "I've another thought, captain: they have her captive and in chains, but took a detour to the Den of Innocence to celebrate the victory."

"Supposed to wait until after," the captain groused.

"Then I'm wrong," Innel said. "They wouldn't do that."

"Pah," the captain replied. "Be just like those bastards to get themselves good and stoned on fine qualan, while I'm here to coil ropes."

Innel felt his own cravings claw through him.

"Should have sent word, though," the captain said. "It's my ship that takes them home."

Innel gave an amused grin. "Who among them could be convinced to come back, while the rest were tucking up qualan in their cheeks?"

The captain shook his head, agreeing, then spat. He gave Innel a sidelong look. "If this goes bad, Arunkin, and I return my vessel empty of its intended cargo, there's no bonus for me either. And no ride home for you. Understand?"

"I understand," Innel answered quietly.

Innel looked back at the harbor town. He would need a plan as to what to do with himself after the mercenaries returned without Amarta, beyond explanations of why it wasn't his fault.

His gaze rose above the town, where the road led up and inland. In the distance he saw gray stone walls of Seuan.

And maybe another plan as to what to do if the mercenaries didn't return at all.

∾

Innel emerged from his tiny cabin the next morning. The captain caught sight of him, his expression dark. He advanced like a storm.

The man was clearly done with waiting, and looking for someone to blame. It was time to take the initiative.

Innel strode to meet him, yelling as he did. "Beyond acceptable," Innel cried out. "An insult to your ship, and my expertise both. Wherever they are, whatever they're doing, they had an obligation to report. Captain, this is outrageous."

The captain stumbled to a bemused stop in front of Innel, his own anger eclipsed by Innel's. An old trick from Cohort days. Innel continued on, not waiting for the other man to recover.

"Captain, someone must go ashore. Find out what in Hells has happened. Track them down, bring them back. The crew is essential; I must insist that it be me. I know you think that I'm a cripple, but I'm entirely capable, I assure you. Please, ser: allow me."

The captain's fury was gone from his sails. "All right then," he muttered. "If you think that's best."

"I do. I'll gather my things."

"No taking any of my food with you, Arunkin," the captain snapped. "We need every scrap for the return voyage."

"I wouldn't think of it. Nothing but what I brought on board, Captain."

~

Innel walked down the ramp of the ship, everything he owned on his back. The docks were wood, and the road of the harbor town of Seute Enta was dirt.

Dirt was dirt. He'd never been here before, but some things crossed all oceans. As Innel walked the streets of the harbor town, he was struck by the quiet of the townspeople, who stood in doorways to watch. Their faces had reddish, dark skin, with striking pale eyes. They tracked him with their gazes.

Innel stopped a polite distance away from an unsmiling man in a heavy apron who stood by a small shop. A fishmonger, by the smell of him.

"Good day," Innel said. "Do you speak Arunkin? Perripin?"

"Perripin."

"Excellent," Innel said, switching languages. "I am looking for some friends of mine. They came ashore five days ago. Perripin. A few more than fifty. Lightly armed. Have you seen them?"

The man stared at him for a long moment. "Those were your friends?"

"Yes. They were headed to—" should he say where? Well, why not? "To the city. To Seuan. To fetch someone, then return."

"Eufalmo," the man said.

"Eufalmo?" Innel asked.

The word was dimly familiar. Some Cohort study, somewhen, a lifetime ago.

"Eufalmo," the man said again. He held one hand

parallel to the ground, then wiggled his fingers, as if to demonstrate something crawling.

Ah, that's right: a traveler's journal Innel had once read in the great palace library that mentioned Seute Enta. A carpet of colorful beetles. A fantastic sight, the traveler asserted.

"And my friends?" Innel asked, thinking that his question had been misunderstood.

The man exhaled through pursed lips, and took a wary step backward.

"Please," Innel said, hands up. "I mean no offense. I only want to know where they are. The Den of Innocence, perhaps?" He grinned a little, but it faded at the man's increasingly fearful look.

"Not the Den. The Eufalmo. Your friends are gone."

"Gone to the Den? Is that what you mean?"

A creeping chill climbed up Innel's spine.

"Their bones lie on the ground. Outside the walls of Seuan."

Innel looked back at *A Splendid Catch*. At this distance, the captain and crew were small figures at the railing. He looked at the fishmonger. "Were they going to Seuan, or returning from it?"

"Bones, after the Eufalmo pass. Bones. Do you understand this? In piles. Not going anywhere."

"Was there... was there a woman among them?"

The man's mouth fell open slightly, as if dumbfounded. "Listen to me now, Arunkin-man: bones and weapons. Then the scavengers come. I got me a rare Duri knife. You want to know how many died? Go there and count the skulls."

Innel swallowed. His mouth was dry. He swallowed again. "Which way?" he whispered.

The man pointed up the rise.

This doesn't sound good, brother.

"And," Innel said slowly, "The Den. Which way is that?"

The man's arm swung to point south.

"But they are not there, Arunkin-man. You understand this?"

Innel nodded, trying to corral his thoughts as they darted around in his head.

The Seer killed them. With your help, brother.

"Or they found her, and now she's bones, too," Innel muttered in reply.

Do you want to know which it is?

"No, I don't think I do."

The fishmonger quickly backed away from the muttering Arunkin man, into his shop where he shut the door, barred it, and put a finger to his lips to silence his curious wife.

Chapter Seventeen

THE ROOM WAS full of answers.

Amarta looked around. One long wall was covered in cork and pinned paper notes, some connected with lengths of string. The notes contained dates, events, descriptions. A forest of details, from floor to ceiling, corner to corner.

She read the notes. Storms. Floods. Tides and seasons, moons and days. Winds, directions. Cistern levels. Crop yields. Ship schedules. Trade winds. Symbols that denoted levels of uncertainty.

Eufalmo.

The Seuan words for bone, blood, and water. The castes of Eye and Ear. Foreigners. Mages.

Then blanks, underlined. Questions that the Heart did not yet have answers to.

She was looking for one thing in particular, and then she found it. *The Seer of Arunkel.* The date she had arrived in Seuan. A symbol for sorins in an amount that came to uma-sorins.

So it was true: the Heart had sold her—or tried to—in return for a small fortune.

Who, she wondered, was now the poorer for the Perripin mercenary force's failure to acquire her? And where did the trail of coin lead? The Heart's notes did not say, but Tayre once had speculated that those after her came from the Arunkel Houses.

It didn't matter; there would always be people after her.

She began to understand how the Heart thought, as if she glimpsed an opponent's hidden hand of Rochi cards. She realized that she could spend days in this room, or months, and still not understand it all. She would need to come back.

Particularly interesting were the blanks he had left.

Off the main room was an alcove lined with books. There she found ledgers and journals. An entire set was devoted to the Eufalmo. When they had come and how many. How long the horde stretched into the distance as the first ones reached the city walls. Sketches and descriptions of the various kinds, including the Eufalmo queen, who stood as high as a tall man.

A list of the Eufalmo that Seuan had managed to kill across decades. A short list. None had been captured alive, though from the descriptions, it had been attempted once.

Amarta flipped pages to the most recent entries. The Eufalmo swarms had last come to Seuan three years ago, and it seemed to her they were coming more often, and in greater numbers.

She considered the blank pages that followed the last entry, her fingers tracing the page, to read words that weren't there, but might be some day.

On another wall, a fireplace with various objects atop the mantelpiece. A figurine of a man assembled from gold, silver, bronze, and pewter, the parts fitting together in a puzzle. A long, lean feline carved from green stone, caught in the act of stretching. At this, a sharp pang went through Amarta, as she remembered Tadesh.

Next, a red-gray godstone, a face with a wide, oval mouth showing teeth, from Punaami. Then a huge opal, bigger than Amarta's fist, milky white with an inner glow. Past that, three curved knives with handles of agate, turquoise, and bloodstone, laying on a small velvet pallet. Amarta recognized them from the Kailo. At the last, a stone jar with a tight-fitting lid. Within was a fine, gray dust.

Amarta looked back at the expanse of handwritten notes across the wall. The Heart of Seuan was famous for his predictions, but Amarta now knew that he did not foresee as she did. Rather, he used the signs of the world and the records of history to analyze facts and speculate about what was to come.

He was no seer. He was a pretender.

She studied until the night was nearly done. She left the Heart's secret room just before he returned.

~

A marta told their Seuan keepers to find her and Tayre another apartment, one closer to the center of the city, and they did. It was a mark of Amarta's new status that there was no objection.

At dawn, they were moved. They looked around the new apartment, and the door that bolted from the inside, as the last one had not.

"Amarta," Tayre said, touching her hand. "Something's upset you. Tell me. Let me help."

So gentle was his touch that she felt herself melt. His expression of concern—the hint of desire in his eyes—stirred both her emotions and her body.

A beautiful performance. Subtle and effective. She felt the pull to tell him everything, as he had no doubt intended.

"Dirina and Pas," Amarta breathed. "Someone is after them in Arunkel. They are in danger."

"And?" A slight change to his face, to his tone.

Amarta's display would need to be at least as convincing. How?

She sought out a vision—a brutal, violent future and stared into the horror.

"Pas's smile is broken," she whispered. "His mouth twisted. He limps to me, grabs my hand, and makes a sound over and over. I can't understand him. Then I can. He's saying my name. They cut his mouth. They cut out his tongue."

She looked at Tayre, her eyes filling with tears.

A risk, she knew, to examine this trail so closely, to give it the power of her regard. But Tayre must believe her, so she must believe it.

And she did: her chest felt torn open. She rubbed away tears, pushing herself to continue. "Pas somehow makes me understand that Dirina is dead. I want to see her body. He gestures and gestures. He can't. They fed her to pigs. There's nothing left." She gave Tayre a bleak look: "My sister."

Tayre nodded, to all appearances unmoved. "Is this future avoidable?"

Amarta cleared the vision as best she could. "Yes, thank the Fates. If you go to Arunkel—if you see them to safety—they may survive."

He tilted his head. "Me? Don't you mean us?"

"I can't go. Not yet."

"What in Seuan could be so important to you?"

"The Emendi slaves. They need—"

"Amarta."

"There are children here, rejected from the order of Eye and Ear. They are bled, so that—"

"Amarta. Slaves and children. Again?"

"Yes, again," she snapped. "You can't know. You don't see what I see."

"I am certain it is wretched and intolerable. It always is. But is it more important than your sister and nephew? Choose."

"I do not need to choose. It is better that you go without me, anyway. You'll be faster, more effective. And you are the only one who can save them."

He laughed, but there was no humor in it. "The only one? Truly? Well, you are the seer. I say we go back together." His smile hardened. "On the monthly trade ship, leaving in days."

What to say now?

He studied her. "What is there for you here, Amarta? Another doomed rescue of the weak and enslaved? Can you save all the world's victims?"

"This is different."

"So you say, though you refuse to tell me how. I don't see what you see, but this I know: had you let the people of the Island Road live as they wished, Olessio would be alive and with us now."

Amarta tore from the apartment, striding the city streets without direction, furious.

Then, all at once, she stopped in her tracks, realizing that Tayre had baited her, and she had bit the hook.

He was attempting to unbalance her, because he didn't want to leave her side. He would fight to stay with her.

She blinked back tears, and stared up at the clouded sky. He was right about the Island Road and Olessio, of course. But he was wrong about the rest.

She turned back to the apartment, taking less-traveled routes as the day brought Seuan units into the street. She passed through a narrow gray-stone walkway between two buildings. A faint midair glint brought her to a halt.

A spider had built a web between the two walls, but in no future did the web and the spider survive the morning's foot traffic.

As she watched, the spider dropped and climbed on the web, diligently continuing its work, creating new lines.

Such a lot of work for something that soon would be destroyed. Amarta could duck under, and leave the small thing to spin what it could in the time it had left.

Or she could break the web, force the creature to the ground, to crawl away from its work, and give it a chance to live.

Was it better to live only a short while, but in accordance with one's nature—one's gift-curse—or to have someone destroy your work before a tragic conclusion that only that someone could see?

If only she could ask the spider what it would choose, but the spider would understand the question no better than Tayre would; he had lived too long in the shadow of his own death to consider it important.

And so she must decide for him.

Amarta walked forward. She waved her hand in the air, breaking the web. The spider dropped to the ground, and scurried away.

❧

Her hands groped for Tayre's in a frenzy of hunger fueled by the sure knowledge that, one way or another, their time together was ending.

She would not go back to the land from which she had so painstakingly liberated herself. She could not; it would make her too small.

But he must.

In the hours of touch and tangle, she immersed herself in

him, the future and past swept away. When at last their passion settled, Tayre brought his face close to hers.

"Amarta, how important is this, that I leave you to protect Dirina and Pas?" There was an intensity to his whisper. He put his hand on hers, lying between them on the bed.

"Very," she replied.

He stroked her hand gently, his voice suddenly harsh. "Then release me."

Her breath caught. Her mouth opened. He moved closer, holding her gaze in his own.

"How can I fulfill the terms of this mage-witnessed contract that binds us if I am not by your side? If I am across the ocean? In another land? How?"

He is not like others, Olessio said. So true. By any standard, Tayre was singular.

Had she really ever wondered if he had taken the contract for a single, scratched nals coin? Absurd. Nor had he taken it for curiosity, though his delight in puzzles was surely some part of it.

He could have ended the contract a long time ago, had he wanted to. Amarta had ached for him so much, for so long, that she would have been easy to steer. He could have made her act in any way he wished her to, including being free of her. He hadn't.

Whatever his motives had been at the start, they were something more now. What?

You are already my people, Amarta. Can you not feel this?

Sudden understanding was sudden pain: Tayre was her people, just as Olessio had been.

And that meant that in the choice between releasing him or watching him die, there was no choice at all. She must protect him.

Amarta felt forward in time. *I release you.* All at once, the futures in which she felt those words come from her throat multiplied into the thousands.

She thrust them away. Silently, she reached for him again. Just as silently, he reached back.

~

In the tower room, a room of windows and doors, high enough to see over the walls of the city, Amarta stood at the side of the Heart of Seuan.

He gazed out of the windows, his hands clasped behind his back, his gray robe brushing slippered feet. On his face, Amarta saw light lines of advanced age against smooth skin.

The city, its clusters and packed structures, sat under darkening, overcast skies, but the streets were dry.

"The cisterns levels are low," the Heart said. "A storm in four days will bring them up." He spoke as if to himself, but Amarta knew what game he was playing. "Light rains only. What do you say, Advisor to the Body?"

Amarta must convince him that she understood his priorities, without revealing just how well. She must keep secret that she had been in his inner sanctum and knew all that he had written there.

She must, somehow, arrange for him to keep his high self-regard, yet not let him lose sight of how useful she was.

A six-player Rochi game seemed easy by comparison. She would need to learn fast.

"Yes," Amarta replied. "The rains are light. Perhaps three days hence."

"In three days," The Heart said, as if he had himself changed his prediction.

In the streets below, a unit of Seuan Feet drew a heavily laden wagon. Supplies from one caste to another, a task reserved for the Feet.

"Forayers seen." The Heart said. "A day to the west. The full swarm could come next month. Or next year."

He would not ask her, so she could not answer directly. Yet. He was better at the game of pretending to know the future, but actually guessing, than she was. He had many years of life lived.

He was clever. Experienced. She must tread lightly.

"I am certain that you know when they are to come, Heart," she said, trying for the right mix of respect edged with challenge.

He was silent for a moment. Then: "Here in Seuan, we say this: once is test, twice is fortune, thrice is guess, and fourth is truth. To speak a prediction is the easy part. It is true only when it happens."

Amarta nodded agreement. "Surely, the swarm's increasing size and frequency in recent decades makes precision difficult."

He frowned, perhaps wondering if Amarta could see into the past as well as the future. He did not, after all, know how her ability worked.

"If we knew with certainty," the Heart said as he continued to stare out the window at his city, "we could open some of the cisterns now to nearby farms who require water to achieve a second harvest before winter."

"We could," she said, ignoring his sidelong look at her use of *we*. "And yet..." she trailed off, staring distantly, pretending to be deep in thought, letting the quiet lengthen.

"And yet?" he prompted at last, tightly.

A fine line, making him respect her enough to keep her close, but not so much that he began to fear her.

She took a breath. "It might be best not to plan for a second season of crops this year."

He made a thoughtful sound, then let the room fill with silence.

Another game of cat and mouse.

Amarta hoped she was the cat, but she knew that the Heart believed the same of himself, and she had been the mouse too many times before to let herself be too certain.

❧

here is something you need to know.

Amarta stood in the doorway, ready to go, but turned back, drinking him in.

His hunter's brown eyes. His hair curled around his ears. It tore at her to leave him here this day, knowing that there would not be many more of them.

He looked back impassively. "What aren't you telling me, Amarta?"

How long had she been standing here, staring? Had Tayre spoken in the actual now, or in some potential near-future?

Had she perhaps returned from a similar moment in one of the multitudes of futures she had been tracking? Hearing him say that very thing, again and again, but in the now, he had been silent?

She blinked as if waking, confused, and looked around the room. He had spoken in this moment, she decided. The actual now.

Again, she tracked forward along the trails of his life, returning back to reach the moment before someone—the Heart, most likely—realized how much he mattered to her, and how broken Amarta could be made with his violent death.

One misstep on her part, one moment beyond that key point, and she would be helpless to protect him.

Simpler to save a city than this complicated man.

It was beyond selfish to hold him here. And so: in what

future did she draw him to the docks, and onto the trade ship coming, in mere days? In what farflung scenario—perhaps no more likely than Rhaata and his mushroom—did Tayre agree to leave Seute Enta without her, for Arunkel, for a land in which he might yet survive?

In the actual now, he was speaking. Saying her name. Demanding answers. Amarta stared into the future long enough to be certain that he would be alive when she returned and then she left.

That night as he slept—or, more likely, pretended to—she stood at the window and watched the castes of the Body of Seuan light lamps in their caste clusters' windows, chant devotions, and snuff their flames to sleep.

The night passed. Amarta gazed into the wilds of the moments to come, as a full moon slid across the sky. By dawn she was as certain as she could be.

There is something you need to know.

Chapter Eighteen

ELLA FROWNED. "It's essential that she cooperate."

Tokerae chuckled. "She will."

Ella's frown turned into a questioning look. "You're certain?"

"After last night, I am." He smiled wide.

Last night, Tokerae had gone to see Citriona in the grand palace room that he had arranged for her, near his own. She had broken down in tears.

With a gesture, Tokerae dismissed the servants, and sat by her side. She lay on her bed, face down, head in her arms, sobbing.

He pried one hand gently from her face. It was wet with tears. For some reason, this made her cry even harder.

"Tell me what it is, my dear."

She rolled to her side and looked up at him. Her eyes were red.

"Father says you're a good man, smart and strong. Eparch. Cohort, too. And you've been so kind to me."

"All true," Tokerae said. But for the accompanying weeping, these seemed to be good things. "What is the matter, Citriona? You must tell me, if I'm to do anything about it."

She sat up on the bed, snuffling. "The Ministerial Council declared Cern dead yesterday."

"Yes," he replied. At long last, after another visit from himself and Ella.

"Along with her children. Poor Estarna! The baby, too!" Citriona's lips trembled. "Our very queen. Dead."

"Yes, it's very sad. But—"

"They called me inside! The council! Tok! I thought they would tell me I had done something wrong. Maybe this apartment that you gave me, and I shouldn't be here. But no!" She turned an earnest look on him. "I'm next on the succession list! A month ago I was twenty-third."

Tokerae let his smile grow wide. "Congratulations, my dear."

Citriona wailed and began to sob. "But I don't want to be queen!"

This Tokerae had not expected. "What? Why not?"

She gulped air, her sobbing paused. Her voice dropped. "Because I heard about the mage."

A most unattractive image of Undul Etris Tay flashed into Tokerae's mind.

"What mage?"

Her voice barely a whisper, she leaned toward him. "The one who killed the queen, Tok. Before the impostor took her place. Who else could have gotten through all the guards and the dogs, too? And Sachare? It has to have been a mage. Everyone says so."

"Ah," Tokerae said, nodding slowly. "I have heard this as well."

"Illegal mages, in the palace! I can't imagine. It's outrageous." She gave him a horrified look. "Is it true?"

"If everyone says so," Tokerae replied, "there might be something to it."

"Oh, Fates spare me," Citriona whimpered. "Cern is dead. Her children are dead. If I'm monarch, I'll surely be next."

She began to gasp, as if she couldn't get enough air.

Tokerae brought Citriona's hand to his lips and kissed it in a way that he knew was very distracting.

"Could you," he asked, "be monarch for only a little while? A few hours, perhaps?"

"Hours? I think it's supposed to be longer than that. What do you mean?"

"I'm Cohort, Citriona. This is what I was raised for." His look confident, her gaze latched onto him as if she were drowning. He brushed a tear from her cheek. "Here is how it works, my darling. First, you and I will wed. An extravagant, splendid ceremony of which your parents will be proud, and for which you will be the gem that sparkles most brilliantly."

Her panicked expression eased and her mouth went slack.

"Soon after," Tokerae continued, "you will ascend to the throne, and I stand by your side as Consort."

"But a mage could come right through you, Tok! They can do that, you know."

He held up a finger to indicate he was not done. "It need only be hours later that you abdicate to me, thereby satisfying all your duties: you honor the Council, your parents, your Anandynar ancestors, and your empire, all by setting on the throne a man who was formed from his earliest years for the purpose of protecting Arunkel from all threats. And you—you will be out of harm's way."

"But you would be monarch!" Her voice dropped again. "The mage would kill you."

"No. I have taken care of the mage."

"You have? Already?"

"Of course. I'm Cohort. We're taught to think ahead, Citriona. To plan, as if for battle. The mage is no longer a threat."

For a moment she was silent, seeming to Tokerae poised to ask him how. Instead, she heaved a great sigh of relief, flopped onto her back, and wriggled her head into his lap, like an insistent cat. She smiled up at him.

"You like me, don't you?"

"Oh, darling Citriona. Very much."

Tokerae had intended to sound sincere, but the open delight in her face was so charming that the words came quite easily.

~

"Please don't move, Your Illustriousness. I've got a pin."

Tokerae gave his sister a grim, suffering look. From the corner of the room, she gave back an amused smirk.

"Have you found the cursed torq?" he asked her.

Tokerae was being dressed and addressed by tailors from both Houses Murice and Sartor, who moved around him as if he were a dress form, shooting glares at each other like children.

Murice, House of Dye, and Sartor, House of Needle and Knot, had been in uneasy association since Sartor had lost the amardide armor contract to Murice decades ago. At the announcement of a royal wedding, both Houses had insisted that they be the one to dress Tokerae.

There was no choosing between them; it would be an insult to decline either one.

"We will find it," Ella promised.

Tokerae saw the glint of a needle in Sartor's fast hands as the tailor glowered at Murice around Tokerae's legs.

"You. Be careful."

"Yes, your Illustriousness," both replied at once.

"If only we had the damned seneschal," Tokerae muttered.

"Another traitor, deserting his post," Ella replied.

Escaped alongside Cern, she meant, with some two hundred or so that had yet to be found. And where the Hells were they all?

"He knew where things were," Tokerae said.

"All will be found, brother. The Consort's torq, and the many other things that have gone astray."

Meaning Cern and her people. Tokerae didn't have Ella's confidence. Too many days had gone by since Cern had last been seen.

"In time? A wedding in two days? The coronation a day later?"

Ambitious, to say the least. But Ella had insisted. He had reluctantly agreed.

She was right. It was a delicate situation; having convinced some twenty-odd Anandynars to step down, the moment was unstable. Best not to give the royals warning enough to reconsider putting the formerly twenty-third successor on the throne, or the ministers a moment more to round up House resistance. Speed was their friend.

"It is generous of us, brother, to arrange for the many royals and dignitaries who must travel to the wedding not to need to make another trip for the ascendancy. I shall see to it that they understand this, along with enjoying the palace's most excellent hospitality."

The ascendancy was still as secret as it could be, with the necessary planning in motion. Tokerae had convinced Citriona not to tell her parents or any relatives—and certainly not the Council—until the very day that she abdicated.

"How is our dear Citriona holding up, brother?" Ella asked, meeting his gaze over the heads of the two tailors who were in a whispered argument about Tokerae's hemline. "She would doubtless enjoy something imported and exquisite."

Intoxicating, Ella meant.

In private, that morning, when they had been able to speak freely, Ella had urged him not to take any chances with Citriona's compliance.

"A Seuan elixir," she had said, "would soften any resistance."

Tokerae understood: everything hinged on Citriona, whose innocent and guileless actions would be an implausible ruse coming from any Cohort sib. Raised at the palace, yes, and perhaps only paces from Cohort intrigue, but she was so naive and credulous that she might as well have come from the rural provinces. There was not a drop of pretense in her.

A delicate flower. A simple, trusting, delicate flower.

"She'll do as I direct," he told Ella.

"If she's anything other than what she seems, brother..."

"Then I deserve what comes." Tokerae laughed at his joke, but Ella did not.

"You would, but I wouldn't. And our House wouldn't. This had better not explode in our face, brother."

"I have her in hand, sister."

The wedding was lavish. Chains, silk, and velvet draped from the balconies of the Great Hall, glittering in Anandynar red and black alongside Etallan's silver and copper. It was a message no one would miss.

Citriona beamed through the ceremony, her face full of delight, eyes and smile wide as she looked across the packed room where her family and the aristocracy stood watching, adorned in their finest. She gripped Tokerae's hand tightly.

When the event was over and they were, at last, in her room, Citriona eagerly drew him to the bed. Laughing, she playfully pushed Tokerae backward. Obligingly, he fell backward onto the bed, pulling her on top of him. She kissed him breathlessly, her enthusiasm infectious.

Tokerae remembered himself at her age. The Cohort had done a great deal of bed-hopping, but he could not remember anyone as full of unbridled joy as Citriona was now.

Yet she seemed so young. He held her up from him so that he could search her eyes.

"Did you have an anknapa?" he asked.

"Of course," she replied. "Doesn't everyone? I had many. The best."

"Good," Tokerae said, relieved.

"But sex always seemed like such a lot of work." She touched his nose with her own. "What I like best..." Her eyes shone. "Having my feet licked. Did they teach you to do that in the Cohort?"

Cohort anknapas had been outstanding, the very best that royal status and money could obtain, not only in the arts of sex, but in all the ways that touch might be applied, for pleasure or influence. As it happened, that covered a great range of study. Feet must surely have been on that list, though Tokerae could not recall that lesson.

No matter; whatever he had forgotten he would invent.

He examined Citriona's face, adjusting his expectations for the evening, and promising himself that when Citriona was asleep he would have a slave come to his room and do to him—all of him—what he was about to do to Citriona's feet.

"Absolutely," he assured her.

Even in normal times, a royal wedding would not compare to the splendor of crowning a new monarch.

Tokerae now saw the wisdom of Ella's plan to have the coronation so closely follow the wedding. It gave momentum to events, priming attendees, from royals to Houses to artisos, to accept the glamour, glitter, and legitimacy of the ceremonies.

The Great Hall was packed even tighter than it had been for the wedding, where some Houses had been only minimally present, most notably Kincel and Nital. Tokerae would not forget that.

For the coronation, though, all were in full force, with eparchs and heirs all in attendance.

The First Minister began the ascendancy ceremony, reciting the formal litany that was required. Perhaps less enthusiastically than Tokerae might have preferred, but at least he had all the words in the right order.

The key moment in the ascendancy was the one in which the monarchy was legally transferred from the old ruler to the new. No words need be spoken; the act alone was sufficient, as had been demonstrated when king Restarn sullenly handed the scepter to his daughter Cern years ago.

Alas, there was no current monarch to pass on the scepter to Citriona, Cern having been declared dead. The Council itself had not performed this act in some generations, but the histories clearly indicated that it had been done before, so it could be done again.

Tokerae and Ella had persuaded the First Minister of this, showing him the records, while also assuring him of their most ardent good wishes for his continued robust health.

The ceremony was not long by Arunkel monarchical standards—no doubt a reflection of generations of both rulers having little tolerance for waiting for the damned thing to be over—and thus, the First Minister was quickly coming to the important moment. He spoke of the history and gravity of the scepter that he was holding, of the significance of the act that was about to follow, the one in which Citriona would stand, from where she now knelt on pillows that were used for no other ceremony. The one in which he himself would hand her the royal scepter, and then, she would be queen.

Then, just before the final words, the First Minister stuttered to silence, his mouth hanging open.

It should have been a simple thing: recite the words, hand Citriona the scratched, dented, gem-encrusted and oversized stiletto, and it was done.

Instead, the minister stood mute, scepter shaking in his tightly clenched fist. The packed hall went quiet.

Citriona gaped upward at the minister, while he stared past her to the watching crowd as if hoping—what? That Cern herself might pop up from the audience and tell him to stop?

Tokerae and his sister, standing to the side on the dais, exchanged alarmed looks. Her wordless instructions were clear: *Do something. Do it now.*

"First Minister," Tokerae hissed. "We wish you a long life."

The First Minister blinked, as if waking. His face flushed red, a frightened gaze darting to Tokerae and away. He heaved a deep breath, and muttered the final phrase, directing Citriona to stand.

She did. Their hands slowly met, mid-way between their bodies, as if the minister couldn't quite summon the strength to close the distance. Citriona grabbed the royal scepter out of his trembling hand.

Maybe not such a long life, after all, Tokerae thought.

No matter, it was done: Citriona held the long, gaudy thing over her head and grinned widely at the many standing before her. She waved it, and they cheered.

～

"I don't understand, Tok," Citriona whined.

"You speak to the Ministerial Council," Tokerae said again, as gently and reassuringly as he knew how.

"I don't need permission to see them?"

Tokerae considered this absurd notion, then reminded himself that she was neither Cern, nor Cohort. In no way had she been trained for the position that she now held.

Only an accident of birth had put her on the succession list at all. Far down.

He stifled a sigh of frustration, instead giving her a fond smile. "You may wish to give the Ministers a bit of notice, so that they might dress appropriately for the royal presence." At this, Citriona's face began to brighten. "To look their best for you," he added. "A bell's warning is all they need, though. A royal attendant can set this in motion. Shall I summon one now?"

Citriona's smile faded. "I am to do what, again? Walk into the Council? What do I say?"

Tokerae stifled annoyance. This was the third round of a similar conversation. He took Citriona's hands and looked into her eyes.

"You say that you abdicate to me. Speak my full name, so that there is no confusion in their small minds. They will try to talk you out of it and attempt to intimidate you. I'll be right outside—simply call my name and I'll come in to explain the matter to them. But you must speak first."

"And then, what will you say to them?"

Tokerae blinked, and blinked again. She had asked this before, nearly word for word.

For a moment, he wondered if he had been wrong about her, and if she were playing him after all. She was not Cohort, no, but Anandynar blood flowed through her veins. Could this be subterfuge?

He heard his mother's mocking tone.

No; Citriona would need to be a brilliant dramatist for it to be so, and she was not. This was a Cohort-level performance, at least.

Nothing more than fear and lack of understanding. The Council's authority unnerved her.

He reviewed what he knew of the young woman before him. Her parents were from a line of Anandynars many steps removed from the crown, enjoying generations of wealth and palace life by virtue of their name, without having to do anything to retain their position. There was, among them, not a single Cohort child.

So she had been raised in luxury. Well-educated, yes, but very gently educated, and without challenge.

Ah. She needed flattery.

"I will say nothing," Tokerae replied, with a widening smile, "Because you are the queen, and I am only the Royal Consort."

She dimpled, drew herself to stand tall, her head coming to his chest. He embraced her.

"Then I shall be monarch today," she said into his shirt. "And you can be monarch tomorrow." She pulled back, grinning. "I think you should treat me very well tonight."

"What a brilliant plan, Your Excellent Majesty," Tokerae

said, bowing. Out of the blue, he thought of Innel, who had been married to Cern for years. Had the traitor-mutt needed to work this hard to keep Cern happy? "Have you seen the royal bath?"

Citriona's eyes went wide. She shook her head.

"I think I know what splendid thing we'll be doing tonight."

~

"**W**hy today?" Citriona pleaded, her head in his lap as she looked up at him. "We put it off yesterday. Why not tomorrow?"

Citriona's hair spread in a wild, curling honey-colored storm about her head.

Perhaps, Tokerae thought, he should have objected more strenuously the first time they'd had this conversation, or the second, but she had been so unrestrainedly delighted in the bath, that he had found himself telling her about the gardens. After that, they made an adventure wandering Cern's rooms, exploring the racks of cloaks and chests of wondrous children's toys, and puzzling over Cern's odd collection of wire, wood, and fabric.

Citriona was so full of astonishment and pleasure at these trinkets that Tokerae mentioned the royal inventory.

That took them another day. They walked through rooms of art, mirrors, carved gemstones, walls decorated with lush tapestries, glinting armor, cutlery, textiles. All the myriad and priceless gifts that a monarch might receive across generations. Even Tokerae had been impressed. Who knew that the Anandynars had amassed such a dazzling treasure trove?

Well, it would be Etallan's soon enough.

Everywhere she went, Citriona blossomed like a rose,

taking in the bows and obeisances and forms of address as if they were air itself.

It would only be a few days, Tokerae told himself. It built her confidence. That would serve when she abdicated.

This morning, he strode the hallway to arrange for a repeat performance of the royal bath. Rose petals across the water, this time, he decided.

Ella came from a doorway and grabbed his arm, fingers sinking deep into his flesh. She yanked him into an empty room, and shut the door.

"What in Hells is is wrong with you?" she demanded.

"What do you mean?"

"We did not bank the work of generations, spend souvers as if they were grains of sand, and call in every debt Etallan is owed, to put another Anandynar on the throne. What are you doing?"

Tokerae rocked back as if slapped. His breath caught in his throat. He shook his head adamantly.

"Nothing is wrong. She will abdicate. Tomorrow. Or the day after."

Ella gave him a stunned, incredulous look. "Shake off the spell, brother."

"There's no spell. I'm building her confidence."

"Oh? Well, you've succeeded. She is becoming accustomed to this role. Get her unaccustomed and fast. Or do you need my help with that, too?"

He stared back at Ella, felt his stomach drop.

"I do not."

"Should have been me," Ella said, under her breath, revealing a rare bitterness.

Tokerae snorted to cover his shock. "You'd have no hope of getting her pregnant, sister." He grinned, hoping to lighten the mood.

"Best you hold off on that as well, until you have the

throne secure, so she can't decide you're a clumsy oaf in bed
—which you probably are—and divorce you the next
morning. Nine words is all it takes, brother. Nine words.

I divorce you, said thrice.

"I know how this works, sister," Tokerae snapped angrily.
"I am Cohort. As you are not."

Tokerae immediately regretted his words. He looked
away.

Ella took a deep breath, then another. She put a hand on
his shoulder, and spoke with a gentleness that rocked him
again.

"Brother, we are so close to our goal. Our ancestors spent
metal and blood to deliver us to this moment. Tokerae dele
Etallan, the honor of our House and lineage is in your hands.
Now is the time to act. Only you can restore us. Only you."

When she spoke like this, Tokerae felt her words shake
his very bones.

What had he been thinking? And doing? Ella was right.

Citriona was not particularly clever, but her very lack—
her naive charm—had taken him unawares.

It would not happen again.

"I will address this. Today." Then, at Ella's arched
eyebrow, he added: "Now."

Chapter Nineteen

CERN STOOD from where she had sat on the riverbank, feeding Nipatas. Nearby, Sachare was changing Estarna's clothes.

The camp was busy. One tencount was serving everyone breakfast, while another readied supplies and packs, and a third fetched water from the river.

Cern's gaze ranged the camp, seeing in her people diligence and cooperation, a smooth handling of the business of food and shelter as they continued on the run, creeping eastward away from the capital.

The days in the tunnels had been terrifying, but not one person had cried out, whether from fear or an intent to betray. After they had emerged, Nalas and Lismar had kept count of every person so they would know if anyone walked away.

None had. Not one.

Perhaps the hardship of the tunnels, combined with the relief of being alive day after day, had changed them, convinced them that their continued freedom depended on working together. Quietly, quickly.

Or maybe they felt fortunate to have ended up with Cern, rather than one of the other two companies that had just left camp.

With Estarna's clothes changed, Sachare took the baby from Cern and began to clean him.

Even Cern's seneschal, Natun, had undergone some sort of transformation. He had lost his sour expression, his imperious tone. Just now, he complimented a man's work, patting him on the shoulder amiably. He even smiled.

Nalas rode into camp on one of their recently acquired horses, a sturdy gelding who behaved well as long as he was given enough fodder.

Perhaps that was the explanation, people not being so different from horses. Cern had managed, daily, to keep everyone fed, Lismar procuring for them supplies from loyal households along the way.

Nalas dropped from his horse, letting a queensguard take the reins. He strode to Cern, his gaze sweeping the surrounding rise, where sentries stood guard.

"They are away, Your Majesty," he said.

"Fates protect them," Cern muttered of the two companies from the division of the whole that were now moving in different directions from the one that Cern's people would soon take.

Decoys, each with a woman, a small girl Estarna's age, and a bundle that might have been a baby, riding at their center.

Cern still felt the weight of her failure to lead and protect those she had left at the palace, who had fought the overwhelming attack to defend her and her throne while she fled. Add on the many who lived in the palace, the survivors whose lives would be held cheap even if they swore fealty to the usurper.

It was a daily shame to swallow, as she looked into the

drawn faces of those who had left families behind in the usurper's control. Nalas's wife and son were merely two among many more.

In the oppressive tunnels, there had been little time for her to ruminate. Now, during long days of walking and nights of listening to every sound that river, trees, and wind might make—an attack? a betrayal?—Cern faced the challenges of her own mind, the questions that could not be answered.

What signs of betrayal had she missed? Who had she mistakenly trusted?

Reluctantly, her thoughts turned to Innel. He had lied to her—there was no doubt of that.

But which time? And for what cause?

Some day she would ask Nalas what he thought. But today was not that day.

Today, Cern must keep herself and her children alive, and lead those at her side to some form of refuge. Then they would recover and she would rebuild. Only then could Cern look back to the Arunkel capital, the palace, and her throne, where her ancestors had reigned for nearly a thousand years.

She would reclaim her throne. Of that she was certain. Her questions would be answered. The betrayals would be remedied.

She fervently hoped that the usurper would leave his Cohort sib Putar alive and whole, because when she regained her throne, she would make Putar Minister of Justice, and Tokerae would be his first performance.

"We are ready to go, Your Majesty," her seneschal said.

"We'd best move," Nalas added, "if we are to seem a third decoy."

The other two companies were not merely decoys. They were targets.

When Cern sketched the plan, Lismar and Nalas quickly

assembled a list of those women who might stand in for Cern.

"Volunteers only," Cern directed.

"It is their duty and privilege, Your Grace," Lismar objected, "to stand for their queen."

"It is their lives," Cern answered.

"What if no one volunteers?" Nalas asked, speaking Cern's own silent fear, to which Cern did not reply.

That was not a problem. It seemed that every woman in the camp came forward to offer herself, and parents and siblings urged forward girlchildren who were Estarna's age.

Stunned, Cern looked into their eyes, struggling to keep the emotion from her face.

There was no time for it, but Cern spoke to each of them, asking them their names. As young as they were, the girls might not understand what they volunteered for, but she spoke her gratitude anyway, assuring every woman and child that this brave service would not go unrewarded when she reclaimed her throne.

When.

One of the girls chosen piped up, promising Cern that she would never let harm come to the queen or the princess, as Estarna looked on. So young, but the girl made herself understood.

Cern swallowed hard, a lump in her throat. To her surprise, she discovered that her determination to redeem the sacrifices of her people could be further fortified. She brought Estarna's hand to the girl's hand, and held both in her own.

Even in Cern's own company, another woman stood in for her, and a girlchild for Estarna. Those two rode on one of the few horses, a mild, pale dappled mare. Cern and Estarna walked, Nipatas under a cloak in Sachare's arms.

The woman who rode in Cern's place was a scullery

maid, now dressed in Cern's clothes, a bundle that might be a baby strapped to her chest. The girl who rode in front of her was her younger sister.

The woman's name was Atabasca, and the girl was called Pulegan.

Chapter Twenty

AMARTA GENTLY HELD the shifting world of *soon* that slithered through her mind. If she held it too tightly, it would slip her grasp. The trick was to follow, fast and agile, as the future forked and forked again.

The serpents of the future twisted in her mind, turning and hissing, possibilities dying and being born every instant.

Step by step, Tayre walked with her from Seuan to the oceanside harbor. Step by step, she walked the fine line between his curiosity and his caution. At each moment, he might turn away.

Zung-Resch—the Third of the Ear—had privately urged Amarta to take more defense. But no; Amarta knew that if she had, he would not have come.

Trailing them were three Left Thumbs, those Seuan warriors who fought threats external to the city walls. Their armor glinted like the Eufalmo themselves, dusted with a dark powder whose scent Amarta would never forget: the Eufalmo repellent.

They walked the stone streets of the town, the wind full of sea and brine. From doorways, townspeople watched.

At the dock, the merchant seaship *Fast Wind* prepared to depart. Crew dashed across the deck and dock, shouting back and forth. Stevedores carried bundles and crates up the ramp.

Gulls cried. Someone swore.

"Am I leaving?" Tayre asked mildly.

Amarta dug a hand into her pocket and then into a further, nested pocket, from which she brought forth the last of the treasures she owned: a small seashell, striped blue and white. It had been her mother's.

The ship's first mate, a scowling Arunkin man, strode toward her from the ramp.

"I said noon, damn it," he growled. "These tides and crosswinds are no joke, woman."

Tayre's gaze seemed so easy as he looked around, as if he were simply curious. Amarta knew better: he was counting men. Assessing. Preparing.

"Dirina and Pas," she said to him. "Their lives are in your hands." She held out the shell to him.

He made no move to take it as he snorted softly. Amused? Annoyed?

"You ask me to believe that if I don't go, you'll let your sister die. Your nephew be maimed. Hard to credit that story, Seer."

"You can move faster without me." Amarta felt the press of time. "You can find anyone, anywhere. As you found me, again and again." When he had been under contract to the Lord Commander of the Arunkel empire. Before she had given him a nals coin.

Tayre's gaze swept past her, to the docks and the ship beyond.

Still she held out to him the shell. "Will you do this for me? Please?"

Tayre's look snapped to her, hard enough that she felt it.

"Release me."

The first mate had been turned away, looking over the ship. He addressed Tayre. "Your passage is paid for, ser. Get on board, if you're coming."

But Tayre's gaze was locked onto Amarta.

"I release you," she said quickly, softly.

Tayre nodded slowly, then took the shell from her outstretched hand. "Again."

"Got a tide to catch, lovebirds," said the first mate. "Give you the count of ten, then we leave without the man. And no refund, woman. One."

Tayre's stare at her was weighty.

We are aggrieved, the Heart would say, in some increasingly likely future. His murderers will be found and punished, Advisor, I assure you.

But Tayre would still be dead, and Amarta's spirit torn to shreds. A mountain of grief to put next to the one named Olessio.

"I release you," she croaked through a tight throat and an ache heavy in her chest.

Tayre glanced at the ship. Speculatively. Then back to her.

"Once more, Seer, and we are done." There was something about his tone, something resolved. Was it also sad? She couldn't tell.

"Two," shouted the first mate.

"You will save them," Amarta said.

"Say it a third time," Tayre snapped.

But once released, he might decide not to go. And then...

All his futures came through this moment, like a funnel. Mishandled, Tayre died here in Seuan, refusing to leave her side.

Don't miss, he had once told her.

There were too many moments in which he did not walk

up that ramp, did not sail across the Nelar Ocean to Arunkel, and did not escape his narrowing future.

She took a step toward him, then another.

"Three!"

Close to him now, nearly close enough to touch.

"There is," Amarta said, "something you need to know."

The wind shifted suddenly. She could smell him. It almost undid her. She gripped tight to her resolve, blinking back tears.

From the ship, a sailor yelled, tossed down a coiled rope.

"Four!"

"Amarta dua Seer," Tayre said to her, "release me from my sworn contract to you, and I will go."

The future said that he might. Or he might not.

She opened her mouth to say the words, these final words. Only three of them—how hard could it be? But they were stuck inside her mouth. She might as well have been mute.

The wind changed again and the future solidified. She knew what to do. She raised an arm, gave the signal.

From behind boxes, climbing from under piers, standing from hiding, and jumping down from scaffolding, came sixty Left Thumbs, their dark, blue-black armor glinting. In a blink they had arranged themselves into a smooth curving shape that faced Amarta and Tayre and the ship. They advanced.

No weapons, she had told them firmly, remembering all the times that she had seen Tayre, outnumbered, turn arms against the attackers. She didn't want anyone getting hurt.

"Five!" called the first mate as he eyed the advancing Thumbs uneasily.

Tayre dropped slightly into a ready crouch. Few futures showed him attempting to take on sixty armored Seuan warriors, futures in which he would be captured, bound, and bodily put on that ship.

But Thumbs would die.

She waited a moment, then another, and raised her hand again. The Thumbs stopped closing.

She took a breath. "Long ago, you told me that you wanted to see me strong. You wanted to see what I would do. Do you remember?"

"This is your strength, to coerce me through overwhelming force?" Tayre laughed. "Show me your strength of honor instead. Say it one more time. *Release me.*"

"Six," yelled the first mate stepping backward from the Thumbs.

"Listen, there is something—"

"I need to know," Tayre interrupted, with a voice like steel. "Something that you think will change my mind and convince me to leave, to break a contract to which I am sworn. Well, then, Amarta dua Seer. Get to it. Let's see if you're half as clever as you think you are."

The words lashed her. She knew they would.

"Seven."

"Your uncle," Amarta said, enunciating clearly, precisely, to make sure he heard her. "Is in Sio."

"My uncle is dead," Tayre said.

"No. You never saw the body." A guess, but from his sudden, blank expression, the words had landed. *Look to disable*, Tayre had taught her. *Waste nothing.* "Alive, but dying. There is not much time. You must go now."

"If you lie to me, Seer—"

Nothing will keep me from my vengeance, he was about to say, but did not. Did not need to. She heard it clearly in the future. As he knew she would.

"I speak truth," she said.

"Eight!"

"With Dirina and Pas at your side," Amarta said, "there is a future in which he is restored to health."

Tayre's blank expression fell away like a dropped curtain, replaced by something that she had never seen in him before. On another man it might have been agony. Or passion. Or fury.

On him, it was something else, something she could not name. Something fierce. Something naked.

In a blink it was gone. He took her by the shoulders, gripping painfully as she frantically opened her hands in a gesture to stay the Thumbs behind her, to keep them from defending her.

"Come with me," he said, and repeated it. Not a suggestion. Not even a command. Something more, full of urgency and seduction that somehow held all the best moments between them, every splendid touch, every intimacy. His tone and expression poured over her like honey. She felt as if the breath had been stolen from her body, the resolve from her spirit.

Olessio, she thought to herself ruthlessly. She could not stop the tears, but she could remember. She pulled forward into the future against which she navigated: the one in which Tayre did not die by her side as another casualty in her journey through the world.

"You must go," she managed. "I stay."

His captivating expression changed again, as if swept away by the ocean wind, and he pushed her, but as he did, it was he who stepped away, not her. He gave a final assessing look at the force arrayed against him, then his gaze locked on Amarta's.

A backward step and another, and another, until he was at the ship's ramp. There he stood, staring at her.

"Nine!" the first mate shouted from atop the ship's ramp.

"Amarta," Tayre said. "What is this that you do?"

247

The sea wind whipped the tears from her eyes across her face.

"What I must," she called back. "What I must."

It was almost a nod, his response. He climbed the ramp onto the ship and stood at the railing, turned away.

The captain barked orders. Sailors dashed up the ramp, unlocking the ramp. Dockhands pulled the plank back on to the dock. Ropes were cast off.

"What I must," she said, again, but only she was close enough to hear herself now.

Minutes passed and the ship began to pull away, out of the Seuan harbor, sails unfurled and raised.

Slowly, so slowly. And yet so fast. Too fast.

The sails caught the wind. Tayre had not moved from where he stood, looking eastward, toward his destination.

She stood there and watched as the ship shrank against the horizon and at last vanished. Then she stared at the empty ocean as gulls rose and fell and cried on the winds.

It was hours later, perhaps, that she turned and began to walk, her footsteps slow and heavy and shuffling.

Scraped raw inside, stunned at what she had done, she wondered if she would ever see him again.

Vision moved to answer. She slammed the door on any answers. It was a future she could not afford to want.

She felt like an old woman, hunched, slowly ascending the road to a city that held an apartment that would be empty of him. The townspeople gaped at this odd foreigner woman, weeping as she walked from the harbor, trailed by sixty-three Seuan warriors.

From the loss of Olessio and the loss of Tadesh, Amarta had come to understand that grief was a road all its own. It must be traversed, and nothing could make it shorter. No act, no effort, no good intention, could lessen the time required for the shard of glass to dull.

She should have released him. Said it one more time. It would have been the right thing to do. But in the end, it had been the one thing that had been entirely beyond her.

I am sorry.

By the time her plodding climb led her to the gates of Seuan, which opened wide for her, her eyes were red, but dry.

It was done. She could go forward. There was nothing and no one left to lose.

～

"Tueb is sweet and friendly. She will not harm you, Advisor to the Body," said the woman, a sorog keeper. The keepers were clearly not of the Body of Seuan, living outside the city as they did, in the caves with the great sorogs.

Amarta's foresight agreed with the keeper, yet as she stared up at the huge sorog, she felt daunted.

Around her stood various people, waiting. Left Thumbs, Fingers who toted bags of water and food for the day's journey. Eyes. Ears. All watched Amarta silently as she studied the sorog nervously, thinking about how to mount up on the great beast.

Was this a test?

The Second of the Ear, called Aka-Etero, had earlier told her: "You must ride, Advisor to the Body. The Eufalmo may sweep the lowlands. We cannot risk you."

Amarta could have told Aka-Etero how unlikely it was that the Eufalmo would cross their paths today. Unlikely, but not impossible.

No reason to have that discussion, though, other than to avoid this moment.

Amarta nerved herself and took hold of the handles built

into the high leather saddle that formed a sort of ladder. She hauled herself up, and up some more, and finally sat atop the great, broad creature's back.

This was surely as high as if she sat on Souver, though Souver, of whom she had been so fond, seemed to belong to another life. There was no other similarity; so wide across was the Tueb that Amarta's legs must splay out to the side to sit the saddle. The creature's nose came to a sharp, horned point and her hide was a dusty black, thick and hard as if it might be armor.

Tueb snorted, stamped her front feet, and shook her huge head from side to side. Panicked, Amarta gripped the edge of the thick leather saddle with both hands.

Laughter cut the air, and the sound of it shocked her. She looked for the source, finding that the amusement came from the sorog keepers, not from her Seuan escort, who did not even smile.

The rest of the party split itself onto the other sorogs, mounting multi-seat saddles, a Thumb or two on each huge, horned beast.

But Amarta had Tueb all to herself.

Yes, it was a test.

From the ground, her amused sorog keepers showed her how to steer, though there was no need, since once on the road, Tueb compliantly followed the other sorogs.

The great creature's heavy gait and rolling sway was nothing like riding a horse. More like a boat. Amarta's thoughts turned to the last time she'd been on the water. She circled the memories, keeping them at bay, then dismissed them entirely.

The entourage toured the outlying villages and farmlands that were just ending their first harvest of the year. Villagers proudly displayed produce, and children, and talkatively explained how they defended themselves from the Eufalmo.

Some villages sheltered in a common underground structure that was lined with heavy rock and thick mortar. Some withdrew into many, low-ceilinged houses, much like those that she and Tayre had used, so that if the Eufalmo breached one, the rest might survive. Others wrapped themselves in dung-heavy fabric and buried themselves, with straws in their mouths for air.

But the villages closest to Seuan relied on speed.

"We run," a village elder told her from the ground. "Very fast. If we are lucky, we arrive before the city gates seal. After the swarm passes, the Body makes a feast, and we are allowed to join! We waddle home!"

They did not need to say what happened if they were unlucky.

The village elder laughed uproariously at his own words and so compellingly that Amarta found herself joining him. They were the only two.

Amarta knew from her eavesdropping on the caste clusters how private a thing humor was among the Body. Only rarely had she even heard soft laughter.

Unbidden, memory served up the loud bark of Olessio's laughter, unrestrained and unapologetic. *To see the world in its many shapes and colors.* Somehow she was sure he would have loved this strange land.

As they rode to the next village, Amarta turned to a nearby sorog. To Second of the Ear, Aka-Etero, she said, "I would like to know more about the sorogs."

"They serve defense," Aka-Etero replied. "In long-ago times, foreigns from the western mountains or from across the sea mistook Seuan for a fruit, ripe and easy to pluck. With the sorogs, we showed how incorrect was their thinking."

"Also the Eufalmo," said Ugo-Resch, the Third of the Eye, speaking in Seuan.

Amarta stared at the man, at his mottled tunic and stained hands and feet. It was the first time any man of that caste had spoken to her.

"Yes," Aka-Etero agreed, answering in Arunkin. "The sorogs will walk through an Eufalmo line if they must."

"With risk," said Ugo-Resch.

"With risk," Aka-Etero echoed, smoothly switching to Seuan, observing that Amarta seemed to be following without trouble. "All Eufalmo consume, but some, that we call chewers, that we see infrequently, cut through even hard sorog hides. The sorogs will protect themselves by stamping and rolling and crushing. It is their instinct. But if chewers latch on, the beast may be lost."

Still vivid in Amarta's memory was the Eufalmo forayer line that in mere moments consumed fifty and more Perripin mercenaries.

This was why Seuan was so focused on defense. They could afford no mistakes.

Doesn't have much of a sense of humor, does she?

Amarta understood.

∾

Of the many knots Amarta sought to untangle, the first was the man called the Heart of Seuan.

At his command, Amarta's quarters had been relocated to a small room, in the temple of the Eye, near one of the many raised walkways that connected to the Heart's temple.

Most evenings, the Heart went to his private sanctum, stayed a few hours, then returned to his own quarters. Amarta entered, when he left, to see what notes he had added to his board, to journals and ledgers, and what vision might show her anew in the blank spaces he had left.

She had no doubt that she had been relocated to keep

better track of her movements. The Heart must have been disappointed in the results, because day or night, Amarta was in her quarters when he summoned her and came quickly. The rest of the time, she walked where and when she liked.

When she allowed herself to be seen, she was of course followed. Sometimes by Thumbs, lesser Eyes and Ears, or a subcaste of the Third Left Finger, whose primary work was the making and keeping of records.

Often she would double back, watching as her pursuers stumbled to a halt, looking about in confusion as Amarta seemed to have turned a corner and vanished.

Yet another game of cat and mouse, once in which Amarta played both roles.

During one of her untracked wanderings, Amarta discovered that the source of some of Seuan's rarest extractions were the Emendi slaves themselves. These were Emendi who did not meet the Seuan aesthetic ideal, or who had been injured, or who simply failed to behave in a sufficiently docile manner.

An ancient Emendi woman was led through the city to the cluster of the Right Pointing Finger, whose caste was responsible for such work. The Emendi woman limped forward, slack-jawed, eyes wide in fear. Sedated, Amarta decided, though not enough: she knew what was coming.

Amarta looked through a window into the room where it was done. A man, a Finger, hit the Emendi woman hard at the back of her neck, stunning her. As she crumpled, he wrapped his arms around her head and twisted, once, sharply. She went limp.

Amarta doused the fire of fury that came over her with the vivid memory of what she had wrought at the Tree of Revelation, at the Island Road. Had she not promised herself that outrage would not longer guide her hand? *Olessio.*

Trembling all through, she watched.

The rest was meticulous butchery: organs removed and deposited in silver bowls. Hair, skin, and bones likewise. All the bowls, glinting in bright sun as they were delivered to other castes.

Nothing wasted. Nothing but the old woman's life.

You want to understand the knots of Seuan? Understand this.

Amarta observed variations of this same scene. Again and again, she knew that each Emendi life taken was a life she could have saved.

But it was not enough to save one stranger's life, only to need to save the next and the next in endless succession. The knot must be properly untied.

Living inside the temples, it was easy to return to the rooms of the singing children. Then, one day, they were gone.

Alarmed, she searched, to find that they had been moved: the boys to the Temple of the Eye, the girls to the temple of the Ear, where they began their testing.

Amarta spent more and more time with the Heart. At first, when he summoned her, they would stand in silence, staring out at the city together. Bit by bit, he began to speak to her, and then more and more.

No longer did he use any language but Seuan. He told Amarta about the city and how it had become great. He spoke of the Eufalmo.

Amarta learned the signals of the horns that would sound atop the walls, what patterns meant Eufalmo scouts, forayers, or a full swarm. She came to understand how the drums and smoke from the farthest villages relayed news to the city, how Seuan drums and horns sent it back again.

The Heart spoke of exports, of elixirs and salves. Of imports of silks, food, and slaves. Bitterly, he lamented the lost harvest of this Island Road's treasures, especially the sea pearls which were promised but never delivered due to a strange, violent storm.

Amarta listened closely for any hint that he knew of her involvement. But no—all he had were rumors of confused destruction.

He did not know what had become of the Islands. Amarta did not enlighten him.

One night, the Heart took her to his Temple's basement. Deep underground, he showed her his collection of Eufalmo backs: spotted, lined, solid, iridescent. In the lamplight, they made Amarta's green scoop, now lost on the Islands and probably in the sea, seem paltry by comparison.

One Eufalmo back was so large that it hung on the wall like a large warshield. Another was long and thin, coming to a sharp point. "Not carved," the Heart assured her, smiling proudly. "That is the shape of the creature itself."

Amarta needed no pretense to seem astonished at this array of Eufalmo parts, to inhale sharply as he moved the lamp around the room to show off the varying, startling shades, patterns, and colors.

He showed her his collection of mined stones and named them: huge blue sapphires, long slabs of lapis, ovoids of black opal, and cathedrals of amethyst. They glittered and shone with an inner light, taking the lamp flame and turning it into rainbows. She touched them, sensing the ages of time to come. The opals drew her back for a second touch.

The Heart was clearly happy to show her these collections. They were the riches never exported, the greatest of Eufalmo shells and the rocks dug up from Seuan soil. Were they ever offered, they would command fortunes.

There was no need. Seuan was wealthy from the exports of intoxicants, stimulants, poisons and their cures, fertility elixirs, and on and on. Some made from Emendi slaves.

Amarta praised his collections and good taste until she worried that he would think her fawning words false.

But no, he was simply pleased. It must have been a very long time since anyone had been here to see these. Maybe she was the first.

Amarta had, by now, spent a great deal of time hearing the Heart speak, not only about Seuan and shells, rocks, and all the rest, but about himself. Amarta was not used to people talking at such length without demanding answers, and his ongoing attentions and loquacious explanations were a tangle of mystery to her. A puzzle. She mused for days.

All at once, she understood. Seuan was a city full of castes, each of which cleaved tight to its own. As completely loyal as they were to him, the Heart of Seuan was alone. A caste of one.

She only had to look in a mirror to feel his ache.

Chapter Twenty-One

AMARTA STOOD beside the trio of the Heart and Eye and Ear. The four of them looked out the windows of the circular tower room.

"What is heard, my sister?" asked the Heart of Seuan.

The First of the Ear touched her fist to her chest, then her fingers to her right ear. "Signals relayed from northern villages," she said in her mellifluous voice. "A grain silo, a herd of sheep, and seven children are lost. The Eufalmo come no closer."

It took a moment for Amarta to understand, not because she didn't know the Seuan as spoken, but because of the one word: lost.

Grain, sheep, children—lost. *Lost*, like her Perripin attack force.

Eaten, they meant.

No closer meant to the city of Seuan, of course, because everything was about the city. Those who lived outside the wall were not of the Body, though they supplied grain, meat, produce, war sorogs, and more. These outsiders were connected to the body, as food is connected to the one who eats it, but they were not the Body.

Twists of the knots that Amarta was determined to understand.

"What is seen, my brother?" the Heart asked.

The First of the Eye touched his fist to his chest and his fingertips to his brow. "Distant scouts. None approach."

In the fields to the west of the city wall, great pits opened to the sky. Three sorogs ridden by Left Thumbs faced the pits, some forty feet between each sorog, ropes linking them together.

"This is only practice," The Heart said for Amarta's benefit. "In their caves, the sorogs are safe. In the open, they are useful. We do not risk them for a forayer line that could be turned by repellent and flame. But for a swarm, we must."

Amarta nodded, hoping to seem both eager to learn and gratefully respectful, though she had studied the sorogs when reading his records.

"Can the Eufalmo come through the gates?" she asked, already knowing the answer.

He gave her a tolerant, amused smile. "They cannot. Our gates are the finest in the world. Mage-sailor made. Even the swarm cannot breach them, though it might climb the walls and reach the top."

"Only reach?" Amarta asked, though, again, she already knew.

"Only reach. We have ways to repel. The only Eufalmo to touch the ground of Seuan," he said. "have been dead ones." His look flickered to Amarta, then back to the window. "Do the scouts approach the walls today, Advisor to the Body?"

Here was the fine line: make him respect her words, but not enough to think her a threat. Predictions were like sharp, spinning knives; she must not catch them by the sharp end.

And she must not be wrong.

"No approach today," Amarta said, hoping that vision remained consistent. The truth was that the Eufalmo could turn in a blink, far more like weather than a trade ship.

"That is my prediction also," the Heart said.

He was taking her lead and claiming it for his own.

On the field, the three roped sorogs charged toward the pits, the middle sorog running between two of the openings, the others to the outsides. Between them, the rope, barely brushing the ground, trailed over the openings.

Once past, the sorogs came to a stop, then turned in place, stepping with surprising agility over the ropes so that they again stretched between them. Once more, the huge beasts thundered forward, running to pass between the pits, the ropes brushing the earth.

The swarm was coming to Seuan. When exactly—a day, a month, a year—Amarta could not be certain. But it was coming.

She knew this, just as she knew that while scouts and forayers could be guided by Seuan attractant and repellent, a full swarm would not even notice.

Amarta woke suddenly. She rolled out of bed, felt for her clothes in the dark and shrugged them on, then, fled the room. Outside her door, two Right Thumbs guarded. She spoke urgently and ran to the tower room.

Minutes later the Eye and Ear arrived, soon followed by the Heart. He glowered at Amarta in the lamplight, clearly furious at being summoned to his own tower.

From his look, she could tell that he knew why, and what it meant.

"The Eufalmo only come with daylight," he snapped. He

wanted to say more. *You overstep, child,* he said, in any number of now-fading futures.

Instead he gazed out the window into the pre-twilight darkness. "What do you predict, Advisor?"

However she answered, he would claim the prediction for his own. He might doubt her, but he was willing to use her.

At that thought, a lifetime of resentment sparked to flame.

For a moment she said nothing, balancing the urgency that had brought her here against the many ways the near future might yet go.

As she struggled with her anger, a fork loomed before her. On one path lay the challenge that her darkening mood was now forming, the one in which she was attacked by masked Thumbs at the Heart's order—the very encounter she had foreseen in Perripur, under wet skies and Tayre's tutelage, when she had been blindfolded and dodging balls.

When Olessio still lived. Forever ago. She swallowed the ache.

Or she might go forward on the other path, one that must begin now, in which, rather than lash out with her foresight, she gently worked the knot.

Part of her wanted the fight. She craved to show the Heart what she was capable of, that he only pretended to.

In the next moment, she was disgusted with herself. How many times had she seen the future, but overlooked the damage that she would cause, the lives that she would topple?

What did it matter if someone doubted her, or tried to use her? Was it really such a surprise?

While these thoughts circled, the future tightened. She was herself part of the knot that she sought to understand, her own fingers entwined in the tangle, her own self inextricably wound into the events. She must understand more than what was outside herself.

"I predict lines of scouts and forayers," Amarta replied. With a tinge of regret, she chose the second path, the one that declined the challenge, that began with the next words. "But I defer to your greater wisdom, Heart."

The Heart's nod was appeased. "I predict this also."

The future shifted. The path in which masked Thumbs attacked Amarta faded, weakened, then dissipated.

The Heart gestured at Thumbs standing silently by the door who left, returning quickly with narrow, metal lamps. A red-flamed one went to the Eye, a blue-flamed to the Ear. With a fist-touch and bow, a white-flamed device was put into the Heart's hand.

Outside, a faint wisp of dusk lit clouds. The light hinted at the city's form, at the lands beyond.

"There," Amarta said, pointing.

The Eye drew from his mottled red robe a long-lens—a brass bar connecting two finely made pieces of glass. He pulled, lengthening the device, then peered through in the direction that Amarta had pointed.

"Scouts," the Eye confirmed. He held up his red lamp, waving it to signal the wall.

In a blink, horns sounded across the city, the patterns and meanings another language Amarta now understood.

Scouts, northwest side.

Do you hear?

We hear.

At the window, the Ear tilted her head back and forth. "A forayer line follows the scouts."

The Heart snapped into motion, waving his white-flame lamp and passing his other hand before it, back and forth, yet more signals.

Across the city, drums began to beat, quickening to tell

the Body of Seuan to act; some to move, others to hide deep within their caste's understructure.

Sorogs emerged from their caves on the fields beyond the wall. Armored Thumbs mounted.

Soft, fast words passed between Eye, Ear, and Heart as they each moved their lamps and hands independently. It was impressively meticulous, with no movement or breath wasted. A three-person dance that reminded Amarta of Tayre.

Then, barely visible in the predawn dark, the forayer line came into view, where Amarta had pointed. At first it was a trickle, then a rivulet, then a stream. In a blink it was wide across the middle. A sudden river, driving toward the walls of Seuan.

Through the tower windows, Amarta began to hear the familiar muttering hiss. The clicking. The drone.

All the more chilling, now that she had seen what they could do.

Atop the city walls, mangonels—metal contraptions the size of mules—were wound and let loose, again and again, bags of powder and flaming balls of tar flying down into the sides of the undulating river.

The powder broke at the edge of the forayer line, releasing a dark cloud. Then flame. An attempt to change the course of the river, to push it back from the walls.

But the river of Eufalmo did not even waver.

Atop the wall, Thumbs ran to the raised corner watchtowers. This, Amarta knew, meant that the forayer line had reached the western wall's base, hidden from their vantage.

She could easily imagine the Eufalmo climbing the wall. Coming closer. *The only Eufalmo to touch the ground of Seuan have been dead ones*, the Heart had said.

She found herself breathing fast.

The wall's walkway, now clear of Thumbs, roared into flame, thick and high. Heavy smoke boiled off the top. In a moment, Amarta could smell the repellent. She coughed, snuffled, and accepted a thick face-cloth.

"They will not advance," the Heart said adamantly, his pale eyes reflecting the fire on the wall. "They will withdraw."

He glanced at Amarta briefly. She said nothing.

They stared at the wall. On the far side of the flaming walkway appeared heads and horns, the Eufalmo's black eyes catching the flame light.

Amarta' breath left her. For an instant, everyone in the tower room seemed to freeze where they stood.

Then, all at once, the creatures were gone, drawing back, rebuffed by flame and repellent.

The horns blared from the raised watchtowers.

They retreat.

The Heart drew a long breath. He turned a smug look on Amarta.

"Now you see: I am the Heart of Seuan, Advisor. I predict an outcome, and it is so."

"It is so," echoed the Ear and the Eye together.

"It is so, Great Heart," Amarta replied softly, which he might take for humility.

On the field below, the Eufalmo forayer line withdrew, pulling back the way it had come, like a river reversing course.

In moments, the field was clear. The sorogs returned to their caves.

Amarta shook. The Eufalmo had not been close to them, here in the tower at the center of Seuan, yet she had felt terror.

A shadow, no doubt, of what the Perripin men she had sent to their deaths had felt in their final moments.

She was not at all certain that the few minutes' warning

she had given them had made any difference in the outcome. But no matter—it was a demonstration, and a means to understanding the knot of Seuan.

As Thumbs and small Fingers cleaned on the walkways of the wall, removing burnt fuel and repellent, the Heart, Eye, and Ear flashed signals to the tower to assess damage. How many injured? Dead? Had any sorogs been lost?

As they did, Amarta slipped quickly out of the room, counting the ways in which she had proven herself so far, and had yet to.

Once is test, twice is fortune, thrice is guess, and fourth is truth.

❧

"A full swarm?"

The Heart looked from Amarta to the Eye, then the Ear.

It was daylight, so Eye and Ear flashed their signals to the watchtowers using day lamps with built-in mirrors.

"Nothing is seen," said the Eye, as he read the return flashes from the towers.

"Nothing is heard," the Ear echoed.

"A full swarm, tomorrow," Amarta repeated. "This time, the walls will not stop them."

The Heart studied her a moment. A small smile accompanied his hard expression. "A catastrophe, is it? And only you can see it? Is that so?"

This time, she knew, he would not echo her prediction.

Thrice is guess.

This time, from his long lifetime's experience, he was wagering that she was wrong. They had just repelled a forayer line. Amarta knew from his records that a full swarm, so soon, was unlikely.

How certain was she? A wager on the Eufalmo was like a wager on the weather.

She swallowed. "They come," she said firmly. "Seuan will be full of flame."

The Heart scoffed. "We know what we do, Advisor." His tone was dismissive, amused. But beneath that was something else.

He was tired of her being right.

"Not merely chewers," she said, "but also diggers. They will consume—" she struggled to focus on the man in front of her instead of the devastation that the future showed her. "Many. We will survive—" *we*, she had said. "The Body will survive, but the repellent and ready-fire will be spent. When another swarm comes in mere days, we will have nothing left. The Body may not survive."

The Heart's expression darkened. "Now we know with certainty that you guess, *Seer*," he spat. "Swarms do not repeat. They come once a cycle. Repelled, they return to their nests for years. You know so much, but this, you do not know?"

She met each of their looks—his: antagonized. The Eye, curious. The Ear, wary.

"The Eufalmo are not as you have known them to be," Amarta said, struggling to seem calm. "They are changing. If you do only what you have done before, the Body will take a mortal wound."

The Heart's eyes widened in anger as he seemed to struggle with what to say next. *You exceed your position,* he might say. In other futures: *Take her to a locked cell, where she will mislead us no longer.*

Had she gone too far?

She looked down, as he was quiet for many counts.

He took a breath. "What do you propose, Advisor?"

Amarta's mouth opened a moment, surprised. She bowed her head to him in genuine respect.

"The swarm surrounds the queen, Great Heart," she said. "Where the queen goes, they follow." She had learned this in the Heart's library. "I advise a mixture of attractant and repellent, laid on the ground where she passes. Confuse her enough that she will take the swarm elsewhere. Maybe to the villages, where..." Amarta trailed off as she realized what she was suggesting.

Some must die so that others might live. Slowly, she blinked, and in that moment she saw again the Monks of Revelation, crushed by their own Tree, engulfed by the crowd. She heard the screams of thousands as the Islands dove.

She saw Olessio as he sank, covered in blood.

The Heart scoffed. "The queen is at the center of the mass. Impossible to reach. This also, you did not know?"

Amarta shook her head. "We need not reach where she is, if we can put the mixture where she will be."

Closer to the time of the swarm, there would be a handful of places the queen was likely to pass. If the queen could be addled, she might deviate and pass by Seuan, taking her swarm with her.

But there were no road signs out in the wilds of the countryside—Amarta could not direct someone else where to take the mixture. She must place it on the land herself.

On the land where the Eufalmo roamed.

She thought of Tayre, who never hesitated to step into danger when he must, and Olessio, who had stood at her side in the canoe, risking his life to defend them. Could she do less?

"Give me a sorog and a brave Thumb," Amarta said. "As much attractant and repellent as we can carry. I will lead the swarm away."

Brave words. She swallowed, resisting the disagreeing visions that belied her promise.

Always a path to failure, is there not?

The Heart exchanged a look with the Eye and Ear, then settled a pensive gaze on Amarta.

She could almost read his thoughts, that a sorog and Thumb might be a small price to pay to discredit her. Perhaps, as a bonus, feed this difficult foreigner woman to the Eufalmo. Either way, he stood to win.

Amarta must make sure that the same was true for her.

Chapter Twenty-Two

AT THE DEN OF INNOCENCE, Innel was asked many questions.

Does the visitor have a preference as to intoxicant? Qualan, yes, Arunkin-ser, of course. We have the finest anywhere, so close are we to the great Seuan. You wish to begin with the qualan?

He did.

Does the visitor have money? Much money? In what form? Please show us.

Innel displayed some of his stolen wealth.

Ah, is enough. We will make an account for you. You will be very happy. This way, please.

Innel had not known how much the glittering trinkets, gold coins, and chains he had pocketed at Zeted's villa would buy him at the Den, but he did rather like the sound of *enough*.

He was led from the entryway into a large, dim room, with a low ceiling, domed at the center. Cots spread across the floor, occupied by sluggish and unmoving figures.

"It will seem more lovely, Arunkin-ser, after you have settled in," the proprietor said, correctly assessing Innel's thoughts from his expression. She offered him a small palm-sized cube in wax paper. "Our welcome gift. Do you know how to use? Yes? Good. Already sliced, no need for you to do so. No knives allowed. Simply raise your hand and we will come to serve you whatever is needed. Food, water, qualan. As you desire. Here is your place."

She left him at an empty cot. He lowered himself, glad for the lack of light that mercifully prevented a closer examination of his bedding.

Trembling, he unwrapped the cube to reveal what he had missed most while at sea; what he had, perhaps foolishly, set aside to try to save the Seer of Arunkel.

He turned it in the dim light, squinting. Did it have a bronze tint to it?

It did.

Innel took a slice and tucked it up between cheek and gum. Some crumbled in his fingers, dropping to the cot.

A hiss escaped him. He fell prone, touching the tip of his tongue to the bits he barely saw on the fabric, pushing away thoughts of what else might be there, and wondering, belatedly, how many others had done exactly the same thing.

In moments, all those thoughts, as well as the unpleasant stench of the room, were gone. A delicious rush rippled through him. The stink had become delightful scent, reminding him of flowers, wine, and the most excellent sex.

He lay back on the cot. There was no need to go anywhere.

The deepest aches within him—the loss of Cern, his daughter, and the life he had fought so hard for—began to unwind and melt into the cot under him, then to fade away. The lesser pains of these many, many months, of fear and bruise, of cut and break, all followed into a sweet river of bliss.

Innel stared up, into the dark ceiling. There his mind

played only beautiful images. His body offered only joyous sensations.

He wept in relief.

~

Brother.
"No," Innel said to the whisper, denying the voice, denying the memories.

How long had he been here in the Den? Hours? Days?

Surely not months, not yet.

He unwrapped the rest of a new package of qualan, put some into his mouth, holding the last bit expertly between his fingers. Far more deftly than when he had arrived, he was proud to note. No crumbs on the cot this time.

The room began to brighten. Even knowing it was only his perception, Innel realized something that seemed to him, at this moment, profound: this was wealth. All the other things he had sought, across a lifetime, were only poor imitations.

So much effort to achieve and become. How sad it all was. Here he had a stunning prosperity.

"Brother."

Sound moved air. Innel slowly, reluctantly, turned on his cot to look.

One cot over, a skinny man, barely dressed, sat cross-legged, waving his arms, arguing with someone who wasn't there. Innel snorted in amusement, then lay back again to stare into the welcoming dark overhead.

Then, at the corner of his vision, at the edge of his own cot, a figure sat.

He would not look.

The proprietors assured him that this was the finest

qualan in the world. The occasional convincing hallucination was only to be expected.

So solid was the figure, that Innel almost believed that if he reached out his hand, he would touch his brother. "But I don't believe in ghosts."

"No? What do you believe in, then, little brother? Tell me."

Was there any sense in talking to a ghost?

Innel put the last bit of qualan into his mouth, moving it with his tongue until he found a spot on his gums that was not yet sore.

He need only wait moments, he knew, until even that mouth pain turned into rightness. All that was required of him now was to let himself dissolve, along with the qualan.

And that, he could do.

Chapter Twenty-Three

"TOK? Where have you been? I missed you so. What have you been doing?"

As Tokerae came into her room, she ran to him, taking his hands.

The telltale signs of boredom were scattered across the room: a set of cordial glasses, partially full of colorful liquids; a book opened to the second page; an exquisitely carved amardide gittern with a music book atop its four doubled strings.

Tokerae clasped Citriona's hands in return, gazing down into her unhappy face with a fond expression.

"Tending to matters that you would find tedious, my darling. So tedious." He gave her a playful, mischievous smile. "But also arranging some amusements for your rarefied delight. Pleasures worthy of Cern Anandynar. Pleasures worthy of Citriona esse Arunkel."

Her face lit at this flattering comparison.

Tokerae had debated just how subtle to be. Citriona was young, inexperienced, and lacking exposure to the realities of palace life—despite having been raised here.

She might miss subtle signs. He decided to err on the side of the obvious.

Over the next two days, items were found in Citriona's room, in the pockets of her clothes, and in her bed. A small vial containing foul-smelling liquid. A glinting garrote.

A dead wren.

He made sure to be just outside her door when she discovered the bird's body. As she screamed, loudly and satisfyingly, he rushed in.

"What is it?"

She ran to him. Inarticulate sounds came from her throat as she pointed to the bird's carcass. It was lying in a clothes drawer, the one that held the most delicate of her garments.

He gestured to a guard to have it removed. "Not to worry, my darling." Once the guard and bird were gone, he stroked her hands on his arm, hoping to calm her. She had a surprisingly sharp grip for such a small woman.

"Someone is trying to hurt me," she whispered.

"What? You mean the bird?" With his free arm Tokerae waved this away. "Arunkel tradition, my dear. Testing the new monarch. Nothing more."

"Tradition? Test? What do you mean?"

"Part of being queen, Citriona, to survive such foolish pranks. Simply avoid touching anything sharp, or drinking that which has not first been tasted. Not forever," he said, patting her reassuringly. "Give it a year or two. They'll start to die down after that."

She looked appropriately horrified. Tokerae pretended not to notice, telling her where in the great library she could find histories of her family, the ruling Anandynars, and all that they had survived. Might be worth the study, he pointed out.

He knew that she wouldn't, because that would mean

leaving her apartment, nor would she have the books brought, because it wouldn't occur to her.

She became more and more agitated. He bowed deeply. "I beg your forgiveness, my darling—Your Excellent Majesty —but there are a great number of officials across the palace who I must speak to before they make matters of state even more of a mess than they already are. Will you excuse me?"

He didn't wait for an answer.

It didn't take long for Citriona to see signs where they weren't. She had Tokerae summoned again and again to show him things.

A guard with a half-ear who she thought certainly must be a traitor. Wine that didn't taste right. An odd-smelling pillow she was certain was dusted in poison.

That night at dinner, Citriona stood from the table, backing away so abruptly that her chair fell to the floor. A dessert had been set before her, a sugared confection of mint and ground almond, formed in the shape of a snake, red and blue, mouth wide, pale fangs revealed.

"What is wrong, my dear?" Tokerae asked innocently.

Citriona fled to her bedroom. Tokerae stood, stretched, and followed.

From under the covers, the young queen whimpered. He sat at her side.

"I can't be monarch, Tok." Her voice was muffled by blankets. "I won't. I refuse." Her face popped out from the covers. "You could. Still. Would you?"

"Would I what?" he asked, as if truly confused. "What is it, my darling? What can I do?"

"I will abdicate tomorrow, Tok, first thing. Will you take the throne for me? Even though it's so very dangerous? Please?"

Touched by her concern, he put on his best smile. "I

stand ready to serve. If you deem it best, my darling, of course I shall."

She nodded soberly, her eyes bright. "I don't know what I would do without you, Tok."

~

Now was the time to fortify Citriona's resolve.

An early-morning discovery of a creatively carved mouse cadaver left Citriona clinging and sobbing, begging for reassurances.

She would not let his hand go until they reached the door of the chambers inside which the summoned Ministerial Council waited. There Tokerae explained to her, yet again, that she must go in without him if she were to be credible.

At last she did.

Despite the heavy wooden doors, Citriona's voice carried well. With some pride, Tokerae noted that she matched for volume the voices of the other ministers, who, judging by their tone, were doing exactly what he had told Citriona they would: objecting.

Muffled though her voice was, as it rose in volume, there was no mistaking what she was saying or the name she kept repeating.

It was his.

Tokerae waited until the discussion reached a momentary pause, gestured for the doors to be opened, and—Ella by his side—strode into the chamber.

~

While Citriona, Ella, and Tokerae watched, each and every one of the Ministers was invited to repeat, word for word, what the queen of the Arunkel empire had just told them: that she was abdicating the throne in favor of Tokerae dele Etallan. Ella looked over the shoulder of the ministerial scribe as he penned the words for the legal record.

It was thrilling.

After the meeting, Tokerae and Ella ushered Citriona to her apartments, access to her tightly controlled.

It was one thing to be given the throne, another entirely to be crowned.

Citriona was kept compliant with a gentle balance of nurturing and terror. Signs of threat continued—small things —but Citriona missed not a one, now that she was looking for them as if her life depended on it.

Across the palace, a hot political firestorm raged, jumping from mouth to ear, handwritten note to eye, as ministers, royals, House liaisons, and spies all began trading information, favors, and threats. The balance was upset—or was it? Who was in charge?

What to do about Etallan? went the whispers. And: *How do we keep the Anandynar throne Anandynar?*

Tokerae and Ella followed the conversations via informants. They assembled a list of names.

In the middle of the chaos, Ella brought them a seneschal. Kelesk was short, thick, and well-groomed. He claimed to have been the old seneschal's protege and chosen successor.

Perhaps. Perhaps not. As long as he could get the job done, he could claim what he liked.

Kelesk was quickly useful, bringing details of the various political maneuvering that exploded across the palace.

Tokerae and Ella took what steps they must to dampen some flames, and spark others.

Between inducements and threats, they began to settle palace minds into accepting the inevitable.

Next, the coronation.

House Etallan was wealthy enough to fund the entire event without even dipping into their coffers; this went a fair distance to defanging the Ministers of Treasury, Coin, and Accounts, all of whom were assured that if they cooperated, they would keep their positions.

Or better them.

Tokerae and Ella made it known that the position of First Minister depended entirely on Tokerae's successful coronation. Which must be as soon as possible.

"I believe we have the Council in hand," Ella told him. "Citriona is my greatest concern. Will she see it through?"

Not an hour went by that Tokerae did not ask himself the same question.

"She shows no regret for her decision. Impatience to make it fact. Gratitude to me for making it possible."

"Well done, brother. Whatever it is you're doing, keep at it."

"Foot rubs," Tokerae replied glibly.

The next morning, Kelesk brought to Tokerae the news that the Minister of Justice had been speaking with some of the people on Tokerae and Ella's list.

"We may have a problem," Tokerae told Ella privately.

"Leave it to me."

Two hours later, Ella was back, assuring him that they had the Minister's firm support.

"So fast?" he asked Ella, impressed. "How?"

"He has a family, Tok, and secrets. I have been working toward this day for a long time."

"Sister, you are a marvel."

She dimpled at the praise. Suddenly, the smile fled her face.

"What is wrong?" Tokerae asked, alarmed.

"Two days hence, you take the throne, my brother. But you haven't set foot in House Etallan in a month. You must give up the eparchy."

Tokerae felt her words like a gut-punch. "But it's mine," he breathed.

Ella was watching him closely. She laid her hand gently over his clenched fist.

"You are about to become the monarch of the Arunkel empire, a far greater power than mere eparch. But you cannot do both."

He shook his head.

"Put the burden on my shoulders," she whispered. "You gave me your word that if you ever willingly relinquished the eparchy, you would take my cause to succeed you. Tok, think of it: Etallan and the crown, in harmony at last. Imagine what we could do together."

"After I'm crowned," he murmured.

"Before," she countered. "Indeed, right now. We go to Etallan together. You cede the eparchy to me, as swiftly as it was bestowed upon you."

He sputtered. "I have no time for that sort of thing."

"The only thing that can stop your ascension to the throne now is Citriona. You are taking over an empire, brother; surely you can steer a devoted, willing, and smitten young woman. Do you doubt her infatuation?"

"No."

"Do you doubt yourself, then?" She softened it with a smile.

He examined her carefully, his mind spinning across the many ways this could go wrong.

"Would you have come so far without me, Tok?" Gently asked, but he felt the steel behind the question.

She stood, the motion so elegant and shockingly regal that he found himself standing with her. Where, he wondered, had she acquired such poise?

He did not dispute her reasoning, yet he could not seem to bring himself to say so. At his silence, she bowed to him, very low.

"My loyalty to you, your Illustriousness. Your Majesty-to-be. My faith in you, now and forever, pledged without hesitation."

Stunned at this unexpected oath, Tokerae took a half-step back.

"Will you give me your faith as well?" she asked.

He exhaled slowly. Ella had believed in him, when his own mother had not. He would not be here without her.

Do you doubt yourself, then?

"Let us go to Etallan, sister, and put that ancient, dusty robe across your shoulders."

"Your Illustriousness," Kelesk breathed, "He was insistent. We could not, surely, restrain an Anandynar royal?" Seeing Tokerae's expression, he added, weakly, "Could we?"

Tokerae pushed past Kelesk into Citriona's room, to find her sprawled and sobbing across her huge bed.

He had been gone for less than a bell.

A sick old man, her grandfather, yet somehow capable of sowing such discord and agony. The man had been on the succession list once, for a few minutes, in some odd political maneuvering during King Restarn's reign, from which he had perhaps taken the misunderstanding that he had influence. Tokerae berated himself for underestimating the hunger of the Anandynar bloodline to hold the throne.

Only one day to coronation.

Citriona's wailing was muffled by velvet pillows. Tokerae swallowed his temper and went to the bed. He sat at her side, gently turning her to face him. He kissed her forehead reassuringly.

She snuffled. "I'm a horrible, horrible girl."

Tokerae wiped tears from her cheek with his thumb. "No. You are quite marvelous. Tell me what has happened."

"I've damaged the honor of our family, grandda says. The honor of the empire. All my fault, if I cede the throne to you." She began to cry again.

As tempted as Tokerae was to go to her grandfather and explain his mistake to him so that he could correct it, that could be loud and messy. This must be handled quietly. Delicately. He thought fast, tugging on lessons from his Cohort education.

To remove conflict, appear to align with both sides.

Tokerae made a long, thoughtful sound, as if considering the matter.

"You know, he might be right."

Citriona gulped a sob, her mouth going slack with surprise. "What?"

"Hear me out, my darling." Tokerae gave her a confident smile. She drew herself to sit up in the bed, a glimmer of hope on her face. "You know your family's history, surely. You must know, then, that in the forming days of the empire, the Nine Families gathered together to hammer out the covenant. It was agreed that the Anandynars would take the throne in perpetuity, and Etallan would be one of the Great Houses."

She hung on his words.

"A very long time ago," Tokerae continued, "but we Etallan gave our word to support the Anandynar monarchy. Your virtuous and noble grandfather is simply pointing out that what we are about to do might seem a breach of that promise. An important point, and not one to be disregarded. Etallan's word is not merely a convenience; it is our bond. If our word cannot be trusted, what are we?"

Citriona's eyes were wide as she nodded.

"You must also know," Tokerae continued, "that in the hundreds of years since this covenant was made, many Etallan worthies have married into the royal Anandynar line, producing heirs, and thus furthering the Anandynar rule. When we have children, you and I, they will be Anandynars, just as those were. Yes?"

"Yes," she said uncertainly.

"I am, surely, Etallan, and worthy." He grinned at her enthusiastic nod. "You are, without question, an Anandynar. What is the difference in this situation?" He raised an eyebrow and waited for her to consider, as if he were a tutor and she his student.

She shook her head slowly, unsure.

"The difference," he said, "is one of name. Mine— Etallan. But names matter, don't they?" He nodded slowly, and she nodded along with him. "Let us not only satisfy the sacred word of my ancestors, but also honor your esteemed grandfather's wishes."

"Tok! Is there a way?"

"There most assuredly is. After I am crowned, I will change my name to Anandynar. In that one act, we gratify not only your grandfather's legitimate concerns, and your wish to cede the monarchy to me, but also the covenant that forms the backbone of our empire."

"Yes," she cried, clapping. "I'll tell him. He'll be so happy."

Tokerae held up a finger. She lost her smile.

"This is a delicate time, my darling. Coronations always are. The time for words has passed, my dear; now is the time for action. Demonstrate your virtue. Let your grandfather see it." When this did not seem to entirely convince her, he added: "You and I will rule together, Citriona. I am simply offering to wear the monarch's target on my back, so that you need not." He smiled wide, hoping this image would settle her final doubts.

"Yes," she said, but her tone did not hold the conviction that he hoped for.

Now what?

He took a breath. This particular metal required a hotter flame to forge. A much hotter flame.

Abruptly, Tokerae's smile was gone. He gave her a disapproving look.

She flinched.

"You seem undecided, dear Citriona," he said sternly. "I can't have that, not with all that I'm doing and risking for you. This matter is far too important for you to have even one small doubt." He stood. "I shall cancel the coronation immediately. Of course, I'll double your guards to keep you safe and have a mage sent for, to protect you against the other mages who will yet come for you."

Her eyes went wide, her expression full of horror. "The coronation is tomorrow. You can't just cancel it." On her knees on the bed, she gripped his hand fiercely, looking up at him. "I understand what you've said, Tok. I won't talk to grandda. Not to anyone. I promise." She looked around the room frantically, fearfully, then back at him. "Please."

Tokerae drew a long, slow breath, giving her every reason to think that he was conflicted.

In a soft voice that was catching in tiny gasps, she said, "I beg you, Tokerae dele Etallan, please be monarch for me."

Ah. Now that was what he had wanted to hear.

He watched her impassively and let the moment stretch, allowing her to consider what might happen to her if he said no.

All at once, he gave her the warmest smile he had.

"As you wish, Your Majesty."

Chapter Twenty-Four

WHAT I MUST.

Tayre stood at the bow of the ship, watching the horizon. He had just seen a subtle swelling at the dark edge of the ocean.

They were nearing the journey's end: Northern Arunkel, the Yarpin harbor.

The ship's crew remained quiet. That would change soon, the moment they caught sight of what he saw.

Tayre had stood at this bow for much of the ship's voyage, finding the vast scope of the Nelar ocean a useful canvas for his churning thoughts and unsettled plans.

What would he do now? If Amarta dua Seer had released him from his sworn word, he would be free to decide as he saw fit.

But she had not, so he remained bound. He reviewed the words of his oath: *help you learn about yourself and the world.*

How was he to do that from across an ocean?

In those last moments, as Amarta's eyes filled with tears, he had done everything he could to get her to say it a third time.

I release you.

She almost had. Almost.

Instead she had gotten Tayre onto this ship by arranging overwhelming force against him, while at the same time dangling the lure that his uncle might still be alive.

Threat and bait, a classic trick. He didn't remember teaching it to her, but she had learned it nonetheless. A better student than he had thought, perhaps. Or perhaps vision had always been her teacher.

The outcome didn't suit him, but he to admit that it was effective work, what she had wrought. Thorough. He would set foot on Arunkel soil, just as she had intended.

He certainly knew what she wanted him to do next: rescue her family.

Would he?

Dirina and Pas had nothing to do with his still-intact contract with Amarta dua Seer. He could even make a compelling argument that letting them die would do more to teach the Seer of Arunkel about herself and the world than anything else he could do. Or not do.

Though to whom he would make that argument, he had no idea. The only person who had witnessed the contract's making was Marisel dua Mage. She would not, he was nearly certain, have any interest in seeing Tayre again, let alone enforcing the words to which he was bound.

Amarta had sent him away. Like a servant. With instructions. That was not the contract.

He saw no way to maintain his part of the bond; his word and honor were compromised. An untenable position, the one into which she had put him. Did she understand what she had done?

Probably not. His welfare had never been a card on the table between them. Nor had he expected it to be. But he had expected to be released before he left her side.

What was there for her in Seuan? He was certain that it was more than merely saving helpless children and slaves. What?

It wasn't that she was tired of him, of that he was certain, from her responses to his touch, even the night before she had maneuvered him onto the ship.

She had foreseen something. What? That he would somehow work against her plans?

He didn't know. He couldn't know. But she was rid of him, at least for now.

Whatever she was doing in Seuan, in time, he thought it likely he would hear, in time. The Seer's exploits could not be kept secret, not at the scope that she shaped events. Reports of her actions would continue to ripple across the world, as had the destruction of the Monks of Revelation, and the drowning of the Island Road. Stories not originally crediting her as the cause now did. On this very ship, sailors told tales of the stranger woman who could raise her arms and draw lightning from the sky, who could pull waves from the ocean.

Sooner or later, Tayre would know what Amarta was doing in Seuan.

For now, though, he must step into his own future.

"Hoi!"

"Land! Land!"

Roars and cheers filled the ship.

～

There is something you need to know.

Tayre descended the ship's ramp, traversed the docks, strode through the gates and into the bustling, stinking capital city of the Arunkel empire. Here he would gather messages, check his caches, assess the political situation, and decide what to do next.

Your uncle is in Sio. Alive, but dying.

He knew what the Seer wanted him to do: find and protect Dirina and Pas, then take them to Sio to look for his uncle. But Sio was a long way from here, and it was a large province.

Amarta had gotten surprisingly good at deception at the last. It might have been a ruse to get him on the ship, her saying that his uncle Sarat was still alive.

But it might not. He needed to be certain, which doubtless she had known.

And in truth, it would not be unlike Sarat to pretend his own death. He had done it before.

With Dirina and Pas at your side, there is a future in which he is restored to health.

He had no choice. Tayre must seek out Sarat. And to do that, he must first find the Seer's family.

So be it.

Tayre located the house outside the city where Dirina and Pas had once lived. It had been given to them by then-Deputy Lord Commander Nalas, before the downfall and execution of the Royal Consort.

Dirina and Pas were long gone, the house staff still employed to keep the place ready for their return.

Tayre made friends with the servants. Over the meal for which they insisted he stay, he told stories and made them laugh. He learned that the staff was as mystified at the departure of their mistress and her son as anyone else.

He also learned that he was not the first to come to asking, and the others had not been nearly as polite.

As he stood at the front door to leave, the housekeeper touched his shoulder. "I hope you find them, ser. With everything that's happened in the city..." her voice dropped. "We worry. If you find them, will you make sure they're safe?"

"I will," he assured her, though he had not yet decided.

As he left, he mused on the situation: an empty house, yet someone was still funding its expensive upkeep. Who?

Whoever they were running from.

~

In the time that Tayre had been gone from Arunkel, staggering political changes had swept through the city and the palace.

He did not even need to ask, merely pause for a moment, as if he were a lost traveler. Whether in tavern or on street, strangers would excitedly tell him all that had happened.

Queen Cern and her children had been killed by an impostor. Brutally beaten. Poisoned. A bloody decapitation. Drowned in the Sennant River, wrapped in priceless tapestries.

The details were both abundant and flexible.

Cern's impostor had then attempted to take the queen's place. The Houses, Etallan in the lead, breached the palace to rescue their beloved queen.

But too late: Cern was dead.

The captured impostor was identified by the lack of a certain royal birthmark on her thigh. The teller would describe the birthmark with prurient relish and inconsistent precision.

The impostor was executed, of course, but in private. There was a good deal of grumbling about this—the people deserved to see it happen, didn't they? That digression led to further complaints about the dull display that had been the hanging of the mutt-traitor.

A disgrace, these modern executions.

Tayre took it all in.

Whatever had truly befallen Cern or her supposed

impostor, there was no question about what happened next: one Citriona Anandynar, an obscure royal, had wed Tokerae dele Etallan at the palace. The next day, she was crowned Queen of the Arunkel Empire.

Stunning enough, those events. But within a tenday, in a shocking move, unprecedented even across Arunkel's bloody and dramatic history, Citriona abdicated the Anandynar throne to Tokerae dele Etallan.

At this point in the story, the teller would typically pause to let the gravity of their words settle on Tayre, then would take a long sip of whatever they were drinking. Thirsty work, Tayre was assured, an unsubtle hint that he might buy them another, which he often did.

Clearly, Etallan was reshaping the governance of the empire. No surprise there, at least not to Tayre; that Great House had been quietly—and expensively—angling for the Anandynar throne for generations.

And Cern?

There had been none of the traditional public funeral rites for the dead queen. The lookalike impostor, if there were one, was not a good enough match for Etallan to display the body as if it were Cern, which they would have done if they could, in order to make Citriona's claim to the throne—and thus Tokerae's—more secure.

So, in all likelihood, Cern was not dead, but alive, escaped, and in hiding.

Could she have taken Dirina and Pas with her?

No, the timing was wrong; Dirina and Pas had left their house while Cern was still queen, well before the Etallan overthrow.

A very nice house it was, too, so something significant must have happened to inspire them to leave. Tayre suspected that they were warned. Were he to track that warning, it would, no doubt, lead back to the palace and new monarch, Tokerae dele Etallan.

But that wasn't the man's name. Tokerae Etallan esse Arunkel. Even that wasn't right, as Tayre understood from drunken lectures and overheard arguments.

The new king was going by the name of Anandynar as well as Etallan, via some intricate legal maneuver in which he claimed rights to both names, then used them interchangeably.

Whatever name the man used, if he or his people had Dirina and Pas, their house would have been repurposed for someone else in the new government rather than held ready in the hopes that whoever had lived there might yet return.

So Tokerae didn't have Dirina and Pas. That meant that they, too, had escaped and were on the run.

At his caches, Tayre selected weapons, money, and what papers he might need.

He came across a writ of safe passage signed by Innel sev Cern esse Arunkel, the former now-executed Lord Commander. Worse than worthless, now; if Tayre presented the writ to authorities today, it would gain him nothing like the liberty that it promised. More likely, he'd be imprisoned and tortured for what he might know.

A shame: he'd worked hard for that priceless passport: he'd tracked the stunningly evasive Amarta across the continent and back again.

Now he had neither.

Despite the years away from Arunkel, Tayre's reputation was solid enough that all he needed to do was to put out the word that he was available and lucrative offers found him.

Tonight, he sat across a table from a broker who knew him as Tukar. She was nearly breathless at the chance to persuade him.

"A year and more," Tayre said, when she had finished describing what she wanted, then shook his head. "This trail is cold."

"Many hunters are still tracking them."

"Many hunters are fools."

"I'll pay you well. Even for rumors." She leaned forward, staring at him intently. "If anyone can find them, Tukar, it's you."

He made an undecided sound. "I won't take a contract."

"For you, none needed."

"There's money behind this. Whose?"

"Get them in hand, Tukar, and I'll pay you a fortune," she grinned, not answering his question.

"An agent of the new monarch?" he suggested.

Her pupils widened, the tightening around her eyes barely discernible. "You know I can't tell you that."

But she already had. He nodded as if accepting her answer.

"Show me," he said.

She eagerly slid a sketch of Dirina and Pas across the table.

The boy was a good deal older than the last time Tayre had seen him, but Tayre knew his face well.

He remembered the first time he had seen Pas, from atop Horse, on a rocky bank, as Amarta, Dirina, and baby Pas gaped at him from the river, trying to free a raft to escape.

It was the first time Tayre had laid eyes on Amarta. He did not yet know what she was. But as she stood from the raft, daring him to shoot her, he saw her courage. His contract had been to apprehend, not to kill, and he was too far away to get them in hand. He had no choice but to lower his bow and began to track them again as they sailed away down the Sennant.

As Tayre left the tavern with the sketch in hand, he thought of how Amarta had looked the last time he had seen her, on the dock in Seute Enta. How changed she was.

In that moment, he had considered taking from his pocket the nals coin she had given him years ago, and dropping it at her feet. He almost had, when it became clear to him that she would force him from her side without releasing him.

But it would have been an empty gesture. He had known then, as he knew now, that nothing but her words could set him free.

She should have released him. It would have been the honorable thing to do.

He could not account for Amarta's honor—that was her business—but the bright line of his own was unmistakable to him: he was still bound to the contract he could not fulfill, a puzzle he did not know how to solve.

But he did know what he would do next: locate Dirina and Pas.

Then, perhaps, he would find out if Amarta had been telling the truth about his uncle.

～

Tayre played out enough coin to find out which other hunters were tracking Dirina and Pas. The list was long. From it he selected the ones most likely to succeed, and began to follow them.

The advantage of a well-trodden path was that it served nearly as well as a map. The disadvantage, of course, was that someone else might find them first.

For a number of days, that seemed increasingly likely; a

crew of three who called themselves the Thorns had a woman and boy tied and hooded on horseback.

Tayre followed the team westward, watching until he was certain that their captives were not Dirina and Pas. From the woman and boy's loud complaints, it was clear that they had tried to convince the Thorns of the same thing.

He abandoned the Thorns and their captives, and began again, trimming his list to those hunters on their way to Sio, reasoning that the Seer would not have told Tayre that he must both save her family and be quick about finding his uncle, if both weren't possible, which strongly implied that they were in the same direction.

Through the mountain and into the province of Mirsda, just north of Sio, Tayre followed the promising path of a hunter he knew, named Kestrel.

There, in open countryside of gently rolling hills, he found Kestrel's various camps. She'd been there at least five days, circling one isolated farmhouse.

The farmhouse had a garden to one side, and black and white goats to the other. A glimpse of a woman washing clothes and the boy at her side was all Tayre needed to be sure Kestrel had found Dirina and Pas.

He doubled back and stepped into Kestrel's camp, crunching leaves and twigs underfoot.

Kestrel whirled and dropped into a defensive crouch. She recognized him and gave a heavy sigh.

He flipped a large, octagonal bronze and gold coin across the distance between them. The Perripin uma-sorin glinted in the air. It landed in the dirt at her feet.

"Walk away, Kestrel, and I'll think favorably of you when our paths cross again."

She scowled back. "I've been on this trail nearly a year, Tukar. They're worth ten or twenty of those."

He grinned. "Not worth anything if you don't have them."

"But they're mine."

Tayre shrugged. "You could fight me for them. I don't recommend it."

Her expression went sour, and she gritted her teeth. "Favorably, you say?" she muttered.

"Very."

Tayre gave her a moment to think.

"All right, damn you."

"Good choice."

While keeping an eye on him, she crouched to pick up the coin.

"I waited six days for the old man and his two adult daughters to go check their hillside snares. That's what I get for being patient." She inhaled. "All right, listen: the woman and boy will be alone this afternoon. The boy is charming, the woman compelling. The old man suspects they're running from something that comes from Yarpin. He doesn't want to know, so if the two of them are gone when he gets back, he won't be surprised, and he'll stay silent about it."

It was good information and she'd offered it freely. "Thank you, Kestrel. I won't forget." Then he pointed east. A silent command.

She grumbled but packed hastily, mounted up on her small horse, and rode off. Tayre followed long enough to be confident that she was gone.

Then he turned back.

～

"Ho, the house!" Tayre called pleasantly, waving at the woman hanging laundry on a line in the afternoon sun.

The boy darted to her side. The two of them looked at him like frightened deer, ready to bolt.

As he approached, Tayre adopted a sincere, self-deprecating smile, hollowed his chest a bit, and ducked his head. He launched into an intriguing story about why he was there, that made him seem harmless, his voice lowering until he was close enough to grab her if he had to.

He stopped, his expression changing. "Amarta sent me, to help you, to see you to safety."

At her sister's name, Dirina dropped back a step. "We don't know what you're talking about," she said unconvincingly.

"There isn't a lot of time, so I'll be direct: there are a number of competent and deadly hunters on your trail, one of whom almost took you captive today."

She gripped her son's hand, wary, but not entirely surprised.

"There's a lot of coin being spent," Tayre added, "to bring you both in. Dirina, look at this."

He offered on his palm the blue and white seashell that Amarta had given him. Dirina's eyes went wide. Her mouth dropped open. She reached forward, then twitched back, looking at Pas as if for direction. The boy stared at Tayre.

For a long moment, no one moved.

"It's yours," Tayre said. "Take it." Pas dropped his mother's hand and darted forward, snatching the shell from Tayre and giving it to his mother.

"Mama? Is it hers?"

"It is." Dirina's look at him was full of intensity, her voice unsteady. "Is she all right?"

"Will you trust my answer?" Tayre asked gently.

The pair exchanged a fast look.

"Yes," Dirina said, though she didn't sound sure.

"She was whole and well when I last saw her."

Quite changed from the Amarta they had known, but no reason to say that.

"Where is she?" Dirina breathed.

That answer, once spoken, could not be unsaid. Tayre considered how the knowledge that Amarta was in Seuan might change Dirina and Pas's course, or impede his efforts to find his uncle.

If he wanted the outcome that the seer had predicted, he ought to take the most probable path, and that meant doing whatever he would naturally be inclined to do. He mulled his obligation and his opportunity.

"Not mine to say," he answered.

"Who are you?" Dirina asked.

Our contract is made, Tayre. Enlon. In all your names and appearances.

The many guises that Tayre had worn through the years —the many names he had used in his time with Amarta dua Seer—flashed through his mind, from the first time he hunted her, thinking her no more than a child, to the moment that he had turned away from her on the dock, a woman commanding enough power to force him to leave.

None of those names would serve.

"Call me Feather," he told her.

~

Tayre improved Dirina and Pas's willingness to leave by describing the hunters coming for them.

"If I had not arrived today," he said, "you would be bound and taken, on your way back to Yarpin, to be put in the hands of the new king and his people, who are not your friends."

He said it soberly, borrowing subtly from Amarta's own accent and cadence.

Dirina looked around the place, and at the clothes on the line, a resolved sadness in her stance. "Again we leave," she murmured.

"I think you'll find me good company," Tayre said warmly. "I know many tales, some from distant and exotic lands. I even have Farliosan stories."

"Really?" Pas asked, brightening.

"Yes." Tayre smiled at the boy. "How quickly can you gather your belongings?"

"Quickly," Pas said.

And they did.

Over the next days, Tayre led them east to cross through the Mirsda foothills. They camped nights at the edge of a wide, shallow river as Tayre considered where to go next.

Your uncle is in Sio.

But where? Sio was a large province.

Tayre thought about Amarta, and how she foresaw. What was most likely?

"Do you know where Nalas is?" Tayre asked Dirina as they walked, hoping for a clue to solve the puzzle.

She shook her head, expression tight with suppressed grief. "He was at the palace during the overthrow. I doubt he survived."

"Well..." Tayre drew the word long, gathering their attention. "I don't think Cern died in the overthrow, as has been advertised. If she had, there would have been a showy funeral to prove it. A lack of a body is no small thing. Thus, she may have escaped. While I wouldn't have you wager on it, Nalas might be with her."

In Dirina's face he read hope, painfully barbed for having been roughly resurrected.

Tayre vividly recalled sitting at his uncle's grave. Sarat had been sick for years with something that couldn't be cured, not for money or magery.

A fabricated death, to force a younger Tayre to go off on his own?

"Where?" Dirina asked as they walked. Her breathing was shallow.

"That, I don't know."

"Then where are we going?" Pas asked him.

Alive, but dying. There is not much time.

Assuming her words were true, Tayre would not have long. He could not search an entire province. That meant that it would somehow be obvious where Sarat was.

Obvious to Tayre.

The moment the thought crossed his mind, he knew the answer.

"Otevan," Tayre said.

"Where the battle was? Where it rained gold?" Pas asked, excited.

Tayre nodded, remembering the sky above the battlefield, how it glittered as bits of sunlight floated down onto the field, covering the ground with a gold snow. That was the moment that the battle's outcome changed.

"Were you there?" Dirina asked. "When Amarta was there?"

Tayre smiled.

"Was it amazing?" Pas asked.

"Yes," Tayre answered. "It was."

Chapter Twenty-Five

AMARTA SPENT the day outside the walls of Seuan, riding a sorog named Tueb. Ahead of her on the saddle, steering the beast, was a Left Thumb rider, outfitted from helmet to boots in black-blue armor.

As they rode through the quiet, spare lands, foresight battered Amarta with dire warnings of the Eufalmo that might cross their paths. Masses of them wandered through vision in ghostly flickers.

Dire in an hour. Here and then, but not here and now.

The sorog plodded forward until Amarta had the Thumb halt. And then again.

It must have seemed insanity itself to the Thumb, what she directed him to do. Slow. Stop. Turn the sorog around to face the way they had come. Then ride full out.

"Stop!" she would cry. Then: "That way!"

Again and again, they would stop. Amarta would climb down the saddle's ladder to the ground, where she would play out powder and unguent from sacks tied to her waist, as the Thumb watched from atop the sorog.

Every time she dipped attractant onto the dirt with a

stick, or touched it to a rock, or a bush, vision would howl to her of lethal peril. Each time, she must nerve herself to complete the mixture with the powdered repellent, focusing intently on the open door of possibility, rather than the dead-end alleyway that solidified with each passing moment, here in the wide-open lands.

Trembling, she would remount.

They would ride and she would do it all again.

Once they saw Eufalmo scouts, far distant, a flickering, colorful thread on a rise that rippled with the heat.

"What to do, Advisor?" the Thumb asked, and Amarta thought she heard a touch of fear in his voice as he stared at the distant scouts. They both knew how fast the Eufalmo could move.

"Wait," Amarta answered. "Wait and I will tell you when to ride."

They stared for long moments. The Thumb's face showed her both fortitude and obedience, and in his composure Amarta saw Seuan's greatness, the courage of every caste, the willingness to sacrifice to keep the Body whole.

She lifted her arm and pointed. "That way. Ride!"

They ran, the sorog's feet thundering against the caked dirt as Amarta gripped the handles to stay in the saddle.

By sunset, Amarta was bone-weary, but satisfied: the job was done. They returned the sorog to its keepers and Amarta walked through the gates of Seuan.

The next day, the swarm did not come to Seuan. But a village far to the east was blanketed. No one survived.

~

The Heart stood in his usual pose, staring out the window, hands clasped behind himself, gray robes falling to the tops of his slippers. On one side was the Ear, watching from behind her face-veil. On the other, the Eye, his mottled, plum-colored tunic wrapped tight, his feet and hands stained to match.

The tight three-person constellation made it quite clear to Amarta that she was the outsider.

They all gazed out the window.

"Tomorrow," Amarta said at last, "the swarm comes."

The Heart snorted in doubt. Amarta looked to the Ear, who did not meet her gaze, and the Eye, who did.

Amarta took a breath. "This swarm will be larger than any that has come before. I led the other one away so that we would have supplies sufficient to repel this one, but only if you—"

The Heart made a sharp gesture to silence her. She paused, waiting for him to speak.

When he did not, she continued. "There will be no leading them away this time, Heart. We must use everything, but at the exact right moments."

"We have repelled the Eufalmo," the Heart said in a low tone. "For centuries. Do not tell us our business."

Amarta fervently wished for Tayre's charm, how he could use words and tone to get his way.

Well, she must try.

She ducked her head. "You are great and wise, my Heart. It is so. Thus you know that the swarm has altered these last decades. To triumph tomorrow, we must change the shape of the swarm, from the first moment we see it. The mangonels on the walls..." In vision, a flaming tarball launched from a metal mangonel, landing in the center of a sea of moving brilliance, yet still the Eufalmo came. "Put the mangonels near the towers."

"You overstep, Advisor," the Heart scolded in rough Seuan, using words to speak down-caste or to an errant child.

Amarta felt herself warm. "Yesterday I saved our city."

"Or you spent precious reserves of attractant and repellent and risked the life of a sorog and Thumb for nothing."

Amarta gaped at the Heart, as shocked by his words as she was by her own lack of having anticipated them. She had spent so much focus on the myriad ways that the swarm could attack tomorrow—*would* attack tomorrow—that she had not foreseen this.

"We know what we are about, Arunkin," he said. "Your advice is unneeded."

Arunkin. Not her title.

She opened her mouth to object, then shut it quickly. Another word now, and he would have her removed from the tower room. That future led nowhere that she wanted to go.

The Eye tilted his head to stare at her.

"What is heard, my sister?" the Heart asked softly.

"Nothing is heard, my Heart," replied the Ear.

"What is seen, my brother?"

"Nothing, Heart."

Pointedly, The Heart did not look at Amarta.

With a sinking feeling, Amarta realized that she had made the most fundamental and foolish of mistakes: preventing a disaster to prove herself. It proved nothing to those who had not seen it coming.

For a moment she saw herself as he must: a small, foreigner woman who somehow knew a few things that she shouldn't, and who was, above all, unknown, with mysterious and threatening agendas.

Unlike the Eufalmo, which he thought he understood.

If this conversation of rising stakes had been a hand of Rochi, it was past time to fold.

But what to do? Tomorrow the swarm would pour over the walls, for the first time in Seuan's long history. Eufalmo would fill the streets, climb the towers, and dig into the castes' understructures where they thought themselves safe. It would be a wound from which the Body of Seuan might never recover.

Amarta thought of how dearly she had paid to stay in Seuan, to be here in the path of approaching carnage. She could be at Tayre's side right now, taking her chances in Arunkel. A far safer bet.

She missed him. Was he there protecting Dirina and Pas, despite the manner in which she had sent him away?

She might never know.

And was there enough time to leave before tomorrow? Save herself and let the city fall?

Memories of Olessio flashed through her mind, of his beautiful smile, of his passion. Of his last moments. Of the Islands as they rose and sank into the ocean. Of Rhaata and his mushroom. The edges of the edges of the possible.

The Heart's expression was stormy. He was, she foresaw, on the verge of ordering her out.

Amarta touched her fist to her chest three times, in the most respectful of manners, her head bowed to the Heart with all the obeisance he might believe he was due.

It was the first time she had done so, and foresight told her it would be the last.

Amarta entered the tower room in the predawn dark, relieved to find that the guards at the bottom of the stairs did not move to bar her way.

The tower room was crowded. Thumbs, Fingers, Eyes, and Ears. The Heart—whether from his own assessment or Amarta's predictions—had summoned a good many people, some of whom Amarta had never seen before.

She looked out the window at the darkness beyond. The future lay in bright, bloody, spiraling strands.

So many paths to failure. Each had its own shape. The shape she intended to fashion out of what was coming was...

Outrageous. Nearly impossible.

The circular tower room had many windows, and some walls. Between two windows, back to the stone, stood a pair, a woman and man. They were from the Left Pointing Finger, a caste that delt with on all things that affected Seuan from the outside, particularly the Eufalmo.

From her studies, Amarta knew that they would be called Tro-Ast and Tro-Etero, First and Second of their caste.

"An error, surely, my Heart," said Tro-Ast earnestly, in reply to something said before Amarta had entered. "A swarm in two masses? It has never happened."

"Confirm," the Heart said sharply to the room at large.

The Ear listened at the window with an ear-cone. She spoke softly. "Smoke and horns. A mass from the west. A mass from the north. It is so."

The Eye signaled with his red lamp. At the tower, lamps flickered in return. "Two masses," the Eye said. "Confirmed."

"Ready defenses," the Heart said.

All across Seuan, horns sounded. Drums beat.

The sky and land slowly lightened, color infusing the scene before them. On the fields outside the walls, forty Left Thumbs in dusted black-blue armor mounted twenty sorogs, two riders each. Wire nets were set across the field at regular intervals by running Feet, who, Amarta noted, wore no armor. Speed was their only defense.

The firepits, each one twenty feet across, were filled with what seemed to be black char and logs, then soaked in streams from liquid bags, carried on the backs of yet more Feet. The kindling glistened.

The Heart gave Amarta a sour look. For a moment, a

future thickened in which she was dragged from the room by masked Thumbs.

"I beg your forgiveness, Heart," she said quickly, humbly. "For my arrogant words yesterday."

He seemed hardly at all appeased by this, but the future shifted.

"Today you will not distract us with your spurious warnings."

"I will not," she agreed.

Inside the walls, at ground level, Right Thumbs arrayed themselves, spiked clubs held high. Various Fingers helped hoist huge cauldrons of hot tar onto platforms that were then cranked to rise up and up to the top of the walls.

Across the city, mangonels glinted dully on rooftops and behind the wall parapets. Thumbs and Fingers stood by, lidded copper pots of ready-fire at their side, and bladders of fast-flame slung across their shoulders.

Deafening warning horns sounded. Through the gate streamed villagers, children on their shoulders, dogs at their feet, alongside the Left Feet who had been preparing the fields. They sprinted as the gates began to roll shut, clearing it just in time. The gates sealed, a great clacking, squealing sound.

In the streets below, those preparing for the swarm moved fast. No two collided, nor did they slow. Amarta had never seen so many people move so smoothly together at such speed.

Amarta had witnessed the battle of Otevan: a morass of men and horses, a chaos of confusion. By comparison, this was a dance.

This practiced, organized, and interlocking system of castes had kept Seuan safe from the Eufalmo for hundreds of years.

In moments, anyone not active in Seuan's defense against

the swarm was gone from sight, deep underground, in sealed, lined shelters that were the most secure vaults the Body had ever devised.

Amarta looked around the tower room, realizing with a dull, almost alarmed surprise that she had come to care about these people. The Eye in his plum robes and stained hands and feet; the veiled Ear with her magnificent voice; the two Tro who were even now speaking urgently about the motion and nature of the Eufalmo; the masked Right Thumbs that vision had shown her so long ago. She even felt fondness for the gray-robed Heart, his hands clasped behind his back as he intently watched through the window.

They were, like people everywhere, trying to survive what the world threw at them. Doing their best to protect those whom they called their own.

Today, if Amarta miscalculated—or could not soon, somehow, manifest the impossible—they would fall.

She would fall with them.

Well, at least there was one uplifting thought to follow that one: unlike all Amarta's previous disasters, in which she had been an unwilling observer of the destruction she had wrought, she would not need to see the outcome. The Eufalmo were fast.

Dawn lit the land.

First came the Eufalmo scouts: a trickling, distant line, sparkling in the first light of the morning sun.

Tro-Ast and Tro-Etero eagerly shared a long-lens.

"Look," Tro-Ast whispered. "Recall four swarms ago? The brown ones in the center, the red ones holding to the edge."

"But in back," whispered Tro-Etero, "the dark blue ones."

"As three swarms ago. Presaging, perhaps, an increase in chewers, and decrease in diggers, as it did then."

"Quiet, now," said the First of the Ear.

Amarta dipped into vision. Future paths flickered and shifted, like slippery, bright needles, that twisted and pierced. She struggled to find the line she wanted, the future she needed.

No one sees everything, Tayre had said.

No, she could not see every uncountable thread of the rippling weave of what was to come, but somehow she must find the essential line that accounted for the central problem: what she foresaw, she altered; what she touched—however lightly—she changed.

An epiphany came to her: the threads were not paths at all. In truth, there was no path forward. There were only moments, like grains of sand on a beach.

"The swarm comes," the Heart said.

On the field outside the walls, all at once, Eufalmo scouts abandoned their line and spread in all directions. The signal of a pending swarm.

"The swarm comes," said the Ear, formally, her ear-cone to the window.

"The swarm comes," echoed the Eye, his long-lens pointing to the distant hills, tracking a line of motion coming toward them, a river that had not been there a moment ago. "And again," he said, sharply, turning his lenses northward.

There, distantly, another line flickered.

Tro-Etero inhaled sharply. "Two masses. Two queens?"

"One swarm, one queen," Amarta answered, knowing it was a risk to speak, but sensing it was time. "They come in two parts, but they will merge... there." She pointed just beyond the still empty field.

Tro-Ast looked in astonishment from Amarta to the Heart. "They have never come this way before, my Heart."

The Heart glared at Amarta, clearly wishing she had kept her predictions to herself.

"Deploy all?" the Eye asked the Heart.

The Heart blinked and blinked again. Then, with obvious reluctance, he looked at Amarta, who gave the smallest of nods.

"Deploy all," the Heart said.

Signals flashed. Horns and drums followed.

Atop the wall, in the streets, on the roofs, people ran, climbed ladders, dashed across the wall's walkway. None looked uncertain; the Body of Seuan knew what to do.

On the hills beyond the field, Eufalmo gathered, a thickening mass, broadening in vibrant color as the sun imbued the land with light.

The two masses of Eufalmo joined at the place where Amarta had pointed. Their sound increased, almost drowning out the horns and drums of the city. It was a deep thrumming, as thousands of drones overlapped, along with a hissing, like a storm coming through trees, and a high whine that set Amarta's pulse racing.

"There!" shouted Tro-Etero, gesturing and raising his voice to be heard. "That snarl! The queen!"

The Eye drew back from his long-lens. "The queen," he confirmed. Then, unexpectedly, he pressed the lens into Amarta's hands. "I have seen," he said. "Now you."

Surprised, Amarta looked through, roaming her sight across the tide of color and motion.

Revulsion hit her in the gut as she saw the Eufalmo swarm up close. She swallowed and swallowed and kept looking.

There: what had seemed from afar perhaps a boulder in the middle of a fast-moving iridescent river was a tight cluster of creatures with backs of red and pink, surrounding an even larger creature, glimmering in the sun.

The queen. She was green and yellow.

So much. So many. Amarta thrust the long-lens back to the Eye, suddenly overcome with an horrific uncertainty that it was too late.

It was. Too late for doubts. Too late by far.

The front line of the Eufalmo swarm reached the first of the great firepits. The mass flowed around and into the hollows in the ground, crawling through the soaked logs and damp char.

From the mangonels on the wall, balls of fire arced into the air. One firepit exploded into a huge blaze, spraying sparks and beetles out in all directions. Then the next and the next.

At the lip of the firepits, some Eufalmo struggled out, leaving those inside to burn. Each time another firepit ignited, the swarm parted around it and streamed past, unslowed.

The twenty large sorogs stood in a line facing the pits and the oncoming swarm. Riders now grabbed poles between which the nets spread tight. Each pole was set into tubes built onto the sides of the saddle, linking the sorogs into pairs, the net between them.

The pairs of sorogs charged forward. As the beasts slammed their huge, heavy feet into the river of Eufalmo, the wire nets scraped the ground, trapping the creatures. First only a few, then more, and the nets filled with Eufalmo.

The sorog pairs, running against the swarm's flow, passed to either side of the blazing pits. As they did, the riders released the tubes. The nets swiveled, dumping the gathered creatures into the firepits. The nets released from the posts and fell atop the pits, like mesh lids on top of some frying dish.

Free of both cargo and nets, the sorogs passed out of the river of Eufalmo to the clear field on the other side, where fresh nets and posts stood ready. They quickly turned, nets between them, and began another forward charge into the flow, mesh nets again scooping up uncountable Eufalmo, and again dumping them into the roaring firepits.

A sorog stumbled in the swirling mass. It turned and turned, disoriented, crying with a high-pitched squealing sound. The mounted Thumbs struggled to steer it out of the tide, using whips to knock away the Eufalmo that crawled or jumped onto the hide of the sorog like fleas. The great beast limped and squealed again, then bit at its own leg, stomping the ground.

The sorog dropped and began to roll against the carpet of Eufalmo attackers, tossing both rider Thumbs wide and into the flow. In a blink, the Thumbs were covered in a blanket of fast-moving, consuming frenzy.

The fallen sorog, still writhing against the swarm, was soon swallowed by the glittering tide, which flowed over the huge beast. In moments all that was left was a flattening lump of streaming color.

The remaining sorogs paired up again, at a row of posts set further back, charging back into the river of Eufalmo with nets spread. This run, another two sorogs stumbled and were lost.

Another run. Another two lost.

Half. Already half the war sorogs—and the Thumbs who rode them—were gone. How many Eufalmo had the sorog pairs dragged into the pits, removed from the oncoming onslaught?

To Amarta, the incoming hoard seemed not at all thinned or slowed.

From the watchtower came horns, flickers of signal lights. The front wave of Eufalmo had reached the outer base of the wall.

In quick succession, atop each of the four sides of Seuan, on each walkway, smoking flames roared to life, ten feet high. Black smoke billowed from the walls, the stench reaching the tower a moment later.

A Left Thumbs pressed a scarf into Amarta's hand. Across the room, everyone wrapped their mouths and noses to protect against the poisonous smoke.

For hundreds of years, Amarta knew, the flame and smoke had been enough to keep the swarm from passing into the city.

The Eye pointed to the burning walkway. At the outer parapet, the fire flickered, sputtered, and went out.

"They douse the flame with their bodies," said Tro-Ast, voice full of awe.

Coming across the wall was a single line of small Eufalmo, running over the bridge made by the charred bodies of those that had come before them, the cause of the fire sputtering.

It had never happened before.

Smoke billowed around the bridge of Eufalmo bodies. If it slowed them, Amarta could not tell.

Now the trickle passed across the inner parapet and began to crawl down the inner wall of Seuan, descending as if gravity had no tug at all.

They were inside Seuan.

The drums sped. The horns sounded. The Heart shouted commands.

As the first of the Eufalmo reached the ground of the city, Thumbs in armor and high boots swung spiked clubs. The

Thumbs were fast, fearless, and they hit decisively, rarely missing.

One on one, the Thumbs did well; a hard blow could crush or kill even a medium-sized Eufalmo, leaving it dead, or injured enough that other Eufalmo paused long enough to eat it.

But the Thumbs were outnumbered.

Atop the wall, the bridge of charred and dead Eufalmo was widening, as more poured over, dousing the flames and smoke to either side.

The Heart's expression was stark. "Advisor," he croaked, turning to her. "Speak. Speak now."

Amarta looked past him, setting her gaze on the Eye and Ear. They looked back.

"Make me the Heart," she said.

"What?" The Heart cried, his mouth pulled back to show teeth. "You insult us! I strip you of your title! Guards—"

Remove her, he was about to say.

From outside, there came the howls and screams of the dying.

In the street below, Thumbs were being overrun by the rising tide. Eufalmo crawled up their legs, across their shoulders, onto their heads, onto their clubs.

One by one the Thumbs fell, still swinging as they were bloodily consumed and sucked down into the carpet of Eufalmo.

"And fourth is truth," Amarta said.

The west wall was a flooding waterfall of luminous, flickering color, as the Eufalmo streamed over the wall and into the city of Seuan.

Chapter Twenty-Six

IN THE STREETS, the screaming stopped.

On the rooftops below the tower room, Thumbs shot bladders of fast-flame and tarballs into the thick tide of Eufalmo that filled the lanes and boulevards of Seuan. Each time, the colorful tide would pause around the splattering flame, then cover the spot, heedless of the deaths of the few required to smother the fire.

The Eufalmo spread, pouring into doors and windows, climbing up the sides of buildings.

The drums stuttered and stopped.

"She comes," the Eye said, pointing.

The queen topped the inner parapet of the wall, her body sparkling green and yellow in the full sun. She paused, looking around at the city, then her horned head swung down and she dropped over the edge, wings fluttering as she slowly drifted past the waterfall of Eufalmo and into the bug-filled streets.

As one, Tro-Ast and Tro-Etero gasped, then gaped at the Heart. Everyone looked at him, awaiting direction.

The Heart's expression was a stark mix of fury and terror.

His lips pulled back into a snarl. He put a hard gaze on Amarta.

Amarta looked past him to the Eye and Ear. "Make me the Heart," she repeated.

"My sister. My Brother." The Heart's voice rose above the droning. "This is not how the Body selects a leader. You cannot."

The Ear took the Eye's hand. She drew him to the window. Urgent words passed between them.

"A foreigner!" The Heart shouted at them. "You might as well bring plague! She'll destroy us all!"

"Without me," Amarta said, just as loudly, "the Body of Seuan dies today."

And her with it.

The queen found her way to a low building rooftop. She leapt to a higher one, her wings abuzz.

She was coming for them, and they knew it. Amarta had more than foreseen it; she had arranged it. A little attractant in just the right places. Amarta trembled.

"Shall I tell you how this will go?" Amarta shouted over the rising, deafening drone that filled the city.

"Tell us, Advisor," said the Ear.

"You will say that the making of the Heart requires a written, fulfilled prediction." Amarta drew from her jacket a small piece of paper. She held it out to the Eye, who glanced at it long enough to read it, and shared it with the Ear. "Now you will say something else."

A bit of performance art. Olessio would be proud.

The Eye and Ear turned to Amarta, their hands raised just as they had in the Kailo, in the moment that they confirmed the Heart of Seuan.

The Heart roared with fury and lunged at Amarta, the flash of a small blade held in his hand.

Coated with poison, vision informed her. One cut, one stab, and Amarta would be dead in moments.

Options splayed out before her. She forced herself to wait as he rushed at her, his deadly knife snaking through the air toward her middle.

Now.

She stepped to the side, twisting. The Heart's stab missed her stomach by the width of the blade. His momentum took him just past her, and she shifted her weight into his thigh, sending him stumbling backward.

He tangled in his robes and fell to the floor, the knife skittering across the stone.

The Eye snatched it up from the ground with his plum-stained hands the moment before the Heart reached him. The Eye turned, blocking the Heart's grasp for the knife with his own body. The Heart swore, using Seuan words Amarta only barely understood.

He charged her again, and vision was vivid: in a moment, his hands would circle her neck, squeezing. She would be helpless to stop her own death. Vision offered one option.

She stood, unmoving, letting her eyes widen as if she were frozen in shock, not as far from the truth as she would have liked. The Heart lunged at her, arms outstretched for her neck.

He closed. Amarta dropped hard to her hands and knees on the stone floor. The Heart tumbled, sailing over her back, sprawling across the floor.

All doubt was gone from his face; he knew what she was, and what she could do. Fear turned to despair as he crawled backward until he reached the wall.

But no one was looking at him now. Or at Amarta.

She followed their gazes to the window.

Green and yellow iridescence filled one of the large

windows as the huge Eufalmo queen grabbed at the edges, compressing herself to crawl inside the room. Once within, she folded her wings into her carapace, and turned her horned head to look at those who stood watching, mouths agape.

No one moved as the multifaceted eyes took them in, glittering like black gemstones. A second set of eyes was below the first, on each side of her head.

The Eye and Ear had lost their composure entirely. They backed away. Tro-Ast and Tro-Etero were crouched on the ground, as if being small might make a difference. Amarta smelled terror and urine.

Only the masked Thumbs retained enough self-possession to advance on the Eufalmo queen. They did, clubs held high. One swung at her head, a hard swing, intended to crush.

In a motion so fast that Amarta simply did not see it, the queen's mandibles snapped out. The Thumb's head had left his body and was now in the queen's too-wide mouth, blood dripping down her thorax. She tossed the head across the room. It bounced off the wall, coming to rest by Tro-Ast and Tro-Etero, who stared at it, stupefied.

"Seer of Arunkel," the Ear whispered urgently from behind her, "you are the Heart of Seuan."

"It is so," hissed the Eye, hastily agreeing.

The queen's eyes stopped roaming the room and settled on Amarta.

～

For a blink, the Thumb at the side of the first froze in shock at the fast demise of his fellow. Then he lunged at the queen, swinging a club at her head with efficient, brutal force.

In a blur, the queen's middle legs snapped forward.

The Thumb bent double. A deep gash in his stomach liberated pink, red, and gray insides that slid down the front of his thighs. Moaning, he groped for the floor and collapsed.

Amarta felt numbly distant, as though in a dream. Vision was keening, telling her that life required motion. Yet at some deep, visceral level, her body insisted that to stay unmoving was the only answer.

Fear, she realized, as her breath came hard and fast, her chest pounding. Simple mortal fear.

The queen turned both sets of eyes on Amarta.

Amarta had imagined this moment. The Heart, Eye, and Ear would witness her courage and power.

But terror, it seemed, had an imagining all its own, that demanded one more labored breath after another at any cost. Even the cost of life itself.

Tayre knew how to handle these moments. What would he do? What would he say?

Slow your exhale. That's right. Again.

She did. And again.

As the Eufalmo queen uncurled fully, it became clear that she had not been at her full height before. She drew herself tall, towering a head and more over the tallest people in the room. Her carapace lifted, her wings emerged, spreading wide and huge, making the already crowded room seem small.

Shades of blue and teal and green rippled across the wings, as if they were painted gossamer silk in a metal frame with edged, sharp points.

Vision was howling. Weeping as well. Much like the huddled Tro-Ast and Tro-Etero on the floor behind Amarta.

She must move.

Shudderingly, Amarta pushed herself to inch forward, a mere toe's advance toward the queen. A tiny step. Now the other foot. Again.

The queen stepped forward to meet her, the creature's dainty feet coming to sharp points.

In so many futures, Amarta would soon die.

Seek doorways, not dead-end alleys. Look for the open spaces.

Into vision. This moment, the next, and back. Again.

Amarta opened her mouth and made sound. In some distant, serrated future, she would know what this meant, these convolutions of tongue, the hisses and clicks that were coming from her throat. Whatever Amarta had just said, she said it again.

The queen stopped advancing. The moment stretched.

Sounds issued from the queen's head, much like the ones Amarta had made, but louder. More certain.

Amarta pressed more sounds from her throat as she circled the present and the future. It felt like something between choking and coughing.

Then, all at once, Amarta understood the meaning of what she was saying to the Eufalmo queen.

I have what you want most. I have it.

Show me, Food, the queen had replied.

Amarta reached into her pocket with shaking hands and drew out a fist-sized black opal that she had taken from the Heart's basement, holding it on a flattened palm so that the queen could see it plainly.

Is mine, the queen replied.

Yes, is yours, Amarta replied. *I have more, this, what you want. But these, like me, you must not kill. They are mine.*

The queen looked around the room.

Is food. Hungry.

Not kill, Amarta insisted. *Not kill any more.*

A pause. Was the queen considering?

Then: Give. All.

Amarta set the opal on the ground and slowly backed away. The queen advanced, bent to take the gemstone in her forefeet, then stood tall, drawing it to her mouth. She exhaled audibly.

The opal's darkness began to lighten. Inside, the milky white swirls began to move, to turn. Bits of the outer crust twitched, cracked, then sloughed to the ground, broken bits of shell.

Inside, something dark began to wetly unfurl. The queen shook the changing thing out like a wet rag, her tongue unrolling, long and thin and covered with small hairs. The queen licked the dangling creature, front, back, and again.

As she did, it uncurled, struggled in her grip. Amarta could now see tiny stubs of wings and a black, iridescent shell straightening in the air.

My prince, the queen hissed at it as it stretched, its wings jerking. *Come alive.* She licked it again. Black wings spread and folded, the newborn creature craning its head to look back at the Eufalmo queen.

I have more of these, Amarta said. *Many more. But you must not kill mine.*

Hungry.

Eat what is dead, but only that. I will give you all the princes. But you must leave now, and take yours with you.

The queen scanned the room. When she returned her stare to Amarta, Amarta saw herself reflected many times in the queen's dark, multifaceted eyes.

No more princes you take, clicked the queen. *No more.*

No more we take, Amarta agreed. *No more.*

In the long moment that followed, Amarta held her breath, wondering if the queen found this conversation as strange as Amarta did.

Time seemed to move very slowly as the queen tucked against her side the wriggling prince that moments ago had seemed no more than a gemstone. She folded her wings and climbed up to crouch in the window.

There she looked out into the city of Seuan, her horned head swinging one way and then the other. She dropped, the buzzing sound of her wings fading as she descended.

~

Trembling so violently that she could barely walk, Amarta stumbled to the window.

The Eufalmo queen had reached the ground. She crawled across the top of the river of Eufalmo that rippled and droned and shifted to swirl around her. At the wall, the queen began to ascend as easily as if it were solid ground.

When she was halfway up the side, the tide of Eufalmo through the city streets contracted and flowed to follow her.

A reverse waterfall, drawing itself up the stoned wall, up and up and over the charred, smoking remains of Eufalmo that filled the walkways, and then down the other side.

As Amarta watched, the entire swarm left the city.

It did not take long. The streets of Seuan were silent and bare. All that remained were scattered bones and metal weapons.

~

Amarta knew that one of the very first things she must do was to make good on her word to the Eufalmo queen.

She asked for the sorog Tueb, to ride out into the countryside, but Tueb was among the fallen, now only bones indistinguishable from other sorog bones, raked into piles, shoveled into carts, and taken to Seuan for use in extracts and salves. Nothing was wasted.

Amarta thought to ride out on a sorog as she had before, perhaps a Thumb or two to guide her. But no—that was not how the Heart of Seuan traveled. A good tencount of sorogs and their armored and weaponed Thumb riders accompanied her, along with Tongues, Fingers, Eye, and Ear.

Amarta led them to the mines, where the opals had originally been found.

Not opals. Princes.

There in the dark caves, Amarta placed the black spheres that she had taken from the Heart's collection, setting them into the soil and rock alongside the white ones from his inner sanctum, which were another sort of Eufalmo.

Back in the city again, Amarta turned to address the first of the Eye. After a moment's thought, she spoke his formal Seuan caste title.

"Ugo-Ast," Amarta said to the Eye, "send messages to all the villages. Tell them that any opals are to be left untouched where they are found. Those belong to the Eufalmo, who will return for them."

Ugo-Ast touched his fist to his chest in obeisance.

"Aka-Ast," Amarta said to the Ear. "Is it good, this message, and how I have said it?"

"Yes, Heart," said Aka-Ast. "It is good. Very good, because it is a clear threat, and they understand such things."

Amarta blinked. So it was.

"The man," said Ugo-Ast. "He must be changed."

Amarta did not at first understand what Ugo-Ast meant, because he had used a word she had not heard before.

The man. He meant the old Heart. And the word *changed*...no. The word meant *ended*.

The old Heart, they were telling her, must die.

They led her to the cell where he was kept. Thumbs unbolted the door, held it open, weapons ready against the man they had once sworn their lives to.

He no longer wore gray robes. He no longer wore

anything at all. No longer of any caste, he had been, literally, stripped.

The old Heart went to his knees on the cell floor before her.

"Casteless," Ugo-Ast said of him. "He is no one."

In the quiet, flat tone of one who has lost everything, the old Heart offered Amarta his life. "It is Seuan tradition, to fortify the new Heart with the blood of the old." He looked up with a wry, bitter smile. "I think you'll find it a singular experience."

There was wisdom in this, Amarta saw. A tidy clarity. It would keep the castes pure, yet also waste nothing.

Amarta caught her breath in shock at her own thoughts.

But was it really so different than the death she had already caused, by accident, at the Tree of Revelation and the Island Road? Death followed her. Was it not better to act with full knowing and intention, to take what life she must, with her eyes open?

I don't know if I like what I am becoming.

Revulsion, fear, and confusion swirled inside her. She backed out of the room, Aka-Ast and Ugo-Ast following.

"No," Amarta told them quietly. "He lives."

"It is our way, Heart," Ugo-Ast said.

"Do I not make our way now?" Amarta breathed.

Aka-Ast spoke softly, sweetly, gently. "Great Heart, until the Kailo, we can override you for your own safety, if we must. Even imprisoned, to leave this man alive threatens you. We cannot allow this."

Ugo-Ast nodded agreement. "Never have two Hearts lived at the same time. It would confuse the Body."

"The Body is not an idiot," Amarta hissed.

"The man wants it," observed Aka-Ast. "His life is over, his usefulness passed. Is it not a mercy to grant him a graceful ending in gratitude for his decades of devotion and service to the Body?"

They were clever, these two, and no surprise; their orders drew from the most capable children of all castes, testing them for years, to see if they were suitable to join the orders that helped the Heart govern.

But those children who fell below the line were not returned to their castes. They had another use: their blood formed the rarest of Seuan elixirs, the one that gave the Heart longevity.

"He lives," Amarta said.

Ugo-Ast and Aka-Ast exchanged looks.

"Feet, hands, tongue," Ugo-Ast said to Amarta, countering.

At Amarta's horrified expression, Aka-Ast spoke again. "He has attacked you, with lethal intent. Do you think he will not try again?"

Feet, hands, tongue.

They were not wrong; the old Heart had spent a lifetime —two lifetimes—ruling the Body of Seuan. Canny and powerful, he might seem broken now, but in time he would recover his ambition and ability. There was no caste to which he could return. Some doors allowed only entrance.

From the future, Amarta heard the drums and drone of her Great Kailo. There, the highest of each caste would offer part of their own bodies to demonstrate devotion to the new Heart. Now she understood the words of the chants: *Skin and bone. Heart and home.*

The people of Seuan were committed to the Body, their loyalty unwavering. Amarta had not known this when she came to Seuan with Tayre. Then she had thought the Heart would help her understand herself.

But she had changed. Who was she now?

Who must she become?

Amarta stode back into the cell, Ugo-Ast and Aka-Ast following. From the floor, the bald, naked man watched her with lidded eyes, waiting to find out his fate.

She met his gaze. "Only the hands."

After some back and forth, Amarta knew, Aka-Ast and Ugo-Ast would agree. They would also consent to teach Amarta to do the act herself.

She must, to gain their full respect. And her own.

The man on the floor stared at her another moment, as full understanding came to him. Then he closed his eyes.

Chapter Twenty-Seven

INNEL WOKE in the dark to howling.

It was not the sincere and devoted howl of someone in true physical pain—fingers being twisted off, or skin slowly sliced from the body. That sort of howl, he knew.

He gave a breathy laugh. "Not like growing up under the old king. Eh, brother?"

The sound continued, disturbing and plaintive. It was a woman's voice, and try as he might, Innel could not shake the feeling that her pain, whatever the cause, must be addressed.

He struggled to his feet, swaying a moment, light-headed. He waited for the sparks in his eyes to pass, then hobbled through the maze of cots and bodies to where the wailing woman lay.

Asleep, from all appearances. He knelt down at her side and laid a hand on her forehead.

Her eyes flickered open. Pale green, they seemed, though the light was dim and he was not sure.

For a moment, Cern's face formed atop hers, thickening with Cern's rounded cheekbones, her dark green eyes with gold specks. The woman muttered in some dialect of Perripin, but Innel heard Cern's voice.

"No, no, no," he said, his voice rising. He yanked his hand back from her head. "I did not betray you. No, your grace."

He took her nearest hand in his own. "Cern, listen to me. I only acted to protect you." Was that the truth? His recollection was hazy.

He must tell her everything. He owed her that much, at least.

But her eyes were closed again. She was snoring, the air catching deep in her throat each breath. He frowned at her. Had Cern been so dark-skinned? He didn't think so, but his mind did not feel so keen, his memory not as solid as perhaps it once had been.

He licked his lips. "My queen." He touched his forehead to her hand, still in his. His nose chose that moment to become very wet—blood, maybe. He rubbed his other hand across his mustache, then wiped it on his trousers, hoping she wouldn't notice.

The truth.

"Cern, I beg you: hear me. When you became pregnant, I changed, I truly did. I put your life and our child's life before my own." A sob escaped his throat. "I did not betray you. Etallan—that's who. They wanted me gone and wanted you weak."

Was that all of it? If he was going to reveal his dark corners, he could not hold back.

"Yes, I admit that I had..." he took a breath. "Thoughts."

Thoughts? Did that even make sense? He shook his head, hoping to clear it, and less than pleased with the results. There was a throbbing behind his eyes.

"Plans, then. I had plans." He was whispering now. "In

case you couldn't hold the throne. But then she was born, and I was remade, my loyalty to you whole and complete."

He waited for her to respond, but she didn't.

"I was set up, Cern. I was played. No excuse, that. I should have known. I'm Cohort." He cleared his throat, then again. "But then, so were they. Only Cohort could have taken me down so thoroughly."

Was she even listening? He shook her hand to get her attention. Her eyes fluttered open.

"What?" she asked in Perripin, blinking at him.

"You must believe me," he said urgently, then turned aside to cough, looking again at her shadowed face. "Cern, you must believe me."

She was squinting at him, straining to raise her head. "Jhoa? Is it you?"

Elation filled him. "Yes, Cern, it's me. It's me."

"Jhoa!" the woman called, gripping his hand tightly with her own. "All that I did. You didn't deserve. Not a moment. I have so much regret."

"No, Cern, the fault is mine. Mine and only mine. I should have told you everything. I failed you. I failed our daughter. I am so very sorry."

A moan escaped her. "I should never have let you go, Jhoa. Never."

"What choice did you have? You allowed me to live. You were merciful."

"So much grief!" She began to cry. Innel felt the sympathetic quivering of his own shaking sobs, deep inside.

It's not her, brother.

"It is her! It is!" Innel shouted at the room.

"Yes, Jhoa. It is me. It is!"

He brought his forehead to hers, and they fumbled to hold each other, their tears mingling.

~

Innel came awake, rather more clear-headed than he liked. He looked around the dark room, its dingy canvas dome, and stinking inhabitants.

There was a solution: he took from his pocket the envelope of waxed paper. Too thin; within he found only a few corners of broken qualan rectangles.

He tongued the paper, taking the crumbs into his mouth. No part of his gums, under-tongue, or cheeks was free of small wounds. He tucked the bits back and back, where it hurt less, then lay down again, waiting for the thoughts to go away.

Suddenly he was aware of a figure, sitting at his side.

"I didn't know," Innel muttered to him. "About you and Taba. Did you like her a lot?"

A thoughtful sound. *I would say so, yes.*

Innel remembered the small cabin on Taba's ship and how hard she had hit him.

"She liked you a good deal as well."

A small chuckle. We talked of marriage, if you can believe it. Though she doubted my sincerity.

Innel nodded. "More sense to wed a House than the crown, I assure you." Innel gave a short laugh. It turned into a cough. "Taba could have been Eparch."

Could have. She didn't want it.

Innel considered. "Were you sincere, brother?"

A passel of little Helatan babies? With her height and mine, they wouldn't have been little for long. Yes, I was. I was on the verge of stepping back from the contest with you, giving you a clear path to Cern, so that I could say yes to Taba.

Innel smiled at the thought of his brother having children, and that brought him to his own daughter and how she had looked as she stared at him from the bed, nestled in her mother's arms.

It hit him like a blow: his brother could have had children. If Innel hadn't killed him first.

Innel hunched on the cot, his stomach roiling. He leaned over and heaved a wet, smelly bit of something from his stomach onto the stone floor, feeling some pride that he had missed his bedding.

Distantly, someone swore loudly in Seuan. Two youths came by. Sullenly they cleaned up Innel's mess.

He lay on his back to stare up at the dark, curved ceiling, letting the qualan do its magic.

Some time later, one of the proprietors bent over him, standing. A woman. She scowled down.

"You take too much at once," she scolded. "Save some for later in the day, after the meal. Then it will not upset your stomach."

Innel scoffed. "It is not enough." He gestured at the ceiling. "Not enough. None of this is enough."

She made a disgusted sound. "Is plenty." She turned to leave.

"Wait." Innel struggled to a sitting position. He pulled out a chain from under his soiled shirt, tugging it over his head. He held it up to her. "Will this buy me more?"

She inspected the gold chain. "Will buy much more, yes. But we do not recommend this."

"I don't care. I want more. All of it. Today. Now."

"We do not recommend this."

"You said that already."

~

I nnel impatiently waited for the proprietor to return with
his qualan.

Pohut had been right, of course: the wailing woman had
not been Cern. Innel found his mind clearing, thoughts
returning like birds to a roost.

He sat up on his cot, considering the hundreds of figures
scattered around the dim room. Most lay unmoving, some
on their bedding, others on the floor. A few sat up, as he was
doing.

He wondered if any of them had qualan to spare and
could be persuaded to part with it.

How, he wondered, had each of them come to be here?
Were their journeys anything like his own?

Flashes of his former life went through his mind. So
much time spent in the struggle to ascend. One rung at a
time, as his brother used to say.

And to gain what? Enough height to fall and fall hard.

Innel lay back, glad to at last be free of the desire to gain
anything or ascend anywhere.

"I think I might be ready to go, brother," he said to
Pohut. "To the Beyond, where you are. Then I could tell
you..."

What? How sorry he was?

The land of the Beyond, if it existed at all, and there was
only one way to find out.

He waited for his brother's reply, but none came. No
surprise—he wasn't really there.

Innel chuckled at his own mind, gone so soft. Like mud.
Like the sand at the bottom of a lake. Like sewage.

He liked how the humor felt in his throat, so he tried it
again. The room seemed to chuckle back, a strange
companion that made everything even funnier.

He looked around for someone to share his mirth, but no

one looked back. Even the woman with whom he had cried before lay unmoving. All these people, but he was alone.

Had been alone for a long time. Since the night he had killed his brother.

He had surely killed the rest of his family as well. Likely his mother and sister had been made gruesome examples to further atone for the traitor's crimes.

Perhaps not his sister Cahlen, though; she was an unpredictable mix of simple and brilliant. She might well have slipped through the cracks, like a bird easing itself through bars that had been too close-set for escape until necessity demanded it.

Innel knew all about necessity. Raised to do whatever was needed to achieve—what?

Cern, certainly. Power, assuredly. Wealth, of course.

They had been brought to the palace so young, he and Pohut, thrust into the princess's brutal Cohort. Innocent, malleable, and entirely unprepared for the cutthroat nature of their companions.

Not his fault, what he had become. Catch a child early enough, and you could train it to anything. Turn it into any sort of monster.

By that rationale, Innel could justify every event to which he had put his hand, at any moment along the rocky path of his life. He imagined a steepening trail up a treacherous, bleak mountainside. Could he hope for a plateau at the top? A final cliff?

That thought led to another, one both simple and surprising, that his lifelong efforts to court and marry Cern, to gather influence, to father the heir of the empire, had been, at their core, no more than to show himself equal to the House scions with whom he was raised. He had gained an adult body, and more coins with which to wager, but otherwise little had changed from the posturing and skirmishes of the play yard, when it had seemed so important to prove himself worthy to his Cohort sibs.

Innel snorted in amusement at the realization that this now seemed a meager achievement, a dismally low rung of the ladder to grasp for.

Every one of his Cohort sibs had been similarly educated to reach for power, to hold it at all costs. But to what end? No one ever asked. The goal was assumed to be self-evident.

With astonishment, Innel realized that he had not been ambitious enough. Not nearly enough. So much struggle, and yet he had settled for what he had been taught to want.

It was, perhaps, the greatest absurdity he had ever witnessed: that even with his moments of fabulous power, he had not reached for what he really desired, because he had never stopped to ask himself what that might be.

Once he started laughing, it was hard to stop. He laughed so hard that his bladder began to leak into his pants. His convulsing turned into a fit of coughing, which brought to mind the old king Restarn in his final days, hunched and hacking out his life in his grand bed. How Innel must have seemed to the old man: young and vital and full of arrogant demands and foolish confidence.

That, too, struck Innel as outrageously funny. He fell into another fit of giggling and snorting.

When the proprietor returned to Innel with more qualan, warning him that to take all of what she was giving him now would be the last thing he did, Innel was still laughing.

~

I nnel smiled through the pain in his mouth. He looked around the dimness of the Den and came to a conclusion.

It took a bit of time to get to his feet, and exceptional effort to stay there. He shuffled around the maze of cots. Under the glare of the proprietor's scowl, he pushed out into the day.

The sky was mercifully overcast, yet still too bright. He stood blinking, eyes adjusting.

As near as the Den was to the ocean, it took Innel a good while to get there. The stone road was gapped and cracked, holes filled with slippery sand, so he must move forward slowly, keeping his eyes on the ground so that he did not fall. Once down, he was not sure he could get up again.

With each hesitant step he felt his brother at his side. He dared not look, for fear that he wouldn't be there if he did. Innel wanted him there, now especially.

The road ended at a crumbling edge, where rocks and sand were kept from merging with the ocean below by virtue of determined scrub and hard grasses.

Innel gratefully let himself down to the ground. He trembled. Not from the cold sea breeze, or fear of falling; simply the exertion that it had taken him to get here.

Innel slid his feet over the cliff's edge and looked down. The ocean crashed against rocks below. Swirls of green-gray seawater roiled around huge boulders.

Thirty feet. Forty, maybe. It should be enough.

The coward's way, brother? Pohut asked.

"I am already a coward," Innel whispered.

You owe me.

Innel exhaled, his gaze tracking distant whitecaps as they slowly rolled toward the shores of Seute Enta. In the air, seagulls soared and dove and rose again.

"Yes, I owe you," Innel agreed, a lump in his throat. He looked at the drop below. "Will this pay off my debt, brother?"

No, not even close.

Innel blinked in dull surprise. "If not this, then what?"

Your life.

"My life," Innel agreed, as he fumbled into his pocket for the rest of the qualan. It was enough to make these last moments a certainty.

Not your death, little brother. Your life.

Innel paused, the substantial envelope of qualan resting in one hand. "What do you mean?"

No fall today. No rocks below. No ocean of qualan to sweep away your pain.

Innel shook his head. "But I killed you. I deserve death."

What do I know of what you deserve? Ask the Dragon Sun. The Serpent Moon. The Fates of the Wind. You owe me, is what I know, and I tell you this: you live.

"But, brother, I want to be done. To rest."

No rest. You owe me a life.

"No rest?" Innel gripped the envelope of qualan so tightly that it crumbled in his fist. "No rest?"

No endings today, brother. Go back and live.

Innel heard himself wail in anguish, a long, high sound that mixed with the screaming of the gulls, and continued in his ears even when he paused to draw his next breath.

Chapter Twenty-Eight

JOLON AL OTEVAN and his shaota mare arrived home at Ote, cantering their way along the familiar roads, and stopping at the fork that led, in one direction, to the elders' longhouse, and in the other to the shaota rounds.

He slid off the side and gave his mare an affectionate pat. "Thank you for carrying me. There is no measure for my gratitude and joy."

In reply, his shaota snorted, infusing the air between them with a warm horse scent. She turned and trotted off for feed and water and a rubdown from the youngers of the tribe, many of whom lived in the roundhouses among the small horses.

Jolon wanted his own feed and water, but no time. Not with what he had just seen.

To be gone from home three days, as he had been, meant that he now strode past friendly questions and curious looks. Where had he been? What had he seen? He smiled, waving them off for later.

Likely they'd all know soon enough.

Jolon had been returning from Mirsda, riding the High

Serpent's Tooth Trail. He and his mare paused at the top peak. While she wandered the crest of the crown, sampling delicacies that only grew here, Jolon looked out across the west valley to see what could be seen.

There, approaching Otevan on the Lower Creek Road, was a company of at least fifty. At this distance there was no making out faces, but there was no question that they were Arunkin.

Not the usual refugees and discontents who found their way to Otevan, not in those numbers. Arunkin refugees usually came in singles or pairs, perhaps as many as four or five. Rarely with children and dogs.

They had a few of the dumb, oversized Arunkin horses. At the center rode a woman and child.

Jolon watched a long moment. There was something about this ragged group, approaching his land, that drew his eye. What was it?

They were trying to appear other than they were. Those at the perimeter were watching the woods as if they expected attack. Their clothes were oddly lumped with what Jolon guessed were weapons.

Arunkin, bringing secrets to Otevan.

Again.

A visit from this many Arunkin was usually trouble. Whatever treaty was in force was only as reliable as the latest monarch's word, and their most recent peace treaty—the one that had ended what Arunkel called the Battle of Otevan, and the Teva called the latest Arunkel invasion—had been signed by Cern esse Arunkel, who was reputed to be dead.

When that news had arrived, the Teva had gathered to discuss. Elders, Jolon, Mara, and anyone else who wanted to. Would the new monarch honor the treaty?

History said no. That meant that, sooner or later, Arunkel would come to Otevan with demands.

This time, perhaps sooner.

Jolon whistled for his shaota. Mounting up, he asked his mare to run. She did.

At the longhouse, breathing hard, Jolon pushed open the swinging door.

His mother-elders sat together, working fleece into cord, fingers flying.

"Jolon. From where do you return?"

First Mother wore orange, as always. Second Mother wore blue. Jolon had no idea why. One of the many mysteries of his parents.

Both mothers set down their work on the table, staring distantly, eyes clouded with white.

Their sight was nearly gone, but their minds were keen, and their affection for each other as strong as it had been before father had gone back to ground and sky.

If he were to answer First Mother, Jolon must say that he had gone to Mirsda to see Gallelon dua Mage, to ask him to come to look at their eyes. But this had been a point of contention between Jolon and his mothers, so he hesitated.

"Let us be, Jolon," First Mother had said many times. "The darkness is our reward for long service: we no longer must see the pain of the world. That burden is now yours."

Part of his burden, Jolon was coming to understand, was to sometimes disagree with his wise mothers. So he had ridden to Mirsda to visit Gallelon, who had years ago gained the nearly unheard of bestowal of a shaota filly, offered in the Teva tribe's profound gratitude for the mage's help with Arunkel's most recent invasion.

Jolon told the mage that he was there to check on the shaota, and remind him that shaota were not like other horses, that his young one must know her own kind to properly understand herself. Jolon invited the mage to visit

Otevan, working in what he hoped was a casual question about his mothers' eyes.

The mage was not fooled. "I am not in the business of healing," he had said. "I will come, for my shaota. But that is all."

Jolon had returned home. At his lack of answer, First Mother smiled a little. Had she known where he had gone?

"What urgency do you bring, Jolon, with your hard ride and fast breath?" Second Mother asked.

"Arunkel is at our borders. Fifty by my count. Some armed."

"Another invasion?" asked First Mother.

Second Mother cocked her head. "It has been welcome years since Arunkel has troubled us."

Jolon shook his head. "Perhaps not force. A woman with a child rides one of their huge horses."

"The dead queen, come to give greetings?"

First mother tilted her head sideways, gently touching second Mother's Shoulder. "I told you it would come to this."

"You did, My One, you did."

"Go meet them, Jolon."

"If they want sanctuary, mothers, what am I to say?"

"Listen to your reason and sense, Jolon," said First Mother. "And Mara's. You are both Teva leaders. Now is a moment in which we must be led."

Jolon objected. "But you are the wise ones."

"Tell us what seems wise to you," replied Second Mother, "and we will tell you if we think you are mistaken."

Jolon shifted from foot to foot, considering, uneasy to have such an important matter in his hands when before him sat the guidance he always had relied on.

"Our treaty with the Arunkel queen says nothing of sanctuary," he said. "It speaks of our independence, of mutual fosterage of heirs. So we cannot look to the treaty for answers."

He paused to give his mothers a chance to tell him he was wrong. They did not. He continued.

"No Arunkel monarch has ever asked sanctuary of us before. So neither can we look to the past for answers."

He waited. Still they said nothing.

"Whoever they are," Jolon said, "I say we treat them as we would any who come to us to ask our help."

His mothers were quietly attentive.

"Well?" he asked, feeling the press of Arunkel, soon to be at Otevan's border. "Am I mistaken, mothers?"

"Do you hear us speak?" asked First Mother.

"We are silent," answered Second Mother.

Jolon and Mara arrived at the crossing, at the line of trees and boulders that marked the boundary of Otevan, just as the Arunkin group came into view. From atop their shaota, they gazed down and across the company of fifty or so Arunkin, children, horses, and dogs. All drew to a stop.

After a moment, the company parted to allow the woman on horseback to approach them. She was dressed in fine clothes, rumpled and dirty by Arunkin standards. The woman met Jolon and Mara's gaze.

"I am Jolon al Otevan," he told her. "This is my sister, Mara. We hold authority to speak for the elders of Otevan."

Well, according to the mothers, he was already an elder, but he couldn't quite bring himself to say that yet.

From the horse, the woman looked as though she were about to speak. She nodded once, drew breath, then exhaled silently.

As she continued to say nothing, Jolon and Mara exchanged a confused look.

A moment later, another section of the group parted. A woman, poorly dressed, stepped out from behind others.

"I am Cern esse Arunkel," the woman said to Jolon.

Jolon nodded slowly. "I know your face, monarch."

"As I know yours, Jolon al Otevan, from the signing of my country's treaty with the Teva." Cern raised the clasped hand of a wide-eyed child at her side. "This is Estarna, my firstborn, heir to the Arunkel throne." She gestured to a woman at her side, onto whose back was strapped a baby. "This is my second child, Nipatas. Both are suitable under treaty for fosterage with the Teva. I ask entrance to Otevan for myself and my company under the terms of the treaty."

Jolon gave her a deeply puzzled frown. "You are here for the treaty? You come for fosterage? These ones are years too young, I think, monarch."

Cern took a breath. "Also, we seek shelter."

"Ah," Jolon replied, less surprised. "Then we must ask you the same questions we ask all who come to our lands."

"What? We have a treaty." This affronted reply came from the gray-haired woman to the queen's other side, who Jolon recognized from the battle of Otevan as the general, Lismar Anandynar. "You address Her Most Excellent Majesty, Cern esse Arunkel etau Restarn esau Niala the Conqueror, and you have questions?"

Cern put a hand on Lismar's arm. "I will answer, Jolon al Otevan. Ask."

Jolon took a breath, nerving himself. "Tell us true, Cern esse Arunkel etau Nipatas Two: why do you come to our border?"

Her eyes crinkled slightly, briefly. In amusement, Jolon thought, at his naming her lineage with the first Arunkel monarch to sign a treaty with the Teva, who was also the namesake of her son.

"I tell you true," Cern replied formally. "I have sent two companies like my own in other directions, pretending to be me, to mislead pursuit. To arrive here safely, I pay with their lives. This weighs heavily on me. But I and my children must survive if my throne and empire are to be restored." Her voice dropped. "We are in dire need of a place to hide. We ask Otevan's mercy and sanctuary."

The plea was clear, and her tone unexpectedly humble. It tugged at Jolon.

"Who chases you here?" Jolon asked.

Cern inhaled, and on her face he saw anger, flickering as if firelight. "The usurper, Tokerae Etallan, who has in highest and most reprehensible treason lied and murdered to stand in my place. His time will come."

Jolon exchanged a worried look with Mara. What were they inviting into their home, to let this woman and her people enter their lands, with the trouble that was following her?

Jolon felt the many eyes on him now, waiting for his decision. But he also felt the many more in Otevan who depended on his correct thinking today.

Clearing his throat, he asked, "What do you offer Otevan, and all those who live here, in exchange for this refuge?"

Lismar's expression turned to outrage. Cern gripped her aunt's shoulder tightly. The older woman closed her mouth on whatever she had been about to say.

"We have coin," Cern answered. "Some weapons. These horses." She took a breath. "But our best treasure is our hands, our minds. What we know and have seen. What we can do. We offer freely any service we may be to the Teva and the people of Otevan."

It was a good answer. Jolon nodded. "Lastly, I ask you this: do you give us your sacred word that once you are on our lands, you will respect all those who live here as your equals, and adhere to Teva governance, even when it does not please you?"

Frowns and mutterings rippled through the company. Jolon was telling them, quite clearly, that in Otevan, Cern was not a queen. Not even an aristocrat.

From their faces, Jolon judged this difficult to swallow. One by one, all the Arunkin looked at Cern. She looked at Jolon.

"I do so offer my sacred word and oath," Cern said to Jolon. She turned, meeting the gazes of her people. "I bind you, each and every one, to the same pledge I now make: we respect all who live in Otevan as our equals, and adhere to Teva governance."

Jolon looked across the uneasy Arunkin faces to see if Cern's sincerity was reflected there.

As their many gazes came back to him, awaiting his next words, Jolon felt unsettled. How was he to decide? He gave Mara an inquiring look. Her hand on her shaota's shoulder shaped assent.

Listen to your reason and sense, Jolon. And Mara's.

Jolon might well live long enough to lead Otevan for many years. If his decision was not a good one, he could have a long time to regret it.

He gazed at Estarna, the young Arunkel heir standing at her mother's side. She returned his look. For a moment, Jolon imagined her as a grown woman.

At last, he took a breath. "Cern esse Arunkel and company, welcome to Otevan. We Teva offer you and your people our sanctuary."

Chapter Twenty-Nine

TAYRE HAD NOT BEEN to Otevan in years.

He had been traveling with the Arunkel army, under the command of the former Lord Commander and Royal Consort, Innel sev Cern esse Arunkel. Disguised as one of the troops, he trailed a prison wagon, eating and joking alongside guards who called the captive inside Innel's whore.

During that trip, Tayre had seen the Battle of Otevan and the rain of gold that ended it. If by some chance his uncle were indeed still alive, that would be a tale to tell.

Tayre's purpose that trip had been to give Amarta what aid he could. It took considerable planning to get into the small, hot prison wagon with her for even a moment. There he told her that while the man who held her captive and contract-bound was dangerous and powerful, Amarta was as well.

He is a wolf. But so are you.

As Tayre hiked the road to Otevan with the Seer's sister and nephew at his side, he wondered if Amarta's ability to force him onto a ship at Seute Enta had begun that day, in that wagon.

An amusing thought, that perhaps he had done his work too well to help the Seer of Arunkel understand herself and her place in the world.

This time, there was no advantage to stealth, nor would it go well if Tayre, Dirina, and Pas were discovered by the Teva who regularly patrolled the borders.

So they approached Otevan in daylight, openly, waiting at the border until a fourcount of Teva found them, coming into view atop their small chestnut-and-ocher striped shaota horses.

The Teva drew bows, holding them at the ready. Their quick, assessing gazes took in the three of them. Once, twice, and thrice. The bows lowered.

"Hoi, strangers," said one Teva from atop her shaota. "You stand at the border of Otevan. What do you want here?"

Tayre looked at Dirina and waited for her to speak. Earlier, Tayre had told her what he knew of the Teva, along with his best advice on how to get them across the border.

"We are friends of the Teva," Dirina answered. "I owe Jolon and Mara my life, along with the lives of my son and my sister."

My sister. Dirina knew better than to name the increasingly famous Amarta.

Amarta. The Seer of Arunkel. Tayre wondered how many more names and titles she would amass in her lifetime.

With that thought, in a flash, Tayre knew something of what Amarta intended in Seuan. He smiled inwardly. He would know soon enough if he were right; news of that magnitude, that Seuan had a new Heart, would not take long to reach them, even this far away.

Dirina's mention of Jolon and Mara was enough to get the three of them into Otevan, where they were taken to the town of Ote.

If Otevan had a capital, it was Ote. The town, if it could be called that, was a sprawling collection of structures, both linear and circular, some built into trees, mounds, clefts, and ponds. Teva and shaota horses intermingled everywhere, and there were few structures that did not easily accommodate both.

The three of them were taken into a longhouse with high ceilings and swinging double doors that would easily admit two shaota side by side, should they care to enter that way.

Within, two women elders were in animated conversation with a man and woman. In a moment, there were cries of joy, handclasping, and embracing, as Jolon, Mara, Dirina, and Pas all recognized each other.

"How high you stand!" said Jolon to Pas.

Mara's face was lit with delight. "We must see how you ride, Pas."

Jolon turned to Dirina. "What of Amarta?"

Dirina's expression went sober. She shook her head. "We don't know."

Introduced as Feather, Tayre studied this warm reunion, smiling and nodding in the Arunkin fashion, but infusing his words and subtler motions with the lightest of Teva mannerisms to inspire a sense of familiarity. When it was Tayre's turn to handclasp each of the four Teva leaders, he echoed their movements, cupping his palm as they did, directing his gaze as they did.

He could ask them about his uncle, perhaps name the many names he had known Sarat by.

But no—it would be best to wait until they were settled to take advantage of this connection.

With the Teva leaders smoothing the way, Tayre, Dirina, and Pas were welcomed in the nearby town of Hanatha and given a small room to call their own.

Ote was a long stone's throw and a short walk from

Hanatha. Close they might be, but the towns could not be less similar. As the Hanathan joke went, Ote was for shaota, not the Teva who rode them.

Hanatha was a traditional town, with rows of houses, shops, and public squares. It boasted water wells, good streets, and an impressive set of now-famous double walls, which Tayre knew had been the key to the town's defense against the Arunkin invasion.

Hanatha and the many farms surrounding were populated by those who had gained Teva sanctuary. They gladly provided produce, meat, eggs, and cheese for all of Hanatha and Ote. Under Teva rule, no one paid for food and shelter, and coin was mostly for amusement. Or dealing with foreigners.

In their Hanatha room, Tayre put his bag down and left Dirina and Pas to hunt for his uncle.

~

Tayre's hunt took him to one large Hanathan rooming house after another, thick with Arunkel veterans. Deserters, some outside of Otevan might call them.

"A grizzled old beast," Tayre said, again and again, deciding not to bother with a long list of names. "Tells fabulous stories about battle, sex, and wealth that can't be true, but somehow you believe him anyway. Sick, I hear."

Tayre entered eight rooms before he found him.

"Took you long enough, boy."

The man who had raised Tayre, who had taught him his trade, barked a hoarse laugh from the bed. Sarat struggled to sit up, failed, coughed and coughed again, but all the while, he wore a wide grin.

With a glance Tayre took in the room, noting the scent and signs of serious decline. Two boys sat at Sarat's side, staring curiously at Tayre. At the old man's rasped order, they reluctantly left the room.

Tayre's first touch went to his uncle's head. He raised the lids on each of the man's eyes to see the color. Amarta's prediction had been right: Sarat was declining fast. His complexion was pale, his body far too thin.

"Stop that," Sarat muttered, pulling away.

Still stubborn, though.

"Almost missed me," Sarat whispered hoarsely, his voice betraying emotion.

"I'm here now."

Tayre sat and took his uncle's arm, tracing his fingers down from neck to atrophied arm to wrist, to feel the pulse.

"Too late for all this fuss," Sarat said, annoyed, but he didn't resist.

"We'll see."

~

S arat had as many reputations as Tayre had names. He was widely known to have served in various armies and fought at a number of memorable battles.

Most of that was true. Certainly it was true that wherever veterans gathered, Sarat was welcome.

Each time Sarat had slipped death's grasp—and there had been many—a fine story traveled wide, rooting deep into the bedrock of truth while liberally intertwined with whatever branches, leaves, and fruit Sarat judged the locals would appreciate.

Sarat knew how to sway people to his side, though ask any one of them, and they would swear it was their idea. Even now, sick and infirm and bedridden, Dirina cared for him nearly every moment, pushing aside the boys who had been doing the job. Pas found Sarat so absorbing that he slept at his side.

Tayre encouraged them. It left him free to work on the puzzle of how to make the Seer's prediction come true.

~

With Dirina and Pas at your side, there is a future in which he is restored to health.

Tayre wandered the streets of Hanatha, musing on the Seer's words. He left Hanatha and walked the road to Ote.

What would he be doing, if he were right now on the path to the future that Amarta had dangled as bait?

He would be thinking about how to get there. What else?

He would be looking for circumstances that somehow connected to Dirina and Pas, that might not otherwise have happened.

Such as his personal connection to the young Teva leader, Jolon. Thus Tayre had immediately begun befriending the Teva leader, as quickly as he could, while making it seem entirely natural. He had already wandered through Ote with Jolon, encouraging him to talk, to tell Tayre about his land and people and shaota. His concerns.

Now Tayre walked the curling paths of Ote. There was hardly a straight road through the Teva town. They twisted and turned, doubled back, snaked through tiered roundhouses at one level and exited at another. Some paths topped hillocks, passing terraced gardens, or bridged over—or wandered through—the small river that cut through the town.

Shaota wandered freely, nosing open doors wherever their shaota ways took them.

Tayre paused. A Teva man sat on a log, sharpening a large knife on a whetstone.

"Where might I find Jolon?"

The Teva looked up. Without a hint of friendliness, he tilted his head along the curving road.

Tayre thanked him and continued, coming to a clearing. There Jolon and other Teva talked with a large group of newly arrived, weary-looking Arunkin refugees. Teva would leave with small bunches of them, some in the direction of the elder's longhouse, others to Hanatha.

Tayre watched a time, studying the group, listening and reading lips to understand what was said too softly to hear.

When the busy Jolon at last noticed him, Tayre waved, smiled, and said he would come back later.

Tayre returned to Hanatha, passing through the gates of the town, the double walls, the straight streets, to the room where his uncle lay abed.

Dirina sat at Sarat's side, his hand clasped in both of hers. She was laughing at something Sarat had just said. Pas, his face full of eager attention, sat on Sarat's other side.

His uncle paused in his story and looked at Tayre in the doorway.

"What is known to you, Tavun?"

Tavun was Tayre's childhood name, and the question was a familiar greeting between them.

More than a greeting, it was a teaching. Sarat had always required an answer.

Find the unknown, Sarat had taught him. Make it known to you.

That was a good part of why Tayre had taken the contact with Amarta: to understand.

But instead of answering, Tayre turned his full attention on Dirina. She looked back, puzzled.

"What is it?"

"A company of Arunkin has just arrived in Otevan,"

Tayre said. "I heard the name of someone in the longhouse, with the elders. Nalas."

Dirina shook her head adamantly, tone hard and bleak. "It can't be him. Some other."

"It can," Tayre replied. "And I have reason to believe that it is." Tayre knew that Cern was in that same longhouse, but that he would not say. "Dirina," he said gently. "Go and find out."

That was all it took: hope won. She and Pas were out the door.

Tayre studied his uncle as he walked to his side, adjusting the chair that Dirina had just vacated, and seating himself there.

"All this time," Tayre said, "you were still alive."

His uncle grinned. "Setting you free, Tavun. Feather— that name I recall. Tayre's a new one on me. You know, I think I've heard of you." The grin widened.

Our contract is made, Tayre. Enlon. In all your names and appearances.

By whatever name, he was still bound to Amarta, and so he carried the nals coin she had given him.

How better to learn about the world than for you to choose our way forward? he had once asked her. How well she had learned that lesson. In the end, that was exactly what she had done: choose her own way forward.

Without him. But she had given Tayre a final gift, if he could manage to lay hands on it.

Tayre touched Sarat's spotted, thin arm. "What is known to me is this: I have reunited a family, and thus fulfilled an obligation thrust upon me, in the service of something that I have long sought, something I may yet find. Soon, I hope. What is known to you, uncle?"

Sarat exhaled a humorless, throaty laugh. "The invincible

adversary is just outside the door. This time, Tav, I think I must go with him. I am out of road."

The conversation that Tayre had meant to have with Jolon today, and would certainly have with him by nightfall, had to do with the visitor that Jolon was expecting tomorrow. During their conversations, Jolon had come to trust the Arunkin stranger named Feather, and had confided in him that he had a problem he did not know how to solve.

Jolon had persuaded a shaota-bound mage to visit Otevan, hoping beyond hope to convince the mage to heal the Teva Elders' eyes. But the mage had already refused, and Jolon did not know what to do.

"I've had some success in dealing with mages," Tayre told Jolon mildly. "Will you allow me to help?"

Jolon had gratefully accepted.

Tayre took his uncle's hand in his own, and as he did, he was certain that he had found the path into the future that the Seer had told him was possible.

Tonight Tayre would talk to Jolon. Tomorrow he would convince a mage to heal not only the Teva elders, but his uncle as well.

"I don't think the road is done with you, uncle. Nor you with it. Fight the invincible foe one more day and let me prove myself right." He smiled at Sarat, who gripped his hand. "In the meantime, let me tell you about the Battle of Otevan, and the rain of gold."

Chapter Thirty

AMARTA LED AKA-AST AND UGO-AST, the First of Ear and Eye, into the Heart's inner sanctum, where Amarta had changed nothing.

From the surprise in their faces, Amarta knew that they had not been here before. Their gazes traversed the board and pinned notes.

She urged them to explore the room, studying them as they studied. She followed their trail of thought as they traced lines between pinned notes, whispering to each other.

Before long, they were in the alcove of books, absorbed in the journals and ledgers.

What had been the old Heart's shape in their eyes? What was it now?

A charlatan, she imagined herself proclaiming. Deceived you into thinking he knew the future. I am what he was not: I am true.

She could say that. With the evidence before them, they would believe her. Oddly, she felt no need.

And what was her shape in their eyes? How did they see her now?

How did she want them to?

That thought led her to break the silence that had hung in the room this last hour and more. As she began to speak, they turned toward her.

"He served the Body faithfully," she said. "We will care for him for the rest of his natural life, since he cannot care for himself."

Aka-Ast and Ugo-Ast exchanged a look, one that Amarta judged to be troubled. For a moment their worry caught on her own; could they be regretting making her Heart?

As Amarta dipped into the future to find out, she was drawn back into the present by their abrupt motions.

Ugo-Ast sharply brushed back his robe and knelt on the floor in front of her. Behind him stood Aka-Ast, a hand on his shoulder, her other, fisted, to her chest.

"Those who came for you, Heart," Aka-Ast said, her tone elegant and sorrowful. "The armed Perripin men." Her gaze flickered to the board and back. "We knew of this. We aided the then-Heart to send word to Arunkel, saying you were here, that they should come take you." Aka-Ast drew a long breath. "Thus, the Orders of Eye and Ear are culpable in this act against you. Do you wish reconciliation through life and blood? It is offered. We must be right with our Heart."

In their faces, Amarta saw deep remorse.

After the long moment it took Amarta to understand, her stomach dropped. She held herself rigid, lest she inadvertently consent to the horror they offered. She was certain that all she need do was to nod and these two would begin to slaughter themselves in repentance.

"No," Amarta breathed, "No, and no again. Reconciliation has already been achieved."

Ugo-Ast looked up at her with an unusually skeptical expression. "In what manner has this precious thing been achieved, my Heart?"

How would Tayre have answered this, in his eloquent, convincing manner? What potent story might Olessio have told to make them understand?

Amarta shook her head in frustration, searching for the right words. "You are my people." Her voice cracked. "Can you not feel this?"

As she spoke, the shard of glass that was Olessio inside her cut deep. She blinked back tears.

At the next Great Kailo, these two, along with the first five of every caste, would give to their new Heart an oath of words and skin and bone. Amarta had seen this in the past and in the future.

But even that act of profound devotion did not make the oath by itself. It was a reflection of what already bound the Body together, the bond Amarta herself must form.

Beginning now.

She looked around the room, searching for something she could feel but could not name. She strode to the mantel, touching those things that remained now that the white opals had been returned to the Eufalmo queen.

She laid a palm flat on the set of three knives that had been used in the last Kailo and would be used in the next, though this time Amarta would allow no sacrifice. She took a blade in hand and faced Aka-Ast and Ugo-Ast.

"It is not enough," Amarta said firmly, "that you give of your bodies to the Heart of Seuan in the Great Kailo. I tell you now, it is not enough. The Heart must also give to you."

She stepped close to them. In two fast, circular motions guided by vision, Amarta cut into her own left forearm. No deeper than needed, just enough to make herself bleed, to form droplets that she let fall into the outstretched palms of Aka-Ast and Ugo-Ast.

The kneeling man and the standing woman rubbed her blood between their hands with a fervor that she had not expected, somehow understanding this moment as well as Amarta did. Aka-Ast touched her palms to the sides of her head, over her ears, and Ugo-Ast covered his eyes with his palms.

As they returned their hands to fists that went to their chests, Amarta saw the spots of red that her blood had left on them.

"I hear, my Heart," said Aka-Ast.

"I see, my Heart," said Ugo-Ast.

The red circlet that Amarta had cut into her left forearm began to sting and ache.

"I will need ink," Amarta told them.

A marta shaved her head and took on the gray robes of the Heart of Seuan. Her left arm, where she had used the finest of black Seuan ink to make her *limisatae*, was now bandaged and healing.

She walked the city with Aka-Ast, Ugo-Ast, and others, to inspect the damage from the Eufalmo swarm attack.

Piles of bones and metal were still being raked together and sorted into parts for further use. The bodies of dead Eufalmo beetles were collected, cataloged, sketched, and analyzed.

The dead of Seuan were known only by their lack; there was no other way to identify them from what little was left. The list of names presumed slaughtered grew longer each day.

Among the many things in need of repair were the tunnels that went down into the rock-lined shelters, under the caste clusters, that had been breached by the swarm's diggers. Rock walls had been jolted loose by the earth-shaking, thundering hoard. Where the swarm had passed, anything not metal, rock, ceramic, or bone was simply gone.

Across the city, various castes were hard at work replenishing the substances consumed by the battle. Amarta quickly stepped in to redirect their efforts away from repellent and attractant and toward healing unguents for the injured.

There was no need now, she told them, to prepare for defense. Seuan was safe for a time.

Years, perhaps. Yes, the Eufalmo would return, but when they did, they would come as smaller swarms, as they had in the past. Seuan would easily repel them.

As Amarta walked the caste clusters, Seuans stood in neat lines, bowing to the foreigner woman who had somehow become their leader. Again and again, deep bows, fists to chests. No hint of question.

Amarta worked hard to speak to everyone, even if only a word or two. Elders. Adults. Children.

Emendi.

As she spoke to the Emendi slaves, she signed in the subtle, deniable language of the hidden city of Kusan.

I see you. And again: I see you.

Nothing. And more nothing.

Then, one small Emendi child, barely old enough to stand on his own—perhaps only recently come to Seuan—signed back.

I see you, also.

While her spirits soared, Amarta struggled to show no reaction.

They had not forgotten. Her Emendi tutors had doubtless known the signs, too, but had pretended otherwise. Who knew what companions and family had been wrenched from them by their slavers? Who knew what horrors they had endured? Secrecy was their only defense.

But they knew who they were and where they had come from. That meant that they, too, could be mended.

As eager as Amarta was to begin that process, it must wait until after the Great Kailo, when her authority would be unassailable.

It must also wait for the city to rebuild, so that the Body would know that their new Heart's protection was steady and potent.

Lastly, before she worked to untie this particular knot, Amarta must better understand Seuan and its Emendi.

Every day, Amarta visited the old Heart. She sat with him in his locked cell, the bandaged stumps of his wrists sitting motionless in his lap.

"We will treat you well," she assured him. "You are still one with the Body."

His eyes had not opened in her presence, not since the very day she had taken his hands. Respect, denial, or some other resistance, she did not know, and did not ask.

But daily she would tell him what she had seen across the city and outside the walls, or what she read in the room and library that used to be his. She would ask him questions. She would wait for answers.

He did not speak. It would be months, or years—or never, vision said—before he spoke again, to her or anyone else.

But Amarta heard what he might have said, and despite his silences, she learned.

Chapter Thirty-One

"THE BEST," Amarta told Aka-Ast and Ugo-Ast. "Bring them to me."

Aka-Ast bowed. "Yes, Great Heart. We have already selected one for the Kailo, of bright mind and pleasing body, so that his blood and organs—"

"No. Bring that one to me as well. Whole. There will be no taking of life at my Kailo."

The Eye and Ear fell momentarily silent.

"You wish to breed them, Great Heart?" Ugo-Ast asked.

"We advise against this, Heart," Aka-Ast said quickly. "The imported stock is strong and resilient. Even the small children. Money is plentiful, so we purchase from brokers across the sea rather than breed them ourselves, and sterilize the females to prevent unwanted extras."

"It is sense," agreed Ugo-Ast.

Breed. Stock. Extras.

Sense.

Amarta swallowed, then swallowed again, steadying herself at this talk of Emendi as if they were no more than cattle. She could not be angry with the Eye and Ear—she would not permit herself to be. This was the world they knew.

"The clever ones," Amarta said, struggling for focus. "As clever as if you were choosing for your own orders. Treat them well."

Aka-Ask and Ugo-Ast frowned in confusion.

Dare she say more?

Well, she was the Heart of Seuan and about to be confirmed. She had better dare.

"Beyond clever. I want those you deem to be without..." How to say it? "Docility. Those ones especially."

The savvy and resistant would form the necessary core. The leadership.

Aka-Ast and Ugo-Ast looked uneasy.

"It is our practice to use those ones in other ways."

As ingredients. Amarta knew.

She took a moment to consider her words. "Recall when the Eufalmo came, how that swarm was unlike any other, and we had to reshape ourselves to survive it?" They nodded, soberly, doubtless remembering the moment they had made Amarta Heart. "The Body changes when it must."

After a moment, Aka-Ast touched her fist to her chest. Ugo-Ast followed.

"Where do you wish these chosen ones brought to, these cunning and headstrong ones, my Heart?"

"There are empty rooms in the Heart's... in my temple." Rooms that awaited the next crop of singing children, another tradition that Amarta meant to change. "Plenty of space. If the chosen ones have family, they may bring them as well."

"Family? Heart, they are slaves. They have no family."

Amarta stared at the two of them, reminding herself that they represented the Body of Seuan. To move them to a new place, she must begin with them where they were.

Knots and more knots. Some outside herself. Some within.

It was not sufficient to untie a knot; she must also be able to keep it untied. Or retie it differently.

At last she spoke, almost surprised at the gentleness in her voice. "Let each Emendi decide for themselves who they call kin. Bring them also, if they wish to come. It is their choice."

"Yes, Heart."

Aka-Ast and Ugo-Ast touched their fists to their chests, bowed, and left to obey.

As uncertain as they were, Amarta knew that Aka-Ast and Ugo-Ast would turn her words into action. They did not need to know what she intended, such was their faith in her.

Amarta made a silent oath to herself to be worthy.

Amarta set about to learn how Seuan functioned, so that she could make essential decisions to guide the city to recovery. She immersed herself in the study, relying on Aka-Ast and Ugo-Ast for guidance.

Then, as soon as she could, she set out to visit the villages beyond the wall.

This time, accompanying her were even more sorogs than before, well over a hundred armed and armored Thumbs, and a host of others as well.

As she mounted her sorog, Amarta bemusedly scanned this huge company. The long train began forward toward the first village, which would be the one that Amarta had sacrificed to divert the swarm from Seuan.

Alongside her rode the First of the Left Thumb. She shifted in her saddle to see him.

"Dum-Ast, why do we travel with so many, with such force? The Eufalmo will not cross our paths today."

Nor tomorrow. Nor any time this year. Whatever the queen was doing with her princes, it would keep her busy for a while.

Dum-Ast touched a fist to his chest. "It is as you say, Heart. But also this: we must show strength to outsiders, particularly when the Heart walks among them. Otherwise, they may wonder if a challenge to the Body might succeed. It is my duty to ensure that this thought never enters their minds."

Amarta thanked him, accepting this. The Eufalmo, she reminded herself, were not Seuan's only enemies.

When they arrived at the village, all that remained were stone streets and gaping holes that led into sunken shelters. Inside these subterranean rooms they found scattered bones that told the story of the villagers' last moments.

At her expression, Tro-Ast and Tro-Etero assured Amarta that the village would be repopulated and useful to Seuan again.

Small consolation to those who had lived here. Amarta looked around at the silent town for a time, letting what she had wrought sink into her spirit, into her knowing.

Then she took a breath and remounted her sorog.

Most of the other outlying villages they visited had not been affected by the swarm, though many had seen it at a distance.

Others were simply gone, as if they had never been.

As they rode between the villages, Amarta would, here and there, stop the procession to climb down.

As she did, Thumbs dismounted, ringing her in a wide circle. She might walk a bit to a boulder, or put her hand flat on the dirt, or trace her fingers over the bark of some small tree, all so that she might glimpse this land's many futures to better understand its people, in and outside the walls.

If these strange doings of their new Heart puzzled her companions, they kept it to themselves.

As they traveled, the Dragon Sun passed its zenith. It had descended halfway to the western mountains when they turned back to the city, detouring through gentle hills to a known watering hole for the sorogs.

Everyone dismounted, freeing the sorogs. One by one, the sorog keepers called animals to come and drink from the pond. In moments, some of the huge beasts were rolling happily in the wet, making it muddy.

As Amarta's feet touched the ground, she let out a startled cry. All around, gazes snapped to her.

She spun in place, frantically scanning hills and brush. All at once, she began to race forward.

"Heart," cried the Aka-Ast from behind her. "What do you do? Where do you go?"

Thumbs, Feet, Fingers, Eyes, and Ears surged to follow. Amarta paused to to face them, her chest heaving. "No. You stay here!"

"Great Heart, it is not safe out there. It is very—"

But Amarta was already dashing ahead again, their warnings lost in the hot air behind her.

Panting, Aka-Ast and Ugo-Ast caught up to her to run at her side.

"What is it, Heart?" Aka-Ast asked breathlessly.

"Where do you go?" croaked the Ear.

Amarta shook her head. She could not both follow the thin trail of possibility and explain.

She raced forward.

～

As she ran, Aka-Ast and Ugo-Ast, one to each side, determinedly paced Amarta.

Deep in vision, Amarta was dimly aware of the courage this took. The three of them ran far from the protection of Thumbs and sorogs, in the open, where Eufalmo roamed. The Eye and Ear's presence at her side was a declaration of devotion no words could surpass. If she had had breath to spare, she would have told them so.

Amarta pounded up a rise, then sprinted down the other side. She stamped through a bare trickle of a tiny, seasonal stream, then scrambled up the steep bank of thorny bushes that guarded the other side. Blood welled from the cuts on her arms and legs.

All at once, she lost the trail. She ran in tight circles, howling her frustration to the dusty ground and the pale sky.

Ruthlessly, she cast herself into the future. Again, and again, as if against a wall.

All futures. Any future. The one in which...

There.

Following the thin trail of the barely possible—thin as spidersilk—she ran full out. Up another hill, down the other side. Her breath came raw and hard.

On a flat expanse of ground, her feet pounded the ground. At last, her body could simply go no further. Amarta sank to her knees on the hard-packed ground.

Was she close enough? She wasn't sure.

Then she was.

Gasping for breath, Amarta wept, already in the moments to come. Raising her head, she looked at the hills.

Ugo-Ast pointed. Aka-Ast drew a small knife from inside her robes.

Amarta gestured at them frantically. "Do nothing. Nothing at all!"

Aka-Ast returned the knife to hiding.

In the distance, a small figure was in motion. It ran, tearing left, then right across the dry ground and scrub, zigzagging around boulders, growing larger as it neared.

A blur, but Amarta knew that tiny white face, the dark nose, the striped tail.

Tadesh launched herself into Amarta's arms without slowing, knocking Amarta onto her back on the ground. There she cradled the scrawny, furred thing to her chest.

Amarta buried her face in the quivering, panting creature's ragged pelt, and cried for joy.

Chapter Thirty-Two

EVERY CASTE HAD HEALERS, but those belonging to the orders of Eye and Ear were the best.

They came quickly at Amarta's command. They had never seen an animal like Tadesh before, but immediately devised a plan to restore her health.

With Amarta checking every elixir and salve, touch and treatment, Tadesh recovered quickly. Across days, then weeks, she put on weight. Her fur returned to a thick, healthy sheen.

Before long, Tadesh was riding Amarta's shoulders everywhere, as she once had ridden Olessio's. More often than not, Tadesh dug her claws into Amarta's shoulders, at first for balance. Later, as she regained her strength, to make outrageous leaps from ground to Amarta, or back again.

Amarta rejoiced at every sharp stab, letting it sink into the place where she kept Olessio's memory. Somehow it was a healing salve.

The Great Kailo came. Each caste offered Amarta skin, bone, and their sacred oath.

Not a drop of Emendi blood was shed. No life was taken.

Amarta spoke often with the Emendi living in her temple. She first tasked them with selecting a leader.

Instead, they chose two: the man who had been selected to be sacrificed at the Kailo, and was not, and a woman who, despite looking nothing like her, reminded Amarta keenly of Maris dua Mage, with her intense focus and willingness to speak her mind.

Savvy and resistant, both of them. Amarta was pleased.

The two Emendi leaders stood at her side as Amarta inspected the construction of the new caste cluster at the center of Seuan. The new cluster had required the other castes to adjust their boundaries—no small feat—but they had done so, obediently and without question. A good first step to adjusting their thinking.

"Ours, my Heart?" asked the man, whose name was Bisar.

"Yours," replied Amarta. "The Emendi are the Body's newest caste, and you will lead it."

She gave them a moment to absorb this.

"What is our caste to be called, Great Heart?" asked the woman Emendi leader, whose name was Navend.

Amarta had seen the future and already knew the answer, but she also knew that the path and the destination were never truly distinct.

"You decide this," she answered.

～

One sun-bright day, Amarta gathered an entourage of whomever Aka-Ast and Ugo-Ast thought necessary and useful and led them out into the countryside south of Seute Enta and along the high coastal road.

Tadesh rode Amarta's shoulder, her nose quivering as she took in the sea air. Lulled into an easy contemplation by her sorog's swaying stride, Amarta gazed east at the bright blue Nelar ocean and considered what lay beyond the horizon.

Arunkel. Perripur. Kusan.

She thought of Dirina and Pas and Maris.

How long would it take for the news that Seuan had a new Heart to make its way to those lands? Who, hearing it, would put together the pieces and realize that the new Heart of Seuan was Amarta?

Tayre, certainly. She ached at the thought of him, that shard still sharp within.

But not many others, she would guess. A foreigner as the Heart of the reclusive and insular Seuan? It had never happened before. It would take time for people to believe.

And that meant that the hunters who had been tracking her all these years would continue to do so. With some amusement, she imagined them coming to the gates of Seuan to find her.

Let them come.

The ride south took until midday. At their destination, Amarta and her company dismounted, leaving the sorogs to their handlers.

Tadesh launched from Amarta's shoulders, dashing into the salt marshes in search of good hunting. Now that Tadesh was recovered, there was no constraining the creature, and Amarta did not try.

Indeed, it mended Amarta's spirit to see Tadesh so lively. Amarta smiled as the lush, long tail vanished into the high reeds.

Surrounded by advisors, assistants, translators, and a good many warriors, Amarta made her way into the town via a wide cobbled road. Doors opened and townspeople flocked outside to watch the procession. Excited whispers, gestures. Questions. Could this small, pale woman really be the new Heart of Seuan?

She smiled at them. They gaped back.

When she and her company reached their destination, Amarta let two high-position Tongues press through the doubled doors ahead of her. They each passed the open doors to Thumbs who trailed them, who passed it to another set, and another. Four Thumbs turned in one smooth motion to face Amarta, holding open the doors to make an entrance for her.

From inside, Tongues spoke in the countryside dialect, telling the proprietors of the Den of Innocence about the immense honor they were to receive, advising them to behave appropriately, respectfully, and cooperatively in all things.

Such polite language for threats.

"More lamps," one Tongue said. "Many more."

Amarta entered.

It was a large room, vast and sunken. A low, domed ceiling was made of wood and canvas.

It would never survive a Eufalmo attack. Neither would the guests. But Amarta had no doubt that the proprietors had a well-fortified cellar hideaway nearby in case of Eufalmo attack, and more than sufficient wealth to rebuild.

The room stank. Across the floor were blankets, cots, and bodies in various states of filth and undress. Some squinted back at the lamplight.

Amarta wandered among them, stepping past wadded blankets and bowls of mash. When she paused, Thumbs would turn over prone bodies. At her nod, they would grip chins or heads, showing her faces in the many lamps gathered close by the Fingers.

Amarta had already passed the thin, bearded, slack-jawed man who was slumped double on his cot, when vision and memory slammed together.

She turned around. A Thumb and Finger pulled the man

to sit upright, shifting him to face Amarta. His head lolled. A Thumb drew it upright by its long, tangled hair.

She had already known that he would be some kind of broken, but to see it was shocking. His eyes were lidded, his face lopsided. The stench coming off him made it clear that it had been months since any part of him had been washed.

Amarta crouched in front of him.

"Innel," she whispered. When he didn't respond, she said, more sharply: "Lord Commander."

His exhale was an amused half-laugh. His brows drew together. "Where did he go?"

"Where did who go?" Amarta asked.

"My brother Pohut."

"Your brother is dead," Amarta told him. "You killed him in Botaros, after you found the child seer and paid her to tell you how. Don't you remember?"

Innel nodded slightly in the Thumb's grip of his hair. "The Seer of Arunkel. I remember. I tried to save her from the Perripin attack." He blinked rheumy eyes, squinting at her. "Do I know you?"

He was so unlike the man she had once known. She wondered what he saw right now.

How far they both had come.

"No, I don't think you do."

She put a hand on his thin, shuddering shoulder, and read his body's future. He did not have long. Without her help, he would not live more than a few more days.

His gaze sluggishly searched the room. "I think he's gone, this time. Really gone."

Amarta stood. "No. The dead never leave us. But we must go on without them anyway, until we join them." She held a hand down to him. "Come with me."

He snorted lightly. "There is nowhere to go."

"I proclaim you Advisor to the Body of Seuan. Now you have somewhere to go."

"I have no advice."

She withdrew her hand. "Perhaps not. But you have something to set right. As I do."

At last he looked up. At her. At the many Thumbs, Fingers, and Tongues who surrounded her.

"Who are you?" he asked, bemused.

"I am the Heart of Seuan. Come with me, and I'll give you elixirs that put to shame what they offer you here."

That got his attention. "Truly?"

"Truly."

He struggled to stand. His legs shook so badly that he seemed he would fall. At Amarta's nod, her people were at his side, holding him up, steadying him as he shuffled forward toward the door of the Den.

Amarta matched his slow pace. He was half the bulk he had been when she had last seen him, regally dressed in his elegant Lord Commander's black-and-red uniform, and broad across the shoulders. He had given her a blue-and-white seashell and a golden horse. Both were gone, now.

Once outside, Innel dropped his head and shut his eyes against the bright sun, tears streaming down his face.

Now Amarta could see how damaged he really was. One foot was twisted out. His shoulders were uneven, his gaunt face asymmetrically scarred. Even his eyes were wrong; one lid drooped and the whites of both were yellowing.

Once he had towered above her. Now he seemed very small.

His eyes at last adjusted. He blinked them clear and looked around, at the armored Thumbs, at Aka-Ast, at Ugo-Ast. His frown deepened as his gaze came to rest on Amarta in her gray robes and shaven head.

He stared. A surprised grunt came from his throat.

"You," he exhaled.

Near death he might be, but he was still sharp enough to think.

She squared herself to him. "Me."

He pulled his arms from the holds of those who had been steadying him to stand, swaying precariously and his gaze slid from hers. "I don't want to go with you."

Amarta mused. At a gesture, it wouldn't matter what he wanted; her people would drag him back to Seuan, heal his body, and adjust his attitude.

It was exactly what he would have done to her, when he was Lord Commander. A tight knot, easily solved with a sharp knife.

She felt sympathetic to his resistance.

"I am ending slavery in Seuan, Innel."

His gaze crawled back to meet hers. His tone was quiet but surprisingly adamant. "Good."

"But the world is large and the things that must be set right many. I need you."

Innel took a wobbly step back and away from her. A Thumb briefly steadied him so that he would not fall. Innel shook his head, retreating another step, back toward the Den.

"I have something," Amarta said, unmoving. "Something that you want."

"No, you don't. You have nothing I want. Only pain, and I have enough of that."

Though he could barely step an inch at a time as his legs shook, he was determinedly withdrawing.

"The chance to see her again," Amarta said, answering the question that he would not ask.

He stopped, all of him trembling visibly.

"Not possible."

"If I say it is, it is."

"Which one? Who do you mean? Who, exactly, damn you?"

Still keen enough to think critically. She was pleased.

Amarta smiled. "Both of them, Innel. Both of them."

~

I nnel, who now went by the name Adra, healed slowly.

He was, Amarta's healers told her soberly, very damaged, and she should not be surprised if it took months —or years—for him to regain significant use of his body.

As for his mind, they did not know. Probably he would never be who he had once been.

The same could be said of the city of Seuan, still rebuilding from the Eufalmo swarm.

And yet, the city healed. As it did, it began to move with the cadence of its new Heart. Sensing this, Amarta slowed. Large transformations could not happen quickly.

Amarta walked her city, entering every cluster, every building, seeking to understand the castes more completely. She studied how each of them set about to heal the bodies and spirits of their wounded. She saw how, in their eyes, the new Emendi caste was changing shape.

The Emendi called themselves The Restored.

"What is our caste's work and duty, Great Heart?" Navend asked her.

She studied Navend and Bisar a long moment, their white-blond hair and blue eyes a stark contrast to all the other Seuans.

But then, so was she.

"What does the Body of Seuan need, that you are called to provide?" Amarta countered. "Seek to understand the whole. You are no longer slaves, but a caste among many, and so you have responsibility. Ponder this. Ask yourself the question you just asked me. Ask until you are hungry to do the work. Then you will know what it is."

They touched their fists to their chests.

If the Body of Seuan was a tapestry, it was torn in many places. By the Eufalmo. By the cutting away of the slave class. By the new Heart and her ways.

There were knots yet to untie. Many of them. Others must be cut.

The tapestry must be rewoven.

～

A day came when Amarta felt she could be spared for a few hours. At a small fishing village nestled in the rocky cliffs north of Seuan, she sat at the end of a long, narrow dock, her legs dangling as the ocean surged and fell a few feet below her.

On the land-end of the dock, Thumbs, Fingers, Eyes, and Ears waited. A group of Emendi had come as well, insisting that they were also part of the Heart's protection. Amarta smiled. The Restored were rediscovering themselves.

Beyond her circle was another, looser circle: the village's fishermen and their families, at a safe distance from Thumbs and sorogs.

All of these many were watching her.

From inside her thick, belted gray robe, Tadesh's wedge-shaped head poked out to sniff at the chilled ocean breeze. Amarta stroked the soft fur between Tadesh's ears as the creature's nose quivered curiously. Tadesh turned in place and burrowed back inside, pressing warm and soft against Amarta's side.

Amarta could have come without so many. Alone, even. But her people needed to provide her with protection and support, and the villagers needed to know that the Heart of

Seuan, swinging her legs back and forth over seawater, had not come alone.

One of Amarta's many tasks was to give her people what they needed.

This moment, though, she would take as her own.

At the end of her legs, swinging in the salt wind, were shoes made by the First of the Feet, Kalug-Ast, who needed to make them. They were a compromise between the Heart's traditional slippers, which Amarta had rejected as impractical, and the traveling boots that she had lived in on the road for so many years.

The shoes were exquisitely made, like everything in Seuan, and astonishingly comfortable. She looked at these treasures on her feet, then her gaze rose to the rocky harbor and beyond, to the horizon of the Nelar ocean.

Such a vast stretch of water, the ocean. A sort of a road, really, one the color of steel, of fish scales, of tears. A road that led to all places and all futures.

Somewhere at the end of that road was Tayre. What he would do with the freedom she had forced on him—whether he would find Dirina and Pas and save them from whatever ill threatened them—Amarta did not know.

But she did know that Dirina, Pas, and Tayre were now, finally, liberated from the deadly influence of being close to Amarta and her visions. Free to find their own future.

As was Amarta.

"Remember us," Tumaya of Carugrua of the Island Road had once begged her. Probably dead now, drowned with thousands of others, but Amarta no longer tallied the multitudes of lives destroyed at her touch. The Monks of the Revelation. The people of the Island Road. The village that she had sacrificed to the Eufalmo.

For the many, there was no accounting. No justice, but what she herself made.

The few, though, those she would remember.

Olessio, his death her lifetime's burden to bear.

Tayre, gone, but free and alive.

Tadesh, at her side, whom Olessio had given into her care.

Change was rippling through Amarta's city. The other castes were laboring to change, to adjust, not only to The Reformed, but also to their new and strange Heart. The tapestry Amarta was beginning to weave was huge, and each strand was made of other strands, all essential to the whole.

In truth, it was too big—she simply could not weave it alone. So each strand must also, somehow, become a weaver.

To set all this in motion was a daunting undertaking. It would take time.

She had time.

Tayre had once asked her what there was for her, here in Seuan. She had not been able to answer him then, because she had not known.

Now she did; it was what he himself had taught her: practice in new ways.

Amarta's shape had changed, and it was still changing. As she reformed Seuan, she would reform herself. Not only herself, but her own shape in her own eyes, which would allow her to change even more.

Whatever was required of Amarta to understand Seuan, she would do. Whatever she must learn, she would learn. Whatever she must become, she would become.

Her gaze lazily traced the ocean's horizon, from north to south, then back again as she both remembered and foresaw.

Amarta knew that she was not yet ready for the rest of the world.

But she would be.

Read More!

Be sure to read all the books in The Stranger trilogy!

Unmoored
Maelstrom
Landfall

Available at your favorite retailers!

It's True. Reviews Help.

IF YOU LIKED THIS BOOK, please consider giving a rating and a review. Even a short "Can't wait for the next one!" will do nicely, and help the author to make more books for you.

About the Author

Sonia Orin Lyris's stories have appeared in various publications, including *Asimov's SF magazine*, *Wizards of the Coast* anthologies, and *Uncle John's Bathroom Reader*. She is the author of THE SEER, an epic fantasy novel from Baen Books. Her writing has been called "immersive," "ruthless," and "unsparing."

Her passions include martial arts, partner dance, fine chocolate, and the occasional human critter.

She asks questions and gives answers, but not necessarily in that order. She speaks fluent cat.

A note from Sonia

Thank you for being part of my creative process. I have regular chats for subscribers, on my Patreon account, here:

https://www.patreon.com/lyris

Never miss a release!

I announce new projects on my Facebook feed:

https://www.facebook.com/authorlyris

You can also sign up for my newsletter:

https://lyris.org/subscribe/

Connect with Sonia

Web: https://lyris.org

facebook.com/authorlyris

goodreads.com/Sonia_Orin_Lyris

twitter.com/slyris

CPSIA information can be obtained
at www.ICGtesting.com
Printed in the USA
LVHW081554120622
721093LV00007B/145